W9-BYL-808

BEST OF FRIENDS

NATALIE DUNBAR

Genesis Press, Inc.

Indigo Love Stories

An imprint of Genesis Press, Inc.
Publishing Company

Genesis Press, Inc.
P.O. Box 101
Columbus, MS 39703

ISBN-13: 978-1-58571-220-5
ISBN-10: 1-58571-220-5

Manufactured in the United States of America
First Edition 2000
Second Edition 2007

Visit us at www.genesis-press.com or call at 1-888-Indigo-1

ACKNOWLEDGEMENTS

I want to thank God for giving me life, and the imagination, determination, creativity, and skill needed to create this book and go through the process needed to get it published. A big, heartfelt thanks to my family for supporting me, pulling together, and making do with a lot less of my energy and personal attention. Chet, you knew I could do it too. Chester III, see what you can do when you put your mind to it? Rahmon, this is only the beginning. I'll learn to manage my time better. Barbara and Lillian, thanks for the ready ears and moral support. Mom, thank God you're always there.

Many thanks to my critique group for their dedication and hard work in helping me to refine and shape this book. Good luck with your individual creative efforts. Thanks to Angela Patrick Wynn for her dedication to goal, motivation, and conflict. Special thanks to Karen White Owens for her keen eye and attention to detail, and for being a supportive friend; I know you've got a winner, so get it out there. Thanks to Aubery Vaughn for traveling some the rockiest part of the writing road with me. Keep on pulling. Thanks to Stefanie Worth, for joining the team and adding her unique skills.

A special thanks to the owners of the Paperback Outlet, Betty &Fred Shuelte, and staff members Yvonne and Ruth for their encouragement and support, and Yvonne again for her review and comments. Thanks to Marsha Vosse, who works at a Detroit area modeling agency and patiently answered my modeling questions.

Any errors in the translation are mine.

All the characters and situations in this book are fictitious. Various Detroit area restaurants are used in this book and although their menus may differ from what the characters selected, their food is excellent. The Dumouchelle Auction

Galleries do exist in Detroit, but their business practices may differ from those demonstrated in this novel.

A very special thanks to my editor, Sidney Rickman, for helping to make this book the best.

BEST OF FRIENDS

ONE

"You need to get back to the office right away."

The high quivery sound of Lynn's voice alarmed Mariah even more than her words. With her heart thumping, she whirled to face her secretary. Lynn's eyes were wide and frightened, and her hands shaking. "What? What's the problem, Lynn?" Mariah heard a tremor in her own voice.

"Imani's upstairs looking like death warmed over. I'm afraid it's something serious."

A wave of apprehension coursed through her. "Oh no!" Hurriedly fumbling, Mariah took out a few coins from her open change purse and tossed them on the counter. "What happened?" she asked, grabbing her soda and following Lynn out of the store as fast as she could. As they headed for the elevator, she silently prayed for everything to be all right. Panic rioted within her. *What was Imani doing in her office anyway?* she wondered fleetingly. Then she remembered tonight's charity event at the mayor's mansion. Had there been some sort of accident?

Lynn's fingers fluttered nervously. "I was just talking to her, and she suddenly sort of keeled over on the couch. She's out cold, Mariah!"

"Was she spaced out? Did you see her take anything?" Mariah asked, feeling oddly disloyal. It was a fact that Imani had been a wild teenager. Had she really changed that much? At the elevators, she pushed the up button. Mariah's mind filled with images of the standoffish and often prickly model lying pale, cold, and lifeless on her office floor.

"No, she wasn't spaced, and I didn't see her take anything, but I came to get you because if she has to go to the hospital, I figured she wouldn't want an official record."

Mariah nodded. "You're right about that, but if she's not conscious when we get up there, I'm calling 911. Her reputation is not worth dying for." The elevator doors opened and both women scrambled into the compartment. Mariah's heart thumped madly as she pushed the button for the tenth floor. The elevator doors seemed to close in slow motion. After an inordinately long time, the doors opened and both women ran down the hall to the McCleary Modeling Agency.

In the outer office, Imani lay curled in a fetal position on the couch with her head in the crook of her arm. She lifted her head as they entered, her eyes seeming much too big for her face. "Hello, Mariah. Lynn, I'm sorry, I don't know what came over me. Did I scare you?"

Lynn circled the couch. "Out of a few years of my life! What's wrong with you?"

Imani's hands held her stomach. "I—I must have fainted. I haven't been eating very much. My stomach's been giving me the willies."

"Are you okay? Should we call you an ambulance?" Mariah asked, noticing that despite Imani's reasonable sounding words, her coloring seemed unnaturally pale; her bottom lip trembled, and her hands moved back and forth across her abdomen. Mariah suspected that the thick makeup covered dark circles beneath her eyes. She'd never seen Imani look anything but glamorous.

"Just let me rest a little, and I'll be all right." Imani's head turned sideways and dropped back into the crook of her arm. "I don't need a doctor."

Staring at her, Mariah's thoughts raced. *Oh yes, you do. I haven't seen anyone who needed a doctor more!* "I've got a soft drink you could have." Mariah offered the can, but stopped when Imani slowly rotated her head from side to side. "Then maybe you should try to rest," Mariah added, feeling a little frustrated.

Imani closed her eyes. Mariah and Lynn exchanged glances, then Mariah motioned Lynn into her private office and closed the door.

"She is not all right," Lynn said obstinately.

"Yes, I know," Mariah said, trying to steady her erratic pulse. She dragged her knuckles across her damp forehead. "Imani could have anything from stomach flu and appendicitis all the way up to stomach ulcers." Glancing at her watch, Mariah realized that it was well past time for Lynn to go home. "Go on home, Lynn. I'll handle this."

"Are you sure you don't mind?" Lynn said, not bothering to keep the relief out of her voice. "I've got an appointment."

"No, I don't mind. Imani has an assignment tonight, and I'll probably need to get a replacement anyway."

Lynn lifted her black bag onto her shoulder. "Then I'll be on my way. Let me know how all this turns out."

Mariah nodded. "Sure."

Turning, Lynn headed for the door. "Good night, Mariah."

"Good night," Mariah called softly as Lynn opened the door and exited. She tried to resign herself to the fact that Imani was at least conscious. Mariah knew better than to think she could force Imani to see a doctor right now. She'd let her rest for an hour, then try to reason with her.

With nervous fingers, she found the "worry wart rock" in its spot by her nameplate. Absently rubbing its semi-smooth surface, Mariah paced the area in front of her desk. Tonight's unusual assignment was important for a number of reasons. The client was her best friend, Ramón, and his law firm was in a bid to gather a little positive publicity by showing themselves to be caring, contributing members of the community. She couldn't let them down.

Tonight's event was in support of her beloved Juvenile Diabetes Association. Her eyes sought the family photo gracing her desk and zeroed in on her little sister's face. Reason number two, she thought, biting her lip. Poor Jennifer had died from juvenile diabetes. As a result, Mariah always did everything she could for the organization that had supported her so much. As for reason number three, supporting the community and its organizations made good business sense.

Who could she get to replace Imani? Quickly, she ran through all the possibilities and came up empty. All her models were either on assignments, or not the type requested. In desperation, she dialed the numbers for a couple of models on vacation, and ended up talking to their voice mail. Then she went through her mail.

At the bottom of the stack of mail she found the newspaper with an article on the front page circled. She read carefully:

Jury selection for the Gerald Hatten murder trial is scheduled to begin next week. Hatten, co-owner and operator of a local chain of hotels, is accused of fatally shooting his partner, John Marsh, at their office on the evening of August 10. Marsh had been embezzling company funds while having an affair with Hatten's wife, Belle. Mrs. Hatten told police that her husband was devastated when he found her with Marsh only days before the shooting. Company secretary Cynda Miller told police that she heard Hatten threaten Marsh after discovering his role in the missing funds. Hatten's gold watch was found at the scene. Hatten has secured the services of Abrams, Wright and Associates for his defense. Ramón Richards, son of Judge Clark Richards, will lead the defense team.

Mariah sighed as she got her scissors and cut the article from the paper. It was nice to see Ramón's name in print. With all the pre-trial work going on, she hadn't seen him in ages. Tonight would be the first chance he'd had to get away from all the work since he made the decision to represent Gerald Hatten.

After an hour, her office felt like a cage. She got up and walked into the outer office to check on Imani.

Imani's long, slim, yet curvaceous form hung over both ends of the office's short leather couch like a drooping exotic flower. "I don't see how you'll be able to make that assignment tonight." Mariah's gaze ran over Imani's beautiful features, cringing at the waxy, almost grayish cast to her normally walnut skin tone. Imani's dark fringe of lashes lay against her drawn cheeks; her trademark pouty lips were pallid and slack. Her short, red knit dress barely covered her hips and crotch, and half her full breasts hung out of the low cut neckline. The dress was something her friend, Ramón, would call a classic "ready sex" dress, easy in and easy out. "Are you sure I shouldn't be taking you down to the emergency room?"

Imani's lashes lifted just enough for Mariah to see the sherry brown pupils of her eyes. "Don't worry," she rasped. "It must have been the shrimp I had at lunch. That's all I ate. I'll be fine."

"I don't think so," Mariah replied. "And telling me not to worry is not going to work." She moved closer, her hand behind her back. Did Imani have a fever? Imani hated anyone fussing over her and, until recently, was usually very standoffish. Deciding to go for it, she applied cool fingers to Imani's forehead. Surprise! Imani's forehead, although not exactly cool, was only a little warm.

"Mariah, quit fussing." Imani's lids drifted closed again. "I guess you're right. I can't make tonight's assignment. Get a substitute for me, and I promise I'll be able to make my commitments the day after tomorrow."

"I can't get a sub," Mariah said, becoming more worried by the minute. "Most of the girls are at that fashion show in New York, and Tammi and Linda are on vacation in the Bahamas! There's no one I could call on this short a notice!" Through all the years the agency had been in business, they'd never failed to meet an agency commitment. Mariah prided herself on customer satisfaction. She didn't want to think about the publicity and business opportunities the agency might miss out on.

"Why can't you do it?" Imani mumbled, rolling over onto her side, one hand kneading her stomach.

"Me?" Excitement bubbled within Mariah at the thought. She glanced at her caramel brown features in the mirror on Lynn's desk. Her dark eyes were fringed with lashes that weren't as thick as Imani's, but they were more than adequate. Her nose was small and short; her lips well-shaped and full. Instead of the prominent cheekbones that helped make a model, she had full, dimpling cheeks. Mariah pushed the dark brown cloud of her mid-length pageboy out of her face. She'd never considered herself glamorous, but she knew she was attractive. Could she do it?

In her secret heart of hearts, Mariah relished the thought of showing Ramón that she, too, could be glamorous and exciting. She'd never met a better-looking man, and he was sexy as hell. Mariah sighed. Ramón Richards was the kind of guy women drooled over, and with good reason. She told herself that she had no intention of chasing him or becoming one of the statistics in his little black book. If she successfully covered for Imani, it would be just a morale booster. Mariah had given up any romantic ideas she had about him long ago.

Ramón liked the tall glamorous babes, but none of his girlfriends seemed to have any sort of staying power. She'd never been sure if it was because he dumped them, or they mutually agreed to go their separate ways, but she'd never ventured close enough to find out. Ramón was as close as she was going to get to having a brother.

"Exactly what's wrong with you?" Mariah asked Imani, hedging her bet.

"I feel a little dizzy and nauseated. If it's not the shrimp, I've probably caught a virus, hopefully one of those twenty-four hour ones. I can't go, Mariah. I couldn't even stand up right now." Slowly, Imani rolled over onto her stomach, moaning lightly. "And if I could, I might just barf all over poor Ramón. You've got to do it."

Imani didn't look as if she would get any better. Mariah took another glance at her own face in the mirror. A voice whispered in her thoughts. Do it! Who was she afraid of anyway? Mariah scratched that thought. She knew who she was afraid of. Ramón Richards, that was who. She loved him dearly and had been friends with the man for years, but she worried that she couldn't meet his expectations. Could she go to the fundraiser in her finery and get the kind of attention Imani gathered naturally? In her thoughts, Mariah found the idea attractive, but actually carrying it off would be no mean feat.

"You really like him, don't you?"

Mariah turned to see Imani watching her from the couch. "Yes, I do," she said carefully. "I've been friends with him since our days at the University of Michigan."

"I envy you that," Imani extended an arm and took the glass of water off the coffee table. "I don't know many guys who are willing to be just friends, and I have no friendship as strong as that the two of you share." Her long tapered fingers held the glass to her lips while she drank.

"You know, it isn't just the two of us," Mariah explained quickly. "There's a good-sized group of us alumni who still hang out. We've all managed to maintain our friendship."

"That's great."

"Feeling any better?" Mariah asked, hopefully. Events like tonight were Imani's forte.

"No. I'm just holding on until Ramón comes. He's been so nice to me that I want to tell him personally."

The idea of subbing for Imani grew more attractive as Mariah sounded out her options. "I guess I could get Pierre to do something fantastic with my hair, and Barb to do the makeup." She chewed her bottom lip. "What would I wear? That dress Anthony designed for you would swallow me. I'm only five foot seven. Besides, I wear a size ten dress and there probably isn't a shoe in the back that would fit me."

"I saw some things in the collection that would be perfect for you. Mariah, please go talk to Tony and leave me in peace."

Mariah rolled her eyes at her top model. "All right. I'll go talk to Anthony. I'm also calling you a cab. I want you to go home."

"Let me stay long enough to explain to Ramón," Imani mumbled, rubbing her forehead into the crook of her arm. The rippling waves of her glorious hair covered her arms and shoulders. "If there was any way I could go, I would."

Conceding defeat, Mariah checked her watch. It was seven o'clock. Ramón was scheduled to pick Imani up at eight-thirty. She hurried to catch Anthony on his side of their shared-office suite.

"So you're going to give the famous Imani a run for her money and show Ramón Richards that you too can be glamorous," Anthony said in an easy tone as he looked her up and down critically. "It's about time."

"What I'm going to do," Mariah said, calmly correcting him, "is substitute for Imani, and get a little publicity for my agency and your clothing line at the same time. Heaven knows, we could all use some more business." In contrast to her words, the excitement within her grew.

Anthony pulled a black garment bag from his closet filled with creative designs. "You, my dear, are not a substitute for anyone. You have a unique beauty of your own, inside and out." His Italian accent thickened as he placed the bag in Mariah's hands. "This is my gift to you. Wear it with my compliments and know that it was designed to complement your special beauty. I was saving it for your birthday, but this seems a more appropriate time."

"Thank you." Mariah smiled. Anthony's compliment lifted her spirits as she placed a kiss on his fashionably stubbled cheek. Slowly, she unzipped the bag and uncovered Anthony's creation. Mariah gasped. It was the most beautiful dress she'd ever seen. She stared hungrily at the soft, shimmery, black wrap dress, her fingers caressing the fabric. Flashing rhinestones ran along the neckline, down the front edges, and around the tulip-shaped hem. It would definitely reveal a lot of thigh. The matching belt and headband were fashioned of the same black material and covered with Anthony's initials in rhinestones. "It's gorgeous!" she breathed. "I love it!"

"I'm glad you like it," he said, watching Mariah hold the dress to her five foot seven inch form. He grinned at her obvious fascination. "You and your models have done more for my clothing line than I ever dreamed possible. Business is great. I've been doing wardrobes for some of the local celebrities and I've even gotten a few movie assignments."

"I just hope I can do it justice." Mariah glanced down at her flat brown sandals. "Now all I've got to do is find some shoes and figure out what to do with my hair."

"Anthony LeFarge at your service. Sit down, let me take care of those things," he said quickly, as he opened his black leather portfolio and pulled out a drawing. Mariah's eyes widened when she recognized herself in the sketch, wearing the dress with rhinestoned black heels and matching earrings. The sides and top of her hair had been cut short and curled, to set off the headband and reveal more of her face. He tugged on a lock of her hair. "I can cut your hair if you'll trust me. Before I became a designer, I fed myself by cutting hair. It wouldn't take long."

Mariah hesitated. "I don't know..." She'd worn her current hairstyle for a couple of years now and was attached to it. It was easy to maintain.

"Take a chance," Anthony said softly. "If you don't like it, it won't take long to grow back."

"I...guess." Mariah gave in reluctantly, but she wanted to look special, and Anthony had never steered her wrong.

"We'll knock Ramón's socks off," he said resolutely, indicating the chair she should sit in and producing a clear plastic cape to keep the hair off her clothing.

An hour and a half later, they were behind one of the blue folding screens. Mariah sat in a chair and Anthony stood nearby. Barb, one of the agency makeup artists, was busy applying the last artful touches of makeup to Mariah's face when they heard a firm knock just before the door opened. Mariah heard Ramón call out a greeting to Anthony in warm tones.

Sticking his head up above the cloth partition, Anthony replied, "I'm fine Ramón. How about yourself?"

"Ready for the big bang at the mayor's mansion. I appreciate you supplying my date's outfit."

"I appreciate the extra publicity," Anthony laughed.

"Hey Maria-Mariah!" Ramón continued, a teasing note creeping into his voice. "I heard your voice. Are you back there with Anthony? I'm a little early to pick up Imani, so I thought I'd holler at you."

"Hey Ramóndo-be-yondo!" she laughingly yelled back in her best Spanish accent, her heart skipping at the sound of his sensual voice. "I'll be out in a few minutes. Imani's in my office. I think she wants to talk to you first."

"In a minute," he said. Then they heard the door close.

Anthony assessed her look. "You look mah-vel-ous!" he said in his best Billy Crystal imitation as he twirled her around to face the mirror. Mariah hardly recognized herself. The sparkling black dress draped her soft curves in a way that made it obvious the dress had been made for her. Her breasts looked full, her waist tiny, and her hips round and firm. Short, soft curls of her dark brown hair framed her face and the shimmering headband. A different foundation made her pecan coloring look creamy, and the skillful application of blush emphasized her cheekbones. She stared at her reflection in the mirror, noting that her eyes looked larger, and much more intriguing. Mariah smiled with the lips she'd always secretly felt were too big, enjoying the sultry look they completed.

"I feel almost like Cinderella on her way to the ball," Mariah said, giving Barb and then Anthony a quick hug. It looked as if things would work out after all.

"He'd better not bring you back before midnight," Anthony quipped, hugging her back before giving her a little push towards the door. "Have a good evening."

"I will." Mariah grabbed the little black clutch purse he'd given her and headed out the door. The sound of Imani and Ramón's voices reached her as she walked down the short hallway, grateful for the plush carpeting that kept her sequined heels from sounding like a horse on the way to the stable.

Through the open door of her office, she saw Imani in Ramón's arms, her head on his shoulder. "You know you can count on me," he said, taking hold of her shoulders and pushing back to look into her face. His lips bussed her forehead in a gentle, surprisingly sweet kiss. Not wishing to witness any more of this touching little scene, Mariah cleared her throat. It was a warning signal she and Ramón used to indicate to each other that they were not alone.

Ramón glanced at the door and turned to stare. "Mariah?" he said, surprise in his rich tenor as he got up from the couch. Something sparked and leapt into flame within his gray eyes. His simmering glance swept slowly over her, caressing her, and easing only when he broke into an appreciative smile. "Hell-o Ma-ri-ah!" he said, emphasizing every syllable. "I'd whistle, but I know you well enough to know you'd only slap me!" He took one hand and pulled her into the office, leaning close to kiss her cheek with a wealth of masculine charm.

Mariah shivered beneath the warmth of his gaze, feeling hot and cold simultaneously.

"Mmmmh…you smell good. Hello gorgeous!" he said softly, a sensual note creeping into his voice. The provocative scent of his cologne beckoned like a warm summer breeze. Gently, he lifted her hand and twirled her slowly. His gaze took in the black rhinestone heels, her long stockinged legs, the glamorous dress, and the results of Anthony and Barb's combined hair design and makeup skills. "You're looking really hot and sexy," he murmured in frank appreciation. "You ought to try this look more often. That dress is talking to me." He gazed at her hair. "I like the new hairdo too. Why don't I taste that lipstick you're wearing? It makes me think of a candy apple."

"No," Mariah said, recovering enough to find her voice. "It's called, 'Forbidden Kisses,' Ramón."

"Aren't those the best kind?" he drawled provocatively.

Mariah wet her lips and the sensual sparkle in his eyes deepened. His spirited comments brought her confidence level even higher. Ramón had never looked at her that way before. A sensual heat simmered in the depths of his teasing slate gray eyes. Gazing unabashedly at her favorite friend, she took in his appearance, enjoying the experience. As usual, he simply oozed charm and good-natured masculine virility. The black tux looked like a custom fit on his lean muscled, six foot two inch frame and was a good foil for his golden oak skin tone. His glossy black hair was cut short on the sides, the top filled with flowing waves. Ramón's full, well-shaped lips cried "kiss me," a phrase his mouth said often.

Mariah gave him her most provocative smile. Ramón grinned back at her, flashing even white teeth. The act emphasized his square jaw and prominent cheekbones. Damn if the man wasn't as handsome as the devil. It was a good thing she knew just how much of a devil he could be, Mariah thought, or she'd have fallen for him years ago. Of course Ramón could be a real sweetheart, too. Mariah would never forget all the support he'd given her when Cotter Eastwood broke their engagement, or all the contracts he and his friend put together for the agency, while refusing to accept the proper fee.

Ramón tipped her chin up with one finger. "Can I kiss you anyway?" he said, giving her one of his trademark 'love me because I'm so sweet' looks.

"No, you may not!" Mariah snapped smartly, stepping away from him. He was kidding, of course, but she suspected that he wasn't faking the desire to kiss her. "Did Imani tell you that I'm going to have to substitute for her this evening?"

Ramón nodded, his gaze sweeping over her like a hot summer breeze. "It should be interesting."

That look sent her pulse racing. Deciding to ignore it, Mariah put a hand on his arm and gazed into his eyes. "I'm really sorry to be making a change at the last minute, but you can see that Imani's sick, and I don't have anyone available to fit your requirements."

Ramón covered her hand with his. "Mariah, I'm not complaining. Let's go for it."

Mariah smiled. "I expect you to behave. I'm doing you a favor by substituting for Imani."

"And believe me, I'm grateful," he began, his eyes full of charm and mischief. "It's just that if I'm going to have to fight off three quarters of the male population, the least you could do is reward me with one teeny-weeny little kiss."

Squaring her shoulders, Mariah lowered her lashes and glanced up at him through the fringe. "Play your cards right, sugah, and I might let you come up and see me some time," she cooed in her best Mae West imitation.

"But sugah," he drawled, tilting her chin up with a finger, "there's no time like the present."

Mariah burst into laughter. Leave it to Ramón to get the last word in. She was at a loss for another snappy phrase.

"Sounds like you guys are going to have a good time," Imani mumbled, drawing their attention back to herself.

What was really the matter with Imani? Mariah wondered, noting the sparkle of tears on Imani's lashes.

"Hey, you gonna be all right?" Ramón walked back to the couch and took Imani's hand in his. "I'll call you tomorrow to see how you're doing. Take care of yourself," he said, giving her a soft peck on the cheek.

"Hope you feel better." Mariah called out to her as Ramón took her arm and led her towards the door. "I tried to call you a cab, but Anthony says he's going your way and he'll accept no less than dropping you off." She heard Imani's murmured thanks just before the door closed.

"You know they're still thinking about making me a partner in the firm," Ramón said after they'd settled themselves in the limousine.

"Yes. I think it's great." Mariah turned to smile encouragingly. "With you leading the team for the Hatten case, how could they refuse?"

"Oh, they could. Believe me," Ramón said as the limousine took off.

"But they won't," Mariah said, squeezing his hand.

"I hope not," he said turning towards the back of the limousine. "They've begun a campaign to show that we are responsible, important contributors to the community. That's why tonight is real important." He opened the refrigerated compartment in the rear of the limousine and pulled out a bottle of champagne.

Was Ramón getting nervous? Mariah wondered. "I know this is important," she said. "It's important for the agency too. When Imani does events like this we usually get a lot of other requests for our services."

Easing back into his seat, he began working the wire on top of the bottle. "Wanna set some ground rules?"

Mariah opened the sidebar and produced a couple of champagne glasses. "What's wrong with the usual? No torrid love scenes with other people, no leaving the other alone for hours on end, and if you see someone you really like, get the phone number discreetly and come on back."

In the middle of opening the champagne, Ramón looked up and caught her eye. "Those rules are fine, but I was really asking, is there anyone you think I should meet? Are there some specific individuals you want to impress? How outrageous are we going to be? You know, Imani is well known, and really good at getting publicity and attention." The popping of the champagne cork seemed to emphasize his statement.

He wasn't stating anything Mariah didn't already know. You never knew just what outrageous thing Imani would do, and that was another reason why she was such a popular model. "You don't think I can get us noticed?" she asked defensively, ready for a challenge.

Ramón's glance did a slow scan of Mariah from head to foot, lingering on her cleavage and the length of leg and thigh exposed by the dress's tulip shape. She suspected him of using this opportunity to get another eyeful without raising her hackles and was immediately ashamed of herself. Ramón didn't need excuses to get an eyeful of her. He'd known her for years, and seen her in a lot less without blinking an eye. "Well?" she asked, when the silence went on too long.

"You'll get more than enough attention." Ramón poured champagne into the glasses. "I've had to remind myself several times that you're still the same good friend you've always been."

"Come on, Ramón," she said, handing him his glass. He was definitely up to something. "Come clean. What's really on your mind?"

"I take it that's an Anthony LeFarge original," he said carefully.

"It is," she said proudly. "And it's not a loaner."

"I don't suppose you could afford to get a little sweaty in it?"

Sweaty? Mariah thought, sweaty? As in one body moving sensuously on or within the other in the heat of passion? As in that tall athletic body of Ramón's doing something hot with hers? Maybe she'd been right on track earlier when she thought his mind might be hovering in sensual purgatory. And maybe hers had joined his. This was not good. Whoa girl, cool down time. "And how might I do that?" she asked carefully, not wanting to reveal the conclusions she'd already jumped to. Ramón's wild, sexy scent swirled around them, making her dizzy.

Instead of answering immediately, Ramón put down his champagne glass, grasped hers, and did the same with it. He took Mariah's hand in his and inclined his handsome face towards hers. "Actually, I have a number of ideas," he said in a low seductive tone.

Was he bent on seduction? It had been years since he bothered. His eyes were hypnotic, his smile sensual. Something in Mariah melted. He was playing with her and she knew it, but she couldn't seem to keep herself from reacting. The corners of her mouth turned up. She enjoyed Ramón in all his different moods. His warm lips brushed her cheek, and her heart did a little tap-dance. Could he hear it?

Ramón leaned closer till his lips nearly touched her ear. His warm breath tickled, sending tremors down her spine. "I thought..." he continued in the low tone, drawing his statement out, "I thought we could..." he gently pushed back a curl of Mariah's hair, "dance."

Dance? Mariah's mind started to clear. She'd heard him say they could dance. Mariah lifted a hand to his muscular chest and pushed. "You flirt! Surprise, Ramón, I'd planned to dance with you all along," she said with a laugh, assuring herself that she'd merely been playing along to see how far he would take it. "Now behave!"

His grin was full of even white teeth and boyish charm. "I thought we could do the dance we did for that play in college. We looked something like Fred Astaire and Ginger Rogers. Women asked me to dance for months after that, and the guys were green with envy."

"The tango?" she asked, remembering the play and the disturbing time she'd had acting as his love interest in the play. He'd been virtually irresistible. That was before she knew just how much he loved women. She'd quickly learned to deal with her attraction to him, but it had taken months to get her mother to quit thinking of him as a future son-in-law. Mariah was certain she'd handle things better this time.

"Yeah, the tango." Ramón gave Mariah back her glass of champagne. "Feel up to it?"

"Sure." Mariah settled back against the seat. "I can handle it." She could handle anything if he'd just quit teasing her.

"To Astaire and Rogers," he said, lifting his glass and touching it to Mariah's. "To Richards and McCleary."

Mariah repeated his toast and they clicked glasses again. The slightly sweet taste of the champagne filled her mouth, while phantom figures of Ramón and herself performing the tango danced through her thoughts.

"I've got a friend who's a reporter for Channel Two News." Ramón settled back into the seat across from her. "He was all set to interview me and Imani. I don't know if it will still be on. Need I say that he was more interested in interviewing Imani than talking to me?"

"Why Ramón, I simply don't understand," Mariah said smartly. "Surely any red-blooded American reporter would love to get the get the scoop from the up-and-coming attorney who's working on the famous Hatten case. I read in the Free Press that he made all that money with his computer services company but his partner—"

"That's just it." Ramón grabbed the champagne and began to refill their glasses. "I can't talk about that case right now. Judge Whitfield put a gag order on all of us. It won't expire for another day or two."

"This case could really set your career, couldn't it?" Mariah asked, thinking of the defendant, Gerald Hatten, a local millionaire. It would take a lot for Ramón to prove him innocent of murdering his business partner since the circumstantial evidence against the man was staggering.

"I'm counting on it." Satisfaction crept into his tone as he gave Mariah her champagne flute. "This is the kind of case people dream of."

"I'm surprised you found the time to attend this affair." Mariah lifted her glass. She hadn't seen him for a couple of weeks and, while he looked as handsome as ever, she saw the tiny red lines in the whites of his eyes. No doubt he pored over cases and reference books deep into the night.

"Are you kidding? This event will be in all the papers. The firm virtually required it. They sprung for the tickets and suggested I take Imani. Now let's make a toast to good friends." Ramón said, lifting his glass.

"To good friends." Mariah touched her glass to his. "May they last forever."

"Forever," he echoed, his gaze locked with Mariah's as they simultaneously drank.

Not long after that the limousine pulled up in front of the mayor's mansion. Soft strains of an orchestra drifted on the air. Carefully, Ramón helped Mariah out of the limousine and up the wide steps past a bevy of young, valet parking attendants.

"Good evening." Nodding at their courteous response, a distinguished-looking older man in a tux opened the door and ushered them into the cavernous hall, past a group of tuxedo-clad security guards. "Your tickets, please," he said politely.

Ramón produced a fancy blue envelope from an inside pocket of his suit and handed it over.

"There's dancing to a live orchestra in the Blue Room. Several musical groups have been scheduled up until twelve o'clock. You'll find dinner service with live jazz in the Green Room. The official ceremony is scheduled for nine-thirty in the Blue Room," he explained, handing each of them an embossed gold program with black lettering. "When you're ready, Jack will show you the way. Would you please sign our guest register?"

"Are you hungry?" Ramón asked, after Mariah added their names and company affiliations to the guest register.

"Not really. I'm too excited. Let's get the work out of the way." Mariah located their names among the sponsors listed on the back of the program and showed them to Ramón. Then she turned to the host, Jack. "Could you show us to the Blue Room?"

Sky blue silk wallpaper and electric blue carpet made the blue room an experience in and of itself. The ceiling was a replica of a night sky full of twinkling stars. Several people in evening dress moved on the navy tiled dance floor in the center of the room. Others watched, chatted, and networked. Mariah and Ramón scanned the crowd, Ramón drawing second looks from several of the women. Tonight, Mariah was pleased to discover that she, too, was garnering her share of attention.

"There's my friend John from TV 2," Ramón remarked suddenly. "Let's see if he'll still do the interview."

Mariah recognized the tall, blond, blue-eyed reporter from the local TV station, more handsome in person. She saw him looking her over as she and Ramón approached.

"John, how ya doing?" Ramón said, grinning at John's mumbled response. "Having a good time?" Ramón shook John's hand and patted his shoulder in a friendly manner.

"Not bad," John replied. "My girlfriend couldn't make it, so it's a little lonely."

"I know how that can be. John, this is my friend, Mariah McCleary of the McCleary Modeling Agency," Ramón began. "Mariah, this is my friend, John Corbett, of TV 2."

"Hello, it's nice to meet you, Ms. McCleary." John Corbett offered his hand and a smile. It was just a polite smile, Mariah thought, with no real welcome. There would be no interview for her.

"It's nice to meet you." Mariah shook his hand. "Imani was supposed to be here tonight, but she wasn't feeling well at all, so I'm substituting for her."

"Could we still do the interview?" Ramón asked casually.

John shook his head. "I'm sorry Ramón, but we were all set for Imani. We've prepared all the background information, and I even brought that Essence cover she did. My producer was going to save a spot just for her."

"Mariah is well-known in the community. Her modeling agency supplies models for all of the big designer shows in Paris. One of her other models posed in last month's issue of Vogue. And she's active in the community. Her agency gave two thousand dollars to tonight's benefit for juvenile diabetes..."

"So did you, Ramón," Mariah interrupted, uncomfortable. "And then your firm kicked in another five thousand."

"I think that's great," John said carefully, "but I'll have to sell that to my producer on some other occasion."

"Hey," Ramón shook his hand again, his expression tight, "sorry to put you on the spot."

"Not a problem."

"Maybe we'll see you later." Ramón took Mariah's hand to steer her away.

"Maybe. It was nice meeting you, Ms. McCleary."

Although various unkind statements came to mind, she bit her tongue and responded politely. Ramón was already unhappy.

Quickly surveying the room, she hoped the incident would not set the tone for the entire evening. One heavyset matron stood out in the corner of the room. "There's Mrs. Belson, one of my bread and butter customers. Come on, I'll introduce you," Mariah said, leading Ramón off in a new direction.

"Ma-riii-ah!" Cora Belson cried in her faint southern drawl. Her well-manicured hands took hold of Mariah's shoulders and kissed the air on both sides of her cheeks. A long, gold lame evening gown hugged and caressed her heavy frame, the side split revealing large but shapely legs. Her silver threaded black hair was piled high on her small head. "I haven't seen you in ages, and I've been meaning to call you! All work and no play, you know what they say, huh?" The diamonds in the center of her heavy gold earrings put on their own light show.

Mariah smiled and greeted the owner of an exclusive chain of boutiques warmly. Cora Belson's boutiques sponsored at least two fashion shows a year and often used the McCleary Modeling Agency in addition to several local celebrities. A contract with Mrs. Belson's boutiques would put the agency that much closer to new headquarters.

"We're starting to schedule our yearly fashion experience, and I want you to put us down for at least four of your top models. Your models lend such a professional air to the entire production. Ever since we started using your agency, sales have increased impressively."

Pulse racing, Mariah could barely contain her joy. Her smile was wide, but she managed a calm, professional tone. "I'm glad we were able to make your event more successful. When are you planning to hold the next one?"

"The beginning of November, to give people time to make their purchases before Christmas. I'll have my assistant call you with the details tomorrow."

"You must be dipping into the stock," the woman continued, her appreciative gaze resting on Ramón. "I take it this handsome young man is one of your agency models?"

"No, this is my good friend, Ramón Richards. Ramón, this is Mrs. Cora Belson of the Belson Platt Fabunique Boutiques."

"I'm pleased to meet you, ma'am," Ramón said, clasping the hand she proffered. "I really like the things you sell."

"Well, thank you. Have you ever thought of modeling? You and Mariah make a striking couple."

"No, ma'am. I'm a lawyer." Ramón released her hand.

"What a waste," Mrs. Belson muttered. "You're not a divorce lawyer, are you? Every now and then, John makes me mad and I think about the joys of being single."

"Actually he's working a criminal case at the moment. He's with Abrams, Wright, and Associates," Mariah said quickly.

Cora Belson's eyebrows lifted. "Oh, then you must be really good. I've heard the name of that firm before, and it's always associated with some high profile case. Do you have a business card with you?"

Ramón produced a discreet cream-colored business card with dark brown printing from the inside pocket of his suit.

"Abrams, Wright and Associates," she read aloud before slipping the card into her gold evening bag. She gazed at him in silence for several seconds. "You look awfully familiar," she said finally, still scanning his face. "You're not Judge Richards' kid, are you?"

"Yes, I am."

"That's fascinating. Your dad and I go way back…" Mrs. Belson continued.

Someone tapped Mariah on the shoulder. She turned and looked up into the striking features of Perry Bonds of the Detroit Pistons basketball team. "Hey, good evening, Ms. McCleary. I thought Imani would be here tonight," he began in that deep voice that seemed to shower down from the heights. He was at least 7 foot one inch tall and reveled in it.

"I'm subbing for Imani. She was feeling a little under the weather," Mariah explained, not missing his expression of genuine disappointment.

"It must have been pretty bad, because Imani loves a party and this is best I've seen all year. She'll hate that she missed it."

"Would you like me to give her a message?" Mariah asked, determined not to spread the few details she knew of Imani's illness.

Looking distinctly uncomfortable, he hesitated. "Ah, just tell her Perry asked about her and that I hope to see her next time."

"I could give you her pager number so you could leave a message yourself or call her back…" Mariah offered, feeling pushy, but suspecting that Imani had a more than casual interest in hearing from Perry. For that matter, Imani probably had an interest in hearing from any and all well-heeled eligible bachelors in the vicinity, Mariah thought. She certainly didn't need any help. Still, there had been something poignant and sad in Imani's face. Mariah had never seen her look so vulnerable.

"Sure. That'll work." Perry shifted a little on his size sixteens, furthering Mariah's impression that he had no intention of following up on Imani. Mariah carried business cards for all her agency's models. From the stack in her evening purse, she selected a pastel peach one and handed it to Perry. He barely glanced at it. "Thanks a lot," Perry said easily, "maybe I'll see you later."

"Maybe." Mariah watched him lope off, only to be surrounded by an attractive group of admiring women. They always spoil the good ones, she thought.

"Mariah, Ramón, you kids having a good time?" a voice boomed to their left. Recognizing the source, Mariah and Ramón turned quickly. Ramón's parents had just arrived.

"Dad! You're looking well." Ramón shook his father's hand enthusiastically and then turned to his mom, his eyes wide with admiration. "Mom, you're gorgeous!" He embraced her fervently and kissed her cheek. "Save a dance for me." Gloria Richards chuckled at the antics of her handsome son. It was no secret that she thought the sun rose and fell on her only child.

"Hello, Judge Richards," Mariah said, planting a reciprocal kiss on the cheek of the impeccably dressed gentleman. He looked like an older, heavier version of Ramón with silver touches to his tightly curled hair.

"Hello, *amiga*!" Gloria Richards cried exuberantly in her thick Puerto Rican accent, her arms opening to enfold Mariah in a quick, heartfelt hug. "Are you feeling better these days?" she inquired in a soft whisper only Mariah could hear. At Mariah's slight nod, she continued: "I thought I saw your doctor friend at the entrance."

Mariah's stomach fluttered. She hoped she wouldn't have to speak to Cotter Eastwood. She hoped she didn't see him at all, but if she did, she'd just have to get through it. Despite the butterflies dancing in her stomach, Mariah smiled brightly at Gloria Richards. In the background, she heard Ramón and Judge Richards conversing with Cora Belson. "Thanks for telling me." She gazed admiringly at Gloria's shimmering red sheath with its plunging neckline. "I love your dress!"

"And I love yours. That's one of Anthony's, isn't it? I thought so. His clothes are always so uniquely classic."

"Honey," Judge Richards broke in, "I'd like you to meet Cora Belson. We go way back."

Mariah heard them announce the orchestra's last song, a tango, before they changed performers. She caught Ramón's eye.

"Excuse us," he said to his parents and Mrs. Belson. "They're playing our song." Quickly, he led Mariah out onto the sparsely populated dance floor. Ramón and Mariah faced each other, his hand at her waist, her hand on his shoulder. He clasped her other hand, and they began their dramatic walk across the dance floor. After four steps, they turned their heads in unison and went the other way. Around them, the dance floor cleared even further as couples stopped to gather around the sides and watch. Playing to the audience, Ramón's steps grew more dramatic, his strides longer as his knee moved forward between Mariah's. When he dipped low with her, swerving their bodies from side to side, she felt the rippling play of his muscular body beneath her fingers. Carefully, she matched his strides, curling back sometimes, and maintaining an erect posture at others.

After several passes up and down the floor, Ramón extended his arm to whirl Mariah out, then contracted it to reel her back into his arms until their faces were so close their lips touched. His wild, masculine scent, mixed with Polo cologne, filled her nostrils, lulling her senses. Mariah threw her head back, lifting her face to his. At the end of each inward whirl, she raised her knee and curled herself back on his arm. Sometimes she gracefully kicked her leg all the way out. Varying their dance, she pranced behind Ramón, twirling on her toes. It was a romantic dance, Mariah thought. Anyone observing the rapt expression on Ramón's face and his tender handling of her would think they were in love. Their dance ended with Mariah at a forty-five degree angle in Ramón's arms, his lips on hers, his eyes sparkling with mischief.

A series of camera flashes and applause from the crowd that gathered around the dance floor brought Mariah out of her daze. She straightened, warmed by Ramón's vibrant smile. They took a little bow. Yes, she thought, they'd managed to get a bit of attention, and had a lot of fun doing it. Two reporters from the local newspapers came up and got both their names and occupations.

After their dance, they went around the room networking with several of the city's most prominent citizens. When they'd completely circled the room, Ramón turned to Mariah. "Are you hungry?"

Taking another sip of her wine, Mariah shook her head at Ramón's question. "Not really, but I guess we'd better eat soon." She glanced at her watch. It was close to eleven.

"I'm not exactly starving, either. I just don't want you to get sick from drinking all that wine on an empty stomach," Ramón murmured, his smile failing to disguise his concern.

"I like this band. If we go eat now, we'll miss their performance," Mariah countered, glancing up at the group on the stage. Sounds of their rhythm and blues performance filled the room.

"I'm going to get you some of those appetizers. Let's make a deal, two more songs, and we go eat."

"Deal." Mariah watched her friend cross the room to the appetizer table. Resolutely, she put her empty glass on the tray of a passing waiter.

"Hello, Mariah."

Mariah jerked around, her body trembling at the sound of the one voice she thought she'd never hear again. Gloria's warning had been right on the money. Mariah had foolishly hoped that Cotter Eastwood would have no interest in speaking to her.

Cotter devoured her with his dark eyes. He'd lost weight since he'd broken their engagement, but his dark tux complemented his tall lanky frame in a way that used to send shivers down her spine. He'd been an exciting lover. The streak of white in his black hair had widened, and his eyes were shadowed against the walnut tones of his skin, but he was still as handsome and debonair as ever.

"Cotter..." she managed, her tongue suddenly thick and uncooperative. This was the first time she'd seen him since the breakup. With her heart pounding in her chest like a sledgehammer, Mariah drew on that inner reserve of strength that always seemed to pull her through the rough times.

"How've you been?" he asked as if they'd parted amicably.

She'd been a basket case, but she wasn't about to let him know. Her lips compressed. "Fine," she lied in a perfectly normal tone. Conflicting emotions pulled at her. Part of her wanted to let him have it for the past, and a deeper, shame-filled part was glad that he asked, and hoping he'd realized the enormity of his mistake. No, she didn't really want to get back with Cotter, did she? No, she wasn't that sick, but the thought disturbed her.

How could he look her in the eye and converse politely after skipping out on their wedding? Just looking at him caused her mind to replay the entire sorry episode. She hadn't really known him at all. Dry-mouthed, she clenched her teeth and straightened her shoulders.

"I need to talk to you in private..." Cotter faltered, his eyes pleading for understanding as he moved closer to her.

Where were all the things she'd planned to do or say if she ever saw him again? Months ago, she would have jumped for joy. Now, she instinctively backed away, refusing to believe her ears. "Why?" Mariah asked. Her fingers clutched the little evening purse. "There's nothing left to say." Cotter had been her dream man, her future husband. She couldn't let him back into her head, or her heart, to ruin the dreams she had left. A quick glance around confirmed her guess that they were already drawing unwelcome attention. Was it any wonder? Cotter Eastwood was a famous surgeon and local celebrity. If she were going to chew him out, it would have to be in private.

He winced, his expression compellingly sincere. "I know I made a terrible mistake. Everything was all set and I just…I lost it. Mariah, I've missed you more than I ever thought possible."

"I suppose that's why I haven't heard from you in months," she said smartly. "I—I don't want to talk to you, so go away."

Ramón came to stand beside her, slipping a warm, comforting arm about her shoulders. "Hello, doctor. Aren't you on call tonight? Shouldn't you be down at the hospital saving lives?"

As opposed to ruining her evening? Mariah thought, as Ramón ripped into Cotter.

"Stay out of this, Richards. This is between Mariah and me," Cotter sneered.

"Last I heard, you'd broken your engagement," Ramón said in a dangerously soft voice. "We were having a pleasant evening until you showed up."

She threw Ramón a quick glance. He usually tried to stay neutral when she argued with someone. "Let me handle this," she told him.

His pitying look had her swallowing and straightening her shoulders. She was going to get rid of Cotter whether

Ramón believed her or not. When her gaze hardened, he nodded and appeared to back down. She could see it cost him a lot.

"Mariah?" A poignant note crept into Cotter's voice. "I've been calling you all week. I need to talk to you alone." He threw a wary glance in Ramón's direction, then continued. "If you'd just listen to what I have to say, we could both continue with our separate evenings."

He sounded so reasonable that she almost agreed, then caught herself. She really didn't want to talk to Cotter. He'd already scrambled her thoughts and emotions, and she hadn't exchanged more than a few words with him. She had to take better care of herself this time. "No. Call my office sometime this week. I'll make sure your call gets through."

He seemed to acquiesce, but then he moved closer, his eyes on Mariah, his trim, well-manicured surgeon's hand extended.

Stiffening, Mariah tightened her jaw. "Cotter, don't push it. This is as good as it gets."

Ramón gave the plate of hors d'oeuvres to a passing waiter. "Get away from her," he warned Cotter in a threatening tone.

Cotter's gaze held Mariah' s, ignoring Ramón. "Give me your hand." he murmured in a voice for her ears alone. It was one their rituals, one he used in public to let her know just how much he wanted to make love to her. Before she'd really thought about it, she'd placed her hand in his. In the background, she heard Ramón curse softly under his breath.

TWO

Cotter covered her hand with both of his, and raised it to his lips in a sensually romantic gesture. The heat of his soft mouth burned the skin on her fingers in the spot his engagement ring had occupied for several months. His gesture underlined the distinct possibility that she was still his.

No. This was all wrong. Speechless, Mariah tried to pull her hand back, succeeding on the second try. She nearly jumped when Ramón's arm snaked about her waist, steadying her. His action distracted her on a totally different level.

"I still love you." His words were barely a whisper, but she heard them anyway. Mariah shut her eyes, forcing his image from her mind. How many times had she heard Cotter speak those words? They had meant nothing when all was said and done. She couldn't afford to let him back into her head and heart. When she opened her eyes, she saw Cotter making his way to the entrance.

"Are you going to be all right?"

"Yes, but I think I've had enough for tonight," Mariah moaned, wishing she could disappear.

"You can't go home. Not yet," he said roughly. "Look around you."

Mariah turned her head just a little past Ramón's chest. Several people stared, mesmerized by the soap opera-like drama that had unfolded. This wasn't quite the attention she'd imagined receiving when she'd taken on Imani's assignment. Mariah swallowed her tears, looking to Ramón for a cue.

"Don't give in to the bastard," Ramón bit out, his expression virtually daring her to show any sign of weakness. "He's playing you like a violin."

"Give me a break! I did get rid of him," she bit out.

"Yeah, I guess you did," he said in an unconvinced tone. "I think he was feeling merciful," he muttered under his breath.

Mariah glared at him.

The band began to play its own rendition of the Temptations song, "Since I Lost My Baby." Shrugging, Ramón opened his arms. "Let's dance to some of these golden oldies." Mariah lost herself in his arms, closing her eyes, and snuggling her face against his chest in the next best thing to a hug. "That's my girl," he whispered in a husky tone.

"Do we still have an audience?" she inquired as they moved around the dance floor for the second time.

"What do you think?" Ramón answered in a flattering tone. "I'm with the most beautiful lady in the room." One hand gently smoothed her back in a comforting gesture, and then settled back at her waist. Mariah relaxed in his arms.

Half an hour later, they made their way to the Green Room and were seated for dinner. "Try to eat something," Ramón suggested patiently as the waiter arrived.

With all the highs and lows of the night's excitement, and the resultant cramping in her stomach, Mariah didn't think she could eat. After perusing the menu several times, she settled on a plate of appetizers and a glass of wine.

"What now?" Ramón asked after she took a sip of her wine.

"Hmmm?" Taken out of her thoughts, Mariah turned her attention to Ramón. She hadn't spoken to him for several minutes. Some date she was. But it wasn't a date, she reminded herself. It was a publicity assignment.

"You don't have to say anything." Ramón shifted in his chair and took a sip of his own wine. "I know you're going to talk to that jackass. I've never known you to say you were going to do something and then renege on it. It's one of the qualities I really admire in you; however, this is one instance where no one would blame you..."

"I still have some feelings for Cotter." Mariah stared into the depths of her wine. "Maybe I still love him."

"After all he's put you through?" Ramón said roughly, his expression full of disgust. "You cried on my shoulder for two months straight. And it took another three months for you to get rid of that kicked-dog look."

"Maybe I'm just stupid."

"Maybe you're just gullible."

Tears stung the back of her eyes, tears that would never fall. Mariah bit into the soft skin of her bottom lip. Get hold of yourself, she thought. Ramón was right again. It had taken a lot for her to get over the broken engagement to Cotter. When a warm hand covered hers, Mariah glanced back up into Ramón's softened expression. He took her hand in both of his, with a charming yet rueful smile.

"I'm sorry, Mariah. I try to mind my own business, but I just can't stand to see you get mistreated. Cotter Eastwood and his high society friends and family stink!"

Before Mariah could reply, the waiter returned with their plates. They spent the rest of the meal in silence. An hour later, the limousine pulled up in front of Mariah's home.

"I'll walk you to the door," Ramón said, jumping out and extending a hand to Mariah.

"It's not necessary." Mariah leveraged her hold on his hand to climb out of the limo gracefully, then leaned close to kiss his cheek. "Thanks for putting up with me."

"Trying to get rid of me already?" Ramón maintained his firm hold on her hand. "And I don't call that a kiss. You're going to have to do better than that."

Mariah whirled around with a half grin, surprised that she could. Ramón had an uncanny ability to bring her out of a deep funk. "I can't believe you're giving me such a hard time."

"I'm giving you a hard time because I know that all the dates you'll never see again don't make it to the porch. Now I'm your best buddy, so you can at least put up a pretense.

"Come on, Maria Mariah, I'm not settling for less. Let's get this show on the road."

It was hard to be depressed with Ramón teasing and cajoling her. She considered his teasing demand. "All right. You can walk me to the door." Taking his arm, she headed for the steps, then pressed the key into his hand.

"Wait here," he ordered when they reached the door. With quick movements, he unlocked the door. Then he made a quick check of the interior. "Now what about my kiss?"

"I think you've already gotten your kiss," Mariah said stubbornly. It was then that he put his arms around her, enfolding her in a warm hug. Burrowing deeply into his embrace, she wished the warm, comforting feeling could last forever. After a while, he leaned back and took her face in the long fingers of his hands.

"Except for the presence of a few negative people, I had a good time tonight," he said, a provocative expression in the depths of his amazing gray eyes.

"Me too," Mariah murmured.

Then he surprised her by leaning forward to gently touch his lips to hers in an affectionate kiss. Mariah breathed in his scent, reveling in the feel of his arms around her. The kiss ended and another began when his warm lips caressed hers, his tongue outlining the sensitive opening, and then darting in to move sensuously against Mariah's in a deep soulful kiss. It made her dizzy, sending the pit of her stomach into a wild swirl. She leaned into him, giving herself up to the kiss, enjoying the arousing touch of his fingers on her face, while the other hand caressed her back. Her hands settled in the soft hair at his nape. When this kiss ended, her eyes popped open and wide-eyed, she pulled away, her fingers on her tingling lips. There'd been a lot more than friendship in that kiss.

"Your lips were made for kissing. I enjoyed that, Mariah," he said impishly, his gray eyes sparkling. "Now, don't get mad. I just wanted to give you something to think about besides Cotter Eastwood and his sexy hand-kissing ritual."

"Oh, you did. That was a first."

"Well, maybe I've improved over the years."

"I'll say." she agreed, still in awe of what had just happened.

"Goodnight, Mariah," he said with a flash of even white teeth.

"Goodnight, Ramón."

Within seconds, he'd turned away, and headed back towards the limo. "Don't forget to lock the door," he called softly before climbing into the back.

Mariah stepped into her hallway and closed the front door. She heard the limo drive off as she locked it.

In the bedroom, Mariah removed the dress and put it on a padded satin hanger. Then she removed the undergarments and put on a sleek blue satin gown. She'd felt beautiful and glamorous all evening in Anthony's creation, and Ramón, bless his heart, had only added to the effect.

She touched her lips again. Ramón had knocked her socks off with that kiss. She wondered if he'd be quite as good in bed. His girlfriends always looked pretty satisfied and anxious to get him back to their hotel rooms or cabins when she and the others in their circle of friends went on group trips with him. She could almost imagine herself in bed with him, but thoughts of the morning after intruded. If things did not work out, or if he eventually tired of her, she'd lose more than a lover. In the past year, she and Ramón had become so close that she considered him her best friend. There was no way she would put such a valuable friendship on the line because of lust.

She stepped into the bathroom and carefully washed the makeup from her face. Too bad Cotter picked such a public occasion to stage a comeback. She'd had no idea that he had been calling her all week. But her secretary, Lynn, probably did. She'd given Mariah a number of probing looks, and she'd seemed uneasy about something. How could Lynn, who'd been with the agency since she'd started, have kept his calls a secret? But Mariah could guess the why. When Cotter had broken their engagement, she'd prided herself on the fact that she hadn't fallen apart. With the exception of Ramón and a few other close friends, she'd kept her pain and heartache private. Apparently, she'd been a lot less successful than she'd imagined.

Going back to the bedroom, Mariah grabbed the brush from the dresser and brushed her hair as hard as she could. She didn't know if she could forgive or forget Cotter's betrayal of her. All Mariah could think of was waiting and waiting for Cotter to show at the wedding rehearsal. She'd blithely ignored the pitying looks thrown by her maid of honor and the bridesmaids. At first she'd thought there'd been some sort of medical emergency requiring his professional expertise, and then she'd become convinced that he'd been involved in an accident. Finally she tracked him down to his river front apartment and discovered that he'd simply lacked the courage to tell her that he didn't want to marry her. He didn't want to marry anyone. Cotter explained that he'd simply been bowing to family pressure. That explanation was the crowning glory for the entire situation. They hated her. They'd probably pressured him not to marry her, and it had worked.

Weary, and too keyed up to sleep, Mariah crawled into bed alone. Cotter had rarely been there in the night to hold her, as she thought her dream man should. There were always patients, surgeries, meetings, and more meetings. She wondered, would things have been any different if they'd gotten married? Turning over on her side, she settled in for the night.

Hours later, the jarring sound of the phone awakened her as no other sound could. Mariah startled, and then sat up in a hurry. Blindly, she patted the nightstand and the plush carpeting beside the bed until she located the phone. "Hello?" she managed when she finally got the receiver up to her ear.

"Hey, wake up lady! You must have overslept." An impossibly cheerful voice came at her from outer space.

"Ramón, this had better be good! I'll never be able to get back to sleep," she growled irritably.

"Check your clock, sleeping beauty. You've only got an hour to wash, get dressed, and get to work!"

Mariah turned on the bedside lamp and stared at the clock through bleary eyes. It was eight o'clock! She felt as if she'd barely slept. "Okay, Sir Galahad, it seems I owe you an apology. To what do I owe the pleasure of this early morning wake-up call?" she said with a yawn.

"I thought you might want to take a look at today's paper, the front page, to be exact."

"Why don't you just tell me what it says?" Mariah stood and stretched, and then resolutely headed for the bathroom.

"A picture is worth a thousand words."

"Ramón! I've already wasted ten minutes talking to you."

"It's been more like two, but now that you mention it, I've got to get down to court early today. See you later!"

"Don't you dare hang up that phone!" she virtually screamed.

"Okay," Ramón said contritely. "Have lunch with me. We should celebrate."

"Celebrate what?" Mariah cried in frustration. This call probably had something to do with last night's fundraiser, she thought.

"Go to the front door. Get the paper off the welcome mat. Check out the front page of the Metro Section. See you at oh…eleven-thirty, okay?"

She was free for lunch, wasn't she? If Ramón could fit her in despite all the pretrial activities she could make time, Mariah thought as she headed for the front door. "Yeah, we can have lunch. I'm heading for the front door now." Hiding behind it, she grabbed the paper off the mat. That's when she noticed the dial tone. He'd hung up on her. "Hmmmmph!" Mariah clicked off the phone in disgust and closed the door.

Still waking up, Mariah unfurled the paper and then gasped. There they were, on page one of The Detroit Free Press, Metro Section, in the very center, in living color, in the dramatic clench at the end of their dance. The caption read: Pictured here: Mariah McCleary, owner/operator of the McCleary Modeling Agency in an Anthony LeFarge original, and Ramón Richards, associate attorney at Abrams, Wright, and Associates make it look romantic at this year's fundraiser for juvenile diabetes. "Yes!" she cried, then quickly checked the headline of the article below: $100,000 Goal Met During Fund Raising Event for Juvenile Diabetes. "Yes, yes, yes!" she sang as she danced her way to the bathroom. "Thank you, God."

By the time she'd showered, dressed, and driven to her office downtown in the Buhl building, it was nine-fifteen. Her secretary, Lynn, was away from her desk when Mariah came into the office, but there were several copies of the picture of her with Ramón in the center of her desk. Mariah removed her navy blue suit jacket and put away her purse. She was staring wonderingly at the photo again when she heard a sound from the doorway.

"Good morning! That's some photo of you and Ramón Richards. I love it," Lynn said, coming into Mariah's office with two large foam cups and a white bag. "Here, I went down and got us a couple of cappuccinos and Danish to celebrate."

"Thanks. I could certainly use something strong right now." Mariah gestured towards her conference table. "Let's eat it over there."

"Anthony's dress looked like it was custom made just for you," Lynn said, placing the packages on the conference table, and opening the cappuccinos.

"It was. He gave it to me as a sort of birthday present/thank you for-all-the-agency-has-done-for-me gift."

"You mean there aren't any copies of that dress?"

"I don't think so."

"It's still early, but in the coffee shop, I saw Elaine, and she said she's already had calls from two people trying to order that dress, and it's not even nine-thirty."

"Hallejeulah!" Mariah lifted her cup. "Let's drink to success!"

"To success!" Lynn touched her cup to Mariah's, and then they both drank their cappuccinos. "The two of you look so romantic in that picture," Lynn continued carefully. "I've already called the paper and ordered a few color copies of it."

"Great." Mariah bit into her Danish.

"I'm glad to see things working out for you again."

Mariah swallowed. "Ramón Richards and I are still just good friends. I was simply subbing for Imani in that publicity assignment last night." Mariah leaned forward. "Did you forget to tell me that Cotter Eastwood called several times within the past week?"

Lynn glanced up from her drink with a guilty expression. "Yes. I'm sorry. I really am." Her head dipped. "I should have done my job and minded my own business." She shifted in her chair uneasily, her brown eyes filled with regret. "It's just that you'd just recently gotten over that broken engagement with him, and here he is calling and trying to start it all up again. I meant to tell you about the calls, in fact, I planned to tell you this morning."

Mariah took another sip of cappuccino. "Thanks for trying to be a friend, Lynn, but in the future, please remember that I need to make my own decisions," she said carefully.

"Of course. It won't happen again," Lynn assured her. "How did you find out?"

"He approached me at the fundraiser."

"That man has a lot of nerve."

"Yes, and sex appeal, talent, good looks, personality, and money," Mariah countered. "There aren't a lot of men like that just floating around. Too bad he's such a rat. I'm not welcoming the renewed attention, but if I send him away for good, it's got to be my decision."

"Good morning. Is this meeting for ladies only?"

The question from the doorway caught Mariah and Lynn by surprise. They both turned their gaze to intercept Anthony dressed in a long-sleeved natural cotton shirt that was open at the neck to reveal a trail of dark hair, and black belted matching pants that complemented his slim frame. Mariah heard Lynn's faint murmur of appreciation. A lock of his curling black hair fell across his forehead, emphasizing his smoldering good looks. Anthony was an attractive man.

"Anthony! Come on in and join us," Mariah said, reopening the bag of Danish. "I see you've got your own coffee. There's a lot of Danish left."

Anthony settled into one of the wingback conference chairs. "I assume we're celebrating your success at last night's fundraiser for juvenile diabetes."

"We are." Lynn gave him a copy of the picture from the morning paper. He studied the picture for a moment and then glanced at the article below.

"Mariah, you were magnificent!" Anthony pulled one of the pastries from the bag.

"Thank you. We were lucky," Mariah grinned.

"I heard in the coffee shop that you've already received a couple of orders for the dress Mariah wore," Lynn put in excitedly.

"Yes." Anthony turned to Mariah. "Would you mind terribly if I had a few copies of the dress made for my special customers?"

"How could you even ask me that?" Mariah said, setting down her cup. "We're all in business to make money. You designed the dress. I'm glad you gave it to me."

"The dress was designed just for you. I hadn't planned to make others, and I think you know that." Anthony took Mariah's hand and squeezed it gently. "I'll tell you what. I'll make it up to you by creating another dress, just for you."

"Anthony, no."

"Yes, Mariah, yes. When you are ready to get married, come see me. I'll make a very special wedding gown, just for you, a special dress for a special lady."

"Thanks, Anthony." Mariah leaned over and kissed his cheek. Her gaze met Lynn's as she lifted an eyebrow.

"You're welcome. Will you be needing a wedding dress very soon?" Anthony asked, the exchange of glances not lost on him.

"I'm not engaged or anything, if that's what you mean." Mariah settled back in her chair. "However, you never know when some dream man might come along and propose."

"I guess not." Anthony gulped his coffee. "I already have a few ideas for your wedding dress. You'll be a beautiful bride."

"I meant to ask you earlier, Mariah, who did your hair?" Lynn asked admiringly. "I like that cut. It really emphasizes your facial features."

"Thank you." Mariah and Anthony replied in unison.

"Anthony?" Lynn asked in wonder, her eyes caressing his facial features. Mariah wondered for the umpteenth time how Anthony could be oblivious to the way Lynn felt about him. It was so obvious.

"Yes, I cut Mariah's hair," Anthony answered seriously. "Before I made enough to feed myself as a designer, I cut hair at one of the salons." Anthony's dark eyes assessed Lynn's face and the thick length of hair she wore hanging to her waist. "That style would not look good on you, but I could suggest something else."

"Would you?" Lynn asked, winding a length of her hair around one finger.

"Not now of course, I need to get measurements and make arrangements for the copies of Mariah's dress." Anthony finished his coffee.

"That's all right," Lynn said quickly, backtracking on her request.

"Patience, Lynn Ware." Anthony stood up and fingered a strand of Lynn's hair. "You've only worn your hair this way for the last five years. Another week or so certainly isn't going to hurt."

Lynn's mouth dropped open in amazement. Anthony didn't seem to notice. Mariah struggled to keep a straight expression on her face. So Anthony was at least aware of Lynn and the way she wore her hair. It wasn't long before he took off to work on his orders. Mariah and Lynn went back to their desks and began to work.

Around ten-thirty, Lynn buzzed Mariah with a phone call. "It's Paul Blair on line one." Lynn said in a voice filled with concern. Imani was supposed to be doing a magazine spread for *Health and Fitness Magazine*. Had Imani failed to show up?

Mariah's stomach tightened as she took a deep breath and then picked up the phone. "Good morning, Paul," she said in as calm and relaxed a voice as she could manage. "I know you're shooting those photos for *Health and Fitness* with Imani. Is there a problem?"

"Yep. She looks terrible! She obviously needs to be at home resting. Mariah, there's no way anyone could look at her today and think she's in good health. We did all we could with makeup, but she spent most of the last two breaks in the bathroom. I just sent her home in a cab."

"I'm so sorry, Paul. Imani wasn't feeling well yesterday, and we were hoping it was just a twenty-four hour bug. Could we send you someone else? Linda is just back from a show in New York. She has a very similar look." Mariah crossed her fingers, awaiting his response. As a top model, Imani demanded a high rate. Linda was less well known, and her rate would be considerably less, but the agency had its ten-year reputation to consider. The agency also needed the percentage income it would receive.

"I'm up against the wall. You realize we've lost a couple of hours already. In the interest of salvaging something from all the time and money spent, I'll give her a try."

"Thanks, Paul. We'll send her right away," Mariah said, glad to obtain some measure of customer satisfaction. Sighing, she hung up the phone and quickly dialed Linda's private line. The phone rang for five minutes straight with no answer. Where was Linda? Mariah opened her Rolodex. Carmen Delane, a relative newcomer to the agency, had much the same look as Linda and Imani, despite her lack of name recognition. Biting her lip, Mariah called Carmen's paging service, and left her number.

Five minutes later, Lynn buzzed Mariah with Carmen's call. "Carmen, are you free for an immediate assignment?" Mariah began. "This would be a wonderful opportunity for you."

"Sure! I mean, what do you want me to do? There's no nudity involved, is there?" Carmen's youthful exuberance bubbled through the phone line.

"No, there's no nudity. This is a layout for *Health and Fitness Magazine*. All you have to do is show up, and pose in the outfits. They'll do your hair and makeup, and you'll get a premium on your usual rate."

"I'll do it. When do I have to be there?"

"Five minutes ago. Get over to the Talon Center, Suite 35C. Do you know where that is?"

"Isn't that near the River Front apartments?"

"Yes. Take Jefferson Avenue east; turn right at Jos Campeau. You'll see it on the left, near the end of the block." As soon as Mariah got Carmen off the phone, she called Paul Blair back and asked him to accept Carmen instead of Linda. Very grudgingly, he agreed. Mariah had the feeling that he would be reluctant to use her agency services in the future if Carmen did not work out.

Having dealt with the crisis, Mariah called Imani's apartment. The phone rang numerous times to no avail. Where was Imani? She'd had ample time to get home.

Mariah went through a stack of picture portfolios featuring several new applicants and identified those she wanted to interview in person. She was determining her priorities when Lynn buzzed her on the intercom. "Yes?"

"Your eleven-thirty appointment is here." A male voice intoned in a simpering imitation of her secretary's voice.

"Get in here, Ramón!" Mariah laughed, pushing back her chair, and retrieving her purse from a bottom drawer. When he opened the door to her office, she was standing, her purse in hand. The scent of his cologne swirled in the air around him. Hugo Boss, Mariah thought, at the sight of his expensive gray suit. It really complemented his tall muscular frame and the color of his eyes. Light bounced off his dark glossy curls. He caught her checking him out and flashed her a dimpled grin full of even white teeth. The man looked good enough to eat.

"You're looking good," he murmured appreciatively, his slate gray eyes warming her.

"Thanks. So are you. Where are we going for lunch?"

"Where do you want to go?" Ramón asked, going to the coat rack and retrieving her navy jacket.

"I don't know. We could go to Greektown."

"Let's go to the Rattlesnake Club," Ramón suggested as he kissed her cheek, his warm lips lingering a few moments more than necessary. When Mariah turned her head in surprise, he was already helping her into her jacket. Ramón was certainly feeling affectionate these days.

"I've never been to the Rattlesnake Club, but it sounds interesting," Mariah said as they closed the door to the inner office. Lynn wished them a good lunch. "Do you want to come along?" Mariah asked, feeling generous.

"Oh no," Lynn replied quickly, "I brought my lunch, and I'm dieting."

Ramón opened the outer door. "Maybe next time," he said smoothly, smiling at Lynn's polite reply. He waved Mariah out of the office, then shut the door. It wasn't long before they were headed for downtown Detroit.

"You haven't heard from your friend yet, have you?" he asked as he turned down Blank Street.

Mariah's gaze briefly locked with his. Sometimes Ramón knew her better than anyone. "No, Cotter hasn't called yet. He probably had surgeries all morning."

"Then what's the problem? Something's bothering you," he said astutely.

"Imani lost the *Health and Fitness* assignment. I was really counting on the income."

"Let me guess. She didn't look very healthy."

"You've got it. Apparently, she's still sick. I've called a few times, but I haven't been able to reach her."

"Losing two assignments in two days is enough to make anyone take notice," he said carefully. "Maybe she went to the doctor."

Mariah stared at him, certain he knew exactly what was wrong with Imani. She refused to ask him to break a confidence. "I hope so," she said finally.

"You can practically smell those new agency offices, can't you?"

"The agency has been in the Buhl building since Mom bucked the system and started it ten years ago. I've just got to continue the tradition by taking it farther."

"You'll get those new offices," Ramón said as they pulled into a parking lot near the Rattlesnake Club. "Your mother would have been proud of all you've done with the agency."

Mariah gazed at the ornate entrance, thrilled with the highly polished natural wood and cool green glass decor of the interior. In no time, they were seated at a table in a corner with a view of the river.

"Is it my imagination, or are you becoming more affectionate?" Mariah asked after they'd put in their orders. He was also quieter than usual. She glanced pointedly at Ramón's hand caressing hers on the table.

"You've just come out of a slump. Don't you need a little extra loving care right now?" he asked in a low voice so filled with emotion that Mariah swallowed hard.

Her startled gaze met his. How could he know? How could he know that she'd only brought it up because she found herself enjoying his caress too much?

"You're a beautiful woman, Mariah, inside and out. I think you know that I have true feelings for you. You've always been more than a casual friend."

Her mind wandered onto all the other neglected parts of her body that had gone without a loving touch for so long that she was vulnerable. Was that why Ramón was suddenly pushing all the right buttons? She couldn't help thinking of Ramón in the role of her lover. He'd be very exciting, yet loving, tender and caring, with her. Mariah wet her lips, not knowing what to say. Finally, she nodded, unable to say the words. One of the rules for her relationship with Ramón was that they were always honest with each other. She saw his gaze riveted to her mouth. In response, her lips burned.

"We're both lonely. Can't I be the one to give you what you need?" Lightly dipping a finger into his wine, he gently shaped her ups with it. She entertained a fleeting thought of touching his finger with her tongue, but didn't feel free to practice such wanton behavior in public. His intense gaze was as potent as a kiss when Mariah tasted the wine on her lips.

"Let me be the one to give you what you need. I'd like to," Ramón continued in a burning whisper close to her ear. One hand stroked her from cheek to chin. "I'd like to cancel the food orders and take you someplace where we can have each other for lunch instead."

"No." Trembling, Mariah took hold of his wrist and gently moved his hand away from her face. Things were going much too far. Fleeting thoughts of sleeping with Ramón were one thing, but the threat of those thoughts becoming a reality inexplicably frightened her.

"No?"

"Ramón," she managed in a teasing tone, "listen hot stuff, you're my best friend and I like it that way!"

"So you think I'm hot, huh?" He maneuvered his chair around the table so that he was sitting next to her. "Can you think of anyone better than your friend to give you what you want? What we both need?" he asked with a smoldering look. Endearingly, a lock of his dark hair had fallen onto his forehead. Mariah's pulse did a two-step. What did she want? she wondered. Could she really do something like that? Sex went together with love and caring as far as she was concerned, but he was tempting. The waiter chose that moment to bring their orders. He set a lobster plate in front of Ramón, and a plate of steaming crab legs in front of Mariah.

"This looks great!" Ramón said as he started in with the crackers. "You can't image how hungry I am!"

Mariah thought of Ramón's offer to cancel their food orders and go somewhere for some hot sex. "Oh, I'm sure you're starving," Mariah replied wryly, and was rewarded with his grin, though a sensual heat still simmered in his gray eyes. The newness of the situation still had her inwardly shaking her head. Ramón with the hots for her? When had he shifted gears? She'd long ago come to the conclusion that she would never be the recipient of the full force of his lethal charm. Had she been wrong?

"Tastes good too," he added between bites of juicy white lobster tail. "How are the crab legs?"

"Fantastic. We'll have to come back," Mariah replied over a forkful of sweet, succulent crab. Every now and then she found herself staring at Ramón when he wasn't looking.

His heated words still rang in her ears. All too soon, the delicious meal was over.

"Would you like dessert?" His voice broke in on her thoughts as she wiped her face and hands with the hot, lemon-scented cloth. Her eyes met his and her face burned in reaction to the blatant suggestion she saw there. She was sure he'd meant, Do you want to be dessert?"

"Please stop," she said, feeling as if she couldn't take anymore of Ramón's teasing.

"All right," he said easily, his expression contrite. "If I made you uncomfortable, I'm sorry." He took her hand and squeezed it. "Are we still friends?"

"Of course. You may get on my nerves every now and then, but I still love you." Mariah squeezed back.

"Really?" he asked innocently, too innocently. There was the 'love me because I'm so sweet and charming look' on his handsome face again. And he was, handsome and charming, that is. He was also the best friend to have around when you really needed one. How had she managed to see him at least weekly for the last ten years and not be seriously affected by all that sheer male beauty and attractiveness? She had to chalk it up to the fact that they'd each maintained relationships with other people during that time.

Mariah raised an eyebrow. "I don't know about you, but I've got to get back to the office."

"So do I. That case starts up in court tomorrow," Ramón replied as he started looking at the bill. "Wish me luck."

"Good luck." Mariah relaxed a little. This was more the type of behavior she expected from her friend. "So what would you have done if I'd taken you up on your offer?" she couldn't help asking in an exasperated tone. "Sometimes you go too far with your teasing and kidding around."

"I hit a vulnerable spot, huh?" He gave her a devilish grin and she considered pounding his head. "Who said I was kidding? Don't I always make time for you?"

"You're pushing it, Richards. Keep it up and it'll be a long time before we have lunch again," Mariah said in a low voice between clenched teeth. Why had she let him get her all worked up?

"Sure you're not just frustrated?" he asked, his expression too serious. The truth in his words sent her pulse racing all over again. She wanted to hit him. What was she going to do with her wayward friend? She'd never seen him so persistent. "Frustrated with me, of course," he added quickly, cleaning it up, and making Mariah feel marginally better.

"I've had a lot of excitement today," Mariah admitted truthfully. And too much of it was related to her dear friend Ramón Richards, she added to herself. "I'm sorry if I seem irritable."

"No need to apologize to me." Ramón reached into the opening of his suit jacket and pulled out his wallet.

"What's my share of the bill?" Mariah asked, grabbing her purse.

"This is my treat."

"Really?"

"Really. I think we did great last night, and between the sponsor list on the back of last night's program, and our pictures in the paper this morning, we've had a number of calls come in this morning for the firm. Never underestimate the power of suggestion."

"I won't. Well, thanks for lunch. I really enjoyed the meal."

"Me too. We'll have to do it again sometime." Ramón threw a large bill on the table and stood up to leave. As easy as that he slipped back into his usual self, and Mariah relaxed. By the time they arrived back at her office, they were joking and laughing as they usually did. Mariah barely noticed the tension headache until he was gone.

"How was lunch?" Lynn asked when Mariah walked past her.

"It was great," Mariah said with a smile. "You should have come along."

"Three is a crowd."

"Ramón and I are just friends," Mariah insisted stubbornly, clenching her teeth.

Lynn nodded with a half smile; it was obvious from her expression that she didn't believe that statement.

Mariah continued into the inner office to shrug out of her jacket. She hoped the rest of the day would be boring, because she'd already had all the excitement she could take.

At four o'clock, Lynn buzzed Mariah over the intercom and said, "Dr. Eastwood on line one."

Mariah took a deep breath and then picked up the phone. "Hello?" She hated the hoarseness in her voice.

"I badly needed to hear your voice," Cotter said on the other end of the line. "The last five months have been pure hell."

Mariah cleared her throat. "Cotter, you chose to end everything. You got what you wanted."

"I didn't get you. I'll never forgive myself for that. We should have postponed the wedding."

"Why?" Mariah's question pulled down a curtain of silence that lasted for several moments.

"Do you really want me to explain on the phone? I want to see your face. I need to talk to you in person." His words and tone of voice made it seem as though he'd come a long way from the proud, almost arrogant man she'd been engaged to. Mariah still resented his attempt to play on her sympathy. She was the injured party.

"And why should I care? Why can't you just leave me alone?"

"Because...because I love you and I know you loved me. The question is, do you still care? Do you think you could ever..."

Mariah broke in on him. "I've had some pretty negative feelings for you these past months, and that's an understatement. Just let it go, Cotter."

"I can't. If you... Excuse me for just a minute, would you?" Mariah heard muffled whispering, and then Cotter was back on the line. "I've got surgery in five minutes, I've got to go. Mariah, think about you and me, would you?"

"I'll try and think on it. Good-bye, Cotter." Quickly, Mariah hung up the phone. Her fingernails strummed nervously against the surface of her desk. Did she still want to be Mrs. Cotter Eastwood? It was something she hadn't thought about for a long time.

The rest of the day proved uneventful, except for several calls from friends who saw her picture in the paper. At five-thirty, Mariah went home in the pouring rain and kicked off her shoes. Then she took off her suit and changed into more casual clothing. Instead of enjoying the solitude as she usually did, she paced the floors like a caged animal. An unusual sense of restlessness drove her to distraction. To get relief, Mariah went to sit out on the enclosed porch, and breathe in the fresh air flowing through its screens. After a while, she became accustomed to the violent patter of the rain on the roof.

What was she going to do about Cotter Eastwood? she wondered briefly. Since the night of the fundraiser, she'd tried hard not to think of him at all. Taking no action was also making a decision, she decided. It was equivalent to a no. Mariah felt oddly disappointed. She hadn't contacted him, he'd come to her. Except for their broken engagement, he'd always been a man of his word. That's why his past rejection had been so unexpected and devastating.

Mariah pushed back in the white wooden porch swing, and stretched out full length on the bright green, forest print pillows. As the swing moved back and forth, she thought about the first time she'd met Cotter Eastwood. Two years ago, they'd been introduced at a Detroit Medical Center fundraiser she attended with her friend Dr. Sonia Martin. Sonia had been certain that her colleague and her friend would like each other.

Prior to their relationship, several women had pursued the tall and debonair Cotter Eastwood, but he chose Mariah. He was fifteen years older than she, and handsome in a distinguishably elegant sort of way, with a streak of white in his curling dark hair. Sparkling sherry brown eyes stood out against his walnut skin tone. He pursued her relentlessly for months, treating her like a precious diamond, and spoiling her ridiculously. For a while, Cotter had been like the handsome prince in a fairy tale, wooing her with dinner and dancing, the theater, and weekend junkets to different Caribbean islands. Mariah had welcomed the attention. What woman would not have been flattered? Cotter was also a genuinely kind and caring individual.

His family, rich for generations, had been the only snakes in their paradise. Mariah's background worried them. Her father, a major in the army, had died in Vietnam. Her mother died several years later, after Mariah finished college, leaving her the modeling agency. Mariah was no debutante, and never would be, but Cotter didn't seem to care.

Why had he broken their engagement? At the time, he'd been just as emotionally distraught as she, and for months she'd been positive he'd come back. She was certain he'd never been completely honest with her.

Feeling melancholy, Mariah sat up in the swing, picked a copy of the latest bestseller, and began to read. When she wasn't reading the book, she stared out at the dreary landscape. No matter how hard she tried, she couldn't seem to concentrate. She found herself reading the same page over and over again. When had the comfort gone out of her time alone? Finally, she went back into the house and fell asleep around ten o'clock.

THREE

A persistent ringing pulled Mariah from the depths of sleep. She sat up, disoriented in the dark, and blindly patted the nightstand for the phone. In a fog, she picked up the receiver and put it to her ear. "Hello?" A dial tone answered her. The determined ringing continued. Then she recognized the sound of the doorbell. Checking the luminous dial of her clock, Mariah turned on the light. It was seven-fifteen. Jumping out of bed, she stepped into a blue silk caftan.

"Hold on, I'm coming!" she yelled as she ran across the peach living room carpet to the front door, fluffing her hair with her fingers. If Cotter Eastwood stood on the other side of the door, he wouldn't see her at her worst. He was the only person who'd ever had the nerve to show up at her door this early in the morning. A quick check confirmed her suspicion. He stood on her porch with a large package in his arms and a big woven basket at his feet. I'm not going to let him in, Mariah decided, focusing on how she would get him to leave quickly.

Detecting Mariah's movement at the peephole, Cotter faced her directly and said, "Please let me in, Mariah. I've been waiting for hours to talk to you." Slowly, Mariah opened the door, surprising herself at how easily she responded to his request. She'd talk through the screen, she told herself.

Cotter's gaze was like a physical caress. "Good morning, beautiful."

Mariah immediately thought of all the mornings she'd been awakened by Cotter with a kiss and much the same phrase.

"May I come in?" he asked, looking as if she'd already kicked him, his hand on the screen door.

Where had all her anger gone? Mariah wondered as she hesitated. She didn't know what she wanted to do.

"Sweetheart?"

Mariah's awareness snapped back to his face at the sound of his voice. Slowly, she opened the screen door.

He looked as if he'd break out into some elegant dance any moment in his gray blue silk suit. "I don't think this is a good idea," Mariah said carefully as he walked into her home for the first time in eight months.

"I do. I owe you some sort of an explanation for abandoning you and all that we'd built. These are for you." He thrust the first, cone-shaped package at Mariah.

"I don't want anything from you."

"Please?" he begged, something she had never seen him do before. Mariah accepted the package. He waited expectantly until she began to tear at the paper, certain that he wouldn't rest until she'd uncovered the contents. "I performed surgeries all day yesterday and didn't finish up until five-thirty. I sat down on the couch in my office for a minute and must have fallen asleep. When I woke up, it was two o'clock this morning. I've been waiting since then to talk to you."

Mariah's eyes burned with unshed tears as she lifted the delicate white china vase with its small bouquet of three purple orchids from the wrapping. He'd always given her purple orchids and called her his queen. Months ago, she would have thrown them in his face. Carefully, she set them on the coffee table in the living room.

"I've brought breakfast and champagne," he said quickly, seeing her distress. "Will you eat with me? Please?"

Mariah nodded and then followed him into the dining room. She watched him pull caviar, croissants, Danish, cheese, silverware, plates, and fruit salad from the basket and set them on the table. Artfully, he arranged the food on the two white china plates with gold edging, and placed gold silverware beside them.

Gently, Cotter took Mariah's hand, and settled her into one of the beige velvet cushioned chairs. "I've never loved anyone the way I love you," he began, his hands on her shoulders. "I've never even loved another woman." He moved to sit in the chair across from her, and leaned close. "You know how close I am to my family, and that they've never appreciated you the way I did. It was a constant source of pressure for me, but I thought I could handle it."

Something flickered in his eyes. Fear? Then he continued. "No matter what you may think, I've never been comfortable with the difference in our ages. I've seen too many older men with young pretty wives that they can't seem to satisfy. Before I met you, I promised myself that I'd never be one of them."

Mariah caught her breath. "You never had that problem."

"No, but it could have happened. It was always in the back of my mind, especially when you spent time with your friends. I was jealous of your friends, jealous of any time you spent away from me, and yet I wasn't selfish enough to expect you to sit around waiting for me to come home."

"Why?" Mariah interrupted. "Why were you jealous of my friends? I never gave you a reason."

"I know that, sweetheart." He brushed her cheek with the tip of a finger. "Your friends and I aren't in the same generation. Heaven knows you're far too young for me. And I've always known in my heart that you would be better off with someone who wants to give you children."

"Your age never mattered to me." She caught his hand and gently moved it away from her face. "And I never said I wanted children."

"I'd bet my life on it. Mariah, you love children. You're just a little afraid because you've never gotten over the death of your little sister."

Mariah flinched. She would never forget her beautiful baby sister. Poor Jennifer hadn't lived past the age of thirteen. It had taken Mariah a long time to come to terms with God for taking her. Biting her lip, Mariah deliberately unclenched her fists. "What are you saying? Have you decided that you want children after all?"

"I'm willing to do whatever it takes. I can do it. These months away from you have shown me just how barren my life is without you in it. I love you." Cotter's warm lips pressed against Mariah's. "All at once everything made the odds against us seem overwhelming and I couldn't handle it. I just couldn't see continuing with the wedding. I got a terminal case of cold feet. Can… you ever forgive me for abandoning you?" Cotter choked, searing her with his soulful gaze.

She actually saw tears in his eyes, and despite all logic, her heart went out to him. "You really hurt me," she replied shakily. "I don't think things will ever be the same."

"I've changed, Mariah. I'm a new man. I'm not staying with my family right now. I've moved out of the mansion. I still see my family, but they don't control me." His fingers tightened on hers. "I know what's important now."

"Maybe it's too late," Mariah whispered. She didn't really know this new Cotter Eastwood. Staring at him was like looking at a lost dream, back to haunt her. Had it ever been real? She suspected that painful memories and heartbreak would never allow her to trust him with her heart again. An old saying played in the back of her mind like a broken record: 'You can never go home again.' Deep inside she was beginning to realize that it was all too true.

With visibly shaking fingers, he grabbed the bottle of champagne and opened it.

"Will you give me a chance? I never stopped loving you."

Hugging herself, Mariah moved away from him. "I…I can't."

He recoiled as if she'd slapped him and stared at her in shocked silence.

"I've just barely gotten over everything. I've got to give me a chance, Cotter," she told him.

In a nervous flurry he produced two crystal champagne flutes from a foam-lined pouch and filled them with champagne and orange juice. Then he pressed one into her hand. "Try to eat something. I know you have to go to work," he said in a strained voice.

Mariah focused on the bubbling orange liquid, and then Cotter. "I shouldn't have let you in." She lifted the crystal flute to her lips and drank, savoring the champagne and orange juice sizzle on her tongue and all the way down her throat. Setting the glass down, she raised her eyes to Cotter. "I'd given up on you."

Cotter stood and pulled her to her feet and into his arms. She stiffened and pressed her hands against his chest. "Let me go, Cotter."

His persistent lips found the skin on her temple. She caught a whiff of Aramis cologne and turned her head. When Mariah gave him a more determined push, he dropped his arms.

"It's over," she said, her voice stronger.

"Just tell me what you want," Cotter crooned, smoothing her hair with one hand.

"I want you to leave." Mariah stepped further away from him. "I've got to get ready for work," she murmured.

A stricken expression flickered across his face. "I guess I should be going."

He was driving away in his dark blue Mercedes when Mariah closed and locked the front door. On her way to the shower, Mariah stopped to touch the orchids. The fact that Cotter had been jealous of her friends jarred her. She'd always been proud that despite the difference in their years, he'd seemed to fit right in with her friends. Boy, had she been way off base! And when she'd noticed Cotter's lack of enthusiasm around children and suspected that he did not want children, she'd been right. But Mariah had had no inkling of the depth of his unhappiness until he had broken their engagement.

The early morning news provided background sound for Mariah as she dressed for work in a rust-colored dress with black suede accents on the sleeves and collar. She paused and ran to the large television set when the newscasters started talking about Ramón's controversial client. The film clip showed Gerald Hatten to be of average height and build. He wore a black tailor-made suit that looked smart as he climbed out of the black Cadillac with Ramón and another lawyer. Ramón stood tall, handsome, and professional in a severely-cut navy Versace suit. He looked as if he could save the world. There was no doubt in her mind about his professional abilities, but those lips of his still looked quite kissable.

Briefly, the news anchor gave the names of the members of the prosecution and defense teams, also mentioning Ramón's law firm, and his connection to Judge Richards. Then Ramón and a co-worker eased Gerald Hatten past a group of reporters while answering each of their rapid-fire questions with the words, "No comment." Mariah hoped Gloria Richards had her video recorder going.

At eight fifty-nine, Mariah strolled into her outer office with a bag full of breakfast leftovers. "I'll set this stuff out on my conference table," she told Lynn. "Feel free to help yourself."

"Whatcha got?" Lynn asked, giving the bag her best x-ray eye.

"Croissants, caviar, fruit salad, and cheese."

"Mmmmh, sounds like the remains of a champagne breakfast..."

Mariah felt the blood rushing to her face. Refusing to react or comment further, she walked into the inner office and began to place the food containers on the table. She didn't appreciate Lynn's comment, because she knew Lynn was thinking of all the times she'd come in with leftovers from other Cotter champagne breakfasts. By bringing in the leftovers, Mariah had practically made an announcement that she was seeing Cotter again. Although it wasn't true, she didn't want to discuss it.

Five minutes later, Lynn stood in the doorway. "I brought you some coffee."

"Thank you."

"That comment just slipped out without my thinking. I'm sorry if it seemed as if I was trying to pry."

"That's all right," Mariah said, taking the top off her foam cup. "Get something to eat and we'll discuss today's schedule."

Lynn fixed a plate with fruit salad, caviar, and cheese, and then sat down at the conference table. "Mmmmmh, there're some good fringe benefits for working here."

"I certainly couldn't eat it all myself, and if I put it in the fridge, I usually forget all about it. When we get through here, why don't take a plate of this stuff down to Anthony's office?"

"That's a good idea," Lynn said, her expression brightening visibly. "We probably won't be seeing him for a while. He's got a lot of new orders."

"Yeah, I'm happy for him." Slowly, Mariah sipped her coffee. "Did Cora Belson ever call? She's starting the planning activities for her yearly fashion experience, and I'm sure we've got just what she needs."

"She hasn't called yet. I can put her on the call list…"

"No, if she hasn't called by Friday, I'm going over there. She was really complimentary to the agency at that fundraiser. I'm sure she's planning to get in touch with us. Did anyone call as a result of our splash in the newspaper?"

Lynn grabbed a napkin and patted her lips. "Actually, a photographer who's doing a sale catalog for Hudson's called as I was leaving last night and a made an appointment to come in and talk to you today. He saw your picture in the paper and liked your looks. I guess the important thing is that he remembered the name of the agency."

"I hope it results in some new business." Mariah set her cup down. "What else do we have scheduled for today?"

"The photographer is scheduled this morning at ten. You have a couple of people scheduled for fifteen-minute appointments to meet you and go over their stats at eleven, and eleven-fifteen. Then there's nothing until your tennis date at four o'clock."

"I'll probably make a few calls this afternoon and then leave early for tennis."

Mariah was nearly finished evaluating a stack of resumes when the photographer, Arturro Felton, showed up. He was an attractive man of medium height, with ultra smooth skin the color of warm cocoa. After introducing herself and getting the details on his project, she asked for identification.

Arturro Felton stared at her the way a hungry chocoholic stares at a Snickers bar. By persisting with a professional attitude despite his obvious admiration and pushing ahead, Mariah forced him to proceed with the business at hand. While he studied the stack of resumes and portfolios she'd put together, she had Lynn check out his credentials. By ten-thirty, he'd made several selections. Mariah took the studio address and instructions to Lynn for copying and gave her half the names on the list of models to call. The other half, she planned to call herself.

With the business portion of his visit complete for the day, Arturro devoted several minutes of his time to the task of persuading Mariah to have lunch with him. He seemed sweet, but she really didn't know a thing about him, so she politely rejected his advances.

She knew Lynn was still at the copy machine when the phone rang, so she answered the phone. "McCleary Modeling Agency."

"Mariah?" She detected a vulnerable note in the husky softness of the woman's voice. "Imani! Imani, where have you been? I was worried about you."

"I...I'm in the hospital."

"You what...?" Mariah started, then remembered her audience. Arturro Felton was feasting his eyes on her and drinking in every word of her conversation. "Hold on a minute." She smiled at Arturro, covering the receiver of the phone. "Mr. Felton, I'll stop by your studio in the morning, help get things started, and make sure you have the models you need, okay?"

"I'm looking forward to it," he replied, getting up to leave.

With Arturro Felton gone, Mariah spoke into the receiver. "Imani, what happened to you?"

"I got sick in the cab on the way home from the fitness assignment. I was so sick that the driver dropped me off at the Hutsel Hospital Emergency Room."

"Are you feeling better now?"

"Much, much better. For a while there, I felt like I was dying..."

"Don't even think it!" Mariah said quickly. "You're not seriously ill, are you?"

"No. I'll recover."

"Why don't I come down and see you at lunch time?"

"I wish you would. Ramón's been my only visitor."

Mariah cursed softly. "That man sure does get around!" she said under her breath.

"I didn't catch that. Were you talking to me?"

"Yes. I said that a better friend can't be found," Mariah quipped, covering her tracks.

"He's certainly been good to me."

"Do you need me to bring anything?"

"Let's talk about it when you get here. I'm in 401 south."

Quickly, Mariah scribbled the room number on a yellow note pad. "It'll be about twelve or twelve-fifteen, okay?"

"Sure, I'll be looking for you."

Mariah ended the call thoughtfully. It was a relief to know Imani had made it to the hospital and was feeling better, but she couldn't help wondering about the nature of Imani's problem. Mariah had a sneaking suspicion that Imani was not going to be able to keep any of her commitments for a long time.

Only one of the scheduled appointments with potential print models proved fruitful. Mariah added his résumé to her files and left him at the office filling out application forms. The lunchtime traffic was only mildly annoying. She stopped by a fast food restaurant and scarfed down a grilled chicken sandwich with ice tea.

It was close to twelve-thirty when Mariah stopped at the information desk for a visitor pass. She took the nearly deserted elevator to the fourth floor and followed the signs around to 401 south.

Imani's private room was flooded with bright sunshine. A large bouquet of red roses filled a crystal vase on the small bedside chest of drawers. Imani sat in the center of the bed, polishing her nails. The soft black curtain of hair hid her exotic face from view. A red and black silk cover-up graced her slim figure. She looked up as Mariah entered the room. "Hi. I suppose you noticed on the way in that this is the maternity section?"

"Yes, I did."

"I really wasn't sure when I saw you last. I did my best to stick my head in the sand and hope it would go away." Imani leaned back to close the bottle of gold nail polish and set it on the bedside table. "I had a lot of assignments scheduled, and I know you've got plans for the agency. Are you angry with me?"

"No." Mariah felt lightheaded as she settled into the guest chair. She was going to have to find someone to take Imani's assignments. "How's the little person doing?"

"Fine, for now." Imani placed a hand on her abdomen. "They're letting me go home tomorrow, but I've got to take it easy."

"Are you endangering your health?"

"Not really. I haven't been eating well because I didn't know I was pregnant. I could hardly keep anything down anyway."

"Do you have someone to help you out? Will the baby's father…?"

Imani's face hardened. "I don't want to talk about him."

Mariah's eyes widened. She bit back a number of the questions that came to mind. "How far along are you?"

"Two months," Imani said, poking out her bottom lip. "He does not want children. I wasn't trying to get pregnant. I simply missed two birth control pills!"

Mariah got up from the chair to sit on the bed and put her arms around Imani. After several moments, Imani pulled away, her eyes bright with unshed tears. "I could never kill my unborn child. Especially when it was made with love."

"Maybe he'll come around…" Mariah said, feeling incredibly sad for Imani.

"No. He won't." Imani settled back against the pillows. "He's still trying to be a playboy. Everybody loves him. Not many people even know I'm his girlfriend. I'm all alone in this."

"If there's anything I can do, I'd be happy to help you out."

"Thanks, Mariah. I appreciate your offer. I may have to call you on it."

"And that'll be fine."

"Do you think we can keep this from the press? He's sort of in the limelight right now, and I don't want to spoil things for him."

That was some pretty unselfish thinking on Imani's part, Mariah thought. It was obvious that Imani really loved the jerk who'd fathered her baby. Imani's references to the limelight reminded Mariah of Ramón. A nasty little thought swirled around in her head. There was no way that Ramón could be the father of Imani's baby, was there? She'd seen him with Imani often enough. But Ramón would never father a child out of wedlock. Mariah felt shame for even thinking of the possibility. "We could say that that you're recovering from exhaustion and taking a break when the question comes up."

"Sounds good to me." Imani smiled. "After I've had a day or two to recover, maybe I could still do a few of the scheduled assignments, at least until I begin to show."

"I'm glad you brought it up. We could certainly try." Mariah relaxed a little. She was glad that Imani was not seriously ill, but the agency still needed to pay its bills. It would be hard to replace Imani. "After your pregnancy becomes obvious, we could also pursue assignments with some of the maternity and parenting magazines."

"I'll do all I can, physically. I have some investments and money saved, but I don't want to go back to ground zero just because I skipped a few pills."

"Hey, your flowers are beautiful," Mariah said, changing the subject. She stood up and walked over to bedside table to touch the soft petals of one bloom. The fresh fragrant scent of the roses filled her nostrils. They'd been organically grown. Mariah recognized Ramón's scrawled signature at the bottom of the short message on the card.

"I love roses," Imani said, stretching out on the bed. "Ramón volunteered to bring me home from the hospital tomorrow during the lunch recess."

"That's great," Mariah said, wondering just how he was going to accomplish that feat and get back to court on time. The man was definitely going out of his way to help Imani. But hadn't he bent over backwards to help her out of the deep funk she sank in when Cotter dropped her like a hot potato? Sunlight from the window warmed her face. "Want to see what I brought you?"

Imani's face brightened. "I really wasn't expecting a thing."

"That's what makes it fun." Mariah lifted a medium-sized package covered with a shiny blue floral print from the shopping bag by the chair and placed it in Imani's hands. She'd done some of her Christmas shopping early, and it was coming in handy. There was plenty of time to get Imani another present, Mariah thought, as she watched Imani carefully tear open the wrapping paper.

"You have such good taste! I just love it," Imani said, pulling the soft beige silk and lace cover-up from the tissue paper. She held the silky material up to her chest, rubbing her hands across the material. "This is nice. I think I'll change into it. Thanks, Mariah."

"Oh, you're welcome, Imani. I saw that in Saks and just knew it had your name on it." Mariah glanced at her watch. "I've got to get going. Let me know if there's anything I can do to help, okay?"

"Sure."

When Mariah left the hospital minutes later, Imani was getting up to change into the dressing gown.

Later in the day, Mariah arrived at the Franklin Center. She'd already stopped by the house and changed into a short white tennis dress with a v-neck and pleated skirt. Taking her racquet from the bag, she placed her purse and bag in a locker. After pulling on a white headband, Mariah put two balls in each of her pockets. She checked her watch. It was four-twenty. Mariah hurried to the court.

Sonia Martin was busy hitting balls on an empty court. She looked up as Mariah approached. "Hey Mariah, did you see Phil anywhere in the club?"

Mariah quickly scanned the immediate area. "No, I haven't seen Phil, but I think I see Mitch over there on court six." She heard Sonia's frustrated sigh. Phil was always late for their twice a month tennis game. "We could always play two on one, you and I against Mitch," she added half-heartedly.

"This is the last straw. We need to get another doubles partner," Sonia fumed. "Why do we put up with Phil?" She slammed her last ball to the other side of the court, then went to collect them.

"You're not looking for Phil, are you?"

Mariah turned at the sound of a familiar voice. "Ramón, what are you doing here?"

"Subbing for Phil. He's the expert on our juror selection team, so I get to take the break right now. I have to go back to the office in a couple of hours, of course."

His eyes touched on the short white tennis dress she wore. Mariah warmed under his appreciative gaze. "Poor Phil, lucky us." She saw Ramón check his watch. "You'd better put your stuff away, because it's almost time to start." Mariah enjoyed the view as he hurried away on strong, tan, muscular legs. He had a nice butt too, she thought, her eyes moving past his firm rounded hips to his well-defined waist and muscular arms and shoulders. There wasn't much she didn't like about Ramón Richards. Briefly, she wondered who was enjoying Ramón these days. He wasn't talking about any one woman, and she hadn't seen him with anyone. It was no wonder people thought she and Ramón were dating.

In an effort to start her warm up, she hit a few balls to Sonia when he disappeared. "Ramón's subbing for Phil," she called out.

Sonia nodded, visibly relieved. As she passed Mariah on her way to take her court position, she said, "Did you know that Cotter's been asking about you?"

"Yes, he managed to catch up with me."

"I know that things didn't work out the way they should have, but he's a good man, Mariah. You could do a lot worse."

"I'm inclined to agree with you," Mariah countered. "But that does not mean I'm ready to repeat past mistakes."

"Touché!" Sonia grinned. "Just had to put a good word in for one good friend to another. I thought you guys made a great couple."

"I thought so, too." Mariah tested her grip on the tennis racquet. "Shall we toss the coin to see who goes first? Here comes Ramón."

Mariah couldn't have wished for a better partner. Ramón's style of playing tennis complemented hers more than either Mitch or Phil's. She liked to play close to the net, easily acing back several balls. She quickly worked up a sweat. Ramón stayed in the back of the court, returning Mitch's hard and fast forehand with aplomb. He was a speed demon, all over the court, but never crowding her space or territory.

Near the end of the match, Mariah made a nearly impossible save and got a leg cramp as she put the ball away. She fell backwards, clutching her leg. Ramón got to her first, his gray eyes filled with concern as he brushed her protective hands away in order to message the muscle. "Ahhhh!" Mariah moaned under the gentle yet firm pressure of his hands. Sonia and Mitch stood by and watched for a moment, then ran to get a quick drink from the sidelines. After a while the cramp eased and there was only the pleasant feel of Ramón's hands on her leg. What would it feel like to have his hands move up her legs and on to her entire body? Mariah relaxed, and then caught herself. What in the world was she doing?

"All better?" Ramón asked, his intent expression not hiding his knowledge of her enjoyment. "Ready to finish the game?"

Mariah bent her leg and shook it experimentally. Did she hear Ramón put a little extra emphasis on the word "game"? She tried to gauge his expression as he helped her to her feet and decided that it must have been her imagination. "Yes. Thanks for getting the cramp out. Let's finish the slaughter!" she cried, scooting off towards the front court. Ramón and Mariah beat the pants off Sonia and Mitch.

"I wish you could take Phil's place full-time," Mariah said to Ramón, as she dropped to a bench outside the court. The muscle in her leg was still a little sore, and her legs and feet still throbbed from their vigorous play. "I think Sonia and Mitch are still in shock. The two of them always win against Phil and me."

"I heard that. Great game, Ramón, Mariah." Grinning, Mitch came off the court and shook their hands. "I'd hang around, but I promised to take my son to get new baseball cleats. What are you guys going to do?"

"I don't have a lot of time either." Ramón replied, glancing at his watch. "I'm due back at the office in about another hour and fifteen minutes. I've got a taste for Coney Island."

"That's a good idea," Mariah countered. "Let's go to Lafayette Coney Island." She saw Sonia drag herself off the court. "Got time to stop at Lafayette Coney Island in downtown Detroit?"

"I'm really beat." Sonia ran a hand through her short blond hair. "I'm already dreaming about a nice hot tub and sandwich before I go to bed. I've got patients scheduled all day tomorrow. No, I think I'll have to turn you guys down."

"Still want to go, Mariah?" Ramón stood, patting his face with a towel.

"Sure, I'll meet you by the front desk in fifteen minutes. Then I'll follow you to Coney Island."

Traffic headed towards downtown Detroit on the Lodge Freeway was minimal, but it was a busy night for the Lafayette Coney Island. Their varied clientele covered the entire range of possibilities, from professional people still in their business suits, to homeless people. After searching carefully, they found a table in the back. When the waiter promptly appeared, they gave him their order. Their drinks came first.

"I heard from Imani today," Mariah ventured casually. She leaned forward, trying to gauge Ramón's reaction.

Slowly, he poured his beer from the bottle into the small glass. "I'm glad she finally talked to you," he said carefully, his gaze meeting hers. "Did you go see her?"

"Yes," Mariah said, deciding to stress the obvious. "I went down to the hospital. Why didn't you tell me about her problem, or at least let me know she was in the hospital?"

He visibly relaxed at that. "I had a hell of a time not blurting it all out to you, but it was not my secret to tell."

"Aren't you taking her home from the hospital tomorrow?"

"Yeah, I promised, but I'm going to have a hell of a time making it work because of the trial. She'll have to be ready to go when I arrive, and I won't be able to stay and do anything more."

"I'd be happy to help, and I told Imani that." Mariah thanked the waiter for the steaming Special he set down in front of her. The spicy scent filled her nostrils and her mouth watered at the sight of the hot dog and bun covered with the rich ground beef gravy. She brushed half the chopped onions from the top.

"I wish you could help, but Imani is so depressed right now that she would probably interpret it as me abandoning her. She's a very lonely lady."

So am I, Mariah realized. Except for her friends, she'd been alone for too long. She and Imani couldn't ask for a better friend. She sprayed mustard and catsup across the top of her Special and broke into it with her fork. "Do you know who the father is?"

"Yes, but that's another secret she wants to keep. When I saw her, she still hadn't told the poor guy. I think she's putting him on trial."

"Do you know him personally?" she asked carefully, not wanting to risk his anger by simply asking if he'd fathered the child.

Ramón stopped chewing to give Mariah a penetrating stare. He knows what I'm thinking, she thought. "I've met him and seen him socially a few times, but we're not friends or anything."

She let her breath out slowly while she poured her own beer into a glass. She'd been right in thinking that her friend would never father a child out of wedlock.

"Why do you ask?"

Mariah chewed a mouthful and swallowed, her mind working furiously. "I was just wondering, do you think he'll stand by her, or offer her some form of support?"

Ramón chewed thoughtfully, shaking his head. He'd already demolished one of his Specials. "He's still playing the field. I think that he really does care for her, just isn't aware of how much. She just sprung the pregnancy on him, so he's just reacting right now. The guy's in the media a lot, so he'll want to keep this quiet."

Mariah shrugged her shoulders and drank her beer, enjoying the bittersweet taste of the cold gold liquid. A quick glance at Ramón assured her that he was no longer suspicious of her questions. She decided to change the subject. "I saw you on TV this morning."

"What did you think?" Ramón wolfed down the last of his meal, licking his lips.

"I was so proud of you!" Mariah threw him a teasing glance. "You looked so handsome and professional! I'm sure the women viewers thought you could handle anything."

"And I can."

"And you're so modest!" Mariah wiped her lips with a napkin. "Do you think your mom got it on tape? They certainly showed that clip enough times."

"I'd bet money on it. Mom was in seventh heaven. She had a front row seat during the jury selection process today. She asked about you."

"Really? And what did you say?"

"I told her we went to lunch. I didn't know I'd be subbing for Phil."

"How is my second mom?" His mother, Gloria Richards, was always making sure Mariah knew she was a welcome part of her family. It made Mariah miss her mother just a little bit less. Ramón's parents treated Mariah like one of their kids.

"Oh, she's fine. I guess you guys have a lunch date?"

"Yeah, we're going to Fishbones. How's your dad?"

"Happy to have the spotlight on someone else for a change. Of course he's proud. I've got a lot to live up to because of him."

Mariah grabbed his hand and squeezed it. "You can do it."

"I appreciate your confidence." It wasn't long before they finished their meal. Ramón glanced at the bill and pulled out his wallet. Mariah gave him ten dollars. Ramón threw a few bills on the table. "So, did the good doctor finally call?"

"Yes, he did, and then he dropped in on me unexpectedly this morning."

"Wait a minute! You didn't let him in, did you?"

The blood rushed to her face. Mariah shifted in her seat and threw him a sheepish look. "I wasn't going to. I need my head examined. I don't know, he was just so persuasive. Before I really thought about it, I'd already opened the door and let him in. Do you think he hypnotized me? Don't answer that."

His answering silence surprised her. She saw his jaw tighten and a myriad of quickly suppressed expressions cross his face. He almost looked as if she'd somehow disappointed him. She felt like a pushover for letting Cotter in, but why should it matter to Ramón? "Ramón, just what are you holding back?"

"Did you sleep with him?" he asked in a low, stilted tone.

Mariah dipped her head, pushing the hair back from her face in a nervous gesture. "Excuse me?"

"I said, did you sleep with him? Lately, you've been vulnerable." His eyes burned with something that looked like anger.

"You've got some nerve!" Mariah exploded vehemently. "I don't believe you asked me that. Number one, it's insulting that you think I'd be that stupid! Number two, it's none of your damned business!"

"I think it is." His gaze was unflinching. "Sometimes you're too nice for your own good. You want to give everyone a chance. Mariah, the guy's no good for you. I really don't want to see you go through the wringer again."

"Then you can imagine how I feel about it! Ramón, I don't think Cotter is a bad person. I'm not that bad a judge of character. Sometimes good people do bad things, or foolish and stupid things. We all make mistakes, and people shouldn't judge us or our entire lives negatively because of it."

"You really believe that, don't you? That is what I'd expect to hear him say to you. Sometimes you're just too nice." He wagged a finger at her and said, "If you don't watch out, he'll worm his way back into your life."

Mariah resented his words and his finger wagging. Cotter had made a colossal mistake, but prior to that, he'd been the stuff dreams are made of. The decision on whether he got another chance or not would be made by her alone. "Are you so sure it would be a bad thing?"

"I've never seen you so hurt and demoralized as you were when he did his cold feet act. I remember..."

"I'd rather you didn't." Suddenly so angry she could barely speak, Mariah stood up. "I don't need you to remember how devastated I was. You're talking about the past. I'm trying to go forward with my life."

"Why are you so angry?"

"Ramón, believe it or not, I don't need you to direct my life. I was doing just fine before I met you. And I've got a personal question for you," she said, feeling reckless. "Did you sleep with Imani?"

"What?"

"You heard me, did you sleep with Imani?"

"As you said, that's none of your damned business, but the answer is no. When we started dating, she'd already formed an attachment for the baby's father. We're just friends. I don't play second for anyone." His eyes narrowed. "You thought the baby was mine?"

"I thought it was possible."

"You don't think too much of me, do you?" he asked incredulously.

"Ramón, it's not about that. You like women in quantity and variety."

"That's been true in the past, but I've never gotten anyone pregnant, and I won't until I'm married. We've discussed this before. What has any of that to do with you and Cotter Eastwood?"

"I wanted you to get some inkling of how I felt when you asked me about sleeping with him."

Ramón got to his feet. "I wish you'd quit being so huffy. I was only trying to help. I want the best for you."

"And I want what I want." And what I need, she added mentally. She followed him over to the cash register by the door, not caring that they'd become part of the night's entertainment for some of the patrons.

"I promised to bring Phil a carryout," Ramón explained as he ordered more and paid for everything. Then he opened the door to let her out. "I'd better get back to the office," he said, checking his watch again.

The short walk to her car with Ramón was very quiet. It had gotten dark outside, and few people milled about the area. Her thoughts churned endlessly, failing to adhere to any coherent pattern. Mariah opened her car door and turned to Ramón. "Hard as it may be for you to believe, Cotter Eastwood is a good person. I don't like what he did, and I haven't forgiven him. Maybe I never will. I don't know. But I truly feel that if you ever really love anyone, even if you end up going separate ways, you still care about them. I can't just turn it on and off, Ramón."

"Are you getting back with Cotter?"

"Can you predict the future? I don't know. I'm not planning on it." Did he think she was stupid?

"Why don't you go out with some other guys, give someone else a chance?"

"Why don't we talk about something else?"

Ramón threw up his hands in defeat. "Excuse me. Excuse me! I'll try to keep my nose out of your business, Ms. McCleary. Don't forget to call my office when you get home, so I'll know you arrived safely."

Mariah rolled her eyes, steaming in silence. She wanted to continue arguing, but beneath his easygoing exterior, Ramón could be quite sensitive. She didn't want to risk hurting his feelings unless it was absolutely necessary. Glancing up at her friend, she noted the closed expression on his face. He was obviously annoyed with her. Well, that was just too bad. "Kiss me," she said perversely, watching him suppress a surprised expression.

Still angry, he lifted an eyebrow. "Forget it, McCleary," he growled.

Deciding to push it, Mariah leaned over on tiptoe to slowly brush her lips against his stiff cheek. It should have softened him up, but it didn't. Feeling a little perturbed, she climbed into her car and started the engine. Through her open window, she called out as she put the car in gear and drove off. Ramón's reply came to her on the wind.

Her hands trembled slightly as she turned the first corner, wondering if she'd been angriest at Ramón for dwelling on her mistake, or herself for letting Cotter into her home. She was going to have to find a way to make Cotter leave her alone.

FOUR

Ramón drove back to the office in a blue funk. Things were definitely not going his way. A long night, which included a minimum of two more hours at the office, stretched ahead of him. He'd probably get home about ten-thirty, and there'd be no one there to care, no one to warm his bed, and no one to fill the rest of the evening with sparkling conversation. He definitely needed a new girlfriend. He wanted Mariah, but it was beginning to look as if Ms. Mariah McCleary was not going to give him the time of day.

Silence reigned when Ramón walked into the conference room and set the carryout bag on the table. The group was obviously taking a break. Phil sat alone at the conference table, the harsh lights shining on the olive tanned skin revealed by the receding tide of his tightly curled brown hair. Carefully, he pored over a list. He looked up as the bag hit the table. "Hmmmh, what's this I smell? Could it be? Could it be?" He opened the bag and lifted out one of the Styrofoam covered Specials and smiled. "Yes! My man, you've already repaid half the debt you incurred when I let you sub for me today. Did you at least get a kiss for your trouble?"

Ramón's mouth twisted at the thought of her kiss to his cheek. He knew Mariah had simply been pushing him because she knew he was annoyed. "Yes, yes I did." He should have kissed those pouting red lips of hers, but she would not have been amused. She'd been a lot angrier than she let on, much more than the situation warranted.

Phil opened the white carton, pulled out the Special and took a bite. He chewed silently for a minute and swallowed. "You guys beat the crap out of Sonia and Mitch?"

"You would have been proud." Ramón pulled out a chair and wearily fell into it. He'd had a hell of a time helping Mariah win and making it look easy. He couldn't remember having more fun, but his muscles throbbed and ached. Instead of running down to Lafayette Coney Island, he should have stayed at the center and gotten into the hot tub.

"Then why aren't you dancing around the table?"

"The girl's got her blinders on, Phil, and her mind's made up. She's not taking any input. I'm just 'good pal Ramón,' and I'm going to stay that way."

"Don't give up. Haven't you heard? Only the best things are worth fighting for, and the best comes to those who wait." He bit off the second third of his Special and chewed. "So what's really bothering you?"

"The good doctor is rearing his ugly head. You know, he showed up at the fund-raiser and upset Mariah. Now it looks as if she might rethink the whole thing." Ramón clawed a hand through his hair. He could imagine all the things Cotter would say, the things he would do.

"She didn't say she was thinking of letting him come back, did she?"

"No, but she treated me to a little speech on good people doing bad things and not having their whole lives judged negatively because of it."

"Boy, that's a new tune for Mariah."

"Not really. She's got a soft heart and she really did love him. Cotter Eastwood is real smooth. He knows which buttons to push."

"I really feel for you, man. I'd feel even more if I didn't think fate was getting you back for some of the hearts you've broken. You know, what goes around, comes around."

"Ha!" Ramón pulled his briefcase from one of the chairs and opened it on the oak conference table. For years he'd suspected that Mariah could be the one, yet he hadn't moved on it. Neither had been ready to settle down and make a commitment to anyone. Somehow Cotter Eastwood snuck in when Ramón wasn't looking. Ramón slapped a couple of files onto the table. He'd grown tired of waiting, and none of his recent attempts to shake things up had been successful. Again, he told himself, if they were meant to be, they'd get together in time.

Phil slid a document down the conference table, and Ramón picked it up to study. After a moment he began to nod his head. "Nice strategy. Good work, Phil. Man, you're the best."

Minutes later, the remaining staff members began to drift back into the conference room. When everyone was seated, Ramón began to speak. "All right, everyone, we'll discuss the strategy for tomorrow, and then we can all go home."

The next week proved to be depressingly uneventful for Mariah. She spent the time calling on businesses that had used the agency services in the past, and some that were new to the area. No matter how hard she tried, she seemed to be running in place. She reminded herself that sometimes customer calls drew results that weren't immediate. The situation wouldn't have bothered her as much except that the days on her riverfront property option were ticking away.

If the lack of business activity wasn't enough to bring down her spirits, her personal life was. Though she needed to get out and meet new people, she felt too fragile to go on the two blind dates her friends arranged. Yet she hated the silence when she got home in the evenings. Several times she'd picked up the phone to call Ramón and then stopped. Although she missed him, she wasn't ready to initiate contact and do whatever was necessary to smooth things between them. Instead she spent the time alone cleaning her house and catching up on her reading.

By Wednesday of the following week, even the current bestseller was not enough to occupy her mind. Mariah lay stretched out on the couch in her living room. She could barely keep her eyes open.

The sound of the ocean swishing back and then pounding forth to reclaim the land formed a pleasant backdrop. Sparkling sunshine filled the fresh salt air and played against the exposed parts of her body. Mariah lay on the warm sand, her senses attuned to Ramón's sensual message. She moaned softly in pleasure as his hands moved from her legs to sculpt and caress her thighs. Opening her eyes, she met Ramón's searing gaze. He leaned forward, his warm provocative mouth moving against hers, his tongue tasting and teasing until she trembled. "You taste good," he murmured in a low sexy voice. Then his fingers lightly caressed the soft petals of her moist heat, and then entered fully in a rhythm that turned her inside out. He continued the caress, one hand sculpting her back and hips while the force of the orgasm shook her in an earthquake of pleasure. Mariah gasped when he maneuvered his lean muscled frame between her legs and entered her, hard, heavy, and hot. Her hands slid up the curling hair of his chest and down his arms. His hungry mouth moved down her neck and onto her breasts. Mariah rode the waves of a sensual heaven. She met each thrust as if it were the last, until they collapsed together in a haze of pleasure.

Ramón held her tenderly, whispering softly, "So good, so good." It was then that Mariah wondered what those other noises were. She opened her eyes to see a line of beautiful women curving around the rock that sheltered her and down the beach.

The girl closest to Ramón and Mariah pulled at her tiny white bikini and tossed back a head full of black curls. "You've had your turn. Time's up. Time to move on."

Mariah pushed at Ramón's chest in an attempt to get his attention, but he seemed oblivious to his surroundings. He continued to whisper sexy nonsense in her ear.

"Look." The woman pointed in the direction opposite of the line of women. Reluctantly, Mariah turned to stare. Several women moved away into the distance. The footprints in the sand seemed to indicate that they'd originated from her spot on the beach. The implication was that they'd all had their turn and left. Surely the joy and passion-filled moments she'd spent with Ramón had been more than her taking a place in a long line of women.

"You've had your turn. It's time to move on," the woman said again, and this time the other women joined her in repeating the words over and over.

A loud thud sounded close to her ear, startling her.

Mariah sat up on the couch, her eyes blinking in the glare of the lamp on the coffee table. She saw that the book she'd been reading had fallen to the floor. What a crazy dream! Remnants of it still ran through her mind, her body humming with remembered passion. Had she really dreamed of sex with Ramón?

Slinging the hair out of her face, Mariah got to her feet, yawning and stretching. She'd been so tired that she'd never made it to her bed. She glanced at her watch. It was seven-thirty, time to get ready for work.

Uncomfortable with the silence, she turned on the bedroom television on the way to the bathroom. Video footage featuring Ramón flashed on the screen. Handsome and confident in a dark designer suit, he was leaving the courtroom with his associates. Mariah listened as the news anchor talked about the start of the jury selection process, and said a quick prayer for her friend.

Instead of going straight to work, she went to Arturro Mann's studio in the Eastern Market area. Noting the discreet sign on the front of the building, she parked in front and followed some of the arriving models into the building. Mariah was impressed with the way he'd renovated the top floor of the old warehouse in the style of a loft. Large sparkling windows looking out on the Eastern Market area and Grand River Avenue dominated the room. A large circular skylight rained sunshine down from the center of the room. Walking across the parquet floor, Mariah stopped at the carved oak desk.

"I'll be with you in a minute." Arturro Mann spoke as he scanned a stack of papers. After a moment or two, he looked up. "Ms. McCleary! I'm honored."

"I said I'd come by and help get everyone processed this morning."

"And I'm glad you did! I have a small staff for this project, just the hairdresser, a wardrobe person, and a makeup artist besides myself." His eyes took in Mariah's appearance, covering her from head to toe. "Could you sign in your models for me? I made a few notes when we talked yesterday. The people needed for this morning have asterisks by their names." He stood up and pulled the chair out for Mariah.

"Seems simple enough." Mariah sat down, glancing at the list. She spent a couple of hours checking in models and filling in with Arturro's staff where needed. He ran a very professional operation. Although his staff was small, they all were very friendly and worked well together. Mariah was impressed with the imaginative ways he photographed the clothes and models for the catalog.

When everyone took a lunch break at eleven, Mariah got her purse to leave. She was feeling pretty good about her prospects of moving the agency again. Arturro had utilized five of her models in the morning session and scheduled four more for the afternoon.

"Let me take you to lunch," Arturro said quickly as she headed for the door. "I appreciate your helping me out today, and I've got a proposal I'd like to discuss with you that could bring in a lot of income."

Torn, Mariah considered his suggestion for a minute. She was always willing to consider a business proposal, and she seriously needed to increase her income, but she had other plans for the afternoon. It was too late to cancel anything. "Can I take a rain check? I've already got a lunch date."

Arturro pulled out a pocket calendar and leafed through it. "How about Tuesday?"

"What time?"

"Can I pick you up about eleven-thirty?"

"Sure, it's a date." Mariah pulled her appointment keeper out of her purse and punched in the lunch date.

As she drove to the restaurant, she used her cell phone to call the office for messages. Mariah listened as Lynn reconfirmed her afternoon appointment with Cora Belson and summarized a few new appointments. She knew her secretary well enough to know that there was something she wasn't saying. The excitement in Lynn's voice was unmistakable. "All right, Lynn," she said when she couldn't stand it any longer. "What's going on? Did Anthony cut your hair today?"

"Actually, he did," Lynn admitted, drawing out every syllable. "Just wait until you see it. The man's a genius."

"I wouldn't argue with you there. I can tell you're quite pleased with your hair."

"I am. I asked him to lunch as a sort of thank-you gesture," she said a little too casually.

Mariah wasn't fooled. So Lynn had finally started to put the moves on Anthony. "That's great. Where will you take him?" She whipped around a corner and accelerated.

"I like what you said about the Rattlesnake Club, so I'll make a reservation for tomorrow. He's too busy to go today."

"He wasn't too busy to cut your hair."

"Yes, wasn't that sweet of him?"

"Yes. Anthony never ceases to amaze me." Mariah paused a minute, trying to picture Anthony at lunch with Lynn. They'd make an attractive couple. "Well, I've got to go now. I've got a lunch date."

"Speaking of lunch dates, I think you should hear the latest proposal made by Dr. Eastwood on the Neighborhood Speak radio show this morning."

"Proposal? What are you talking about?" Mariah stopped at a red light, her fingers tightening on the phone. This was certainly a day for proposals. She had a feeling she would not like this one.

"He casually mentioned on the show that he'd called the Juvenile Diabetes Association and told them he'd donate an additional five thousand dollars if you'd agree to have lunch with him at a restaurant of your choice. Then he called here. You know, a lot of people still remember that the two of you were engaged."

"Damn it! I wish he'd just leave me alone." Mariah slapped the steering wheel with the palm of her hand. "Does anyone else know about this?"

"Only the radio station's listening audience and certain members of the press, who've already called to see what your decision might be. Naturally, they think it's terribly romantic."

"He's trying to manipulate me, and I resent it. My personal time is not for sale."

"What do you want me to say when the press calls back?" Lynn asked carefully.

Mariah gritted her teeth. "Just tell them that I'm thinking it over."

"Sounds good to me. Have a good lunch."

"You too," Mariah murmured before clicking off the phone. She pulled up to valet parking at Sinbad's. After the attendant took her car, she hurried into the restaurant and found Gloria Richards sitting in the back near the large tinted glass window with a view of the St. Clair River. Mariah could see small boats drift past the window and people going into the Roostertail Restaurant situated next door.

"Been having a good day?" Gloria asked with her thick accent, after they hugged and Mariah sat down.

"Sort of." Mariah picked up her menu. "I just left a studio that's using nine of our higher rate models."

"I'm glad. What are you having?"

"Do you even need to ask?" Mariah looked up from her menu and saw the waitress standing at their table with her pad and pencil ready. "I'll have the Alaskan king crab legs and a glass of white zinfandel."

Gloria put in a similar order. "So how did things go after the fundraiser?"

"We made a lot of money for those kids."

"What about Cotter Eastwood? I saw him talking to you. Did you ever really get over him?"

Mariah thought about it for a moment. "I—I think so," she admitted. "He couldn't have been the man I thought he was and just abandon me the way he did. He's been trying to apologize and explain, but I don't think I can trust him."

"That's understandable." Gloria thanked the waitress for her drink and salad and waited while Mariah got hers. "We were worried about you. I'm sorry you've had to experience so much pain. After your mom died, I thought maybe Cotter…I'm sorry, *niña*, it's best not to dwell on it."

"You've got that right." Mariah sipped her wine. "If I didn't have you guys and my friends from college, I don't know what I'd do."

"You've got to keep moving forward."

"I'm trying to, but sometimes the past keeps coming back to haunt me." She took a fork of salad into her mouth and chewed.

"Cotter?"

"Yes." Mariah put down her fork. "He's pledged money to the Juvenile Diabetes Association and publicly offered to give another five thousand dollars if I'll have lunch with him."

"Some people might think he made a romantic gesture," Gloria said carefully.

"Do you?"

"Seems a little manipulative to me, especially when you consider the past."

Gloria munched a breadstick. "Are you going?"

"I don't know. He's upped the ante by making such a public declaration. A few members of the press have already called the office."

"What do you really want?" Gloria's dark eyes were filled with concern.

"I want him to leave me alone." Mariah set her glass down. "But I'd like to see the Association get the extra funds. I guess that means I'll go."

"How far will you let him take this?"

There was an unnatural pause in the restaurant noise and chatter, as if everyone waited to hear her answer. Mariah tossed that thought aside. "I don't know. He's pretty close to the limit now. Cotter's really not a bad person, he's just determined to get back into my life."

"And why shouldn't he be? You are a prize, Mariah. Always remember that." Gloria patted her hand. "Any man with you on his arm is blessed." She turned to let the waitress place a steaming plate of crab legs in front of her. "Looks good, doesn't it?"

Mouth watering, Mariah stared down at her own plate. "The food is always good here," she said beaming at Gloria. Then they settled down to eat the succulent crab before it could cool. Conversation was minimal. Finally, full and content, they were enjoying the view of the activity on the river when the waitress brought the check and took away their plates.

"I know I've still got a few months, but I want your promise to help me with Ramón's surprise birthday party," Gloria said as she looked up from the check.

Mariah wasn't about to mention that they'd exchanged words and she hadn't seen Ramón except on television for a week and a half. She'd picked up the phone to call him at several times and stopped herself. Apologies were difficult for her. She'd only been venting her anger. He should have known that no matter how gullible she'd been to let Cotter in, she would never have slept with him. Ramón's question had only made her angrier. Aloud, she said, "I'd love to help. Where do you plan to have it?"

"Somewhere new and different, or at least so ordinary that he won't suspect a thing."

"We'll have to work on that." Mariah picked up her black leather purse.

"This is my treat," Gloria warned, as she set a large bill on top of the check. "I invited you to lunch."

"All right! All right!" Mariah laughed, placing the purse back at her feet.

"I like having lunch with you, Mariah. We need to do this again sometime. Maybe next week?"

"Yes, we should. I don't know what my schedule's like next week, but let's talk," Mariah said. By the time she'd left the restaurant, she'd agreed to call Gloria on Monday to set up a new lunch date.

On the way to her one o'clock appointment, Mariah briefly stopped by the new building site on the river and took in the view, dreaming of making the site her own.

With a few quick mental calculations, she realized that she still needed more than half the money required.

The drive over to Cora Belson's office in Southfield didn't take long. Cora welcomed Mariah as warmly as ever, chatted for a few minutes, and then went over the select group of model portfolios. Four of the models had looks suitable for Cora's needs. Mariah carefully noted their names. When Cora asked for Imani, Mariah explained that Imani was having problems with her health and would not be available. Sensing Cora's acute disappointment, Mariah promised to find a replacement with a similar look and attitude.

Friday was a dreary day. Mariah felt so melancholy that she refused to accompany her friends to a new jazz club in downtown Detroit. An odd restlessness prompted her to drive to the mall and wander through the various stores. Immersing herself in the kaleidoscope of sounds, sights, and smells of the shops and shoppers, she started at one end of the mall and worked her way down. The aroma of freshly baked cinnamon buns filled the air. A number of fashionably dressed shoppers traversed the mall like participants in a fashion show. In the background, a local radio station played golden oldies over the loudspeakers.

As usual, shopping improved her mood. By the time she'd gone through half the mall, she was fairly dancing in and out of the shops to the beat of the golden oldies. She'd already purchased a couple of items when she noticed a tall, handsome, familiar figure in an expensive gray suit at a nearby bookstore. Rising excitement furiously pumped the blood through her veins as she tightened her grip on her bags. Had he seen her and pretended not to notice? Mariah wondered. She was so glad to see him that she really didn't care. After a few minutes of contemplation, she strolled over to him and tapped him on the shoulder.

"Hey there, stranger."

"Mariah, where'd you come from?" Ramón looked up from the display of bestsellers. Was it her imagination, or was his expression a little cool? His gray eyes were polite, his mouth unsmiling, but he still looked good enough make any woman look twice and drool. It felt good just to be in the presence of her friend again. She'd missed him.

"I was throwing money around in the store over there," she said, pointing. "I didn't feel like going to the new jazz club with the group."

"Me either," Ramón said, closing the book in his hand. "This trial has me too wound up."

Mariah shifted her packages. "Well I'm glad to see you getting away from the office a little. I bet you guys have been down there till all hours of the night all week long."

He nodded. "You've got that right."

"That University of Detroit law professor on Channel 4 gave you good marks for your court performance today. I did a little channel-surfing, and that's the general consensus."

"Yes, I heard. I'm trying to enjoy this relatively positive interval. Things are going to get worse before they get better."

"I'm rooting for you, Ramón." Mariah put a hand on his. "You're one of the best."

"Thanks," he said quietly. A small awkward silence followed. Mariah knew then that if she didn't get on with her apology, she never would. She cared too much for her friend to let a few careless words ruin their friendship.

"I—I want to apologize for being so prickly the other night and jumping on your case," Mariah stammered from uncooperative lips. Perspiration trickled down her armpits at the sudden rise in the temperature. She hated to apologize for anything, even if she was wrong. "I was just mad and mouthing off." She stared at him, trying to read his expression. Her hand fisted tightly into the tops of her bags. "Are you still mad at me?"

Ramón's lips twitched, and a slow smile spread across his face. It was like the sun coming out. "I was." His warm hand clasped hers firmly. "Apology accepted if you'll grovel just a little bit more by buying me a soda at that little café over there."

Her breath came out in a rush that she covered with a little laugh. This was almost too easy. "Deal," Mariah said, watching him fumble with an inside pocket of his jacket. "I hope you understand that I wouldn't just grovel for anyone."

"Special measures for special people." Ramón raised an eyebrow, then winked at her.

"Yeah." Mariah tried to wipe the silly grin off her face as she shifted the strap of her purse to her shoulder. "Are you going to buy that book?"

"Sure, I need something to think about besides the trial." He strolled over to the counter and plunked down ten dollars. In minutes they were headed for the café.

"I know you've had a lot on your mind," Mariah began, as they sat down at a booth. "I missed talking with you." She couldn't have described how much she'd missed him in the past couple of weeks. It had been a learning experience.

"I missed you too." His gaze met hers as he gave her one of the menus. "But I knew the whole thing would blow over. It wasn't about anything."

She felt such warmth that she wanted to hug him. Instead, she gave him a sunny smile.

"What have you been up to?" he asked.

"I'm working on a proposal with a new photographer," she answered, kicking off her shoes and folding her feet beneath her on the cushion of the booth. We're going after new business with that new upscale store."

"Sounds like a good idea. Does your photographer know what he's doing?"

Ramón settled back against his side of the cushioned booth.

"Yes, he's great. He used several of our models for a Hudson's catalog, and his work was excellent. As a direct result, reserved more of our models to use for the circular advertising of Hudson's next sale."

"Wow. You can't beat that." Ramón turned and gave his attention to the waitress who'd just arrived at their table.

"Does all this business activity mean you'll have the $150,000 to exercise that option on your new agency site before it expires?" he asked after they'd put in their orders.

"I'm not sure. I hope so." Mariah leaned forward on her elbows. "I've got two more months to get the money."

"I could float you a loan..." Ramón offered in a smooth, mellow voice.

"No. I want to do this on my own. But thanks for the offer."

"You're a stubborn lady, Mariah McCleary."

"And you're too nice for your own good," Mariah said with a grin, then added, "to me anyway."

In the next hour they ate their meal and talked about their friends and their projects. When the mall started to close, Ramón leisurely walked her to her car.

"I'm not the least bit tired, are you?" Mariah asked Ramón when she was settled in her car. She leaned out of her open window to talk, not quite ready to end the evening.

"No, but I should be. We've been going strong all week. The only reason I'm free tonight is that we're going to meet on Sunday."

"Want to come by for a little while?" The words were out of her mouth before she'd even thought about it.

"Sure." Ramón's expression brightened. He pulled his keys from a pocket. "I'll follow you."

Although the traffic leaving the mall was slow, it took less than twenty minutes for Mariah to drive home. Ramón walked up the steps with her and waited while she unlocked the door.

"Let's play cards," Ramón suggested as she ushered him in and closed the door. "We haven't done that in a long time."

"Not since I finally got over Cotter Eastwood," she said, thinking of all the times Ramón came over and argued, pushed, cajoled, and teased her into thinking about something beside herself. She'd been so hurt and depressed. Was any man worth all that? She didn't think so. Thank God she'd gotten over Cotter.

"Have you?"

Mariah eyed him warily. "I don't think you want to go there."

"I think I do—" he said quickly, and then added, "but not right now. Why spoil a perfectly good evening?"

Mariah raised an eyebrow.

Ramón threw his jacket onto a chair. "Got any beer?"

"Sure, your favorite brand." Mariah headed for the kitchen with him following close behind. "And I'll make popcorn."

She took a bag of microwave popcorn from the cabinet, removed the cellophane, and placed it in the microwave. Ramón sat on the kitchen step stool and joked with Mariah while it popped. When she opened the microwave to retrieve the full bag, he took a large Tupperware bowl from the cupboard and placed it on the counter, then got a couple of beers from the refrigerator. The fragrant aroma of hot buttered popcorn permeated the air. Carefully, Mariah opened the steaming bag, and poured the hot kernels into the bowl.

"Blackjack?" Mariah asked as they headed for the thickly carpeted den.

"For money!" Ramón jingled the change in one pants pocket. "Unless you want to play strip poker, that is."

"You wish." Mariah turned on the track lights in the den and set the bowl of popcorn on the coffee table. "I ought to take you up on it and put you to shame."

"You're on." Ramón grabbed a couple of coasters and put the beers on them. He took a pack of cards from the drawer in the end table, then settled on his knees on the other side of the table.

"That's what I ought to do," Mariah continued, "but I've decided to be merciful tonight."

"Chicken." Ramón flashed his pearly whites. "I'll deal, okay?"

"Sure." She shrugged and relaxed into the space between the sofa and the coffee table.

"Fifty cents a game." With effortless skill, Ramón shuffled the cards and then waited while she cut them. "Last chance to change your mind."

Ramón's teasing and playing around had gotten a lot more provocative. Ignoring his comment, Mariah opened her beer and took a sip. She took a handful of change from her purse on the couch and slapped two quarters onto the table. Slowly, she drew her knees up to take off her cuffed black boots. Then she placed the boots on the side of the dark navy couch, curling her toes into the soft beige carpeting as Ramón dealt the cards. One peek at the hidden card and she grinned, turning it over. "Blackjack!"

His incredulous expression as he stared down at her cards was priceless. Mariah chuckled. His uncanny luck at cards just might be nonexistent tonight. "Don't worry, I'll try to be merciful." Then she proceeded to win another six out of eight hands. Then they played bid whiz and spades.

Again, Mariah won the majority of the games. Luck was definitely with her. Tired of cards, Mariah stretched. "Want another beer?"

"Sure, I'll put on some music." Ramón got up and headed for the oak CD cabinet.

Mariah glanced at the rectangular Lucite clock on the kitchen wall. Eleven-thirty already? Where had the time gone? She didn't plan on doing much tomorrow anyway. Grabbing two more beers from the refrigerator, she headed back to the den. Sounds of a smooth sexy saxophone beckoned to her.

"I see you've got some new music." Ramón sat on the couch.

"Yeah, I joined one of those clubs. I get something new every month now." Mariah put the cold bottle of beer into his outstretched hand, then sat down on the love seat across from him with her own. "So what have you got planned for the weekend?"

"Not much." Ramón took a big gulp of the beer. "Pop in to see my parents, go check on Imani, enjoy a little time off, before heading back into the office on Sunday."

"No date?"

"Can I count tonight?"

"Hardly. Ramón, you're the lover, remember? Always ready, willing and able?"

He gazed at her silently for a moment. "Maybe times have changed. Maybe I'm ready to move on to something more permanent."

Mariah laughed. "How gullible do you think I am? You'll never get me to believe that!" When he didn't return her laughter, Mariah studied his expression. If she didn't know better, she'd think she'd hit a sore spot, but since when was Ramón sensitive about the number of women going through his revolving door?

"And how many women have you seen me with lately?"

She considered that for a moment. It had actually been a number of months since she'd seen him with someone on his arm, especially if she didn't count Imani. "It's been quite a while, now that I think about it," she said, feeling a little warm. Every time she thought she had him all figured out, he'd show a new side. "Why, Ramón?" she asked, trying to fathom his serious expression. "What's going on?"

"You are."

"What?" Her pulse speeded up a little and she leaned forward, anxious to hear the words he might use to explain his provocative statement.

"What do you think? I really value our friendship and you needed my support."

Mariah's pulse eased back to normal. She hadn't expected him to declare undying love for her, had she? So Ramón had actually slowed down to help her get over Cotter. He was a true friend. "I really appreciate all the time you spent making me feel better."

"Hey, what are friends for?"

"I just hope I can do the same for you sometime," she said, smiling warmly.

"Oh, you'll probably get the chance," he said with a half smile. "I hear I'm overdue for a little heartache."

"I don't think so." Mariah curled her legs up onto the love seat. "Do any of your lady friends stick around long enough to get broken hearts?" Ramón lifted an eyebrow and Mariah backpedaled. "I can't believe I said that! You're just going to have to ignore me, that's the beer talking."

"Is it?" Ramón's tone was dangerously soft. She knew she was going to pay for that remark.

"Of course it is," she replied quickly, searching for a way to change the topic of conversation. "By the way, how is Imani? I stopped in to see her last week, and she still looked pretty green."

"I think she's getting over the hump. Her doctor says she'll be a lot better when she's passed the three-month mark. What do you have planned for the weekend?"

"Just rest and relaxation mostly, but I did plan to go through Mother's financial papers," Mariah said slowly. "She left me some stocks I could probably sell to help get the money for the new site. Last time I checked, they weren't worth very much, but you never know."

"Need some help? Want some company?"

"No, I'll probably sit around in my PJs, and make a lazy day of it," she said quickly. He'd already seen her looking her worst too often. Mariah stifled a yawn, and Ramón followed suit.

"I should probably be getting along home," Ramón said, getting to his feet.

"Thanks for coming over. I really had a good time." Mariah took his jacket from the sofa and held it while he put his arms into it. Carefully, she smoothed it up and over his shoulders, then walked with him to the front door. Instead of turning the lock, she lifted her arms and enfolded him in a quick heartfelt hug. Her head barely topped his shoulders, so her face met the warmth of his muscular chest. Darn, the man smelled good enough to eat! His arms closed around her waist just as she started to pull back.

"Kiss me," he demanded, his gray eyes daring her.

What a proposition, Mariah thought. He had a pair of the most kissable lips she'd ever seen. Full and sensual, they were made to drive women crazy. She had no doubt he knew how to use them expertly. Although it was sometimes difficult, it was something she tried not to dwell on. "Kiss me" was one of his favorite phrases.

Slowly, she leaned toward him and gently bussed his chiseled cheek with her lips. Before she could move away, he turned his head, and his lips found hers in a deep, affectionately teasing kiss. She could stand the heat, she thought, letting him push the envelope a little. When she relaxed, he deepened the kiss, drinking from her lips and savoring them like a fine wine. His hands moved along the length of her back, stoking the fire within her, stopping just short of her buttocks.

Carefully, Mariah took both his hands in her own and removed them from her waist, the action causing the length of her body to sink into the sensual heat of his. She couldn't remember ever being so thoroughly kissed. Was it any surprise that he kissed better than anyone she'd ever kissed? With the heat of his body searing her, there was no doubt that he wanted her. Mariah trembled, too close to the edge for comfort. With limited success, she struggled to collect herself. She dragged her lips from the warm, arousing magic of his. Her body vibrated with sensual longing, unconsciously offering itself to him, but her mind played a note of discord that stopped her short of actual surrender.

"Hmmmh," he murmured close to her ear. "Essence of Mariah. I've never had anything better. You're intoxicating..." He held her close for seconds more, as if she were oh so precious, and then gently pulled away. "We really need to rethink the focus of this relationship," he said in a low, husky tone.

"What?" Mariah asked, as if coming out of a fog. She saw Ramón unlocking the door. Her body ached for more of the special attention he'd been giving her, but she was almost relieved to see that he was leaving. Ramón was much too tempting.

Ramón opened the door and turned to kiss her forehead. "Good night, Mariah. Sweet dreams."

"Good night," she replied automatically, her body still humming with excitement.

He opened the screen door and stepped out on the porch. "Now close and lock the door. I'm not leaving until you do."

Mariah closed and locked the door, then collapsed against it, closing her eyes. When she heard his car drive off, she took a deep breath and let it out slowly. Was she really that attracted to Ramón, or was she just too needy these days? The answer was obvious. It had been much too long since she'd been in a love relationship.

She recalled his words about refocusing their relationship and a thrill of excitement ran through her, but Mariah shook her head. It wasn't an option anyway. Her heart was still too fragile. Ramón was her friend and an integral part of the only family she had now. Despite her obvious attraction to him, she could never risk their friendship by joining the line of women going through the revolving door of relationships with him.

FIVE

Ramón made a point of sticking by his friends, no matter what. After spending the morning washing his clothes, cleaning his apartment, and all the other tasks he'd been too busy to get to during the week, he used Saturday afternoon to check on Imani in her exclusive downtown Detroit apartment. Was she losing the baby? She'd seemed much too ill on his last visit. He would have given her more time and space, but he suspected that she would have a problem getting help from her boyfriend. He hoped he was wrong about Perry. Imani didn't have anyone else.

The doorman, a retired cop, joked with Ramón as he signed him in. Instead of taking the elevator, Ramón put a hand on the carved oak banister, walked up the thickly carpeted stairs to the second floor, and down the hall to apartment 5B.

She'd dressed for his visit. Imani stood in the doorway, looking pale, yet beautifully exotic, in a cream silk hostess ensemble with her hair falling about her shoulders. Perry Bonds had to be the biggest fool there was, Ramón thought, because she was not only beautiful, and a lot of fun, but a surprisingly sweet-natured person beneath the veneer of sophistication. If he wasn't so crazy about Mariah, he'd have given Perry Bonds a run for his money. Not that it would have made any real difference. Imani was as crazy about Perry as he was about Mariah. Maybe more.

He noted the slight redness in the whites of her eyes. Imani had obviously been crying. She accepted his kiss on her cheek and smiled when she saw the carryout he had brought from her favorite restaurant. "You're spoiling me," she murmured as she ushered him into her apartment.

"All expectant mothers should be pampered and spoiled," Ramón said as he threw his jacket across the back of the cream-colored leather couch and sat down. He saw the basketball game in progress on the television set across the room, the Detroit Pistons and the Denver Rockets.

"Well, I've decided to enjoy it, so thank-you very much," Imani said, sitting beside him on the couch, but angling herself in such a way that she could still see the screen. "Can I get you something?" When Ramón shook his head, she continued. "I've been watching you on the news. You've become a local celebrity."

"It is the case of a lifetime," Ramón admitted. "But it's also a hell of a challenge. We've been burning a lot of the midnight oil. I'll probably get a few gray hairs because of it."

"It'll be worth it," Imani chuckled as she opened the white carryout bag. "Do you think he's innocent?"

"I know that everyone enjoys the presumption of innocence until proven guilty, but I never represent anyone I don't personally feel is innocent."

"I admire your integrity." Imani pulled out the foam bowl and plastic spoon. "I bet you've had to give up some lucrative cases."

"Yes, I have, but it was worth it." Ramón's gaze met Imani's, briefly. "It didn't hurt that the firm is so large. There are plenty of lawyers to go around."

Imani popped the top off the bowl and grinned. "New England clam chowder! Ramón, you're the best." She dipped the spoon into the mixture and slowly savored the first spoonful. "I was craving this very thing all morning. Do you have ESP or something?"

"Or something," he replied, noticing that her eyes had strayed to the television set. He followed her lead and saw Perry Bonds dancing across the floor with the basketball.

Imani's eyes watered and she began to blink rapidly. A fat tear rolled down her face. Several others followed in quick succession. "I've got something in my eye," she explained before setting the bowl of soup onto the table and jumping up from the couch.

"Need any help?" he asked politely, not taken in by her performance.

"No, I can take care of it," she said, disappearing into the bathroom.

Imani was still in the bathroom when the quarter ended. Cautiously, Ramón got up from the couch and went to stand by the bathroom door. When he heard the unmistakable sound of retching, he called out to her. When there was no answer, he opened the door. She was on her knees in front of commode, clutching her stomach. Carefully, he gathered her hair in one hand as she began another bout. A dim sheen of moisture gleamed on her forehead.

"I guess I won't be able to finish that soup now," she said, smiling faintly when she had finished.

"I'll put it in the refrigerator. You can eat it when you're feeling better." Ramón wet a cloth in the sink, put a little of her facial cleanser on it, and washed her face. Then he poured her a small cup of mouthwash. "Feeling better?" he asked as he helped her to her feet.

Imani nodded. "This little person is going to be the death of me. Do you know my stomach aches from barfing all the time?"

Ramón nodded, watching as she began to gargle.

When she was finished, she walked towards him, weariness evident in every step. "I'm going to lie down on the couch."

"I can carry you," Ramón offered, wondering if she would make it.

"No, I can do it," she said stubbornly, making her way out of the bathroom. When she'd made it to the couch, he fixed the pillows and pulled the blanket up over her. "I told him about the baby," Imani said, grasping his hand. Her words tumbled out in a rush. "He wants me to have an abortion. He says he's not ready to be a father. He thinks I've tried to trap him." Her hands tightened on Ramón's. "I made a stupid mistake, but it wasn't planned."

Ramón nodded sympathetically. He wanted to give Perry the benefit of the doubt. Things weren't always the way they seemed. "Didn't your doctor also suggest an abortion? This pregnancy is really affecting your health," Ramón put in, reasonably.

"I won't do it. I won't have an abortion," she said, her lips settling into her famous pout.

"Even if it means your life?"

"No matter what the cost. This baby is all I have now."

"Imani, what about your family? Your mother..."

"Kicked me out and abandoned me when I was only seventeen. I'll never go back there."

"People make mistakes. Maybe you should give her a chance," he said, certain his words had no positive effect on Imani.

Still clutching his hand, she closed her eyes and was silent for several moments. Ramón glanced at the crystal clock on the glass coffee table. "I'm going to have to leave soon."

"Don't go," Imani begged, opening her eyes, her expression contrite. "You're one of the few friends I have now. How are you doing with Mariah? And don't think for a moment that I don't know how you really feel about her," she said when he winced involuntarily.

Did everyone but Mariah know? Was he that obvious? he wondered.

As if in answer to his thought, Imani continued: "I see how you look at her when she's not paying attention, and you're so happy around her. Did you tell her how you feel?"

Ramón shook his head slowly. "Not exactly. I've tried to show her. I'm beginning to think that she'll always see me as her playboy buddy."

"I don't believe that," Imani countered gamely. "I'd swear the green-eyed monster briefly reared its head when she saw your card and flowers at the hospital."

Hope arced within him, growing rapidly until it reached a peak that his common sense suppressed. "No." Ramón shook his head again. "You wouldn't believe all the girlfriends she's seen me through. If she can't see me being truly serious about anyone, I guess it's my own fault," he said, thinking he should get more aggressive. "It's time to try something new." Yes, he thought, it was time to put his cards on the table and go for broke.

"I know you, of all people, don't need advice on how to let a woman know you think she's special," Imani said softly. Ramón noticed that her head seemed to be sinking into the pillows and that the faint shadows beneath her eyes were more pronounced.

He fitted the lid back onto the Styrofoam bowl and stood. "I'll go put this in the refrigerator."

"Promise me something," Imani said when he came back from the kitchen.

"And what would that be?" He settled into the chair next to the couch.

"Don't give up on her until you've flat out told her how you feel and she rejects you."

"That, I can promise." Ramón knew he was nearing the end of his rope with Mariah anyway. Having to smile and pretend to be happy for her through her near marriage to Cotter Eastwood had been more than enough to shake him up, to let him know just how deep his feelings were. And then supporting her through the pain and heartache of her broken engagement... Could she ever feel as strongly for him? Doubts filled him, weighing him down like a ton of bricks.

Ramón stood. He couldn't keep agonizing over the possibility of Mariah's rejection. He would take her to dinner in a romantic setting and spill his guts over the wine. He would... what? He was running out of ideas. Ramón retrieved his jacket and pulled it on. "If you need anything, give me a call. I'll be back sometime this week." He leaned over and kissed Imani's satiny cheek, then stood again.

"Thanks for stopping in to see me, bringing the soup, and just being a friend."

"You're welcome." He saw that Imani's lashes were already weighing heavily against her cheeks. She'd fall asleep as soon as he left. "Don't get up. I'll let myself out and lock the door."

Mariah's weekend did not go as planned. Instead of spending most of the weekend going through her mother's papers in search of opportunities to obtain much-needed funds, Mariah finished the task by two o'clock Saturday afternoon. She stared at the small stack of stock certificates and said a little prayer. The companies were young and aggressive enough. It had been more than six years since she'd even checked the stock prices. She'd been too busy with school, and then too busy trying to build the agency, and after that she'd been planning her wedding, and now…

Mariah put the certificates in her briefcase, and her mother's papers back into the strongbox. Then she stretched out on the sofa with some paperwork. She felt more than a little distracted. What was the matter with her? She clawed her fingers through the mop of her hair. She'd found Ramón much too attractive last night. If he'd been the rascal she often pretended he was, they would have ended up in bed, and she wouldn't feel so frustrated now. She thought of his scent, his kisses, the way his hands moved on her body, and got hot all over. Oh lord, she thought, she was lusting after Ramón.

Maybe if they did it just once and got the mystery solved... No, she couldn't do that. There was a definite pattern to Ramón's relationships. After he slept with his women, their days seemed numbered. She'd never seen him be anything but charming to any of them, but sex seemed to be the beginning of the end. If she slept with Ramón, could they maintain their friendship once the fireworks were over? She didn't think so, and that was the problem. She loved her friend very much.

Restlessly, Mariah rolled off the couch and stretched out on the plush carpet. Hormones raging out of control! Determinedly, she began a series of leg lifts and sit-ups. Nothing like a little exercise to work off frustration. She hadn't exercised in a while anyway. Fifty sit-ups and several leg lifts later, Mariah realized it wasn't working.

Cotter's Sunday morning call to set up lunch with Mariah went very smoothly because he went out of his way to be charming. Charm was one of his major assets. He was almost apologetic about his very public methods of persuading her to go to lunch, but reminded her that if he'd sat back and waited to hear from her, he'd be waiting forever. Mariah was honest enough to admit he had a point, but she resented his trying to push his way back into her life. The more she thought about the past, the more certain she was that she would never, ever feel the same way about him.

It was one thing to forgive him for abandoning her, she was working on that, but it was something she couldn't forget. Practically everyone she'd ever loved, her parents, and even her sister, Jennifer, had been involuntarily taken from her. Cotter's decision had been a deliberate one.

Mariah felt like an intruder when she walked into her office on Monday morning. Lynn and Anthony were in their own little world. Anthony sat leaning forward in Lynn's guest chair, both talking in low animated tones. Lynn glowed with happiness. Mariah did a double take on the short, asymmetrical style Anthony had given her. It was so incredibly unique that she was sure she hadn't seen anything like it. Lynn's hair was curled in a swirling pattern that was very short on one side, with looser curls at her crown, and curls that lay in loops in front of her ear on the other side of her face. It was a really sharp cut, and it suited Lynn's oval-shaped face, giving her a very chic look.

Not wanting to disturb them, Mariah walked quickly to the inner office and opened the door as quietly as possible. Lynn chose that moment to look up. "Good morning! Can I get you anything?"

Busted! she thought as she returned both their greetings. "When you get your coffee, I'd like one." Mariah put her briefcase on the desk and shrugged out of her jade green suit jacket.

"I've already got you covered," Lynn said, pointing to the large foam cup on Mariah's desk.

"Your hair is gorgeous!" Mariah said, trying to figure just how Anthony had accomplished the look. "Anthony, if you keep this up, you have to open a hair salon in addition to your clothing boutiques."

Anthony came to stand in the doorway of her inner office. "No, I won't cut hair for money. Except for you and Lynn, I haven't cut hair in years. I did this because you ladies are my special friends." He fingered a lock of Lynn's hair. "This is a personality cut, and so is yours."

Mariah stared at Lynn's cut and saw that it was true. "What do we do when we need a trim?" she couldn't help asking.

"Catch me when I'm not busy, and I'll be happy to do it." Lynn and Mariah gave him a chorus of their heartfelt thanks.

"Well, come on in and sit down," Mariah said, gesturing towards the conference table and chairs as she settled into her own. "Did you get doughnuts or something?"

"Lynn made cheesecake," Anthony said, disappearing into the outer office, and coming back with something that could have come straight from the pages of *Joy of Cooking.*

"I—I made that one for Anthony, as part of my thank you," Lynn stammered sheepishly.

"It was not necessary," Anthony said gruffly in his heavy Italian accent. "I've already let you take me to lunch."

"I wanted to do it." Lynn smiled. Mariah smiled too. She'd never seen this side of Anthony. Lynn would be good for him, if his family gave her half a chance.

"Here's the one I brought for us." Lynn pulled a much smaller cake from the bag already on the conference table. This time Mariah had an even harder time hiding her smile behind her cup of coffee. Lynn was obviously a lot less concerned with impressing her boss. Lynn looked a little embarrassed.

"Will you cut me a slice, or shall I do my own?" Mariah asked quickly, coming to her rescue.

"I'll do it." Lynn's grateful gaze met hers. While Lynn cut the slice of cheesecake, Mariah pulled the electric bill from the stack of mail on her desk and tore it open. The magnitude of the bottom line caused the bottom to drop out of her stomach.

"Mariah?" A shadow fell across the bill. Anthony stood at her shoulder. "This is one bill we don't need to split. I personally caused a lot of that with all the work on those dress orders and the new spring collection. I made plenty of money. Don't worry. I'll take care of that."

"Good." Mariah smiled in relief, making a determined effort not to think about the other bills she'd seen in the stack. She'd go through them when she was alone.

"Here's your cheesecake." Lynn set a large slice and a fork in front of her.

Mariah dug her fork in and took a mouthful. Closing her eyes, she savored the rich flavor. "Lynn, it's really good! I want the recipe."

Amid Lynn's murmured thanks and promise to provide the recipe, Mariah saw that Anthony had taken a small slice of his own. "My grandmother would swear I gave away her secret recipe," he said, licking his fingers.

"She must be quite a lady." Lynn sat at the conference table with her own slice.

"Yes, she is. And she's straight from the old country." Anthony took a seat at the table and gave Lynn a speculative look. "Maybe you'll get to meet her sometime."

"I hope so," Lynn spoke softly between sips of coffee, a serene, but hopeful look on her face.

"When did you guys go to lunch?" Mariah asked conversationally.

"Saturday," Anthony said quickly, his gaze meeting Mariah's and straying to Lynn's. "We went to a little Italian restaurant near the Fisher Building."

"Anthony had them fix something special," Lynn added, a dreamy note creeping into her voice. "I love Italian food."

And a certain Italian man, Mariah thought. Wasn't love grand? For everyone but her and Imani, it seemed.

They chatted for another ten minutes, and then Anthony left, and Mariah went to work on finding a replacement for Imani. She took an hour or so to go through all the pictures and stats. At the top of her list was Linda, who'd already filled in for Imani on another assignment.

It took a lot of phone calls, and an even greater dose of persistence, but by the end of the day, Mariah had several models lined up to see Cora Belson. She crossed her fingers and hoped at least one would meet her needs.

She got a carryout salad on the way home and ate it while she sat in the swing on her front porch. Warm spring air blew through the screened porch, caressing her skin. Closing her eyes, she listened to the sounds of birds chirping and a pair of squirrels playing tag in a tree nearby. It was so peaceful. When the phone rang, she sat up with a start. She had fallen asleep. She talked to Sonia for half an hour, and then went in the house to take a bath and get ready for bed.

Mariah poured her favorite bath salts into the blue marble tub and adjusted the water temperature. Sipping a glass of wine while the water ran, she went back into the bedroom and selected a black silk nightgown.

She'd already undressed and settled down into the warm, scented water when the phone rang again. Mariah lifted the portable phone and pressed the TALK button. "Hello?"

"Hello, Mariah. Are you alone?"

"Except for you," she said in a teasing tone.

"Feel like talking for a while?"

"Sure." Mariah reclined on the hot tub pillows as Ramón's voice washed over her.

"How was your day?"

"Pretty busy actually," she replied. 'I'm trying to find a replacement for Imani in Cora Belson's Fashion Experience."

"Imani's pretty special. You must be having a hard time."

"Tell me about it. I can line up the possibilities, but there's no guarantee Cora Belson will accept them." After a moment, she asked. "I haven't seen the news yet. How's the trial going?"

"Things are starting to heat up. We had a hostile witness on the stand today, and we're having a hard time shaking him."

"Did he complete his testimony today?"

"No, we've been strategizing for tomorrow. I just got home, but I'll be back in the office at six-thirty. I don't know what made me watch the news, but they toasted my rear royally."

"You poor baby," she cooed sympathetically as she took a sip of her wine. "I'm so sorry. I've got faith in you, babe. You'll find a way to shake him up tomorrow."

"It wouldn't be so bad if there wasn't such a public rehashing of the case each evening." His voice vibrated with injured pride and annoyance.

"You said the tide would turn, didn't you?"

"Yeah. Sometimes I really hate being right."

"I know it hurt, and I sympathize, but you're going to have to toughen up, hon," Mariah continued carefully. "That was just the first kick." Ramón said nothing for several moments. Mariah imagined steam coming out of his ears. "You still there?" she asked finally.

"I'm still here."

"Are you still talking to me? I can tell I've pissed you off. I should have been more tactful," Mariah said. She spoke from the heart.

"Hey, you didn't do a thing but speak the truth," Ramón growled. "What you've been hearing from me is part of the toughening-up process. A few more days of getting kicked, and you won't even hear a moan."

"Hopefully, it won't come to that." Mariah searched for something else to talk about. "Where are you anyway?"

"I'm on the couch in the den."

"Did you eat something?" Mariah scooted down in the water, resting one foot on one of the jets. Her mellow mood was coming back.

"No, I'm not hungry. I had a big lunch. I hear water," he said suddenly. "Did I call at a bad time?"

"No, I'm just relaxing." Mariah smiled into her glass of wine.

"What are you doing?" Ramón's voice took on a low, husky note.

"I'm in the garden tub, and I've got the jets going."

"Are the lights on?"

"No, I've got a few scented candles burning."

"What color?"

"Red."

"What scent?"

Mariah hesitated, and then thought, what the hell? "Passion's Promise."

She heard Ramón force the air from his lungs. He was silent for several moments. Then he asked, "Who's that you've got playing on the CD player?"

"Barry White," Mariah laughed softly. "You shouldn't be able to hear that. I've got it on real low."

"If Barry can't set the mood, no one can," he murmured.

She found herself reveling in the sound of his voice. When had he become so sexy? She'd known him for years and never thought he could affect her so strongly. Not her.

"I wish I were there. We could help each other...relax." His voice oozed past her eardrum and danced along the surface of her skin. A series of erotic scenes played in her head and she felt warm and mellow all over. Mariah sighed. Damn the man was good!

"What do you have on?"

Mariah bit back her first thought, and said, "My best bathing suit."

"Is that the really sharp-looking, caramel-colored one your mom gave you some twenty-eight years ago?"

She laughed aloud then and swiveled onto her side, so that a jet hit the calf of her leg. "Yes, that's the very one."

"You've got to wear it for me sometime. I'd like to see if how it fits," he continued in a voice full of promise.

"I think I should go now," Mariah chuckled, deciding she'd had enough titillation for the night. "I'm ready for bed."

"So am I," Ramón said in a smooth sexy tone that curled her toes. There was no way she could mistake his meaning.

"Good night," Mariah said quickly, ending the call. She stared at the phone, expecting him to call back, and then got out of the tub, glad he didn't. What would she say if he wanted to come over?

The frustrated feeling she'd been carrying around had momentarily eased. She felt more relaxed and at peace than she had in a long time. After toweling off and applying baby oil to her skin, Mariah pulled on the black silk nightgown.

She looked ready for a midnight rendezvous, she thought, catching her reflection in the mirror. Her eyes appeared dark and mysterious, her mouth full and sensual. The silk gown hugged her form, its seams opening to reveal a long, caramel-colored length of leg and thigh.

In the background, Barry White sang on about sensual lovemaking. When Mariah turned off the light in her bedroom and climbed between the sheets, the soft material seemed to caress her skin, reminding her of a lover's touch. Her frustration grew stronger than ever. She'd really enjoyed her conversation with Ramón, she thought as she drifted off to sleep, maybe too much.

Ramón stared at the phone in disbelief and then replaced it. She'd hung up on him! Well, not exactly. She'd said good night. He started re-dialing her number. With his finger on the last digit, he changed his mind and slammed the phone down in frustration. His common sense won that particular war. He would call her before he went to court in the morning. When he revealed his feelings to Mariah, it would be in person. There'd be no way she could misunderstand.

The old motor was running in overdrive. He hadn't been this turned on in a long time, he thought. Not unless you counted last Friday night when he'd kissed the hell out of Mariah. It had taken every bit of will power he possessed not to schmooze her into her bedroom and put an end to the growing sensual tension between them. She wanted him. He was sure of it. And he'd been wanting Mariah for a long time. He had a feeling he'd always want Mariah.

Ramón got ready for bed, but was too tense to sleep. He switched on the television and got really frustrated. Several channels featured couples in bed, in the various stages of making love. Finally, he turned off the television and stormed into the bathroom for a cold shower.

The cold shower cooled his jets. Feeling much better, Ramón went over the day's transcript of the trial. A new line of questioning came to mind. He made a few notes in his planner, then turned over and went to sleep.

Mariah and Lynn spent most of Tuesday morning interviewing applicants for a local commercial. By the time Mariah left for her lunch appointment with Arturro, her stomach was growling. She arrived at the Greektown restaurant early and took a seat with a view onto the street. To ease her hunger pains, she ordered a cup of soup. The people walking on Monroe Street provided more than enough entertainment as they walked in and out of the various restaurants and bakeries.

Arturro arrived at twelve, looking sharp in a blue suit and a blue and gold patterned tie.

"You didn't have to wear a suit," Mariah said, as he sat down at the table.

"Yes, I did," he insisted. "When I go to business meetings, I wear a suit."

After they put in their orders, he began to talk about his proposal for a joint venture. Mariah was so interested in his proposal that she barely touched her food. His ideas for forming a production company fired her imagination. By the end of their meeting, they'd formed a plan and decided to take the first steps.

At five, Mariah got home and parked the car. She knew from listening to the news radio station in her car that Ramón had had a much better day in court. His critics were upgrading his performance to slightly better than average. She felt happy that her friend would probably find it easier to sleep tonight. Ramón had helped her get to sleep last night by helping her release a lot of built-up tension.

Mariah chuckled to herself as she let herself in. She flicked on the television in the living room, put her purse on the table, and kicked off her shoes. Flopping down on the couch, she stretched luxuriously. Quickly, she dialed Ramón's number. When he didn't answer, Mariah left a short, flattering message on his machine. Although she tried again that evening and a number of times the next day, he was unavailable.

As she was driving home from work two days later, the announcer on the news radio station began to talk about the trial. Stopping at a light, she turned up the volume when they began to talk about the day's activities and listened with increasing dismay. Cursing softly under her breath, she slammed down a hand on the steering wheel. The defense had had a really bad day. By the time the two local legal experts were through dicing up the defense team and its methods, Mariah had turned the car around to head towards Ramón's office. Poor Ramón was going to have another sleepless night. In the name of friendship, she decided to scrap the relaxing evening at home.

"Mariah!" Ramón's secretary, Gail, said in surprise as Mariah came into the office. She gathered a stack of collated papers. "He didn't tell me you were coming."

"He doesn't know. I heard the news on the way home and thought he could use some moral support," Mariah smiled.

"You're right about that. We all could. Shall I tell him you're here? We're just about to wrap up."

"Yes. I'll wait in his office."

"It shouldn't be long." Gail touched her arm. "It's nice to see you."

"Same here," Mariah replied. She really liked Gail.

She walked into Ramón's office, crossed the light gray carpet, and went behind the rich mahogany desk to sit in his big, soft, leather chair. He had a nice office. She stared out appreciatively at his view of the river and Canada, and then at his degrees and certificates lining the wall. Up-to-the-minute news flashed across his computer screen, a benefit of his screen saver.

Visiting Ramón's office always exhilarated her. The present circumstances failed to dampen her feelings.

Impulsively, she curled her legs up and whirled around in his executive chair, enjoying the air on her face and the dizzying sensation. Going around for the third time, she heard him call her name and stopped, grinning sheepishly.

"Hey, Maria Mariah," he said quietly. He stood by his desk, looking tired and worn, but with a little fire in his eyes, and a lot of quiet dignity. They hadn't beaten him yet. "I'm glad you came by," he said, a slightly questioning expression on his face.

"I came by to cheer you up." Mariah swung her legs to the floor. "I was on my way home when I heard today's court report, and I just couldn't stay away. How are you holding up?"

"If words were lasers, I'd be a dead man," he said ruefully as he placed a couple of folders in the bin on his desk.

"Are you free this evening?"

Ramón's expression brightened. "Sure, what did you have in mind?"

"Dinner and a movie? Or a movie and dinner later, if we're still hungry?"

"I like your idea. What do you want to see?"

"That new comedy they keep advertising?"

"Yeah! That was on my list. It's playing over at that complex near my apartment."

"Good," Mariah said, standing. "We can drop your car off on the way."

Ramón pinched the bridge of his nose, rotating his fingers back and forth.

"Got a headache?" she asked, frowning, one hand on his arm.

"Just a little. I'm glad you're driving, because I don't want to be in charge tonight."

She moved closer and gave him a warm, heartfelt hug. Poor baby, she thought. He was really letting it all get to him. After a moment his arms moved forward to lock about her waist. "Kiss me," he whispered in a voice that sent tremors down her spine.

Carefully, she leaned closer and placed a couple of gentle kisses along his cheek. She felt drawn to his beautifully shaped lips, wanted to place a kiss upon them too, but the very thought disconcerted her. There were kisses, and there were kisses. Hadn't they been kissing too much lately? And they'd been more than friendly kisses. As if he sensed her desire, Ramón turned his head, and his lips touched hers in a kiss that barely was. It felt so good, too good.

Lust can be a terrible thing, Mariah thought as she pried her lips away from his. It certainly was twisting her in knots. She wanted to cheer her friend up, not make out with him. She focused on this goal as she stepped out of his arms to look at him.

But Ramón had other ideas. He pulled her back into the circle of his arms till his cheek rested against hers. "Let's do that again," he purred. "Now I know what they mean when they say, 'Her kisses were like wine.' You make my head spin." His lips touched hers twice more, as if she were the most precious thing in the world.

Mariah found herself clinging to Ramón's shoulders, shaking just a little. "You silver-tongued devil you," she managed in a teasing tone. Her body tingled from the contact with his, but she felt some security in the fact that they were in his office. No matter how tempted she became, she knew that making love in his office was simply not going to happen. "Don't you ever run out of flattering things to say?"

"Not when it comes to you. Let's skip the movie and go to my place instead. That would cheer me up and set my mood for the month." His hands gently framed her face. He looked as if their kisses had affected him just as strongly.

"Seriously," she said, unable to look away from his sexy gray eyes.

"Seriously," he replied his eyes guileless as his restless hands smoothed up and down her waist. "You are so special to me. You must know that my feelings for you run a hell of a lot deeper than friendship."

Eyes widening, Mariah struggled with conflicting emotions. Deep in her heart, something soared at Ramón's words, words she'd never expected to hear. She knew from first hand experience that he was a wonderful man, kind, generous, and giving. Because he was so dear to her, his words also frightened her. She still felt much too emotionally fragile to deal with what a relationship with Ramón would mean.

Mariah clutched Ramón's shoulder with cold fingers. Her heart hammered her chest. She didn't want to say the wrong thing, and yet she couldn't encourage him now.

He smiled at the inarticulate sound she made in her throat and continued. "This feeling I have for you is like nothing I've ever felt before. Just seeing you brings me joy, makes me happy, and makes me smile. It has no bounds and I...I just can't hold back the flood any longer, Maria Mariah."

"Ramón..." she croaked, searching for the right thing, anything, to say.

His warm fingers brushed back the hair from her face. "You and I were meant to be together. And when we become one, it's going to transcend sex. We're going to set the world on its ear, because there's nothing we can't do." Awareness danced along her nerve endings as Ramón's finger stroked her cheek. "I really care for you, Mariah. And I know you so well," he said slowly, a look of sadness creeping into his facial expression. "You're going to turn me down, aren't you?"

"I have to." Mariah said breathlessly, wetting her dry lips. "Please Ramón, that's not why I'm here." Her eyes burned. "I'm not ready for this. Not now. I just want to be your friend." She felt an almost irresistible urge to cry, and her normally efficiently functioning brain refused to give her the words to end this situation as painlessly as possible. "If I've been a tease, if I've been leading you on..." she stammered. Shaking his head, Ramón pulled her closer, and Mariah found her head resting on his broad shoulder. "Maybe I shouldn't have come."

His hands smoothed her hair back and gently massaged her neck. Who was comforting who? she wondered shakily. If only she could get her emotions under control.

"You haven't been leading me on," Ramón said, his husky voice tickling her ear and sending chills down her spine. "I've been holding everything in so long that it had to come out sometime. I'm glad you came." He tilted Mariah's head back and kissed her on the forehead. "Just being around you makes me feel good."

Mariah's finger clutched his shoulders. Anxiously, she scanned his face. "We should talk about our feelings. I…I'm…."

"This hasn't gone the way I planned. You're upset." His penetrating gaze left her no secrets. "I put you on the spot. This isn't what I had in mind."

Was there a hint of injured masculine pride in his voice? She placed her hand on his. "You're my best friend, and I love you." Her teeth tortured her bottom lip. "I'm going home."

"No." He gripped her hand. "Take the time to cheer me up, just as you'd planned. Can you do that?" Something simmering in the depths of his eyes made her stomach clench.

"Yes, if that's what you want," Mariah said, glad of her temporary reprieve. Relief seeped into her voice, but she knew that this new wrinkle in their relationship was far from resolved.

"It's what I want," he assured her, dropping his arms. He even managed a smile, but she felt uneasy. This reprieve would not last for long. Ramón was too intense about this. How was she going to move their relationship past this obstacle without ruining it? She waited until he nodded in agreement and then took a deep breath and let it out. Carefully moving away from him, Mariah tried to assume some semblance of normality. "All right, I'm the cruise director for the evening. I'll do my best to take your mind off work, and I'm going to spoil you, Mr. Richards. Are you ready to go?"

"Sure. Just turn off the computer," he said, grabbing his jacket from a hanger by the door. He held the door open for Mariah, his eyes like a physical caress. "I'm gone for the evening," he called to Gail as he locked his office.

Gail sat at her desk nursing a cup of coffee. "I'm leaving in a few minutes myself," she said. "Have fun, you two."

They ran into Phil on the way to the front door. "How's it going, Phil?" Mariah asked.

"I've had a lot better, that's for sure," Phil said, lodging a pencil behind his ear. "Did you come down to spread a little sunshine?"

"Yeah, I thought I'd come down and get Ramón out of the office, you know, cheer him up."

"What about me?" Phil asked plaintively.

"I'll bet Marcy's got something planned," Mariah replied, referring to his wife. She let Ramón pull her towards the door.

"You're not going to Lafayette Coney Island, are you? I've got a yen for…"

"No, Phil," Ramón said shortly. "We're not going to the Lafayette Coney Island."

"Oh." Phil raised his bushy eyebrows, and then began to retreat. "Well then, I'll see you at tennis next week, Mariah."

"Okay. Good luck with the case." Mariah saw Ramón open the door.

"Thanks, Mariah," Phil called as Ramón urged her into the hallway and shut the door.

Mariah was a little uncomfortable with Ramón's silence as he walked her to her car. What had she let herself in for? When she started the car, she saw him still standing by the driver's door. She rolled down her window.

"See you at my place," he said before turning to go to his own car. Mariah took off.

SIX

The thought that Mariah came by to cheer him up, to take his mind off the trial, comforted Ramón as they drove to his apartment in rush hour traffic. He'd been thinking about her as the team finished rehashing the day's activities and going over the plan for tomorrow. How he'd needed to see her, to touch her, feel her presence. She'd been a part of too many of his dreams lately. She'd said she loved him, but he was certain she hadn't admitted to romantic love.

In his rearview mirror, he spotted her car in the next lane, three cars back. His beautiful, sweet, sexy, smart Mariah. How was he going to keep her from running away from him? She'd seemed torn by her need to support him, and her desire to keep their friendship clear of any romantic nuances. He was going to have to show her that she belonged to him. She always had. Cotter Eastwood's engagement had been a fluke, a mistake.

Ramón pulled into the parking lot for his complex and found a parking spot near the front entrance. Pent-up energy rippled within him like a train with no wheels. His nerves were still taut from spending hours in court, thinking on his feet. His fingers drummed the steering wheel impatiently. If she hadn't dropped by the office, he'd be inside his condo, drinking himself under the table. This was a much better scenario. Briefly, he considered going in to change clothes, then scrapped the thought. Mariah was still dressed in her work clothes.

A car pulled into the handicapped space beside him and he looked up. Mariah waved at him, a silly grin on her face.

The sight warmed him all over. At that moment he decided to just relax and enjoy her company. He rolled down his window.

"You're not going in, are you?" she asked. When he shook his head, she added in a commanding tone, "Then come on! Get in the car."

He found himself returning her grin as he got in the passenger seat of her car. The sounds of an upbeat tune by Earth, Wind, and Fire filled the air. She waited while he pulled on the seat belt, then took off with uncharacteristic speed.

It must have been a big date night for a lot of people because the ticket lines at the movie complex were long. By the time they got up to the ticket counter, the comedy tickets were sold out except for the late show. Instead of going to a different theater complex, they opted to see another movie.

Ramón knew there would be trouble when the mystery movie became an erotic thriller. His libido had been in overdrive for weeks and did not need additional stimulation. He risked a glance at Mariah and saw her jaw drop as the hero began a particularly sensual exploration of the heroine's body.

Mariah stared at the screen. Oh no! Her hands clenched in the tub of popcorn she shared with Ramón. This was not the type of movie she had had in mind. This was soft porn, and something about the darkly handsome hero made her think of Ramón. He was definitely as competent in the romance department. She looked nothing like the sexy and smart blonde heroine, but she found herself identifying with the woman.

When the hero brushed aside the sculptured black lace and kissed his way down the heroine's body, Mariah's jaw locked. The touch of Ramón's arm against hers on the shared armrest sent a chill down her spine. Swiftly, she pulled her handful of popcorn out of the tub. Her hand brushed against his. She suddenly felt very warm. She spared Ramón a quick glance and saw he was watching her. Mariah grinned to cover her discomfort. Stuffing the popcorn in her mouth, she forced herself to chew. Then she turned back to face the screen.

The man lovingly explored the heroine with his hands and mouth. From the joyful sounds the woman made, she'd died and gone to heaven. Mariah crossed her legs. This was too much. Especially after all the sensual kissing and innuendo she'd endured from Ramón lately. Endured? Carefully, she wiped her hands on a napkin and unbuttoned her jacket. Then she grabbed one opening flap and discreetly pulled the material away from her body to let in the crisp surrounding air.

All right, she admitted to herself, she'd enjoyed all the physical flirting they'd engaged in, but things weren't going any further. Her ears were still ringing from Ramón's confession, which sounded awfully close to a declaration of love.

Slowly, Mariah let out the breath she'd been holding and focused on the screen action. They'd made it to the bed. It had certainly taken them long enough! Mariah hooked a finger in the front of her camisole and lifted the fabric. The small, cool current of air generated felt good against her hot skin.

The camera focused on the man's dark head, and when he turned, his face became Ramón's. Mariah swallowed, hard. The lips he kissed sensuously became hers. When his dark head disappeared between the woman's thighs, Mariah's body tingled all over. Slowly, she eased down in her seat, her mind translating the screen's visual images into physical sensation.

"Mariah?" she started at the sound and feel of Ramón's whisper close to her ear.

She turned to look at him, her hands loosening their grip on the armrests. "Yes?"

"Is everything okay?"

"Yes," she said as casually as she could. In the background, she heard the couple on screen bring their lovemaking to a satisfying end.

Ten minutes and two sex scenes later, the mystery was solved, and the killer led away in handcuffs by the hero and his FBI buddies. Then the loving couple headed for marriage and a honeymoon in Hawaii. The credits came up. Mariah sighed. Her suit was definitely the worse for wear, and so was she.

The lights came up, and people started leaving the theater. Mariah re-buttoned her jacket and said, "Let's get something to eat." She and Ramón stood up in unison and quickly exited the theater.

"I wouldn't say that cheered me up," he confided on the way to the parking lot. "But it certainly took my mind off the trial."

She laughed and changed the subject by suggesting several restaurants nearby. A nervous excitement still ebbed within her, begging for release. For the first time in months she regretted that she had no love interest, no steady boyfriend. Self-discipline only went so far, she noted as her handsome friend opened the driver's door for her. Would it really be such terrible a thing to sleep with her best friend? Yes, it would. She imagined the change in Ramón and the certain end to their friendship. She'd have to get a new best friend and a new boyfriend. Ramón would be difficult to replace.

"Where to?" she asked, when he'd settled himself in the passenger seat of her car. As she drove off, she hoped he wouldn't notice the dampness beneath the arms of her suit.

They finally decided on Fishbones in Greektown. Mariah parked in a nearby lot. A varied crowd roamed the streets of Greektown, some still dressed for work in the corporate environment, some dressed for the theater, and others casually dressed in jeans and sweats.

The high level of energetic conversation in the restaurant welcomed them. They were seated at a table with a view of the front door.

"Would you rather go home?" Ramón's voice broke in on Mariah's thoughts. She focused on him guiltily.

How could he even think that? Her mind had been replaying the things he'd said in his office and she'd been wondering how she would respond if he tried to continue the conversation. Her feelings and emotions were one big jumble that she'd long since lost the ability to balance. If she'd had more control, she'd have moved her chair over to his side of the table so they could talk without seeming to shout. She smiled ruefully, a teasing note creeping into her voice as she answered his question. "No, I wouldn't rather go home. I enjoy your company."

"Then get over here!" The dare in his gray eyes told her that he was reading her like a book. What didn't he know about her?

"What's the magic word?" she asked, prolonging the inevitable.

"Please." His expression softened. "It would cheer me up."

Scooting her chair around to his side of the table, she smiled in spite of herself. "What are you going to have?" Mariah ordered shrimp jambalaya, and he ordered crawfish etouffee. Then they sipped beer and chatted while they waited for their food.

At one point she saw him scan the restaurant and do a double take. "I don't believe this," he muttered under his breath.

"What is it?" Her gaze followed his to rest on Cotter Eastwood and a companion nestled in a tight corner of the restaurant. The woman was attractive, with dark hair and eyes, and skin the color of café au lait. Her tasteful blue silk evening ensemble looked expensive. The couple sat close, deep in an engrossing conversation. Was this a new love on the horizon? Somehow Mariah didn't believe it. Cotter wasn't giving his companion "the look."

Mariah thought about "the look" and suppressed a wry smile. "The look" was a pure Cotter Eastwood mixed facial expression displaying male charm, love, adulation, and his own potent brand of distinguished sex appeal. He'd given her that look clear through to the end, when he'd broken their engagement. She'd never known what hit her.

Lifting her glass, she drank her beer, noting the absence of pain and anger when she thought of Cotter and the way it used to be. It was finally over. When had this happened? She saw Ramón watching her, his dark eyes too full of knowledge about her and Cotter. He signaled the waiter for another couple of beers when she set the empty glass on the table.

"I thought the old boy was still pining away for your love and affection," he said.

"That's the impression he's been giving," Mariah replied, glad Cotter hadn't spotted them in the crowd. Her evening had been exciting enough, and when it came to her, Cotter was like a dog with an old bone. Would he ever give up?

"He's like an old sore that never heals. There's no way Cotter's given up on you."

Mariah rolled her eyes and sat back in her chair. The waiter set fresh glasses of beer on their table. She drew lines in the sweat covering her glass with the tip of one finger.

Ramón read her expression. "So what did he do now?"

"I've been getting bouquets of flowers every day for the past week, and I'm sure you've heard about the WETX Morning Show fiasco."

"No, I've been too absorbed with this case to notice much besides the news on the trial each night."

She took another sip, then set the mug of beer down. "Hal Thomas, Cotter, and the other guests were talking about the Juvenile Diabetes Association and Cotter's contribution. Cotter explained his offer to give another five thousand if I go to lunch with him at a restaurant of my choice. Then the calls started coming in to the office." Her gaze met Ramón's and held. "You know how I feel about that organization."

"Yes, I do." His hand squeezed hers gently. The contact sent ripples of awareness throughout her body. She stiffened slightly, unable to forget the words he'd said earlier. "Anything to help them find a cure." His lips twisted and he was silent for a moment. "I can't stand the turkey, but that was good thinking on his part. He gets an 'A' for effort. So when are you guys going to lunch?"

"Next week. He's taking me to the Whitney."

"I'm impressed."

"I'm not." Mariah lifted the glass and took another sip. "Would you want to go to lunch with him?"

"He's not my type." Ramón winked at her. "Don't be so resentful. The guy has good taste."

The waiter chose that moment to bring their food. She realized then that she really had no appetite. Butterflies circling in excitement filled her stomach.

"Are you feeling okay?" He fell on his food with the zest of a true seafood lover.

"I think I got full off the beer," she said politely. He shot her a glance that spoke volumes. "Quit trying to read my mind!" she snapped irritably.

His grin didn't help things. "So you admit that I can?" His gray eyes sparkled, drawing her like the sun.

"Sometimes." She pushed her plate to the side, deciding to take it home for later. "We should have gone to a comedy club. It would have been a more effective way to cheer you up."

"You hate comedy clubs."

"I'd have gone for you."

"I'm flattered, but it wasn't necessary." He chewed a mouthful of food. "I'm feeling better. You've been a good friend."

"I'm glad, because I think that true friends are right there with you when you need them."

"And you know I feel the same way."

"I hate to see you stressed," she sighed.

"Most of the time, I love the excitement," he explained. "When it's a high-profile case like this one, the stress is just part of the job."

"When this trial ends, I bet they make you a full partner." Giving up on her meal, she set her fork down. Lifting a hand, she caught the waiter's eye and pointed to her untouched plate.

"Are you unhappy with your meal?" the waiter asked as he approached their table.

"No, I'm just not hungry. Could you wrap this up?"

As the waiter bustled off with her plate, Mariah leaned back in her chair.

"You're sure it's going to happen, huh?"

"Of course. Ramón, you're a great lawyer, one of the best." His expression brightened.

The waiter quickly returned with a carryout bag. Towards the end of his meal, Ramón excused himself, and headed for the men's room. Mariah sat toying with her empty beer glass, lost in thought. When she glanced up, Cotter was standing nearby, as handsome and debonair as ever. She didn't feel particularly susceptible.

"You look beautiful. How are you?" he asked, his gaze intent.

"I'm fine," she replied carefully. "My office is getting a little crowded with all those flowers, though. It was a nice thought, but it's beginning to seem like harassment."

He smiled charmingly. "I didn't want you to forget me, no matter how much you wanted to."

"You definitely got your wish."

"And will you grant my other wishes?" He raised both eyebrows hopefully.

"I don't think so." Mariah placed her chin on the palm of her hand. Why didn't she just say no?

"I've been thinking of taking some time off. We could go to Hawaii. It would be a wonderful opportunity for us to rediscover our..."

"No," she said unequivocally. "I'm not going anywhere with you."

"Except lunch."

"Except lunch," she conceded in a softer tone, while scrutinizing his expression. Was he trying to imply that he'd manipulated her once and could do it again?

"I'm simply trying to spend a little time with you," he said, sensing the direction of her thoughts.

Mariah pushed the short curls back from her face. "It's not a good idea."

"Let me be the judge of that," he urged.

"And what are you judging this time?" a voice interjected.

They both whirled around.

"Ramón." Cotter nodded, acknowledging him, but ignoring his question.

"I saw you with your companion other there, and hoped you'd be too wrapped up in her to notice us." Ramón pushed past Cotter to take his seat at the table. Mariah found herself viewing his actions in an entirely new light. How could she have been so blind? Ramón's behavior had been more than protective in regard to Cotter for some time. He was jealous!

"I couldn't help but see Mariah, the light of my life. I've been merely existing in the dark for far too long," Cotter said, focusing on her. "I'm here because my colleague and I are collaborating on a book. I'll introduce you if you like."

"No, that's not necessary," she replied, noting how hard the woman worked to look nonchalant as she avoided looking in their direction.

"Then we'll talk further at lunch," he said, making it sound more important than it was.

"Yes, let's do that," Mariah shifted in her seat, searching for a way to get rid of him. "I think your friend looks lonely."

Ramón added. "This is unusually rude, even for you, Eastwood."

"I probably should be getting back," Carter told Mariah apologetically, obviously very reluctant to leave.

"Yes, well have a nice meal," she replied, determined not to encourage him. In his present state, he could take a social pleasantry and make it into a personal declaration. Why did she feel sorry for him? She was the injured party!

Ramón said, "I should have known he wouldn't stay away."

"No harm done." She downed the last of her beer and glanced at her watch. She felt the sum of the evening's excitement weighing her down. All she wanted to do was relax.

"You're tired," Ramón said between forkfuls of spicy seafood.

"It's been a long day."

"Yes, and it's going to be a long night."

"What do you mean?" She scrutinized his expression, sensing a hidden meaning.

"I'm too wound up to sleep. You want to help me with that?"

"This is about as far I go, Ramón Richards. When I take you home, you're on your own." Her gaze touched his face and she sensed a wealth of energy surging within him. He lifted an eyebrow and shrugged. "You really need your rest," she said on a softer note.

"Tell me about it." He finished his food and sat back with a sigh. "I just need to relax."

When the waiter brought the bill, Mariah whipped out her charge card. "This is my treat," she stated in a voice that allowed no argument.

"Yes ma'am." He gulped down the last of his beer. "Can I at least take care of the tip?"

"I guess."

He threw a few bills onto the table and shrugged into his jacket. They spared a glance for Cotter Eastwood, still engrossed in conversation with his lady friend. Mariah muttered a prayer of thanks. She was over him.

Ten minutes later, they were back in her car and headed for his downtown condo. As they stopped at a red light, she glanced at Ramón, not missing the way his fingers beat a tune on the armrest.

"Let me get my car and follow you home," he suggested.

"No, I'm a big girl. I can get home by myself," she retorted, wishing she could ignore the almost physical vibes she felt emanating from him.

"I'll just worry about you."

"Then I'll call you when I get there." She maneuvered the car into a space in front of his condo.

Ramón took her hand. "I had a good time. You should cheer me up more often."

"Thanks."

His hand slid to her elbow. "Kiss me."

She hesitated. "I don't think that's a good idea right now."

"Why not?"

"Because of what you said earlier. It almost sounded like...like a declaration of love." She bit down on her lip.

"I don't recall using the word..."

"You didn't."

"But I do have very deep feelings for you. What I feel could move the earth. Does that scare you?"

"Yes."

"Why?"

"Ramón, I love you like a brother."

"I don't want to be your brother!" The intensity of his tone shook her. She quickly focused on his simmering eyes.

"I love you dearly, but..."

"There goes the L word again." A light, teasing note crept into his voice, belying the tension in his expression.

"But I'm not your type. I can't play your games."

"I've never played games with you." His steady gaze and the conviction in his tone shook her. He'd never been more sincere.

"No, but to tell you the truth," she admitted carefully, "I think it has a lot to do with good old fashioned lust."

"How can you sit there and judge my feelings? You can't even carry on an honest discussion about them."

She cringed, heat rushing to her face. "I'm sorry. I didn't mean it the way it sounded. I'm just worried. I can't get past wondering, when it's all said and done, where will our friendship be?"

"Why not better than ever?"

"I can't believe that." Mariah moved away from him.

"Maria Mariah, we will always be friends."

"I hope so. It's important to me." He was all she had now. The thought of losing one more person she loved was more than she could bear.

She heard a click as he opened the passenger door. "Take care of yourself," he called as he started to get out.

Feeling cold-hearted and alone, she shivered. "Ramón." she called, coming to a decision.

"Yes?"

She leaned over into the passenger side of the car and pulled him into the brief hug they both needed. "Try to get some sleep."

His lips brushed her cheek. "It's going to be all right. You'll see."

She blinked, and he was closing the car door and going up the steps of his condo. Sadness welled up within her. How she longed for the days when their relationship was simple. Had things been the way she'd thought, or had she been fooling herself? Mariah sighed and brushed the moisture from her face. What was she going to do now?

She dialed his number when she got home to let him know that she'd arrived safely. He was unusually quiet. That bothered her. She felt as if he were angry with her. Common sense told her that he was more likely hurt. She had to stick to her guns on this, didn't she? Why, oh, why had she ever started flirting with Ramón? The kissing had been out of hand for some time now. But sleeping with Ramón was not the answer. She simply wouldn't do it, no matter how tempted she got.

The decision weighed heavily upon her. Mariah found it hard to sleep, despite a hot bath and soothing music. At twelve, she made a relaxing herbal tea and skimmed through the local pāper. Around one o'clock, she drifted off to sleep.

The bright early morning sunshine seemed to mock Mariah's foul mood as she drove in to work. It was hard to stay cranky with birds chirping all over the place, the sun warming your skin, and everyone smiling. By the time she arrived at her office, she'd lost the frown.

The scent of roses permeated the office like an expensive sachet. "Good morning," she called out to Lynn as she passed her desk on the way to the inner office. Lynn's subdued reply got her attention. Mariah put her purse in a desk drawer, pushed the latest bouquet of yellow roses to the side, and glanced back at Lynn. "Is everything all right this morning?"

"Sure." Lynn glanced up from her stack of files and smiled nervously. Her navy suit and cream silk blouse made her look both soft and efficient.

"What's wrong, Lynn? You don't seem your usual self."

"I've got a big date tonight, and I'm just a little apprehensive." Her fingers pushed against the edges of the folders, making the stack neat.

"Do you have a date with Anthony?" Mariah walked back to stand near Lynn's desk

"Yes. I'm invited to dinner, and his grandmother is cooking. I'm flattered, but what if she doesn't like me? I mean, how could she? I'm not Italian, and I don't think he told her I'm black." Lynn's voice trembled a little.

Mariah put an arm around Lynn. "It's really important to you, isn't it?"

Lynn nodded. "It seems like I've loved Anthony forever, and it has nothing to do with what he looks like or how much money he makes. He's a beautiful person, Mariah."

"Yes, I love him too, just not in the same way," she said. Her love for Anthony was not the same as her love for

Ramón, she thought. Never would she ever even think of kissing Anthony the way she'd kissed Ramón, but both were very dear friends. "You really should give him and his grandmother a little more credit. Anthony would never knowingly put you in an uncomfortable situation. I think he really likes you."

Lynn's hand combed restlessly through her hair, and then stopped to twirl a short dark curl around her finger. "I guess I'm just being silly. It's not as if he's asked me to marry him or anything."

"But you want him to, don't you?" She moved to sit in Lynn's cushioned blue guest chair.

"It's much too soon. Besides, why would he bother with me when he could have his pick of all those gorgeous models?"

"Oh, Lynn," Mariah sighed, "don't sell yourself short. If the two of you are meant to be together, it'll happen no matter what."

"I keep repeating that to myself. Maybe I'll believe it one day." Lynn opened the brown paper sack on her desk. "I forgot to set out our coffees." She lifted a large foam cup from the bag and gave it to Mariah. "Thanks for making me feel a little better."

"You're welcome. Thank you for getting the coffee." She popped the plastic lid and took several small sips of the hot liquid, savoring the strong flavor. Lynn did the same.

"How's Ramón doing? I thought they were pretty vicious on the news last night."

Mariah started, burning her tongue. She cursed softly under her breath. "He's fine. I took him out last night to cheer him up." She marveled at the smooth, normal sound of her voice. No trace of the worry that plagued her there.

"That was sweet of you. When you consider the evidence, his client looks guilty as hell. Do you think he's innocent?"

"Ramón thinks so, but I don't know. The evidence seems overwhelming, but the defense has had a good explanation for everything."

"Yes, that's true, I'm beginning to feel like a pendulum, swinging back and forth. He's guilty, he's not guilty. Why do we even care?"

"Because we're all fascinated by the rich and famous, and many of them use that to try to get away with murder." Mariah drank the last of her coffee. She'd succeeded in changing Lynn's mood.

"You know, I've noticed that Ramón is really good at his job. I'd want him to be my lawyer if I were accused of murder."

"Me too." She focused on Lynn's appointment book. "So what's up for the day?"

Though Lynn ran a manicured nail up the page of her book and began to read the appointments in a calm, steady voice, Mariah realized that Lynn was still nervous when she saw her hand shake a little.

In downtown Detroit, Ramón drove himself to another peak performance in the hot and stuffy courtroom. The need for sleep plagued him like a continuing sour note in the back of his mind. After he'd prepared for court, he hadn't slept much last night for thinking of Mariah. He knew her well enough to know she'd try to avoid him until the situation blew over, but he wasn't going to stand for it. They were really meant to be together; he had to make her see that. She loved him. There was no way their attraction could sizzle the way it did if she loved him like a sister loved a brother. How could she believe that?

Adrenaline and nerves kept him going. Questioning Belle Hatten, his client's wife, was like wrestling with an alligator. She was young, attractive, and deadly. During a particularly intense session, he'd exposed her lies concerning her husband's knowledge of her affair with his business partner. Sure, he'd discredited her testimony, but was it enough? Hedging his bets, he reserved the right to question her further at a later date.

The tension within him eased when the judge called a lunch recess. His associates hustled back to the office to resolve a minor problem. Two uniformed policemen led his client away, and Ramón gathered his things. The courtroom was empty before he'd finished. Snapping his briefcase shut, he began the trek past seats that were usually filled with courtroom observers. If he wanted a decent lunch, he had to get a move on.

"Ramón?" The light, unexpected voice stopped him short. He turned to face the source.

"Imani! What are you doing here?" Her face was as beautiful as ever, but he saw the faint dark circles beneath her eyes, and she looked as if she'd lost more weight. He wouldn't have thought it possible.

"Cheering you on. You were great!" Leaning forward, she kissed his cheek.

"Thank you. Feel like having lunch?"

"Yes. I had a rough night, but I'm determined to have a better day."

"My sentiments exactly." Ramón took her arm and led her from the courtroom. "How are you?"

"The cramps were so sharp last night that I was actually dialing the doctor when they stopped. He said to come into the office if the pains come back." Placing a slim hand on her stomach, she continued, "I've been in a sort of holding pattern since then. I've got my fingers crossed."

"I'm worried about you."

"I'm worried about me," she said smartly.

Outside the courthouse, Ramón helped her into a taxi, and then climbed in himself. He gave the driver the name of a restaurant and then settled back into his seat.

"You look pale. Should you be out and about?" he couldn't help asking. Make-up could only do so much.

"I'm tired of being cooped up in bed. I can't remember the last time I had an opportunity to get out."

He stared at her, not at all taken in by her lie. He knew she was ready and willing to spend the next nine months in bed if necessary. "Now what's the real reason?" he asked astutely.

Startled, her facial expression took on a slightly guilty look. Recovering quickly, she said, "I don't know what you mean."

"The hell you do. You want this baby too much to jeopardize it by running around when you should be at home. What's going on?"

She glanced down at her perfectly manicured nails for a moment, and then back at him. "I broke up with Perry last night. I wasn't getting much from the relationship anyway, with him being away all the time."

The unreasonableness of her statement irked him. "Imani, the man has to go to work. You knew he was a basketball player when you started going out with him."

"I don't want to talk about it." Her eyes glistened with unshed tears. Her lips formed a pout.

He boldly held her gaze, lifting an eyebrow, certain his expression implied she was acting pretty immature. Why would she dump Perry when she loved him like crazy? He'd heard that pregnant women could be pretty emotional, but this was a clear case of smashing your nose to spite your face.

"I've been so depressed. I just need to be around someone who really cares," she said, relenting a little. Her long tapered fingers covered Ramón's. "Let me stay and watch you work. Just let me have today, and I'll go home and recuperate for the rest of the week," she begged, her expression full of charm, despite the unshed tears.

The charm wasn't lost on Ramón, but he was not accustomed to being on the receiving end. He and Imani were true kindred spirits, and too much alike for comfort sometimes.

"All right, but you have to promise get a cab home if you feel the slightest twinge."

"I promise." Her eyes began to sparkle as she flashed him her famous smile. "Now what should I have for lunch?"

The restaurant was crowded, but one of the waiters knew Ramón and had saved him a table in a secluded corner. He ate a grilled chicken sandwich while Imani dined on fruited chicken salad and milk. Many a head turned and watched as she ate, basking in all the attention. Ramón suppressed a smile.

Imani finished her salad. "That was delicious. I didn't know I was so hungry." She patted her mouth with the napkin. "How was your sandwich?"

"It was good. I like everything they serve here. Want another milk?"

"No, it'll just make me sleepy after all this food I've eaten."

"You look sleepy now."

"Nice try, but you're reaching, Ramón Richards. I'm coming back to court with you." She settled back in her chair. "Has Mariah been down to the courthouse?"

"No, she's been busy trying to raise enough money to move the agency to a waterfront location."

"She is dedicated. Did you take my advice and tell her how you felt about her?"

Ramón signaled the waiter for the bill and turned back to find her exotic eyes upon him. "Yes." He didn't want to think, let alone talk about it. If he did, he'd have to admit defeat.

"I'm sorry if I steered you wrong. What happened?"

Ramón's fingers gripped the edge of the table til he forced them to relax. "I don't have time to go into it. We should be getting back to the courthouse." When the waiter appeared with the bill, Ramón gave him a twenty and told him to keep the change. "What made you break things off with Perry?" he asked, feeling a little guilty as pain briefly replaced the sparkle in her eyes.

Her head went down immediately and she retrieved her purse from the side of her chair. "I saw a picture of him with Keisha Lannigan in one of those gossip magazines and she was all over him. It's those pictures of him with other models and starlets that hurt most. He's out there having a ball and I'm so sick..."

"I thought he called you every night," Ramón said incredulously.

"He did," Imani sniffed, "but I wonder how he managed with all those women hanging on."

"Imani," Ramón inclined his head. "Maybe things aren't the way they seem. Who knows what happened before and after that picture was taken of Perry and Keisha?"

"Exactly." Imani pursed her lips. "I've always had a very active imagination. I guess it doesn't matter now."

"You and I should have gotten together. It might have worked without Mariah and Perry in the picture," he said, speaking his thoughts aloud.

Imani smiled slowly. "I don't know about that. I was really attracted to you at first, when Perry and I were apart, but it was never romantic. Now we've become so close."

She tapped his arm playfully. "You're like the brother I never had. What can I say? I just love you. Really, Ramón."

Ramón stood up abruptly, shoving the chair back from the table. If he heard brother and love in reference to himself one more time, he'd break something.

"You're mad," Imani cried in disbelief. "Did I say something wrong? You're not hiding a secret passion for me, are you?"

He responded to the concern in her voice with a wry grin. "No, Imani. I'm not hiding a secret passion for you."

The light of understanding dawned in her eyes. "Oh, I get it. Mariah..."

"Ramón Richards, where have you been? Been hiding in the courthouse?" A low sultry voice interrupted Imani.

Ramón turned in amazement, and the attractive owner of the voice was in his arms, hugging him, and kissing his cheek. "Linda! It's been years. You look good. This is my friend, Imani. Imani, this is Linda."

The women exchanged greetings and then Linda turned back to him and said in a low voice, "You're looking good too, Ramón." She took his hand.

He scanned her classic features. "How's life been treating you?"

"I'm okay, but many a day I've regretted my past. Walking away from you was one of the stupidest things I ever did."

Surprised and flattered, he was at a momentary loss for words. If Mariah felt this way, he'd be a happy man.

"I can see you're surprised," she said, squeezing his hand.

He grinned. "Yes, I am."

Hesitating a moment, she stared at him, as if trying to read his expression. "This isn't going the way I'd planned. You aren't married, are you?"

"No," he admitted regretfully.

"But you want to be," she guessed, her face losing some of its joyous animation.

Ramón simply threw her another good-natured grin. He checked his watch. "Can we talk later? We've got to get back to court."

Linda released his hand, pulled a business card from her purse, and pressed it into his hand. "I'd love to hear from you."

"You will." He felt flattered at the way her eyes caressed him. She was fun to be with, and had been good for him in the past. He didn't want to give up on Mariah, but he needed a back-up plan in case Mariah refused to see reason. Maybe if he started back to dating, he'd connect with someone who felt more than brotherly affection and love for him. "Nice seeing you." She gave a pleasant response, and then moved gracefully through the restaurant to join a friend at a table near a window.

Ramón retrieved his briefcase from under the table.

"Who was that?" Imani asked.

"An old girlfriend."

"It looked like she wanted to jump your bones right here in the restaurant."

He chuckled. "Shall we go?"

"It was a nice lunch. Thanks for taking me." Imani stood up and pushed back her chair. Tactfully, she didn't comment further on what she'd just heard, but Ramón caught her eyeing him speculatively several times on the ride back to court. He didn't need ESP to know she thought he'd be a fool to give up on Mariah, but what could she say? She'd apparently given up on Perry.

When they arrived in court, his associates were already seated at the table with his client. Ramón had ten minutes to read his notes and prepare for the afternoon's testimony. By two o'clock, the courtroom was hot and stuffy again, but he'd plowed through two hours of police testimony on the evidence.

Suddenly a loud thud and then a series of thumps echoed in the courtroom. "Oh!" Cries of shock caused a momentary lull in Ramón's questioning of the witness. "Someone get a doctor!" a man yelled.

Ramón whirled to search the audience and his stomach dropped. Imani lay like a broken doll in the middle of the aisle. A growing stain of dark red soaked her aqua silk suit. For a moment, he stood rooted to the spot, unable to move.

Suddenly Ramón shot forward and barreled through the crowd to her side. Kneeling, he covered Imani with his jacket, cushioning her head in his lap. She was unconscious, her face pale and mask-like. He stroked the silk of her hair, praying silently.

Dimly, he heard Judge Watkins call a recess until the following morning. As the courtroom cleared, his associates stopped to wait with him, quickly hustling out several opportunistic reporters shouting questions. A few had recognized Imani. Sadly, he shook his head. Her secret was out.

She was losing the baby. He was certain of it. She'd been ill for weeks and stubbornly holding on. He desperately wished he could do something. Anything. Imani didn't deserve this. After several nerve-wracking minutes, the emergency crew burst through the door. Gratefully, Ramón stepped aside to let them work their magic. He answered the questions they fired at him as best he could and hopped into the back of the ambulance with her.

At the hospital, he'd barely given the nurse the name and hospital for her doctor when an intern came out asking if he were a relative or the father of the baby. Ramón's negative reply put a lock on the flow of information concerning Imani. Feeling frustrated, he put in a call to Perry's answering service. Imani had given him the number for emergencies only last week.

One of the nurses tried to get him to go for something to eat, but he couldn't bring himself to leave. After a while, she brought him coffee. While he drank, she explained that Imani was still in the operating room. When she went back to her job duties, he found himself pacing the waiting room.

Imani filled his thoughts. He figured she'd already lost the baby, but was she going to recover? She'd lost a lot of blood, and her body was already weakened from being sick the last couple of months. On one of his journeys across the room, he almost collided with someone virtually running down the corridor—Mariah, still dressed in work attire. It had been hours since she'd crossed his mind.

"Ramón!" She hesitated, a worried expression on her face. Her mouth worked as she obviously searched for something to say. Finally, she said, "I came as soon as I found out what happened in court. How is Imani?"

"I don't know," he replied, shifting to the other foot and pinching the bridge of his nose. "She's still in surgery."

"Oh." Mariah dropped down on one of the nearby sofas. "I hope she and the baby come out of this okay."

Ramón, knowing there was little chance of that, spoke realistically. "Me too, but she lost so much blood...she's probably lost the baby." He dropped down onto the sofa beside Mariah. The aching groan and loud whine of his stomach seemed to punctuate his statement. Placing a hand on it in embarrassment, he noted her slight smile.

"I thought you might need this." Mariah gave him a brown paper bag.

He opened it and pulled out a fragrant corned beef sandwich. "Thanks. I wasn't thinking about food, but my stomach has other ideas." There was even a can of pop in the bag. He was hungry. Mariah sat with him in companionable silence while he ate. He still worried for Imani, but having Mariah by his side made him feel a lot better. Her presence soothed his jangled nerves. When had his sense of well being become so entangled with Mariah?

A tall lanky figure in Detroit Piston sweats entered the area and strode quickly towards the desk. Ramón recognized Perry Bonds. The man spoke briefly with the nurse, his tone insistent, until she lifted the phone and made a call. Ramón got up and headed for the nurses' station.

Mariah stared. So that's who the father of Imani's baby was. She wondered why she hadn't guessed. She watched Perry bristle as he talked with Ramón, obviously torn between gratitude and jealousy. Ramón's tone and manner remained firm but cordial.

She ran a hand over her throbbing forehead. Would Imani pull through this all right? Worry made all of them irritable. Dr. Lall, Mariah's physician, entered the area from one of the swinging doors. She saw him acknowledge Ramón and shake Perry's hand as she got up to join them.

"Mariah, I'm glad you're here," Dr. Lall called out as she approached. "Imani considers the three of you her family, so I can give you all the status of her condition at one time." Quickly, he informed them that he'd been unable to save the baby. Imani had internal bleeding and had lost a lot of blood. She'd been sedated and was now resting in her room.

Perry insisted on seeing her first. He rushed into the room alone and stayed a full half-hour before opening the door, looking visibly upset. "I'm not leaving, I'll be down the hall," he mumbled as he strode off with his head down and shoulders hunched.

Mariah understood Perry's distress even more when she saw Imani. She lay against the white sheets, looking extremely pale and much too young without her make-up. Her fine eyebrows and the angular planes of her face were still beautiful, but her overall appearance bordered on the ethereal. One painfully thin arm lay close to her side and the other curled up on her pillow.

When Mariah sat on the side of the bed and spoke to Imani, there was no response. It was better that Imani was out of it, Mariah thought. Her heart went out to Imani, knowing how devastating it must be to lose a child. Inside, she prayed that everything would somehow work out. She sat in the guest chair while Ramón held Imani' s hand and talked to her. Again, there was no definite response, but Mariah thought she saw Imani's features relax a bit.

They found Perry outside the door when they left the room. Though Dr. Lall had suggested he go home, Perry refused to leave Imani until satisfied she was out of danger. Reluctantly, Mariah and Ramón left, knowing they had a full day of work ahead of them.

"Let me drop you off," Mariah suggested, as they headed for the front door. She felt drained.

"I know you're tired. I'll take a cab." He looked exhausted. The designer suit had lost its freshness, and his curly hair had tightened.

"Don't be ridiculous!" she said, a little sharper than she'd intended. "You don't live that far from here." Dropping him off was no problem. They'd both been too involved in Imani's problems to think of their own. Consequently, Mariah felt none of the tension she'd been experiencing in his company.

"True," he admitted, walking her to her car. "I guess I will accept your offer. I didn't know I was so tired."

"I think he really loves Imani," Mariah said as they pulled out of the parking garage and turned onto the expressway service drive.

"So do I," Ramón replied. "I feel kind of sorry for the guy. Imani's really been giving him a hard time because she's been so sick, and he made it clear he wasn't ready to start a family."

"She told me that he thought she'd gotten pregnant on purpose," Mariah answered.

"Most men wonder, okay?" Ramón slouched down into the seat. "He just made the mistake of doing it out loud."

"Well, it wasn't as if she could send it back," Mariah replied, slightly annoyed. "And she certainly didn't get pregnant by herself." It seemed that men always felt they were the injured party.

"Aw, get off the soapbox!"

"You men!"

"You women!"

They both laughed then, and conversation flowed easily until they reached his loft condo. "You look pretty beat. At least come in for a cup of coffee before you drive all the way home," Ramón suggested.

Why not? she thought, dreading the drive home. She was tired, having spent a couple of hours at the hospital after a long day and minimal sleep. In her present state, she was likely to fall asleep at the wheel.

SEVEN

Mariah followed Ramón up the steps of his condo, thinking that she should have gone home. Though the crisp night air had revived her a bit, if she waited much longer, weariness would take over. And what was she doing, going into Ramón's condo with him at this time of night, when he'd been making her hot for weeks? She felt much too vulnerable. "I think I'll just go on home," she mumbled, stepping back as he unlocked the front door.

Pushing open the door, he pulled out his key, turning to her. "Come on in, Mariah." His head dipped, emphasizing his words.

"I'm tired," she insisted, stubbornly.

"So am I, but you're here now. You need to drink some coffee before driving home. Now quit fussing."

Was she just being silly? She felt vulnerable, but couldn't she handle one cup of coffee with a man who'd been a close friend for years? He certainly wouldn't grab her and have his way with her. But would she behave herself? One cup of coffee and she'd leave. "All right," Mariah dragged the words out. Ramón didn't touch her as she passed into the house, but he might as well have. His nearness was like a physical caress on the surface of her skin.

While he closed the door, Mariah went into the living room, dropping her suit jacket and purse on the champagne leather couch. Staring at her shoes, she hesitated. It wouldn't do to get too comfortable. Her feet seemed to speak to her, their throbbing resonating up the length of her legs. She could do this. Deciding to get comfortable, she kicked off the navy pumps and sank her aching feet into the soft, plush carpet. Scanning the room appreciatively, she admired its contemporary look, from the marble and glass tables to the various odds and ends gracing the mantle and tables. Her fingers skimmed the surface of a sculpture full of geometric shapes welded together in a unique design. In the background, his footsteps sounded down the hall, briefly stopping at his bedroom, and then continuing to the kitchen.

"Come on back to the kitchen," he called out.

Down the hall she went and into his blue and white kitchen. Stepping gingerly across the cool blue and white ceramic tiles, she stopped and waited while he washed his hands and began to make coffee. She saw him stop to pop a chocolate mint from the bowl on the counter into his mouth and grin. His love for chocolate was legendary.

"Mint?" He politely offered her the bowl. When she declined, he replaced the bowl. "Make yourself at home," he said, pulling a filter from a pack and placing it on the counter. He'd taken off his suit jacket, tie, expensive shirt. The golden expanse of skin bared by his muscle shirt made her mouth water. Mariah selected one of the thickly cushioned chairs in the adjoining breakfast nook, curling her tired feet beneath her on the soft, geometrically-patterned cushion. Lazily, she observed his quick, efficient movements. Ramón was good in the kitchen. Muscles rippled as he opened cabinets, lifted out the can of coffee, and began to spoon scoops of the mixture into the coffee filter. His hips flexed when he bent down to get the coffee maker from a lower cabinet, and she found herself admiring their size and shape. The fabric of his pants caressed muscled thighs. He'd always been a feast for the eyes. His body was just the way she liked it, tall, athletic, and well muscled, but not to the extent of an Arnold Schwarzenegger. Mariah savored the view, a slight smile curving her lips.

After he'd poured in the water and flipped the switch, he caught her watching him. "What are you thinking?" A smile danced across his face, causing her smile to widen.

"I love a man who's good in the kitchen. There's something about it that gives me goose bumps all over," she teased.

"Yeah, right." He rolled his eyes and got two mugs from a cabinet. "I bet you were watching my butt. Remember, I know you well."

She snickered, surprised that his mischievous comment was so accurate.

"So you were checking me out!" He laughed.

"I know you don't expect me to answer that." Mariah swiveled her chair.

"Did you like what you saw?" A sensual spark lit his eyes and smoothed his lips.

She sensed seriousness beyond his provocative remark. Her pulse picked up like a train gaining speed. He looked good enough to eat. Her eyes fell to the golden skin of his neck and chest, and the black whorls of hair, just visible above his muscle shirt. She imagined those whorls growing from his chest all the way down to his sex. Mariah swallowed, her mouth dry. "You always look good to me," she murmured honestly.

He grinned, and shot her a look full of devilish amusement that barely masked deep longing. And she wanted him. An undeniable magnetism grew between them, increasing with the force of a summer storm.

Her body ached for his touch, yet if he touched her, she knew there would be no retreat. This thing between them had been building for far too long. The thought of his lips on hers and those strong hands stroking her body made her shiver. Mariah gathered the last shreds of her resistance. "Can I have some of that coffee?" she asked, her words coming out in a rush. The fragrant smell of fresh coffee permeated the room, almost forgotten with her heightened awareness of Ramón.

Without a word, he turned and poured the dark liquid into the mugs and added cream. Placing both mugs on the table, he eased into the chair next to her. "Want a cookie or something with that?"

Or something. How about some red hot Ramón? Mariah bit her lip, caught up in the excitement. The scent of him mixed with his cologne drugged her senses. She felt his nearness like an electric current against her skin. When their eyes met, he cursed under his breath, then pushed the coffee away, scooting his chair closer. The warmth of his skin beckoned in a potent invitation.

Lightly, his hands framed her face as he leaned close. "Your lips are calling mine," he whispered, before his lips captured hers in a series of soft, warm, caressing little kisses full of his taste mixed with chocolate mint, making her moan. Her tenuous control shattered, Mariah threw herself into the kiss, floating on a cloud of sensual pleasure. When he pulled her from her chair onto his lap, she came eagerly, throwing her arms around his neck and pressing her tingling breasts to his chest. It felt so good!

He paused, his lips at her temple. "I wanted our first time to be slow and sensual, but you're making me hot," he rasped in a seductive whisper. His fingers worked at the buttons on her blouse, their heat scorching her flesh through the thin fabric.

She looked straight into his eyes and said, "Ramón, I want to burn you up." Then she moved to straddle him, her lips joining his in flowering passion.

Urgently seeking and caressing, his hands molded and traced her body as if she were a work of art, stopping only to flick the hook on her bra and free her breasts. "You've got the body of a goddess," he murmured admiringly, staring at her breasts as he tossed her bra to the floor. Gently, his fingers outlined their fullness. Massaging her back and sides, he nuzzled her, rubbing his face against her breasts, then sucked each nipple as if it were a fine candy.

"Ahhhhhh!" Mariah's head fell back as she sank in the depths of the erotic sensation. Through her clothes, she felt his erection beneath her. She moved against the hard hot length of it on a cresting wave of sensation.

"Oooh lusty Mariah," he whispered against her sensitive skin. His lips traced a flaming path back to hers and their mouths joined in a deep soul-wrenching kiss. "You are hot!"

His words excited her and helped her ignore any lingering thoughts about the consequences of her actions. She opened her eyes, boldly holding his smoldering gray gaze while their tongues danced. This was the beginning of her sexual journey with Ramón, and she savored every precious second.

Tracing a path down the sculpted muscles of his arms, she gripped his shoulders. In a flurry of need, she thrust aside his tee shirt to caress the golden skin and soft hair on his chest.

He gasped when she leaned forward and her tongue circled and tasted the brown berry of his nipple, his hands moving up her legs, and under her skirt to the lace band of her thigh high stockings. He widened her legs, massaging and lifting them higher on his thighs as he traced both edges of the lace with his fingers, sending chills down her spine. "Sexy, sexy, sexy!" he whispered, before sliding his hand up to cup her sex through her damp black silk panties.

Yes! This was what she wanted! She moved involuntarily against his hand, undulating her hips. Two fingers slipped through the edge of the black silk to stroke an erotic rhythm in the hot moisture between her legs. Mariah stifled a scream. Furiously, she sucked his nipples, encouraged by the almost growling sound he made, and the growing tenseness in his body. She gasped, reveling in the erotic sensations, not quite believing that she was here in his kitchen, finally enjoying Ramón's expert yet loving ministrations. Wild noises escaped from her throat, increasing until, panting, she climaxed against his fingers, on a wave of sensual pleasure.

Mariah melted, moving against his hand, glorying in his touch. She couldn't get close enough. She wanted to climb into his skin. She settled momentarily for holding his hand between her legs. "I want you." She leaned forward to kiss him, her fingers working at his belt. "I have for a long time."

"And I want you." His fingers stroked her thighs as he took her bottom lip into his mouth. "You've been driving me crazy. I want to bury myself inside you and stay all night."

Unzipping his fly, she stroked the hot hard length of his sex, his musky scent filling her nostrils. "I'd like that. Do it." She pulled him from the confines of his BVDs, encircling him with one hand and stroking him with the other.

"Oh baby!" he croaked, pulling a couple of foil wrapped packages from a hip pocket.

"That's not enough," she laughed, eyeing the packets and momentarily resting her forehead against his. In her present mood, she was certain, it would take several times to put out the raging fire Ramón had built within her.

"I'm sure I can find more," he said with a sexy grin.

Tilting her head, she kissed him once more, then opened one of the packets with her teeth. With small even movements, she began to smooth the condom down his engorged length. His size was such that it would take getting used to, but she was certain it would be exciting and memorable for the both of them.

Ramón gripped her thighs and buttocks, pulling her closer. He ripped away the soaked black silk and thrust his fingers into her. Mariah cried out in pleasure, riding his fingers.

"Mariah, Mariah!" Ramón laughed. "Baby, you're burning me!" He removed his fingers, and suddenly he was pressing against the slick moisture with the smooth, velvety hardness of his enormous erection. For several precious moments, they strained together. Gently caressing her thighs, he whispered her name close to her ear, until she relaxed against him. She cried out in delight when he entered her, and their bodies began to move in exquisite harmony. Love flowed within her like warm honey; her heart filled with her love and affection for Ramón, and the physical joy they shared. Her eyes drifted open, and she saw that he watched her, taking pleasure from her passion. Slowly, his lips descended and he explored the warm velvet of her mouth with a dreamy intimacy punctuated by the thrill of their primal dance. She shrieked her song of surrender as her body trembled and tensed with overwhelming excitement, then set her adrift down an uncontrollable river of sensation. She held on to him as he followed her down the river, panting and crying out.

Gently brushing her mouth with his, Ramón simply held her. She felt his pulse still racing. "I dreamed we'd come together like this," he said, framing her face in his hands. "This has been a long time coming." The light of love filled his eyes and transformed his caressing touch. He loved her, it was as clear as if he'd spoken. He smiled, and she found herself smiling back, and wishing that the uneasiness at the back of her mind would go away.

"I've never felt quite this way either," she admitted, pressing herself to him. His lips met hers in another drugging kiss and she groaned, her fingers caressing the golden skin on his chest.

"You are a wild woman," he said between kisses.

"And you're everything I thought you'd be."

"Is that good or bad?" His words were light, but his dark eyes were serious.

Mariah floated on a cloud of happiness, her body tingling all over. "Good! I didn't know it could be like this." Her fingers played with his hair, then moved over him restlessly. Being with Ramón was better than any dream. She couldn't have asked for more.

"You are the difference. It's different with you, Mariah." His fingers cupped her breasts, massaging the nipples. With his tongue, he blazed a trail of liquid fire from her mouth to her breasts. "Spend the night?"

She nodded her agreement, her head falling back with the sensation of his hungry kisses on her nipples. Her desire for Ramón's loving blazed within her like a physical ache.

Then he stood up, lifting her into his arms as if she weighed nothing. "I could use a bath, what about you?"

Much later, Mariah turned into the hot smooth warmth of her pillow and awakened. The only sound in the room was Ramón's even breathing. She realized that her "pillow" was Ramón, holding her naked length to his while he slept against the thick cotton sheets. In all of her life, she had never felt so loved or cherished as she had with Ramón tonight. They'd both been insatiable. After their initial explosive coupling in the kitchen, they'd made love in the garden tub, and twice more in bed. A pleasant glow filled her, making her smile. Wrapped in the cocoon of his warmth along the entire length of her body, she slept.

Sometime later, Mariah opened her eyes, suddenly wide awake. She stared out into the darkness of the room. The clock on the entertainment center across the room showed four o'clock in the morning on its luminous dial. Gentle moonlight filtered in from the skylight above the bed. As the warm glow of their lovemaking faded, the voice in the back of her mind grew louder. You've gone and ruined everything for a few hours of pleasure. The thought repeated over, and over and in it she heard a promise of doom. A shiver ran through her, and Ramón, attuned to her even in his sleep, massaged her back gently. Why hadn't she gone home?

She watched the moon fade and the darkness give way to pre-dawn twilight. Slowly birds began to chirp their songs of morning. The pleasant tenderness of the night before grew to sensitive breasts and a dull ache between her legs. He'd been an excellent lover, the best she'd ever had. While listening to the even sound of his breathing, she thought of all the years she'd known him and all of the women she'd seen with him. He'd had plenty of practice.

Mariah sank into the depths of negative thinking. She'd only slept with two men in her life, including Ramón. Now she really was in line with all the other women. It was a fact that he'd had her. She watched him sleep, noting the sweet peacefulness of his expression. One hand reached up to brush the dark curls back from his forehead. In response, he snuggled closer, mumbling in his sleep. Almost afraid to listen, she wondered if he would call out the wrong name. How would she feel if he did? She heard her name among the unintelligible words and sighed with relief. It didn't last for long.

Still unhappy with herself, Mariah moved restlessly in the bed. What was she doing here, in bed with Ramón? She didn't need a lover. She needed a friend. Mariah wanted to go home, but Ramón would get up for work in a few hours, and how could she without speaking to him first? People who cared about each other didn't skulk away in the night after sex, and they still liked each other in the morning. She still liked her friend, but was disappointed in herself.

At five o'clock, she slipped from his arms and slid gently out of bed. Treading quietly down the carpeted platform beneath the bed, she crept into the bathroom and filled the garden tub with hot water and turned on the jets. She found bath salts in the cabinet and added them to the bath. Slowly, Mariah eased herself into the soothing water, glad to let it relieve her body's tenderness. After a relatively sleepless night, she dozed in the hot water with her head cushioned against the hot tub pillows.

The brush of warm lips against neck and shoulder awakened her. Her lids fluttered open to meet Ramón's gray gaze. Dressed only in a pair of BVDs, he knelt by the tub. Her nipples hardened. She resisted the urge to cover her body from his appreciative gaze. Visions of the time they'd spent in the tub last night, the wickedly sensual things he'd done to her, and the ways in which she'd reciprocated, ran through her mind.

"Hey, sleeping beauty." The affectionate whisper sent chills down her spine. His lips captured hers in a smooth caressing kiss, his tongue sliding against hers in a pleasant motion.

Despite her enjoyment of the kiss, she stiffened slightly, but he didn't seem to notice. "Good morning.'

His fingers smoothed up and down her arm. "I want you to know that I am living in my dreams. I'll float all the way to court today! How are you feeling this morning?"

"I was a little sore, but I'm feeling better now."

He nuzzled her cheek. "Want me to wash your back?" At her nod, he produced a body scrubber and soaped it up, dipping it into the warm bath water. Mariah drew her knees up and leaned forward, resting her head upon them. With smooth circular motions, he began to wash her back with just the right amount of pressure. Mariah virtually purred under his expert attention. In no time at all, he was rinsing her back. "I showered in the guest bathroom, but I wish I had time to join you. Could I interest you in a full body massage?" he asked suggestively.

The thought caused a pleasurable ache in the very core of her. "No!" Her head shot up, her gaze meeting the amused sparkle in his eyes. "I—I've got to get to work."

"I guess I'm just greedy, huh? Definitely insatiable as far as you're concerned." He chuckled, his lips brushing hers. She saw that his hair was still damp from his shower. A loose curl fell over his forehead, adding to his appeal. What woman wouldn't want to climb back in bed with him and stay all day?

Getting to his feet, Ramón pulled a large fluffy towel from the bathroom closet. "Come on, time to get out of the bath. I thought you might turn me down, so I made coffee and omelets." He opened out the towel, holding it up in front of him. "I'll dry you off."

It was an offer she should refuse. She'd already demonstrated how weak she could be when it came to Ramón, hadn't she? Mariah stood up, the water dripping from her body, and stepped out of the tub into his waiting arms. Vigorously, he rubbed the soft cotton against her skin, gently drying her most intimate parts, causing her body to tingle all over. When he had finished, he wrapped her in the towel and tilted her back for a romantic kiss that filled her stomach with wild butterflies. "You are hard to resist," she murmured half under her breath, her lips still warm from his kiss.

"Must you? Am I someone who must be resisted?" The touch of his hot breath against her ear made her shiver.

She gathered herself, trying to recover from his sensual assault. "Yes, you are. I've got to get home and change."

His eyes scanned her face critically, as if peering deep into her thoughts. He must have gleaned something of her inner thoughts, because he moved away from her, the warmth gone from his expression. "See you downstairs?"

Mariah nodded and clutched her towel, feeling suddenly cold in the warm bathroom. In her pile of clothing, she found the silken remnants of her panties. They were definitely a lost cause. Crumpling them into a ball, she stuffed them in her purse, feeling sinfully decadent.

By the time she made it to the kitchen, it was seven-thirty. Ramón sat at the table with the morning Free Press, a cup of coffee and an omelet. "I waited for you."

"Thanks, but I've got to go." She wanted to leave now, but doing so would be like a slap in the face, and she refused to hurt him more than necessary. Standing by the table, she lifted the insulated pitcher from the counter and poured coffee into the empty cup across from him.

Ramón threw her a probing look. "What's wrong, Mariah?" He pushed his paper away to focus on her. "Why do I have the feeling you're working up the nerve to tell me something unpleasant?"

The uneasy expression on his face caused a burning at the back of her throat. "I—I'm just having a lot of regrets this morning," she said, lifting the spoon and placing the cream and sugar within reach.

"Because of last night?" His tone sharpened.

"Yes." She spooned sugar into her cup and poured cream in, staring into the caramelizing depths. His sudden silence was all too significant. Biting her lip, she searched her brain for something she could say to get them back on the road to the way they used to be.

"Come on, spit it out, Mariah. What are you trying to say?"

"I…think we made a mistake," she stammered, not missing the way his head shot up.

His cup slammed down onto the saucer. "Mistake?" he asked incredulously.

"You're my friend, Ramón, I want it to stay that way."

"At the risk of sounding clichéd, can't we be friends and lovers?"

"You don't understand, I've treasured our friendship and I don't like the turn we've taken. It's going to ruin our friendship."

"Was making love with me an act of friendship?"

His poignant question made her body burn with embarrassment. The very thought behind his question had caused her many restless hours. She'd been a very willing and active participant in their little rendezvous. Mariah's head dropped as she stirred her coffee with a trembling hand. Lowering her lashes, she forced herself to breathe in and out normally. What wouldn't she give to be able to disappear this very minute?

"Are you going to answer my question?" His hand touched hers and she flinched, then stole a quick look at him. His facial expression revealed no emotion, but his eyes burned with anger. No surprise there.

Gathering herself, Mariah straightened, facing him directly. She swallowed. "The answer is no," she managed in a hoarse voice. "It was not an act of friendship. And it wasn't lovemaking, it was sex."

"Really? Are you speaking for both of us?"

She cringed at the nastiness of his tone. It made her mad. Clinching her fist, she raised her voice. "What do you want me to say? I was attracted to you, we've been teasing each other with all the kissing and innuendo. Last night, it got out of hand."

"I want you to understand that what I feel for you goes beyond description. No one, and I mean no one, has ever gotten this level of emotional commitment from me. And if it really was you with me last night, you'd have no doubt that I made love to you, Mariah." The pain and anguish in his words and tone stabbed at her heart.

"Does it matter what we call it? It's not going to happen again. I don't like myself this morning!" Tears burned the back of her eyes. Why couldn't he let it go?

"It was that bad, huh?" he said sarcastically "And I thought it was something you'd treasure."

Mariah stamped her foot in exasperation, tempted to grab him by the collar and shake him. She wasn't up to tiptoeing around the male ego. "Ramón, stop it. It's a fact that you know your way around the bed."

"That's it, isn't it? You can't believe that next to you, all the others are pale shadows. You think it was business as usual."

"I didn't say that!" she gasped in annoyance.

"But it's what you think. No matter what you think about my past, last night was an expression of our feelings for each other, and it was a moving experience."

Mariah leaned over and grabbed her purse. "Please, Ramón," she said, emphasizing every word, "in the interest of our friendship, can't we try to pretend it never happened?"

"Do you think I could ever forget? I've got years of emotion invested in us. If I see you, I'll want to hold you, to touch you. We can't go back to the way it was."

"Then maybe we shouldn't see each other for a while." Stiff fingers flew to her lips. She couldn't believe she'd voiced those words, because it was the last thing she wanted.

The buzzer on the stove went off suddenly, startling them both. Hurriedly, Ramón checked his watch, then went to the stove and turned it off. "I usually set the buzzer so I don't forget the time. Much as I'd like to resolve this now, I've got to get to court and get ready for today's testimony. A man's life is at stake. Can we discuss this later?"

"I guess we'll have to," she said, glad to get a reprieve. Maybe she could use the extra time to find the right words to say. "Call me this evening, about six, okay?"

"Yeah." He didn't try to kiss her. Instead, he bent down and grabbed his briefcase from the side of the refrigerator. "Do you have all your stuff?" She nodded, patting her purse, and they headed out the door.

Mariah got home at ten after eight and made a beeline for the bedroom. She needed to dress for work and for her lunch date with Cotter. Pausing to stare at the gold-framed photo on the dresser, she whispered, "This one's for you, kid." Her eyes caressed the photo of her delicate little sister lying on a large stuffed dog. The frozen moment in time captured the essence of her sunny personality. Curling dark brown hair massed about her head, above bright brown eyes framed by a thick fringe of lashes and a wide, toothy smile, missing two front teeth on top. Her fluffy yellow sweater contrasted nicely with the large purple stuffed animal and her caramel coloring. Mariah remembered how difficult it had been to get the picture, because her sister had rarely been still for long. As usual, the picture made her smile.

In a rush, she stripped and took a quick shower to freshen up. From the back of her closet, she retrieved the painted blue silk print dress with contrasting jacket and put them on. She found fresh hose in a bottom dresser drawer and slowly pulled them up her legs and thighs. While positioning the lace on her thighs, she thought of Ramón tracing the lace bands with a finger. "Sexy, sexy, sexy!" he'd said.

"No!" Mariah said aloud, pulling down her dress. She wouldn't think about it. She really needed to focus her thoughts on something more productive, like her scheduled lunch with Cotter today. No! She didn't want to think of that either. Lunch with Cotter was going to be a battle of wills and nerves. And then after work, she'd come home and battle with Ramón. Expelling the air from her lungs with an exaggerated huff, Mariah switched on the television set. It wasn't long before she had to leave for work, but she wanted to spend the time thinking of something besides herself, her problems, or the sensual memories of her night with Ramón.

The matching blue shoes were in a deep corner of her closet. Mariah stepped into them, then ran into the bathroom to check her face and hair. She'd already done a pretty good job with her make-up, so she freshened her lipstick. Her hair was gorgeous. She stared at it in amazement, because she hadn't done a thing to it but fluff it on the way out of Ramón's bathroom. She refused to think about the effects of the hot tub and all the horizontal exercise. Instead, she listened as they began the update on the trial and Imani's crisis in the courtroom. Luckily, the hospital staff provided no details of her illness to the press.

It was a quarter to nine when Mariah walked into the office. It looked like a florist shop with colorful vases of flowers covering all the available space. She decided then that she'd have them taken to the hospital after lunch.

Lynn sat at her desk hard at work. She looked up when Mariah walked in. "Good morning. Don't you look nice!"

"Thanks." Mariah went past her and opened the door to the inner office. "How are you this morning?" She stowed her purse in her desk.

"Fine." Lynn's answer was uncharacteristically short.

Mariah took off her jacket, hung it up, and walked back out to Lynn's desk. "I hope you don't expect me to believe that. What's the matter Lynn, Anthony's not giving you trouble, is he?"

Lynn turned weary eyes on Mariah. "No, not Anthony, he's the sweetest man. It's his friends. They don't like me. And he's known some of them since kindergarten."

"Was there a specific incident?" Mariah dropped into Lynn's guest chair.

"He insisted we all go to a club last night, and I've never been so uncomfortable in my life. The women were hostile, and he didn't seem to notice. They all talked to each other, but not to me. I felt as if we were on different planets. The guys, well you know how absorbed guys can get in themselves. They talked only to Anthony. Except for Anthony, hardly anyone spoke to me all night. I think they're waiting for me to go away."

"Oh, Lynn." She put a sympathetic hand over Lynn's. "Anthony's such a nice guy, I'm sure he has other friends."

"Yes, but why should he give up his friends for me? And why should I put myself through this crap?" Lynn lifted a carryout cup of coffee from the bag on her desk, and gave it to Mariah.

Mariah murmured her thanks and continued, "Because you guys aren't just having a fling and you know it. You aren't going to go away."

"But sometimes, I wonder if I should..." Lynn said softly, hunching her shoulders.

"You said things went well when you guys had dinner with his grandmother."

"Yes, they did. She's just a sweet old Italian lady who dotes on her only grandson, but there's something negative about his parents. I haven't met them yet, and he keeps putting it off. I just have a bad feeling about the whole thing, Mariah. Danish?" She proffered a white bag.

Mariah stirred sugar into her coffee. "No, I'm not too hungry. I think you should hang in there. Anthony is worth the extra trouble."

"That's why I'm having such a problem with the whole thing." Lynn ran a hand across her forehead. "I can't talk about this anymore." She dipped her head and closed her eyes briefly. When she opened them, her expression was almost normal. Lynn closed the bag of Danish pastries and focused on Mariah. "You're certainly looking calm and rested this morning."

Mariah blushed in spite of herself. "Oh, so it's like that, huh?" Lynn said with a slight grin.

"I don't know what you're talking about."

"Yes, you do, but I'll try to respect your need for privacy. I hope it was Ramón." When Mariah refused to say anything, she added, "The man loves you."

Mariah drank her coffee. She needed a little time to resolve her conflicting emotions about her night with Ramón. It had been physically and emotionally good for her, but she had too many regrets. "Let's talk about something else. Have you been to see Imani?"

"No, I called, but they say no visitors except for family."

"She's got me, Ramón, and her boyfriend listed as family. We were all down at the hospital last night and heard she'd lost the baby. She had a rough time of it, was still out of it when we left."

Lynn groaned sympathetically, shaking her head. "I feel so sorry for her. Imani tries to be so hip and hard-edged, but her heart's not in it. Let's send flowers."

Mariah nodded. "That's a good idea. This baby was something she really wanted. She must be devastated. I want to go and see her today." Her heart went out to Imani, and Perry too. When they'd left the hospital last night, he'd been at Imani's bedside, holding one of her hands, and gently stroking the hair back from her face. The tortured expression on his face had not been an act.

Lynn opened the appointment book and ran a manicured finger down the list of the day's activities. "You're going to have a hard time squeezing it in. You have several appointments scheduled for this morning, and a two-hour lunch with Cotter Eastwood. After lunch, you're scheduled to go see Cora Belson."

Mariah sighed. "We'll just have to see how the day goes."

Knowing that Cotter would pick her up at eleven, Mariah worked steadily until ten-thirty, and then took a few minutes to relax. Within seconds, her fingers found the "worry wart rock" resting by her nameplate. She sat back in her chair, absently rubbing its semi-smooth surface, trying to clear her mind.

Two sharp raps on the door startled her. Before she could answer, the door opened to reveal Cotter Eastwood, dressed sharp and looking like every woman's dream of the distinguishably handsome and sexy older man. "Good morning. Mind if I come in?" he asked, widening the opening and stepping in prior to her answer.

"Good morning, Cotter," she said, deciding not to make an issue of it. She was going to make it all the way through lunch with Cotter without losing her temper.

"Ready for lunch?"

"Just about." She leaned forward to put the rock back in its place. Rubbing that rock always seemed to make her feel better.

Cotter observed her action. "You're not being a worry wart are you?" he asked, and she smiled in spite of herself. It was no accident that the painted blue surface of the "worry wart rock" her sister had given her was worn thin in several spots. At least she could still see the painted frown and worried expression on the one side and the smiling happy face on the other.

"I've had so much on my mind lately, that sometimes I can't help but worry. There's been too much pressure. Your pushing your way into my life hasn't helped."

Cotter sat on the edge of her desk. "I've tried to be reasonable."

Her eyes fell on the basket of goodies that he'd sent over this morning. An expensive bottle of champagne topped the cellophane wrapped mound. She gave a little sigh. "Sure you have."

Cotter's gaze followed hers. "I like giving you things. I remember when you used to like my gifts of love. You thought it was romantic."

"The operative word is 'was'," she replied, swiveling her chair. The gifts were beginning to pile up. Last week, she'd donated the stack to a local soup kitchen.

"Mariah, do you enjoy crushing my hopes?" He bent towards her, eyebrows raised.

"Now that is a goal I've yet to achieve." Leaning to the left, she retrieved her purse from a desk drawer. "Both of us have changed a lot. Cotter, I don't love you anymore. Don't you think it's time you pursued someone else?"

Cotter changed tactics. "Not when you look so delicious in that blue silk dress. You know, I haven't forgotten a thing about you, the things you like, how insatiable you can be..." His tone dipped low and intimate. With her pulse starting to accelerate, Mariah found herself fighting a blush. His statements triggered thoughts of her night with Ramón, and the things they'd said and done. She'd been insatiable, initiating intimacy with a flaming passion, setting them both on fire with a shattering desire.

Instinctively, he'd known exactly what she needed and had given it to her with an eagerness and explosive style that thrilled her. It had taken half the night to quench the fiery blaze. She would never be able to forget her night with Ramón.

Obviously feeling encouraged, Cotter moved closer. "I haven't forgotten you."

She boldly met his gaze. "I haven't forgotten what you did." Or how long it took me to get over it, she added in her thoughts. She would never allow herself to feel that way about Cotter again, never, never, ever.

"It was the biggest mistake of my life. Aren't you ever going to forgive me?" Warm, firm fingers took one of her hands and stroked it.

"I don't know," she replied honestly, twisting her other hand nervously. "But we'll never be the same again. Cotter, you broke my heart. How could I ever trust you again?" She wasn't going to tell him what a sorry little wimp she'd been, crying over him for months. Her eyes burned at the memory. If it hadn't been for her friends, most of all, Ramón, what would she have done?

Cotter got up and walked around the desk to kneel in front of her, and speak in a low tormented voice. "Mariah, sweetheart. If there's anything I could do to take it back, to make you forget, just name it. I'll do it." His strong, warm fingers covered her cold ones in a caressing motion. He gazed at her with such anguish and love that it was impossible for her to remain totally unaffected. Maybe he did love her. Mariah gazed at him with despair. Why hadn't he pursued her this way during the weeks following the broken engagement? It might have worked, then.

She dipped her head, shaking it negatively in answer to his question. There was nothing he could do. A suffocating sensation tightened her throat as he continued.

"I love you. I was miserable without you, and I'm not going to rest until things are right between us." He pressed warm kisses to the palms of her hands.

Mariah found herself wishing she could find a way to permanently discourage him. They'd long ago gone past the point of returning to love. She stared at him critically. He was loyal and supportive of his friends. He'd met all the requirements on her mental checklist for the perfect husband, and then he'd let her down at the crucial point in their relationship. Would it have helped if they'd been friends first? She took her hands from his. "We'd better get going, because I've only got two hours for lunch."

"You're right, of course." Cotter stood and retrieved her jacket from the hanger near the door. Gently, he helped her into it. "I think I should warn you."

"About what?" Mariah shifted the purse onto her shoulder.

"About the reporters outside waiting for us."

She stared at him in amazement, her stare rapidly changing to a glare as her annoyance grew. "You didn't. Tell me you didn't call them and request they show for this fiasco you've set up!" Cotter's love for the limelight never ceased to amaze her. When she'd been engaged to Cotter, she'd gotten used to having her picture in the paper all the time and having people follow them around, but she'd never liked it. She could understand getting free publicity when it suited her purposes, but when it came to her private life, it was a different story.

"I didn't call them. I swear. But a friend of mine is a reporter for one of the local stations who's doing a series on being romantic. She remembered me setting this lunch up on The Morning Show. She's the one with the camera crew outside."

From his expression, she knew he was telling the truth. Mariah ran an impatient hand through her short curls. "I hate having people follow me around taking pictures, especially while I eat. Damn it, Cotter, this is something private, even if you did set it up in a public forum." This was too much. Mariah's hands formed fists of frustration.

Cotter's expression was contrite. He put his hands on both sides of her shoulders, bringing his face close to hers. "Mariah, I'm sorry."

"Yes, you are." The words burst out in a heated rush as she twisted out of his grasp. The remnants of their past, whatever remained, and whatever happened to them in the future was private. What right did he have to air it all in public? She did not want to see it hashed over on the eleven o'clock news. She ignored the pained look in Cotter's eyes. She knew he'd been trying hard to get into her good graces, and this was a big setback, but that was just too bad. He knew how she felt about making her private life public. Cotter moved away and Mariah reined in her temper. She would be glad when this day was over. Yanking open the top desk drawer, she checked her makeup in the mirror. Her brown eyes sparked with anger, and her bottom lip stood out a mile, but her makeup was flawless. Mariah pulled in her bottom lip and closed the drawer.

He ignored her. "Just let me handle everything." Cotter opened the door of her office. "I'll see what I can do to minimize the effect of their presence."

Flashbulbs popped when they stepped into the outer office. Mariah recognized the petite blonde, Sharyn Sheldon, from the Six O'clock News. "I—I didn't want to disturb you," Lynn said sheepishly. "They said they'd just get a picture of the two of you and request an interview when you came out."

Mariah found her voice. "It's all right, Lynn."

Sharyn Sheldon came forward and introduced herself and her crew. Then Cotter explained that he and Mariah wanted no press involvement in their lunch date. After a series of short negotiations, they agreed to answer a few questions and allow pictures at the restaurant, prior to their meal.

Within minutes, Cotter was settling her into his ice blue Crown Victoria, and they were headed for the Whitney Restaurant. Mariah leaned back in the seat and watched the city go by.

EIGHT

Within fifteen minutes, they were turning into the driveway of the Whitney restaurant on Woodward Avenue and stopping at valet parking. Mariah gazed fondly at the beautiful pinkish gray granite brick mansion. It was the American version of a palace, but much more contemporary as far as she was concerned. She hadn't been in its spacious, antique-filled rooms since Cotter had broken their engagement. It held too many memories of their times together. She thought of the summer jazz and blues sessions in the garden, the annual Whitney River Beer Blast, and the New Year's Eve celebration. Eating here with Cotter today would be a sort of exorcism.

Inside, they were seated in the library at a table near a Tiffany window and one of the antique bookshelves filled with leather-bound books. There were a few other couples in the room, and Sharyn Sheldon and her crew. It took a few minutes for the crew to take pictures of Cotter and Mariah. Then the couple gazed out the French doors in an almost companionable silence, watching warm sunlight play on the cement patio. It was the kind of day that made you want to sit in the sunlight, wiggling your toes in the sand, Mariah thought. In short order, a waiter brought their menus and took their drink orders.

Mariah pored over the menu, unconsciously licking her lips. Pecan-crusted whitefish and seared, soy-marinated salmon with stir-fry vegetables caught her eye. Finally she selected lobster red pepper bisque with asparagus for an appetizer, and a soft-shelled crab BLT on a club roll. Cotter ordered grilled filet mignon of beef with roasted potatoes and seasonal vegetables.

"Will you ever forgive me?" Cotter asked after they'd ordered lunch. His question halted the restless movement of her gaze over the antiques in the room.

She focused on his elegant features. "For the way you finagled this lunch? Yes. I agreed to come, didn't I? I wouldn't be here if you'd simply asked."

"I want us to at least be friends again. I actually want a lot more than that, but it would be a start. What do you think?"

Mariah expelled her breath in a huff. "Cotter, give it up."

"Well, think about it," he shot back. "We had something special. We really loved each other. You said yourself that if you've ever really loved someone, you always feel something, always care."

"That doesn't mean we can be friends."

"Why not?"

"Because you'd pressure me even more to go back to the way we were before the break-up." The heavy fullness in her chest increased. Why, she wondered, should she give him an opportunity to bug her even more? She'd need her head examined. Getting back with Cotter was on the top of her list of no-nos. The only way she could be friends with Cotter was to see him less, and that meant a very distant definition of the word "friend."

"And if I could manage to refrain from pressure, to leave things as they are?"

Could this be a way to get him off her back? She sat back in her chair, arms folded. "Why would you?"

"Because I want to see you. I want you to stop avoiding me. I care about you, and our past history is getting in the way. I almost never see you smile."

"And why will I be smiling with you as my friend?"

Cotter looked hurt. "Don't you think you've beat me up enough?"

"No," she said obstinately. "Because if I had, we wouldn't be sitting here now."

The waiter chose that moment to bring their drinks. Mariah gratefully sipped at hers. This lunch was going much the way she'd thought it would, with Cotter exploiting another opportunity. Unobtrusively, she glanced at her watch. An hour and twenty minutes to go, she thought. Strong, well-manicured fingers covered the face of her watch.

"Stop that," Cotter ordered, his fingers stroking the skin of her wrist. "You've been with me less than half an hour and you're already checking your watch. Mariah, I've been hitting my head up against a brick wall. Can't you give me a chance?"

Mariah moved her wrist out of his range, met his gaze and sighed. "Oh Cotter, I wish you could be satisfied with just friendship. I don't want you sending me gifts and trying to be intimate with me." It wasn't lost on her that she should have had a similar conversation with Ramón and resisted getting intimate with him. She could definitely resist getting intimate with Cotter. He no longer attracted her. Critically, she scanned Cotter's earnest expression. She did still feel something for this man, but it wasn't love. "Can you let it go at friendship?" she asked.

"I can do that," he replied with strong conviction.

She wondered if she could really trust him in this. She wanted to. "Really?"

"Yes." Cotter extended his hand. "Want to make this our agreement and shake hands on it?"

Mariah extended her hand, and he covered it with both of his, clasping it firmly and shaking it gently.

"You don't know what this means to me," he said.

She tugged twice at their still clasped hands. When he reluctantly released her hand, she said, "Let me tell you what it means to me. It means that you stop all the amorous calls and gifts and dropping by my house uninvited. When we talk, it'll be mutually agreeable and will not be of a romantic nature. And it's a given that we will both date other people, not each other. Agreed?"

He gazed at her silently, a pensive expression on his face. "Agreed."

On a roll now, Mariah continued. "If we can't be friends, I want you to leave me alone. For good."

"If things change between us, it'll be because you want them to. All right?" At her nodded agreement, he smiled and lifted his drink. "Let's toast to friendship. May it be long and rewarding."

This is too easy, she thought, I'm too gullible. But what did she have to lose? Except for his promise to marry her, Cotter had always been a man of his word. Surprised by his offer, she was glad to entertain the possibility of an amicable end to their ongoing battle. Studying him curiously, she touched her glass to his. "To friendship." The fruity taste of her wine soothed her tongue. Slowly, Mariah relaxed back into her chair. Maybe this lunch wouldn't be so bad after all.

She concentrated on making polite conversation with Cotter. "How's your family?"

"Fine. Mom's a member of that Bloomington Hills Country Club now. You wouldn't believe all she had to go through to get in."

"Yes, I would. They don't admit just anyone, and even less of the diverse population." The waiter brought Mariah's soup and Cotter's salad.

"Nice of you to ask about her. I know she wasn't very nice to you."

"No, she wasn't, but that's all history now." She tasted the lobster bisque with pepper sauce. It was heavenly. She began eating with gusto.

"How's your purchase of the new site for McCleary Models going?"

"It's coming along." Mariah set down her spoon. "I've got to call my broker. I went through mother's papers and found some old stocks. Some I liquidated, and got about ten thousand dollars, but a couple of them needed researching because the companies were no longer listed on the stock exchange. My broker's doing the research."

"How much more do you need?"

"Another ten thousand in about five weeks."

"Think you'll be able to get the money?"

"I've already raised one-hundred-forty thousand dollars. I can get ten thousand more. I've made a commitment to myself."

"I know how you feel about borrowing money from friends, but if you decide you want help, I've got the money." Cotter always had money, she thought, and he used it to impress people, gain loyalty, and cement friendships. She wanted nothing from him.

"Thanks, Cotter, but I've got to do this on my own. If I don't get the money in time, I…I…" Mariah paused, at a loss for words. This site was the only one she'd even considered buying. She'd get the money in time if it killed her. "I'm going to do it, Cotter. Count on it," she said with a confidence she didn't feel. Stretching, she rubbed the back of her neck. For the past twenty minutes or so, she'd had the sensation of being watched. The back of her neck tingled in warning. At first, she'd chalked it up to Sharyn Sheldon and her crew, but she saw that they were sticking to the agreement and involved in their own lunch conversation.

Turning her head, Mariah scanned the room until she saw Ramón with a male and female colleague. She couldn't believe he'd gone by their table without stopping to speak. The woman chatted in a spirited manner to Ramón, while the man read his menu. Ramón met her gaze, his gray eyes burning with dark emotion. Mariah's stomach clinched. Talking with him was going to be difficult. Beneath the table, her knees quivered.

"Soft-shell crab BLT." The waiter set the plate of food in front of Mariah. It looked like something in an exotic magazine. Leafy green lettuce and fiery red and white bits of plump crabmeat peeked out from the sides of the flaky club roll. Slices of kiwi, strawberries, and pineapple garnished the plate. She took a small bite. It was delicious! Another bite, and she was on her way. Across from her, Cotter dined on filet mignon. They ate in companionable silence. Later, Mariah drank coffee while Cotter ploughed through peach cheesecake.

As Cotter put away the last bite, Ramón went by with his colleagues. His golden skin was taut over the sharp planes of his cheekbones; his sensual lips formed a harsh line. She could only stare at him in mute silence, unable to take her eyes off him.

"Mariah, Cotter," Ramón said politely while inclining his head to each of them. "Enjoy your lunch." His heated gaze avoided contact with Mariah's and he didn't stop to listen to their polite responses.

With her fists balled in her lap, she tried to figure it out. Ramón couldn't be upset about this contrived lunch with Cotter. He didn't have the right to be jealous, and besides, nothing happened. That left this morning's falling out. Her stomach bubbled.

A few minutes later, the waiter brought the bill, and Cotter paid quickly. "I guess Ramón had to hurry back to court," he said a bit too casually.

"I guess so," she replied, certain he was about to bring up old jealousies and determined not to help.

"I've got to get back to the hospital. I need to check on a couple of patients, and I've got a bunch of surgeries scheduled from four o'clock on."

"Yes, I know you're a busy man. I've got quite an afternoon planned myself. Shall we go?"

With obvious reluctance, Cotter got to his feet and came to help Mariah with her chair. "I enjoyed our lunch," she said politely.

"It was worth every penny."

"And I really appreciate your donation to the Juvenile Diabetes Association. I feel strongly about the work they do," she added.

"Mariah, you know I give money to several charities every year. Because I enjoy your company, your charity was included. Of course you're welcome." He pushed her chair back to the table, took her arm, and led her from the restaurant.

When the car stopped in front of the Buhl building, Mariah refused to let Cotter get out. He leaned over and kissed her cheek. "We'll have to do this again sometime, won't we?"

"Yes, we will." Mariah opened her door and scooted out.

"Well, how about next week?" he called before she could shut the door.

"Call me, and we'll talk about it. Good-bye Cotter, thanks again for lunch." Quickly, she closed the car door and hurried into the building.

Mariah's meeting that afternoon with Cora Belson was difficult. They spent about half an hour socializing and another two hours going over plans for the show and the program agenda. Cora kept insisting that Mariah play a larger role in the event, including modeling and interfacing with the customers. Finally, Mariah agreed. Cora also refused to take any substitute for Imani. Seriously doubting that Imani would be willing and able, Mariah could only promise to talk to Imani. It was three o'clock when Mariah left Cora's office for the hospital.

In the downtown Detroit courtroom, Ramón enjoyed a hard won short-term victory in the battle to maintain his client's freedom. He'd managed to expose more of the damning lies of his client's wife. Then he'd had witnesses testify about several other affairs she'd conducted during the marriage. She'd been so upset that she'd temporarily forgot her little game of trying to distract him with her body. When court recessed at three o'clock, he went back to the office for a meeting to summarize the day's activities and plan for the next. Then he headed for the hospital.

Close to three-thirty, Mariah made it to Imani's room. Immediately, she noticed the volatile atmosphere. It seemed that an argument was just beginning or ending. Perry sat sideways on the bed, one of his long legs curled beneath him and the other stretched out in front. A large pair of Nike Airs loomed perpendicular to his legs. He appeared frustrated, tired, and worn. He saw her as she prepared to knock and acknowledged her with a nod and a slight movement of his lips.

Imani, dressed in a delicate aqua lace robe and gown, sat in bed staring moodily out the window. Her lips formed the famous pout, her exotic eyes smoldering with grief and anger.

At the sound of Mariah's courtesy knock, she turned, making an obvious effort to rein in her emotions. "Mariah…"

"I'm so sorry about what happened," Mariah began. "If there's anything I can do to help, anything, please let me know."

A single tear rolled down Imani's cheek. "Imani," Perry murmured softly, wiping it away with a fingertip. Her tried to pull her into his arms, but Imani resisted, virtually fighting him.

"I asked you not to touch me!" she cried sharply. Standing near the doorway and feeling like an intruder, Mariah sympathized with Perry.

"I'm trying to comfort you," Perry replied gruffly, his hands out to either side of her. Mariah could see that Imani's rejection hurt him.

"I don't want your comfort. Why don't you just leave?"

"Because it was my baby, too."

"Really? You wanted me to get rid of it! So how can you sit here and act like you're sorry it died?" Imani blurted out angrily.

"That…that was at first. I was wrong. I'd gotten used to the idea."

"I don't believe you." Imani drew up her knees, resting her forehead on them.

"Ne-ne, the baby was a part of me, you and me. You are a part of me. I could never rejoice at the loss of a part of us. I love you."

Imani's head snapped up at his words, her eyes wide. "You…you! Don't you dare use those words now! You've never said them before."

"I know, but they're still true." Perry took her hands in his. "I've made a lot of realizations about myself, about us. There's a lot we need to talk about."

Imani jerked away from him. "Leave me alone! I've got nothing to say to you."

Mariah cleared her throat. "Imani, I'll come back another time."

Imani's eyes battled with Perry's in a contest of wills. "No, he's leaving," she said angrily. After a moment, she looked away, her bottom lip quivering with emotion.

Perry stared helplessly at Imani, his hands opening and closing, then he abruptly stood up. "I'm going to get a cup of coffee," he mumbled. "I'll be back in a bit."

The room was silent for several minutes after Perry left. Mariah walked around the sunlit room, looking at the beautiful plants and flowers filling most of the available space. She saw a card from herself and Lynn on a bouquet of purple lilies, yellow roses from Perry, and gorgeous tulips from Ramón. In the background she heard Imani noisily blowing her nose.

"Thanks for sending flowers."

Mariah turned at the sound of Imani's voice. "Oh, you're welcome. How are you?"

"Not too good. I still ache inside, and I feel so empty. I just can't stop thinking about the baby." Her voice cracked. "Maybe if I'd taken better care of myself, done things a little differently..."

"Imani, stop it," Mariah said firmly, Imani's words tugging at her heart. "You were very ill. Dr. Lall was seriously thinking of ending your pregnancy before this happened."

Imani's long nails twisted the sheet. "But I'm the one who got mad at Perry and went out when I'd been having all those cramps. I should have insisted on being checked, or stayed home in bed. It's all my fault."

"You've been walking on eggshells for weeks now. I know you wanted this baby. I'll bet that this one slip was not what caused you to lose the baby. You should talk to Dr. Lall about this."

"I will," Imani said fervently. "I need to know for sure. I'm going to ask him when he checks on me this evening."

Slowly walking back towards the bed, Mariah searched for something comforting to say. "I thought you might need something to read." She gave Imani the bag she'd been holding.

Opening the sack, Imani lifted out the book of Bible verses and prayers for times of personal trial. With an appreciative sigh, she leafed through it, tracing some of the colorful illustrations with a finger, and reading one of the verses over and over. "I don't go to church much, but I do read my Bible. Thanks, Mariah," she said as she placed the book on the extra pillow.

Bustling into the room in a flurry of crisp white efficiency, a nurse took Imani's temperature and blood pressure, and then scribbled the results on her chart. In soothing tones, she inquired about Imani's pain, and then, satisfied with the answers, went on to the next room.

Two brisk raps on the door startled them both. Mariah scanned the doorway and her stomach flipped over. "Hello, Imani, Mariah."

Her pulse accelerated. “Ramón,” she managed. He looked incredibly handsome in his gray pin-striped suit. A slight glitter in his smoky gray eyes implied he was still angry with her. Her stomach rumbled uneasily. Was he still angry about her reaction to their night together and this morning’s conversation? Had her lunch with Cotter simply made things worse? Whatever it was, it seemed serious. Ramón was usually pretty easygoing. She gripped the edge of her chair.

“Ramón, I’ve been waiting for you,” Imani cried.

“I came as soon as I could.” Ramón strode to the bed, pulling up the extra chair and taking Imani’s hand. Mariah moved her chair to make room. “How are you?”

“All torn up. It was my fault. I should have gone in to the doctor’s office, or least stayed home.”

Ramón leaned towards her, his expression full of affection and concern. “You can’t know that for sure. Did you talk to the doctor about this?” At Imani’s negative reply he said, “Quit beating yourself up over it.”

His words seemed to have the opposite effect on Imani, because she dissolved into a flood of helpless tears. He put his arms around her, gently patting her back.

Mariah experienced a feeling of déjà vu as she observed Ramón comforting Imani. Sometimes his love of women seemed to be a fault, but he truly seemed to like them. It made him a good friend. How many times had she received much the same comfort as she’d tried to accept and work through the break-up of her relationship with Cotter? Ramón was a guy who would be your friend to the end, a person you could count on, a friend to treasure.

Mariah wet her lips. How she wished she could get a little of that comfort instead of the angry looks she'd been getting today. Maybe it was time to leave.

The door banged open, startling them, and capturing everyone's attention. Imani and Ramón sprang apart.

"What's going on here?" Perry demanded angrily, his caramel-colored features a mask of rage.

"I was only comforting Imani," Ramón said. "There's nothing for you to be jealous about."

Perry's shook his head in disbelief. "Isn't there?" he asked Ramón in ringing tones. Perry moved towards the bed, his tall, lean form threatening them. Imani looked frightened. Mariah's pulse leaped, her eyes widening in concern. Perry was known for his rotten temper. He seemed too close to violence.

"No, there isn't." Ramón's voice remained calm. "Hey man, why don't you chill?" He sized Perry up coolly, his gaze hard. Mariah noted the innate tension in his posture and released her breath. He was prepared to defend himself if Perry resorted to violence.

Perry turned to Imani. "This is what you've been waiting for all day, isn't it?"

Staring at him, Imani's mouth worked helplessly. Mariah was struck by the similarity of his question to Imani's first words to Ramón. She'd said she had been waiting all day.

"It isn't what you think," Imani said finally. She swallowed and reached for a tissue. "Ramón and I are friends."

"Yeah?"

"Yeah. This isn't news to you." Imani blew her nose. "Perry, stop acting stupid."

Perry shifted his feet, his hands clenching into fists. He pointed a finger at Imani. "I'm going to take you up on your suggestion. I'm outta here!" Abruptly, he turned and stormed from the room. Three pairs of eyes watched him in stunned silence.

"He'll be back," Ramón told Imani. She began to cry again.

"For a minute there, I thought he was going to knock your block off," Mariah told Ramón.

"He could have tried. I was ready for him."

"I could see that." Mariah stood, gathering her purse. "Listen, I've got to go. Are you still coming by at six to finish this morning's discussion?"

Ramón's gaze turned wary. "Yes, we've got a lot to talk about."

"I'll see you then." Mariah said her goodbye to Imani, promising to visit again soon, and then hurried to her car. During the drive home, she thought about Imani and Perry. That relationship was going down the toilet. She murmured a quick prayer that her friendship with Ramón would not suffer the same fate. He and his parents were the closest thing she had to family. The fatal difference was that although you could have serious fights with your family, they still loved and put up with you. Could she expect the same from Ramón?

Once home, she was too tense to sit out on the porch in the warm afternoon sun. Her stomach bubbled on, implicitly warning her not to eat a thing. She wondered what she was going to say to Ramón.

Ramón arrived promptly at six. He'd exchanged the gray pin-stripped suit for a black sweatsuit and a pair of Reeboks. Tiny lines creased the skin near his mouth, and his eyes were slightly red.

Ushering him into the den, Mariah poured a glass of white wine and set it in front of him. "How was your day?"

Ramón raised an eyebrow. "It started off really well," he said in a low, sexy tone. His gaze spread warmth throughout her body. He paused for a moment and then continued.

"Then in court, I discredited a lot of Belle Hatten's testimony. Now all I've got to do is figure out why she lied, and who really killed Gerald's partner."

"Sounds like you won a significant part of the battle. I'm happy for you," she murmured, slipping into the plush, fawn-colored-chair opposite the sofa. She sipped her wine.

"There's still a long way to go." He shifted on the sofa until he faced her fully. "What were you trying to tell me this morning?"

"I...I think we made a mistake." Mariah's fingers twisted in her lap.

Ramón pinned her with a glance. The glitter was back in his gray eyes. He looked incredibly dangerous, and sexy. "Hmmmph, mistake is such a harsh word to describe what we did. We made a lot of mistakes last night, didn't we?" he rasped, in a sensual tone, emphasizing the word mistake in a suggestive manner. "I really enjoyed all those mistakes. I thought you did too."

Mariah felt the blood rush to her face. She positively burned with embarrassment. Yes, she had enjoyed making love with Ramón. But that didn't make it right, or the best thing for their friendship. Swallowing hard to force saliva past the lump in her throat, she forced herself to continue. "No matter how much I enjoyed it, I really regret making love with you. Ramón, you're my friend, and I want to keep it that way."

Ramón's eyes narrowed. "And you think sleeping together would ruin our friendship?" he asked in a dangerously soft voice.

Mariah bit her lip. "Yes, I do. Sex changes everything."

"Why?"

Emotion welled within her, causing her knees to tremble. She stammered, "B-because I can't see you sticking with me for long if we continue sleeping together. What about all those other women? I can't remember all their names. Ramón, you don't have a good track record. Why would it be any different with me?"

"Because you are different. That's why we've been close friends for so long."

Mariah's body ached with the depth of her emotions. The tremors in her knees increased. "Well, I couldn't take the rejection. I can't play those games. Let's stop before things get serious. Ramón, I care about you. I need to have you in my life."

She tried to gauge his expression. He seemed on edge, about to explode with violent emotion. "Don't you get it?" Ramón got up from the couch and walked over to her chair.

Mariah's eyes widened. "Get what?" she asked, lifting her chin to maintain eye contact with him.

"Get what I've been trying to tell you." Gently, her pulled her to her feet, and into his arms. "I love you, Mariah. I have for a long time." His arms tightened around her as his lips brushed her temple. "I can't hide it any longer."

A feeling of helplessness gripped Mariah. Her teeth began to chatter. This revelation was what she'd been afraid of. He couldn't love her. She wasn't his type of woman at all. It had to be lust, pure and simple. "No. No," she mumbled involuntarily, pushing herself away from him. "You're like family to me. You are family. Don't you understand?"

Ramón pulled her back into his arms, the heat of his body scorching her skin. Mariah struggled to catch her breath. His body enfolded her in a sensual prison. "No, don't you understand? I'm not interested in being your damned brother. I want to be your lover." His warm, mobile mouth moved against her temple, down to her neck, and back to the sensitive lobe of her ear.

Mariah shivered, drenched in a torrent of thrilling sensations. Close to her ear, he spoke in a low, silky tone that turned her knees to water. "I want to make love to you all night, every night. I want to wake up to you in the morning and start all over again." His hands slid down her back to mold the fullness of her hips, and draw her even closer.

Unable to stand on her own, she leaned against the length of his hard body, virtually lying on him. With her hands, she clung to the gently curving muscles of his arms. "Mariah!" he whispered, turning his head until his mouth caught hers in a deep drugging kiss. His taste, his touch, his presence overwhelmed her senses with a maelstrom of passion. Hot, consuming flames of desire exploded within her. Mariah moaned, her fingers stroking the golden skin of Ramón's chest in a growing fury of sensation. She felt him working the buttons of her blouse.

Sinking down onto the thickly-cushioned carpet, they reveled in the warm magic their fingers made against the skin laid bare by their loose clothing. Her short skirt rode up, and he settled between her legs, his hands gripping her, his fingers tracing erotic patterns against her flesh. This was wrong. The persistently nagging voice in the back of Mariah's mind grew louder. She gasped, her hands pushing against his chest. "No. Please, Ramón," she begged. "I'm weak, I admit it."

He dropped his arms and rotated to a sitting position, his face still flushed with passion, and anger. "Admit it," he said, his jaw tightening, "you want me as much as I want you."

She stared down at her nervous fingers twisting in the plush beige carpeting, and then back at Ramón. "I want you as much as you want me." When he started to move closer, she added, "But I can't do this. It won't work, Ramón." Pulling down her skirt, and holding the edges of her blouse together, she took a breath. "I can't believe I did that!" she vented, slapping one hand on the carpet. She'd almost slept with Ramón again.

The sight of his glittering eyes and sullen expression hurt her. She wanted to take her fingers and smooth out the lines across his forehead and coax his stubborn mouth into a smile. The weight of the silence was more than she could bear. "I'm sorry," she whispered.

"Are you?" His tone sharpened as he pulled up and straightened his sweatpants. "Is that what you told Cotter Eastwood this afternoon over lunch? The two of you looked pretty cozy, looking into each other's eyes, holding hands, toasting each other."

"I don't have to explain myself to you, but that's not how it was," she said defensively, shrillness creeping into her tone. "Cotter and I came to an understanding. We're going to be friends."

Ramón got to his feet in a huff. "I can't tell you how it makes me feel to know that you lump me and your ex-fiancé in the same category."

Mariah scrambled to her feet. "I don't. I..."

"You don't know what you want, do you?" he said cutting her off. "You want me, yet you keep pushing me away. What are you afraid of?"

Anger flared within her. She was only trying to preserve their friendship. Why couldn't he see that? Male pride was scrambling his brain. He had some nerve. "I'm not afraid of anything," she said between clenched teeth. "I simply refuse to join your long line of conquests."

His handsome features formed a smirk. "Isn't it a little late for that?" Scenes of her night with Ramón played in her mind. They'd made love several times. Mariah cringed with embarrassment and shame, the flames of her anger growing. How crude of him to infer that she'd already joined his line of conquests. Her temperature shot up several more degrees, the heat emanating from her body in waves of anger. She pushed him, her voice going up several octaves. "Ramón Richards, get out of my face! I don't need to be listening to this. Maybe our friendship is an illusion."

Ramón put his hands on her shoulders. "No, I shouldn't have said that. I didn't mean it. I said it out of frustration and anger more than anything else. I'm sorry, okay?"

Still hurting, she scanned his face for indications of sincerity and nodded. "That was a low blow. You should be."

"Mariah, think about you and me," Ramón continued. "You haven't had a date in months. Neither have I. We've been seeing each other, whether we admit it or not."

No. It wasn't true. How could Ramón think it was? Mariah shook her head. "That's not true." She moved away from him, backing up to sit on the couch with her chin in the palm of her hand. "It took me a long time to get over the broken engagement. You know that. And then I was too busy to think about dating someone new."

"Bullshit." Ramón followed her over to the couch, his expression grim. "If you'd just stop running away from me, from us, Maria Mariah, you'd see a lot that's been right in front of your face."

She took in all the negative energy and anger flowing around Ramón, her eyes widening. Her heart ran a race all its own. Her stomach clinched and burned. She couldn't take much more. "Stop pushing me, Ramón. You're coming on too strong, and I don't like it."

"No, you don't want me coming on to you at all, do you? You want to forget about everything that's happened between us."

Moisture pooled and dripped beneath her arms. The nightmare she'd been trying to avoid was unfolding and spiraling out of control. "N-nothing's happened that can't be forgotten," she said, knowing it was a lie. No matter what happened, her night with Ramón was something she could never forget, but she'd lost the capacity to consciously treat it as anything but a temporary aberration in their relationship. She was too afraid to do anything else. Reaching, she said something she'd heard often. "Get this, Ramón, it was just sex." Immediately, she wanted to take the cold, crass words back. Biting her tongue, she cringed. She'd put her foot in it this time.

Ramón stared incredulously. "Yeah? This from the woman who doesn't believe in sex without love?"

Mariah gripped the folds of her skirt like a drowning woman clutching at branches in the river. She couldn't explain herself. She couldn't tell him she was afraid. That would only give him the ammunition he needed to pin her down, to force her to confront the fear that was coming between them. "So I fell off my pedestal, okay? I'm not perfect. If you value our friendship, you'll forget it ever happened."

"Is that a threat? Haven't you heard anything I've been saying? I love you, dammit, and I'm not going to let you pretend it's nothing."

"I'm not threatening you!" Standing up on shaking legs, Mariah couldn't take her eyes from his expressive face. She was losing it. She was losing him. "And I'm not taking your feelings lightly. I just don't know how else to respond, Ramón. I'm not ready for anything deeper than friendship. I can't handle it right now. I…I…"

"And I can't go on like this. I won't. I've been holding it in too long." He chewed his lip, his fisted hands clinching and unclenching. "What do you think I should do? What would you do if our positions were reversed?"

"I don't know."

"Can't even throw me a bone, huh? Can't you say that maybe you'll feel differently in a few months time? Can't you give, even a little?"

His words pierced her like knives. Should she give a little? She didn't believe in stringing people along. Her mind refused to consider the prospect of a serious relationship with him. She choked back tears, her hand extending to touch his softly sculpted biceps. "Ramón, there are so many kinds of love. You matter more than anyone. You're my family, and you always will be."

"You're hiding behind a bunch of bull. If God wanted you to have a brother, he'd have given you one. I'm not applying for the position," Ramón said shortly. "I want your love in every sense of the word, and don't want to beg for it." He shoved his hands into the pockets of his open sweat jacket, his golden chest gleaming in the soft light. "This morning you suggested that maybe we shouldn't see one another for a while. I was angry then, but now I'm thinking it's probably a good idea. Maybe we need a break from each other."

Mariah cringed, fighting the pain of his rejection. Her thoughtless words came back to haunt her. She counted on Ramón. She needed to see him. Sure, she had other friends, but it wasn't the same. Mariah's breath came out in a rush. "No, Ramón, don't do this. That's not what we need."

The force of his emotions was so intense that she found it hard to maintain her light hold on his biceps. "Then what is? You're all upset because we made love. You're unhappy because I love you. It seems like I'd be doing both of us a favor." His smoky gray eyes seemed to see clear through to the fear in her heart. He was calling her bluff.

"I don't want you to go away angry with me. I don't want you to go away at all," she stammered, one hand going to her throbbing chest. She was a basket case. "Ramón, we don't have to settle everything tonight."

"I think your position is pretty clear. You're running away from us so fast that you haven't stopped to think why. I'm asking you again, what are you so afraid of?"

"I don't know. I'm not afraid of anything." She pushed damp curls back from her face with a shaking hand. "I can't think like this. I won't be pushed into anything. Ramón, give me a break."

He seemed to consider her plea as he silently gazed at her for several moments. When his facial expression hardened into a look of resignation, she knew she was in trouble. Taking her cold hand in both of his, he leaned forward. "I've got to get out of here. Good-bye, Mariah." His warm lips brushed her forehead.

"Night," she replied automatically. Good-bye? Before she could put what had happened into the proper perspective, he opened the front door and walked out of her house. She made it to the front window in time to see him get into his car and drive away. Hot tears scalded the sensitive skin of her face. Bile rose in her throat, burning her with its bitter taste. Within seconds, she was running to the bathroom to accommodate her heaving stomach.

NINE

Mariah awakened long before the alarm clock went off. She hadn't slept much, and when she had, she'd dreamed of losing the option on the new agency site. Tiny grains of invisible sand filled her eyes. Wincing, she rubbed them carefully with the tips of her fingers. The cream lace vertical blinds at the window drew her attention. Engrossed in the patterns of sunlight seeping in around the corners of her blinds, she pushed back the burgundy and cream sheets to sit up in bed. The birds outside chirped and trilled excitedly.

It's Wednesday, she thought, three more business days on the option for the new site, and a little more than a month since I've last seen Ramón. Ramón, Ramón, always there when I need you, where are you now? She needed the moral support, but she knew how to be stubborn, too. She was not going to call him, and she was going to close on the option if it killed her.

Checking the digits on the clock across the room, she saw that it was only seven o'clock. Grabbing the remote from the nightstand, she turned on the television. The morning news anchor gave quick updates of yesterday's news. Within minutes, he began to discuss the trial and the activities scheduled for the day. Ramón and the rest of the defense team were getting good marks from the news team. Within the past week and a half, they'd been able to show murder motives for two other people besides Gerald Hatten. Consequently, people were no longer so certain he'd killed his partner.

When they did a close-up, she gazed at Ramón's image, unable to look away. The whites of his brown eyes seemed a dingy gray that only seemed to emphasize the mid-sized grocery bags under them. The fine lines around his mouth seemed more like grooves. With a critical eye, she saw that the slate gray designer suit hung off his frame. Had he lost weight? He looked like hell.

Mariah switched off the television and padded into the kitchen to wash her hands. In the overwhelming silence, she made coffee. Alone again. She'd been alone since her mother died. Why did it bother her so much now? She certainly had other friends. It was a lot less complicated this way. And lonely, she thought fleetingly.

In the refrigerator, she found a cantaloupe half and pulled it out. No, it was a good idea, but she wasn't hungry. Within seconds, it was back in the refrigerator. She hadn't really been hungry in quite a while. That's why she was determined to eat something. She forced herself to make toast.

Had she lost weight? Did her clothes hang off her as Ramón's did? she wondered. It didn't really matter, she decided, as she poured coffee and added cream and sugar. Quit thinking about Ramón, she chastised herself. There are plenty of other things to worry about.

After coffee and toast, she showered and dressed in record time. Mariah stared critically at her reflection in the full-length mirror on her closet door. She had lost weight, but her clothes were not hanging off her. The skirt of her suit, which had been a little tight before, now fit attractively.

Determined to shake off her low mood, she dragged herself out of the house and locked her door. Loneliness is a state of mind, she decided as she got into her car. She simply needed to think herself into a better frame of mind. The temporary loss of one friend should be no big deal, but it was.

On the way to work, she drove past people jogging in the park or sitting companionably at picnic tables with coffee and doughnuts. When she stood in the hall outside her office, she hesitated before putting her key to the lock. If all her plans came together, her days in this small office suite were numbered. Down the hall, she heard two of Anthony's staff members discussing the beading for an evening gown. In the office, two figures merged together behind the frosted glass door. Lynn and Anthony sharing a kiss, she thought.

They stood together near the file cabinet when Mariah opened the door. Anthony looked sharp in one of his signature print shirts and black pants. Lynn's soft, gray silk dress had a v-neck and a short, pleated shirt. "Good morning!" Lynn said brightly. Anthony called out a greeting.

"Good morning, Lynn, Anthony."

Lynn's smile widened. "There's cappuccino on your desk and croissants, courtesy of Anthony."

"Well thanks, Anthony," Mariah said, watching him tear his gaze away from Lynn. "Are you going to stay and share them with us?"

"No, I've got a deadline that's looming fast. How are you this morning?"

"I'm fine."

"How many days left on the property option?" he asked shrewdly, his dark brows coming together.

Mariah's grip tightened on the handle of her purse. "The option expires next Monday, so I've got three days."

His facial expression softened with increased concern. "Are you going to make it?"

"I'm working on it."

"If you need help..."

"Thanks, but I'll handle it." Quickly, Mariah stepped into her inner office, pulled out her chair, and flopped down. Absently, her fingers found the oval rock and began to caress its worry-worn surface. Close, she was so close to meeting her goal. She only needed another ten thousand, but right now, it seemed like ten million. Payments due from her clients totaled more than three thousand dollars. How was she going to get the other seven thousand?

Mariah scanned her calendar, her brain working feverishly. She'd already refinanced her home and put the extra money in her account for the property. On Monday, she'd called each client with a due bill and requested immediate payment.

Quickly, she tried to come up with new options, her fingers moving faster on the rock. There were no other assets to consider, unless she counted her grandmother's wedding ring. She'd never considered selling it, but when she'd had it appraised at Dumouchelle's Auction Galleries downtown, they'd offered her an exorbitant sum for it. Mariah remembered her grandmother as the thin but pretty, sharply-dressed woman who used to spoil her outrageously. There were dozens of pictures of her holding and playing with Mariah in the family albums. Grandma had died when Mariah was eleven. No, she decided, shaking her head, selling the ring was not an option. She wished she'd sold her house instead of refinancing it. The future had looked so positive then. Her brain cycled uselessly.

In the background, she heard Anthony tell Lynn he was taking her to lunch, then a short silence. Sighing with frustration, she set the rock back in its place and placed her purse in the bottom drawer of her desk. It was time for that cappuccino.

Anthony stuck his head in her office for a minute, his penetrating gaze cutting through her frustrated state, and summing her up. "Let me know if you change your mind."

"Thanks, Anthony," she said aloud, knowing that she'd practically die before asking his help. She had to do it alone. If she couldn't, what sort of businesswoman could she be?

"Anytime. Well, I've got to go." He turned and moved towards the entrance to the outer office. "See you ladies later," Anthony called in a light, happy tone.

"Bye, Anthony," she answered. The outer office door closed.

Mariah sat at her desk drinking her cappuccino when Lynn appeared in the doorway. "Mind if I come in? We can go over your appointments for today."

"Sure Lynn, bring your stuff," she said, clearing a space. Lynn made two trips back to her desk for cappuccino, her croissant, and her appointment book, and then settled into Mariah's guest chair.

"Things seem to be going your way," she said, watching Lynn sip her drink. Lynn and Anthony's love for each other was on their faces and in their mannerisms for all to see.

"Not really." Lynn stared down into the dark liquid as if searching for an answer. "It's hard to have and maintain a good relationship with anyone, but it's ten times harder when you come from different races."

"Are Anthony's friends still giving you the cold shoulder?"

"No, only a couple of them are still his friends," Lynn replied, fiddling with the corner edges of the appointment book. "It was bad enough for me, but I hate to see Anthony lose friends. Some of those people have known him since junior high and kindergarten. Mariah, it got pretty ugly. It started with thinly veiled references to 'you people', and when I called them on it, the racial slurs flew hot and heavy from his friend Marsha. I was really upset by then, because some of those comments really hurt. I lost my temper." Lynn picked up her cappuccino with shaking hands and took a small sip. "What can I say? She was ignorant, she behaved badly, and I let her pull me into it. Anthony was shocked that one of his friends would go that far. He stepped in before we came to blows. I wish he'd stepped in sooner. I guess you never really know what some people will do in a given situation."

Lynn's comments made her uneasy. People were crazy. Rubbing the back of her neck, Mariah said, "Oh, I can imagine." She hoped things would not escalate into violence. Lynn and Anthony had obviously endured more than enough. No one had the right to tell them they couldn't be together. The thought of Lynn and Anthony enduring any further pain as a result of their relationship angered and frustrated her. She took a small bite of the croissant, trying to concentrate on the flavor. "Just remember, it's not your fault."

"That's what I keep telling myself," Lynn said brightly, her cocoa-brown eyes shining with tears. "He is just so wonderful, so loving. I just never knew I could be so happy with anyone."

The little catch in her voice struck a poignant note with Mariah, making her wish she felt that way about someone. How long had it been since she'd felt that way about anyone? Her memories of how it had been with Cotter were starting to fade, but had she felt as strongly as Lynn felt for Anthony? Doubt consumed her. She really needed to start dating again. "Have you met his parents?" she asked aloud.

"No, he says the timing isn't right." Lynn set her cup on the desk. "I suspect it may never be right, but Lord, how I enjoy that man."

Mariah smiled, glad to see Lynn happy. She knew that Lynn's enjoyment of Anthony did not likely extend to sleeping with him, at least not yet. Lynn was an old-fashioned girl. Mariah watched Lynn pull herself together, open the book and begin to go over the appointments. The day was pretty full. Imani, Arturro, and a few new models looking for work covered the morning hours. Lunch in the afternoon with Gloria Richards, Ramón's mother, provided a welcome break before an afternoon appointment with Cora Belson.

Lynn broke in on her thoughts. "Is there anything I can do to help get the money for the option on the new site?"

Lynn's concern touched her, but she kept her tone light. "Can you tell me today's winning lottery number?"

"Of course not."

"Then I guess there's nothing you can do. Thanks for offering."

Instead of going through portfolios and making calls as she'd planned, Mariah spent the time between interviews worrying about the option on the new site. The yellow pad she'd used to list her ideas was filled with dark scribbling and cross-outs. In frustration, she slammed the worry wart rock down on the desk and stared out the window.

Arturro Mann breezed in at about 9:30, full of plans for a Nordstrom catalog. She was certain dollar signs danced in his head as he chattered on, detailing his idea for the theme. He'd already called the company and made an appointment for the two of them to pitch the idea to a receptive audience.

Arturro paused in his perusal of the pile of portfolios she'd gathered for him. "You seem a little distracted. Is there a problem with my proposal?"

Mariah started in surprise. Was she that transparent? "No. I think it's a great idea." She placed the stack of portfolios in her hand crosswise on the pile in front of her. "I've got a lot on my mind today; too many deadlines looming, and too little I can do about them."

Arturro placed a forefinger between his nose and upper lip. "Is there anything I can do to help?"

His offer made her feel good. She and Arturro were becoming friends. Mariah smiled. "No, but thanks for offering. This is something I have to do by myself." She really did have friends who cared about her. She wondered, would any of them ever get as close as Ramón had? He'd left a void in her life.

Arturro returned her smile, patting her hand. "We could go to lunch. That always seems to cheer me up."

Charmed even more, she said in surprise, "Thanks for caring, but I already have a lunch date. Can I have a rain check?"

"Of course. Give me a call the day before you want to go." He went back to his stack of portfolios.

They had finished selecting the models, and Arturro was leaving, when they encountered Imani waiting in the outer office. In a blue silk pantsuit with her long hair framing her face, she appeared thinner. Her beauty was more vibrant than ever. The sadness in her eyes, combined with dramatic makeup, intensified the mysterious and intriguing aspects of her look.

"Arturro, this is Imani, McCleary Models' top model. Imani, Arturro Mann, my partner in A & M Productions." Imani and Arturro responded to one another in polite but friendly tones. Mariah noticed that when they shook hands, Arturro held onto Imani's hand for several moments longer than necessary. He couldn't take his eyes off Imani.

"Your portfolio was not in the selection I saw this morning," he told Imani.

"I've been ill," Imani replied, "and therefore inactive. In fact, I came in today to talk about some new assignments."

"I think you're perfect for the catalog we're doing." Arturro turned to Mariah. "Don't you agree?"

"Yes, Imani has quite a following," she replied. "I didn't want to put her portfolio in the group until I'd talked to her." Taking a step towards Imani, she said, "That's just one of the things on our agenda this morning."

After Arturro left, Imani and Mariah met in the inner office. Imani agreed to do the catalog and Cora Belson's Fashion Extravaganza. Things were looking up. When Imani and the other high rate models worked, naturally the agency made more, too.

"So how are you?" Mariah asked when they'd finished talking business.

"It's really devastating to lose a child. I'm still healing." Imani uncrossed her legs. "Physically, I can do what I want. Right now, all I want to do is work and keep myself in good condition. Dr. Lall says I can still have children." Lips trembling, she blinked furiously, as if to hold back tears. "When life knocks you down, you find out who your friends really are."

She's still hurting over Perry and the baby, Mariah thought, her heart full of sympathy. She stood and went to Imani and gave her a quick hug. "It's those little bumps and hiccups in life that build character."

"Yeah, I just hope they don't also cause a few wrinkles. I need to work."

"Don't we all?" Mariah laughed, returning to her chair.

"Have you called Ramón?"

Mariah turned at the question, her smile disappearing. Did Ramón discuss her with Imani? She was certain of it. Rarely did she discuss Ramón with Imani, yet Imani knew about her argument with Ramón. Her eyes scanned Imani's face. She didn't like the thought. Carefully, she settled back in her chair. "No, I haven't." In pure self-defense, she added, "Have you called Perry?" She cringed inwardly, biting her tongue when she saw the immediate look of pain and sorrow on Imani's face. It wasn't like her to be so mean.

Within seconds, the expression was gone, as Imani's lips tightened, her gaze heating up. "No. Perry and I don't see each other anymore. It's over with, Mariah, and I don't really want to talk about it." One of her hands gripped the edge of her chair, leaving the imprint of her gold-manicured nails on the leather.

"And I don't want to talk about my argument with Ramón."

Imani met her gaze directly. "You've made your point. I'm sorry for prying, but it's hard not to. Ramón has been so nice to me, and I think you guys would be good together."

Mariah gritted her teeth. Obviously Imani had decided to ignore her wishes. "Imani," she said in an exasperated tone.

Imani blabbed on. "You know, I always sensed something about the two of you…"

Deciding that she'd had enough, and annoyed that Imani would continue to press the issue, she interrupted her. "I need to get ready for my lunch date." She stood up and extended her hand to Imani. "Welcome back, Imani. I hope things work out for you."

For lunch, Mariah met Gloria Richards at Xochimilco's in the heart of Detroit's Mexican town. As usual, the parking lot was full of cars from the lunchtime crowd. Mariah walked through two sets of glass doors and up to the hostess station. The gentle strumming of guitar music filled her ears and the smell of hot nacho chips and salsa made her mouth water. The hostess directed her to the upper dining room, where Gloria had already been seated.

Gloria sat at a table, drinking sangria and munching on nachos and salsa. A flickering candle, carafe of sangria, basket of hot nachos, and a bowl of fresh salsa graced the center of the table. Gloria smiled at the sight of Mariah and stood up to give her a quick, affectionate hug. "Hey amiga, long time no see," she said in her thick accent as she smoothed her powder blue silk dress and sat down. "How are things with you?"

"Fine." Mariah took the chair across from her and helped herself to hot nacho chips and salsa. "How's everybody?"

"Oh, Clark's busy with a new case, and Ramón seems to be on the home stretch with the Gerald Hatten trial. I hope the trial ends soon, because my baby's beginning to look so run down. I've told him to take care of himself, but in this day and age, who listens to mama? Can you add your voice of reason to mine and go talk to him?"

Mariah filled a glass with sangria and lowered her lashes to cover her surprise. "You know he never listens to me either," she said carefully, controlling the slight tremor in her voice. If Gloria didn't know about their fight, she wasn't going to tell her.

"I disagree," Gloria said with a wink and a smile. "He cares what you think."

The comment made Mariah feel sad. Her eyes burned as she sipped her sangria. "I'll see what I can do."

"I'd appreciate it." Gloria opened her menu and then gave Mariah a sharp look. "What's the matter?"

"The usual, my personal life's a mess, and things are going down to the wire on the new site for the agency."

"Feel like having a good cry? Go ahead, I have big shoulders." The large princess-cut diamond in Gloria's wedding ring flashed as she patted Mariah's hand.

"I want to, but that won't solve anything." Mariah stared down at the menu, trying to concentrate on the words.

"You might feel better." Gloria's dark eyes were full of sympathy. Her hand gently squeezed Mariah's.

"The only thing that would make me feel better right now would be the resolution of my problems."

"Do you want to talk about it? I know this is a public place, but we could—"

"Thanks, but no thanks," Mariah said quickly. A Mexican waitress dressed in black and white approached their table. Mariah ordered the meat and cheese enchiladas and drank her sangria.

Gloria ordered the same. "You know we're there for you, don't you?" Gloria asked when they were alone again. She bent towards Mariah. "We love you, Mariah, as if you were our child."

Her words warmed Mariah's heart. She smiled as Gloria caught her restless fingers and shook them gently. "I love you guys, too. You're all the family I've got."

"If you weren't so stubborn about doing this on your own..." Gloria began, then seeing Mariah's expression changed tactics. "Are you sure there's nothing else to be done?"

Mariah considered for a minute, then shook her head negatively. She'd been saving the call to her broker for the last. That way there would be one more option for as long as possible. If that didn't work out, would it kill her to sell the ring? "I need to call my broker about some of mama's stocks. The companies had been sold, so he had to do a little research. Actually, I'm surprised I haven't heard from him."

"As long as you're not thinking of doing something like selling your grandmother's wedding ring..." She stopped at the sight of Mariah's expression. "No, you wouldn't do that, would you? You have so little left of your family. I know that ring has strong sentimental value for you."

"I don't want to, but I may have to," Mariah said sadly. Her mouth settled into a stubborn line. "It's the very last option."

"If it comes to that, I hope you'll let us help you. I will pray for you." Gloria took a sip of her sangria. "Everything will be all right, you will see." She shot Mariah a speculative look and abruptly changed the subject of conversation. "Now, what is the personal problem? Is that the code word for man trouble?"

Mariah took a deep breath. "I don't want..."

"Yes, you don't want to talk about it, but I do, and I can be relentless." Gloria grinned. "If you don't want to tell me the truth, you'd better make something up." She raised her eyebrows and drummed her fingers on the table impatiently to emphasize her point.

Mariah used the edge of one hand to push her limp curls up off her neck. She felt hot.

"Cotter Eastwood isn't the problem." Gloria leaned forward. "Is he?"

"Oh, no," Mariah assured her, shaking her head. "Cotter and I have come to an agreement. We're strictly friends. He's hoping for more, but not being so pushy about it."

"How did you ever manage that?"

"I leveled with him. He was getting on my nerves. If he wanted me talking to him voluntarily, he needed to change tactics."

"I'm glad that worked out. So what's the problem?"

Mariah hesitated and then said, "I did something stupid and it's put a good friendship in jeopardy."

"Did you apologize?"

"Yes, but he was so angry, I don't think he heard." She purposely refrained from making eye contact with Gloria by counting the chips left in the basket. Still, she worried that Gloria would guess that she was talking about Ramón.

"If this person is truly your friend, he'll forgive you. Nobody's perfect, so people make mistakes." Gloria poured more sangria into Mariah's glass. "Care to tell me who this friend is?"

Mariah shook her head.

Gloria gave her a speculative glance. "You need something else to occupy your mind. When are you going to start dating again?"

Mariah grinned sheepishly and sipped her sangria. "Lately I've been thinking it's time to start."

"Good." Gloria put her glass back on the table. "Since you and Ramón have never gone farther than friendship, I've made a list of nice, attractive, career-oriented young men I'd like you to meet."

Gloria's words startled her. Ramón and I have gone too far for our friendship, Mariah thought. She nearly choked as the sangria went the wrong way. She turned her head away from the table with a hand to her burning chest in a fit of convulsive coughing. Gloria jumped up and circled the table. With capable hands, she patted Mariah's back and gave her a glass of water. "Are you all right?"

Mariah nodded, clearing her throat and sipping the water. She wiped her eyes with a napkin. "Some of that sangria went down the wrong way."

"Is this your way of telling me you're not interested in meeting the young men on my list?"

This time Mariah laughed aloud. "No, it's not. I'm willing to look at your list, and meet the best ones. When do you want me to start?"

By the end of their meal, Gloria had lifted Mariah's spirits considerably. Then she insisted that Mariah fulfill her promise to personally show her the new site.

Mariah got into her Toyota and Gloria followed in her dark blue Lincoln Continental.

The drive to the new site took approximately fifteen minutes. Mariah got out of her car and stood on the broken concrete, looking out over the deep blue rippling water. It sparkled with a magic all its own. Just looking at it made her sigh with pleasure. A couple of freighters glided by, and in the distance, she heard the sound of a motorboat. Finding this spot had been a stroke of luck. She could almost imagine the people waiting for her to lose the option so that the property would be back on the market.

"This is a beautiful place, and it's not too far east," Gloria remarked, coming up behind her. She turned left and pointed in the distance. "There's Belle Isle!" Then she turned right and peered down river for several moments. "And there's the Ambassador Bridge to Canada. I like this location."

Mariah looked about with eyes that saw the area as it was: in transition, changing from old abandoned buildings and warehouses to new condos, apartments, and office buildings. She knew that only minutes away, there was an area with big, beautiful, historic mansions. Mariah gazed at some of the rundown buildings and tried to see it as Gloria would. Windows were broken out of many, and they stared at passers-by like blind holes. The gray dilapidated warehouse in front of her looked as if a good push would finish it off. "The city's going to tear most of those old buildings down. I agreed to tear down this old warehouse," she explained. "Believe it or not, this is in that empowerment zone President Clinton's been talking about. I can apply for grants and low interest loans to get the new building constructed."

"That's fantastic! Now what sort of building are you planning?"

"I've just begun to look at a number of building designs and floor plans, but I want something modern, yet relaxed.

I want a wraparound deck for my employees. I want a large, open lobby, facing the water. Of course, my office would be up there on the second floor, and face the river too," she said, pointing to the spot on her imaginary building. "I'm going to promote Lynn and make her my assistant, and hire secretaries for us both. I envision a number of studios for shoots, and a media room."

"I'm sure the agency will grow, but won't this be a lot of space for the staff you have now?"

"Yes, it is, but I really need to expand my staff. We've missed out on some good business opportunities and had to split others with our rivals because we're so small. If all goes well, I'll at least triple my staff and take on several more models. Anthony is interested in renting extra space, and I've had others inquire about my plans." She looked down at her watch. "I've got to get going. I have an appointment with Cora Belson this afternoon, and a few stops to make before I go."

Gloria grabbed her by the shoulders and kissed her cheek. "Hang in there, Mariah." She took a last look around the area and smiled. "Thanks for sharing you dream with me."

"Thank you—for listening," Mariah replied. She hadn't felt this optimistic in days. Instead of rushing through her errands and then pushing on to Cora Belson's office, she drove for a while, deep in thought. Stopping at a red light, she realized she was in the area near the courthouse. Now how had that happened? All right, she told herself, you're close to his turf.

Before she knew it, she'd gone past the courthouse and around the block. A trusting expectancy filled her as she slowed down. Anxiously, her eyes scanned the busy sidewalks and some of the restaurants. She went up the next street and back around again in a slow sweep. This is stupid, she thought, unable to control her jumbled thoughts. She needed a plan. What would she do if she saw Ramón anyway? What did she expect him to do? He couldn't stay angry forever, could he? She only knew that she had to take the first step at clearing the air.

Her fingers gripped the steering wheel as she drove past men and women dressed in a kaleidoscope of colors, walking to and from their offices in the warm summer air. In the lot up the street from the courthouse, she caught sight of a black Jaguar with a golden skinned, curly-haired male occupant, and held her breath. Within seconds Ramón's tall, broad-shouldered form, in a dark blue Armani suit, climbed out. Fate caused him to look up as she drove up the street. His gaze met hers with the effect of an electric shock.

He looked like one of those Aztec statues. A woman on the sidewalk openly stared at him. His golden skin, and face full of planes and angles, displayed an exciting blend of his black and Hispanic heritage. Because he had such a sunny disposition, she wasn't used to seeing his sensual mouth pulled into the tight, straight line. The direct gaze of his slate gray eyes burning with raw hurt seared her, like an angry flame.

Cars lined every available space on both sides of the avenue. Mariah stopped the car in the middle of the street, her heart full of hope. She waited for a sign, a signal, a wave, anything to indicate a welcome, or a willingness to move past their argument. Was it too soon to resolve things? Her heart hammered in her chest and the joints of her fingers ached from gripping the steering wheel so tightly. Though the whir of the air conditioning fan seemed louder than ever, small rivulets of sweat ran down the valley between her breasts.

She sensed his internal battle, saw the indecision is his eyes, despite the closed expression on his face. She'd always sensed that if he turned away from someone, bringing him back would be a struggle. But she'd never expected to find herself in that position. Misery so acute it was a physical pain filled her. For the first time, she really began to believe that their friendship might be at an end. Because he'd always been there for her, she prayed that this was just a temporary setback. Anxiously, she rolled down her window and got hit with a blast of hot humid outside air. The moment seemed to stretch on forever.

"Ramón." Her lips formed his name as she felt their connection slipping away. Slowly his simmering gray eyes became as flat and unreadable as stone and he slowly shook his head negatively from one side to the other. She saw Ramón pull his briefcase from the car and lock the door. Pointedly ignoring her, he began walking towards the courthouse with smooth easy strides. The deliberate stiffness in his back and shoulders was message enough.

He was still furious, she realized, her spirits sinking. She'd hurt him more than she'd thought with her inept handling of their night together. Mariah's heart squeezed in anguish when he deliberately turned his back on her. His rejection hit her with sickening despair. It hurt more than anything she could remember. She bit her lip. Hot tears stung her eyes, and overflowed. She couldn't believe this was happening to her. He'd rejected her attempt to meet him halfway. She hadn't felt so alone and misunderstood since the death of her mother.

The angry sound of a horn drew her attention to the rearview mirror. In the rearview mirror, the driver in back of her angrily gestured for her to move on. A line of cars stretched halfway down the street behind her. Slowly, she eased her car up the street, looking for somewhere to pull over and finding none.

Shaking with grim determination, Mariah turned the corner, went down to the next. Turning another corner, she pulled into a no parking zone behind a Checker Cab. She shifted the car into park and then slumped over the steering wheel. Hot tears slipped down her cheeks as she gulped hard and blubbered like a baby. With razor sharp precision, her conscience declared this was all her fault; she had no one to blame but herself! He was never going to forget what happened. He was never going to forgive her, never let them get past their night together. Mariah grabbed a tissue to blow her nose, then ended up crying through all the tissue in her purse.

She was checking the glove box for more tissue when a sharp rap on the passenger side window of her car startled her. Swallowing the sob in her throat, she looked up. Her blurry vision focused on a blue uniformed figure. Sniffling, she rolled down her window.

"Miss, do you need a doctor? Are you okay?" The olive skinned, heavyset police officer spoke in a kindly tone.

"Yes," she croaked, nodding her head at the same time. "I'm okay."

"You look like you just lost your best friend. Is there anything I can do to help?"

Mariah shook her head, unable to stop the new flood of tears. She had lost her dearest friend.

The officer said sympathetically, "Miss, I'm sorry, but you have to move your car. You're in a no parking zone."

"Yes sir." Mariah turned the key in the ignition and put the car into drive.

"And, Miss," he added placing a hand on the side of the car, "there's a parking lot up the street about a block, if you need to take a little more time to pull yourself together."

"Thanks," she said in a choked whisper as she drove off. Her glance touched on the dashboard clock and she began to pull herself together. If she didn't hurry, she would be late for her appointment with Cora Belson. She couldn't afford to lose everything.

TEN

"This has got to stop," Mariah muttered aloud. Things were going down to the wire. Alone and abandoned, she sat on her enclosed front porch and watched the Friday morning sun come up. No matter how positively she directed her thoughts, the sense of impending doom prevailed. She imagined a dark cloud of ill will hovering above her head, ready to dump rain and hail down on her at any moment. With no new ideas, and no new sources of income, she was going crazy. She could almost see the property option floating away on the horizon.

Mariah schlepped into the house, clad in her old faded brown robe and pajamas, and a battered beige pair of bedroom slippers. In the kitchen, she made herself a cup of tea and sat down at the table. Automatically, she grabbed the remote from its place on the table and turned on the television mounted on the wall. She listened to the weather report, but when the announcer began to talk about the Gerald Hatten trial, she switched it off.

The last person she wanted to see was Ramón Richards. She still smarted from the sting of his rejection. In the last day or so, she'd come to the conclusion that she needed to build her own inner strength. She wasn't going to sit around moping anymore over the apparent loss of her friendship with Ramón. Deep within herself she knew that true friendships were forever, and that meant that Ramón would eventually come back into her life, didn't it?

Reverently, she put a hand in her pocket and lifted out a black velvet-covered ring box. Placing it on the table, she slowly pulled open the top. Her grandmother's wedding ring winked back at her, the large, emerald-cut diamond and surrounding baguettes attracting the light and flashing. With loving fingers, she stroked the antique gold and lifted the ring from the box.

She knew what the inscription said, but she read the fine engraving anyway: "To my darling Marie, I'll love you forever. Patrick." Patrick, her grandfather, had been an inventor, and had made a fortune from some of his inventions dealing with automotive production lines. He'd died when she was just a baby, so Mariah did not remember him. She did remember that her grandmother loved to shop. In fact, she'd continued to shop as bills mounted. Mariah remembered arguments between her grandmother and her mother over bad investments. Her grandmother's wedding ring was all Mariah had left of her estate. The property had been sold to pay off a myriad of debts.

Mariah slipped the ring on her finger. It fit as if it had been made for her. As a child, she'd dreamed of getting married with her grandmother's ring. As an adult, she knew it was the most beautiful ring she'd ever seen. She stared at it, acknowledging to herself that she didn't have a groom right now. The most immediate dream was the new building site. It was past time to take action to insure the success of the one dream she had left. Wistfully, Mariah put the ring back into its box and went to get ready for work.

With her mind knee-deep in ideas for raising more money, the drive to work barely registered. None of her ideas were ones she could implement on her own. She made it into the office and buried herself in work.

At nine-thirty, Mariah called her broker to inquire about her mother's stock. The good news was that although he was still researching the computer company stocks, he'd liquidated the telecommunications stocks and gotten five thousand dollars. Mariah was ecstatic until she did a few quick calculations in her head and discovered that she still didn't have enough money to close on her option. Since she'd been able to collect only about two thousand on her due bills, she needed another three thousand dollars. Her grandmother's ring weighed heavily on her mind. She was going to have to sell it, and there was no use waiting until the last minute.

Instead of going to lunch, Mariah went to the downtown Detroit offices of Dumouchelle Auction Galleries to see Tally West.

"This is a beautiful ring. I remember appraising this for you," Tally remarked as she bent her blonde head to examine the ring through her eyepiece. "I'm surprised you decided to sell it."

Mariah detected a note of censure in her tone. Tally's comment annoyed her. Why didn't the woman just take the ring and give her the money? She didn't want to sell the ring. She was operating on pure nerves right now and trying not to think about losing her grandmother's ring. Having made the decision to trade one dream for another, she still inwardly cringed at the thought. Tiny pinpricks of tears stung her eyes. Pull yourself together, girl! Mariah's lips puckered in annoyance. "I don't have a choice."

"I'm so sorry." Tally's sympathetic gaze depressed her even more. "Family heirlooms like this are hard to come by, and then when you take into account that your grandparents were well known figures in this community—" She stopped commenting, just realizing the effect of her words on Mariah. "Please excuse me. I know you said you didn't have a choice."

Mariah's eyes filled with tears, but she didn't allow them to fall. She tried to swallow the lump that lingered in her throat. "How soon can I get the payment?" Like a magnet, the ring drew her gaze. She was about to do something irrevocable.

"If you're putting it up for auction, we have an auction every month. The next one is in two weeks, and we charge everyone a commission."

Mariah bit her lip, angry with herself for being embarrassed on top of everything else. "I—I can't wait that long." A slight edge crept in her tone and was quickly suppressed.

Tally shifted in the seat behind her carved cherry wood desk. "If we buy it from you, you'll get the money sooner, but you'll also end up getting less."

Mariah's hand covered her nose and mouth in dismay. Selling the ring was bad enough, but to trade it for a small sum of money was more than she could stomach. Frantically she worked to think of another option. "Is there any way I could get an advance on the estimated auction price?" she asked, mentally crossing her fingers.

"Let me see what I can do," Tally replied, picking up her phone and punching in a few numbers. "I'm calling my manager."

When Mariah left Dumouchelle Auction Galleries half an hour later, she carried a check for six thousand dollars in her pocket—and it seemed to weigh six thousand pounds. Sad at heart, she walked to her car. Her mother had never worn the ring because it had been willed to Mariah. Now all she had left of her grandmother were memories and the pictures in the family album. Had she done the right thing? Now she had three thousand dollars more than the one hundred and fifty thousand dollars needed to close on the site option.

Unable to face going back to the office, she picked up a sandwich, drove to Belle Isle, and went across the bridge. A heaviness settled in her chest as she parked in a spot on the shore that was private, but not too far away from people eating lunch in the park.

Why did she always have to do without the things other people seemed to take for granted? In a fit of self-pity she eased the seat back. First she'd lost her family, every single one of them; her dad in the Vietnam war, her grandmother in a freak car accident, her sister to juvenile diabetes, and her mother to a heart attack. Wasn't that enough for one person to bear? Then she'd lost the friendship of a man who meant more than she'd ever let herself admit; a man whose shoulder she desperately needed to cry on. Was he gone forever too? And now she'd been forced by circumstances to give up one of the few remaining ties to her family and its history, her grandmother's wedding ring. She'd given up too many pieces of her heart. When was it all going to end?

Mariah pounded her fist on the steering wheel and cried and cried and cried. Then she sat in the hot car with the windows rolled down and watched the traffic on the river. After a while, she got out and walk up the shoreline. She threw pieces of bread from her sandwich to the birds. It was time to move on, she told herself, with her business and her personal life. On Monday, she'd go to the scheduled closing on her site option at the real estate agent's office.

At four o'clock, Mariah arrived at the club for her tennis date with a guy Gloria laughingly called Eligible Bachelor Number One. She'd introduced the two of them at dinner the night before. Gloria was determined to spice up Mariah's personal life, and Mariah was tired of sitting home alone. Bachelor Number One was Larry Hayden III, a stockbroker for a prestigious company in Southfield, Michigan. He was attractive enough, with ultra-smooth skin the color of milk chocolate, and a muscular build that spoke of hours in the gym. She was thrilled to discover that Larry had a voice reminiscent of Barry White.

Larry was a vision in his white tennis outfit when he met her on the court. Why aren't I drooling all over him? Mariah asked herself. He was friendly, handsome and perfect for her. After three very competitive sets of tennis they took a juice break on the sidelines.

"I'm in a daze. I must have died and gone to heaven," Larry mused. He slid closer to her on the bleacher.

"I guess you didn't know what Gloria would come up with, huh?" she teased.

"Actually, I can't believe my luck. You seem to be everything I had on my list of things I want in a woman."

"You just met me last night, Larry," she said gently, enjoying his flattery nonetheless. It had been a while since anyone but Cotter Eastwood had flattered her, and she'd stopped listening to him long ago.

"I know, but unless you've got an evil twin, I'm hooked. Will you marry me anyway, when you get to know me better?" he quipped.

"Well now, if you keep on playing tennis the way you've been playing today, I'll definitely have to consider it."

"I'm going to have to write this one down," Larry said, looking sheepish. "I've attracted some women because of my looks and some because of my wallet." He paused and gazed at her speculatively. "You are the first to be attracted because of my tennis game."

He was a little arrogant, but he had good reason to be. "Now I didn't quite say that," Mariah said, giving his muscular form a frank appraisal. She smiled when she reached his face, her facial expression belying her words. "But it works for me. Right now, your tennis game is foremost in my mind." A movement at the edge of her vision caught her attention. She blinked and turned her head so that she could get a better look at the guys playing tennis two courts down. She recognized as Phil from the way he hit the ball and ran around the court. The tall, lean-muscled figure moving at the end of the court farthest from her made her heart do a flip-flop. A flicker of apprehension ran through her. It was Ramón, she just knew it. Her fingers clenched the end of the racquet. Was it just a coincidence that he happened to be here playing tennis while she had her first date with Number One on Gloria's list of eligible men?

Number One broke in on her thoughts with a question. "Is that simply because we happen to be at a tennis club?"

"Mmmmph?" Confused, Mariah focused on him.

He smiled charmingly and rephrased his question. "You said that my tennis game was foremost in your mind at this stage in our relationship. Why?"

"I play doubles regularly with my friends, but nobody seems to have the time to play singles. I've been looking for someone competitive to play singles with."

"And here I am," Number One said, taking her hand.

Out of the corner of her eye, Mariah saw Phil and Ramón coming off their court. Momentary panic set her pulse to racing. She didn't want to face Ramón, didn't even want to go through the intricacies of being polite when she really wanted to chew him out for rejecting her overture. Mariah stood quickly, keeping her back to them. "Let's see if we can get a few more volleys in before we have to give the court up," she suggested.

Number One retrieved his racquet. "You're on."

"Hey Mariah!" Phil called out before she could get back on the court.

"Phil!" she replied, faking surprise. "Are you playing doubles?" Facing him squarely with her arms folded in front of her, she saw that Ramón had disappeared. She felt oddly disappointed. What kind of game was this? Did he still have nothing to say to her?

Phil shook his head then lifted his racquet and waved it at her. "I challenged Ramón to a game of tennis to get rid of some of the stress we've been under."

"Really? Who's winning?"

"He is, of course. You know that when it comes to tennis, he's the better man."

Mariah noted Phil's emphasis on the latter part of his sentence. Right now, she didn't think Ramón was the better anything. Her heart beat erratically and her palms were moist. If Ramón had sent Phil to spy on her, she was going to give him something to think about. "Let me introduce you to Larry, tennis partner extraordinaire. He's the best." She gave Larry a dazzling smile. "Larry, Phil is on my doubles team."

The two men clasped hands and exchanged friendly greetings. Mariah ignored the quizzical look Larry threw her. She unobtrusively scanned the area for Ramón and came up empty.

She could have kissed Larry when he brought up the fact that they were going down to the new jazz club in downtown Detroit after tennis if they weren't too tired. She wanted Ramón to know that life went on. Phil declined the offer to join them and moved on.

"Which one of them is the old boyfriend?" Larry asked in a much too casual tone of voice as they started to play.

Stunned by his astuteness, she was at a momentary loss for words. "Neither of them," she said finally, gritting her teeth and sending the ball flying to the far side of the court.

Larry recovered it easily. "You could have fooled me."

Unwilling to explain the circumstances of her relationship with Ramón, she swung her racquet and aced the ball close to the service line.

"Wow, you're deadly when you get riled," Larry teased.

"That's right, so don't mess with me," she retorted, and they began to play seriously.

As Ramón went by Mariah's tennis court, he stopped for a moment to watch her play. Without any knowledge or effort on her part, she drew him like a powerful magnet. He loved her. There was no getting around that fact. With his eyes he caressed the physical beauty of her face and form made even more alluring by her unique personality. Her movements on the court in her short white tennis dress were smooth, graceful, and efficient as she went after a difficult serve. Like a haunting melody, her signature laugh when she got the ball only strengthened his sense of loss. He shouldn't have let Phil talk him into tennis tonight, not when he knew Mariah was here with a date from his mother's list of eligible bachelors.

Ramón assessed Mariah's tennis partner. His mother had gone too far. What had she been thinking of? She had to know how he really felt about Mariah. He couldn't have picked better competition for himself. The man was everything Mariah liked, with attractive features, a muscular body, and a tennis game almost as good as his own. Jealousy gripped him with an iron claw.

Ramón stalked away from the court. He needed to find a way out of their impasse, because he'd never loved anyone the way he loved Mariah. It hurt to think that she didn't return his love.

Stopping back at his court, he retrieved his racquet and bag. She'd shocked him yesterday by showing up at the courthouse. He knew how she thought. It had taken a lot of guts and determination to face him, especially after he'd been the one to say good-bye. A part of him felt vindicated, because she obviously felt very strongly for him, but inside it still hurt to know that she was merely trying to make up with her 'brother'.

Phil was throwing his balls and gloves into his tennis bag. "I guess Mom kind of gave you a poke in the eye with this one, huh?" he asked, knowing the source of Ramón's foul mood.

Ramón merely grunted as he strapped the racquet into its pouch and zipped the bag. He wasn't ready to face Mariah, and had no idea when he'd be able to. It was way too soon to kiss and make up, especially if his only avenue was a platonic relationship. If he could just stay away from her until he got his head together, maybe they could have some semblance of their former friendship. He ignored the voice within that whispered that he'd never be able to sit by and watch Mariah marry anyone else. He strode off the court, heading for the entrance.

"Hey man, where are you going? They were talking about going to that new jazz club downtown afterward and invited us to tag along," Phil called as he tried to catch up with Ramón.

"I've had enough," he replied, glancing back at Mariah's court one more time. "We played well and got rid of some stress."

"And maybe picked up a little more stress," Phil added, glancing meaningfully at Mariah's court.

"I'm tired. I'm going home to hit the shower." He continued walking towards the door. "See you at the office later on tonight."

After tennis, Mariah dragged herself off the court. She could only think of going home and going to bed. Larry was so disappointed that she promised she would go to the jazz club with him on the next Friday night. At her car, Larry's expert mouth moved on hers in a smooth kiss that was pleasant, but failed to stir her physically or emotionally.

She and Ramón had been compatible in every way. On her way home, Mariah found herself reliving Ramón's hot, tantalizing kisses. Her nipples hardened. How was that for brotherly love? Guiltily, she bit her lip and forced her thoughts to her plans for the weekend.

Mariah filled the weekend with work around the house and in the garden. Monday took forever to come. She got up early to shower and dress. With a fragrant blend of Colombian coffee and a bag of glazed doughnuts, she made it into the office before Lynn did. Instead of getting together as usual and talking through the activities for the day, each one drank her coffee and ate her doughnuts alone.

Despite the rising excitement due to the impending closure on her site option, Mariah felt oddly sad. Refusing to mope around, she buried herself in work.

A loud bang broke Mariah's concentration. What was that? Dictionary, she thought, trying to pick up where she'd left off. Lynn seemed unusually clumsy. The file cabinet drawer slammed shut. Suddenly several more loud bangs punctuated with a couple of thumps caused her to get up in frustration and stride into the outer office.

In a pleated lime green dress, Lynn knelt on the floor between her desk and the file cabinets, picking up the dictionary, a couple of portfolio cases, and a statuette. Her fingers shook noticeably as she glanced up at Mariah. "S-sorry about the noise. I seem to be all thumbs today."

Mariah stared at her secretary, noting the wild, almost desperate look in her eyes. "Lynn, what's the matter with you?"

"I—I guess I'm just a little nervous." Lynn stood up and began to replace all the items on the top of one of the file cabinets.

"Why?" Mariah asked, stopping herself short. It was really none of her business. Hadn't she had enough of playing Dear Abby? What business did she have giving advice when she couldn't keep her own life in order?

Lynn put the last portfolio case back and flopped down into her chair, the words tumbling from her lips. "I'm ruined. I did everything I could to get around it, and no matter what I did, things just got worse!"

"What are you talking about?" Mariah demanded, circling round the desk to sit in Lynn's guest chair.

"It's Mama."

"Oh Lynn, is your mother ill?"

"No!" Lynn's head snapped up. "She's coming for a visit, and she wants to meet Anthony."

Baffled, Mariah leaned back in the chair. "What's wrong with that?"

"Mariah, Mama's not a racist, but she's going to have a fit when she sees him. She feels that white people have done enough to black folks. To her, me going out with Anthony is like fraternizing with the enemy. I love Mama, but I love Anthony too. What am I going to do?"

"Tell her what you just told me: you love her, but you love Anthony too."

Lynn smoothed her dress with restless fingers. "It won't be that simple, I just know it." A tear fell down one cheek. "She'll make me give up Anthony."

"She can't make you do anything!" Mariah snapped, pushing the box of tissues at Lynn.

"Oh yes she can. She'll be so mean and manipulative to the both of us that Anthony will decide I'm not worth the trouble." Lynn's bottom lip stuck out as she grabbed a stack of files with shaking fingers and rammed them into the desk.

Mariah gently rubbed Lynn's shoulder. "Lynn, people either love you or they don't. If Anthony loves you, nothing your mother says or does will change that."

"Sometimes I'm not so sure." Lynn's eyes flashed with fire. "We've been through some rough times with his friends and mine. When we go out, it's as if we were on display. And then, we haven't, you know, slept together." Lynn's color deepened and her voice dropped. "I know that he's an experienced man, but I've never slept with anyone. It seems old-fashioned, but I've been raised to wait until I'm married. I keep asking myself, how long is he going to wait?"

"You need to talk about all of this with Anthony, preferably before your mother comes to town."

"Do you really think so?" Lynn sniffed, her fingers closing around her coffee cup.

"Yes, I do. When is she coming?"

"This Friday. She's planning to spend two weeks visiting me."

Mariah looked at her watch. "If I know Anthony, he'll be in here soon, so if you want to take a long coffee break, I'll get the phones."

Lynn blew her nose. "Thanks, I really appreciate it."

As Lynn scurried out with Anthony, Mariah considered her words to Lynn. People either love you or they don't. Did Ramón really love her? Obviously not. It hurt so much to even think it, that her shaking fingers dropped her pen. Get over it, girl. Chewing her bottom lip, she grabbed the stack of due bills and went over them again.

With Lynn gone, the office seemed unnaturally quiet. The phone rang and Mariah answered it automatically. The sound of her stockbroker's confident yet boyish sounding voice perked her up. "Harry!" she exclaimed into the receiver, her mind racing in anticipation of his next words.

"Good news, Mariah, good news!"

"Yes?" Mariah's voice vibrated with excitement. She leaned forward, her pulse speeding up. "What's happened?"

"I knew you needed the cash, so I spent extra time researching those other two stocks of yours, and boy did I hit the jackpot!" he said, his voice ballooning with pride. "Your mother bought stock from a company that got bought out by Starshine Enterprises, one of the big boys."

She said a silent prayer. Please God let it be enough for me to get the ring back. The loss of her grandmother's wedding ring had already spoiled her triumph and happiness in being able to close on the site option. "How much?" she croaked. "How much did you get for the stock?"

"Twelve thousand after commission," he said smugly.

Mariah whistled, falling back in her chair and thanking God. "Harry, you're good, very good. I'm going to recommend you to all my friends."

"I thought you already did that."

"I did, but when I tell them how you saved the day, you'll have lots of new clients."

"Just doing my job, Mariah."

"Well, I like the way you do your job. I'm taking you to lunch. When do you want to go?"

"You don't have to do that. I'm glad to see you succeed. I'll be seeing you this afternoon."

"This afternoon?" Puzzled, she glanced at her appointment calendar, running a manicured nail down the columns. According to her appointment calendar, she had meetings all afternoon, and he wasn't one of them.

"Ah...yes." Harry faltered for a moment, obviously thinking on his feet. "I thought you'd like me to bring you the check."

"That's really sweet of you, Harry," she said, remembering that Lynn and Anthony had planned a celebration. Comforting warmth suffused her as she took a hard look at the appointments in her book. She saw Anthony's name, Sonia's, and even Gloria's. Would Ramón show up? "And thanks for reminding me about the celebration Lynn and Anthony planned."

Regret tinged Harry's boyish voice. "I'm sorry if I ruined it for you."

"Harry, don't worry about it. It's no surprise. I've just had a case of temporary amnesia," she murmured, mentally floating on air. Already she'd found the number for Dumouchelle's Auction Galleries. "I'll see you at lunch. Thanks again, Harry."

As soon as Mariah finished her conversation with Harry, she dialed the number and spoke eagerly into the phone. It took several minutes for Tally West to come to the phone. Mariah spent the time praying. The slight hesitation and inherent regret in Tally's voice made her uneasy. Mariah suspected that her grandmother's ring had already been sold.

Within seconds, Tally confirmed her suspicions. "I'm sorry, Mariah. A number of people tried to buy your grandmother's ring. It was sold yesterday."

Mariah massaged her forehead. Shards of disappointment cut at her insides. In addition to her disappointment, she felt a lingering guilt. Many of her friends had offered to help, and she'd turned them down. Had her independence been worth the loss of the ring? Mariah tasted salt and realized she was crying. She grabbed the Kleenex and dabbed at her face. Clearing her throat she said, "Could you give me the name and number of the buyer?"

"I'm sorry, but we try to maintain the privacy of our customers. I will contact the buyer and convey your offer to buy it back."

"Thanks, Tally," she said politely, virtually certain the ring was gone forever.

"There'll be a commission if they agree to sell it back to you, of course."

"I'm prepared to do everything I can to get it back." Mariah said, wiping her eyes, certain she'd lost another piece of her heart forever.

Mariah hung up the phone and drank the rest of her cold coffee. You can't have it all, she told herself, but it didn't stop her from wanting it, or trying to get it. She cut off all thoughts of the ring and tried to focus on the late morning closing.

All hell had broken out in the courtroom. As soon as the judge granted Ramón's request for a recess, the defense team and Gerald Hatten crowded into one of the consulting rooms to talk about the new evidence. "This sheds a whole new light on everything," Ramón said, slamming his briefcase on the desk, opening it, and withdrawing a yellow legal pad. His head pounded and his stomach quivered.

He was still reeling from the introduction into evidence of the thirty-two caliber pistol taken from a padlocked locker at Hatten's country club. The police had already verified that it was the gun used to kill Hatten's partner and were busy sorting out the fingerprints found on it. Dropping down into a chair, he scanned Hatten's friendly bulldog face suspiciously, noting the light sheen of sweat covering his forehead. Ramón only took on clients he felt were innocent. Had Gerald Hatten managed to fool them all with his claims of a setup, and pleas of innocence?

Impaled by the steady gazes of the members of his defense team, Hatten began to speak. "I didn't do it. I'm telling you I'm innocent," he insisted desperately, his unwavering brown eyes meeting the gaze of each team member. "You've got to believe me! That gun's been missing for months."

"Then why didn't you tell us about it?" Phil demanded in an accusing tone, his fists bunched at his side.

A tense silence enveloped the room. Hatten dipped his head and looked down at his folded hands. "I didn't think you'd believe me." His normally calm and authoritative voice cracked with strain. "If I were on the jury with all the evidence they have now, I'd think I was guilty."

"Are you?" Ramón's eyes narrowed and his jaw clenched.

"No." His head snapped up. "I swear it."

"Are your fingerprints on that gun?"

"Yes, unless someone else wiped it. It was my gun."

Phil pushed his wire-rimmed glasses up on his nose. "Where did you keep it?"

Hatten grimaced. "There's a locked display case in my study. I keep all my guns there."

Ramón stopped scribbling on the pad. "Are any of the other guns missing?"

Hatten shook his head decisively.

Ramón lifted an eyebrow. If Hatten was innocent, someone had placed the gun in his locker in the hope of framing him for the murder, and had planned it well in advance. "We need to make a list of all the people who had access to that gun. Then we need to connect them all to plausible motives for murdering your business partner." Ramón massaged his forehead. It was going to be a long day.

Mariah wore her red suit, as a symbol of the fire within. Despite lingering sadness and doubt regarding the disposition of her grandmother's ring, she floated into the real estate office, buoyed by her dreams of the future. Her lawyer had already reviewed the paperwork, but she read every line anyway just to be sure everything was in order. At eleven-thirty she handed over a check for one hundred fifty thousand dollars with an air of unreality, and blissfully signed a mortgage for the remainder. She practically danced all the way to her car with the paperwork. She'd done it! She'd actually acquired the site!

When she got back to her office, Lynn had already left for lunch. Judge Richards and his wife, Gloria, were waiting for her. At the sight of them dressed for the party, she found herself looking for Ramón. He wasn't there. Feeling a little hurt, she covered her disappointment with a bright smile as she greeted his parents.

"We're proud of you, Mariah," Judge Richards said, hugging her affectionately and kissing her cheek.

Gloria hovered close, and when her husband released Mariah, rushed forward and hugged her fiercely. "I knew you could do it. Congratulations, amiga!"

"Thank you. Are you guys here to take me to lunch?" she asked.

"Hmm, that is why we're on your schedule for the next couple of hours," the judge said, putting an arm around his wife.

"We did wonders with the ballroom," Gloria said, her voice sparkling with excitement. "I think you're going to like it." She glanced at her watch. "We're supposed to be there by twelve-fifteen, so we need to get going."

"What kind of food are you guys serving?" Mariah asked as she followed them to the door.

"Gloria went over the menu personally," Judge Richards said, leading his wife through the doorway by the hand. "We've got a lot of your favorites."

As she left the suite, she noticed the unusual silence on Anthony's side of the office suite. People usually worked there till all hours of the day and night. She was glad Anthony was allowing his staff to attend her celebration.

Stepping off the elevator, they headed towards the first floor ballroom.

"Ladies," the judge said, pulling open the door.

When Mariah stepped into the room, the applause was deafening. Then the sound of Macarena music filled the air, and a crowd of Mariah's friends and several associates danced towards her. A blissful grin broke out on her face. The turnout was impressive.

"Congratulations, Mariah!" Gloria hugged Mariah again.

"Thank you," she called above the loud music. "You guys—"

"I'm sure this is just another one of the many accomplishments you'll achieve in your lifetime," Judge Richards said, kissing her cheek and squeezing her shoulders.

"Thanks," she replied, returning his kiss. The sight of her friends and associates gathered in her honor filled her with a warm glow.

Lynn and Anthony danced up and offered their congratulations.

Mariah glanced around the room, noting the balloons and streamers, her name in lights above the impromptu stage, and the band playing. "I can't believe all the things you guys accomplished in such a short time," Mariah said, putting an arm around Anthony and Lynn.

"Lynn did, I just followed orders," Anthony quipped with eyes only for Lynn.

"Thanks, Anthony, Lynn. You guys did a wonderful job." She rocked with the music. "Where did you get the band?"

"You mean I never told you that my cousin played in a band?" Lynn drawled.

"No, you didn't tell me that," she said accusingly. "I love their sound. I think you've just added to the list of your job duties. You can find the groups to play during some of our fashion shows."

"Oh no!" Laughing, Lynn went off arm-in-arm with Anthony.

Imani, next in the line, was dressed in a low-waisted blue sundress reminiscent of the dresses worn by flappers in the twenties. The soft material dropped just below her hips to a short layered skirt of a filmy blue material falling to mid-thigh. Presenting Mariah with a glass of champagne, she said, "Congratulations on achieving your goal." She touched her own glass to Mariah's and drank.

Grateful, Mariah thanked Imani, and poured the champagne down her parched throat. Her stomach growled. She was incredibly hungry. Bachelor Number One danced up to her with a plate of appetizers. He was right on time!

"Larry!" she cried out in surprise. "Were you reading my mind?"

"I thought you might be hungry." He put an arm around her shoulders and kissed her cheek. "Congratulations on meeting your goal. You're one hell of a woman. If you wanted to be president, I bet you could do that too."

"I'm glad you have such faith in me," she said, nibbling on shrimp wrapped in bacon. She took one look at the long line of well wishers, and her stomach growled again. It wasn't getting any shorter. Deciding to take matters into her own hands, she went down the line greeting people, accepting their congratulations, and thanking them for coming. In no time at all, she ended up at the head table with Larry at her side. The food was delicious.

Larry got up in search of another bottle of champagne. Carefully, Mariah scanned the room for the third time. She hadn't seen Ramón, and her need to see her friend tore at her insides. If she'd been alone, she'd have cried. Her gaze met Gloria's, and she didn't miss the look of sympathy that was quickly suppressed.

"Did you know the police discovered the murder weapon in Gerald Hatten's locker at the country club?" Gloria began. "I heard the news on the way over here."

"No." Mariah leaned towards her. Maybe he hadn't totally abandoned her, she thought. After all, a man's life was at stake. She sighed. "This really puts the defense's case in the toilet." Ramón and his associates would be working harder than ever.

"The team is probably meeting with Hatten right now. I'm sure Ramón would have come if he could."

"Oh yes, I'm sure he would," she said as confidently as she could. She hated lying to Gloria, but she wasn't up to explaining what had happened.

Mariah's mood lightened when Lynn and Anthony came to sit with her. "Lynn, did your mother ever make it to town?"

Lynn's eyes spoke volumes as she smiled politely and said, "Yes, mama is staying with me for a while."

Lynn was probably going through hell, Mariah thought. She was just going to have to learn how to get her mother to mind her own business. Mariah pictured 'Mama' as an older, heavier version of Lynn, although there was always the possibility Lynn looked like her dad. "I'd like to meet her."

"And she'd like to meet you. She's already asked me to set it up."

"Could you put in a good word for me, Mariah?" Anthony stole a mozzarella stick from Lynn's plate and popped it into his mouth. "I don't think she likes Italians very much."

Mariah sipped her second glass of wine. She had an idea that Mama was already trying to break up the happy couple.

Lynn tapped his hand playfully. "She wouldn't like any man who dated her only daughter."

"Sure, tell me anything," Anthony's voice broke with huskiness. His intense gaze caught and held Lynn's. When Lynn's lips trembled slightly, Anthony's hand engulfed hers. He scooted his chair closer. The sensual tension mounted between them.

For a moment, Mariah thought they would share a kiss. "So when do you want to get together?" Mariah asked, breaking the spell. "I can drop by this weekend, or we can all go to lunch next week."

"Let's do both," Lynn answered. "She's already complaining that she doesn't know anybody and hasn't had a chance to get out."

"Will you come too, Anthony?" Mariah asked, thinking that it would be good for Lynn's mother to see that they were all good friends.

"If I'm not too busy."

"Please?" Lynn's facial expression turned flirtatious.

"All right, I'll come." Anthony caressed Lynn's hand. "Did you see that, Mariah? This woman has been winding me around her little finger."

"And you are full of it." Lynn laughed.

"Hello Mariah, you are beautiful as always."

Mariah turned at the sound of the smooth, cultured voice and looked into his handsome face. "Cotter. How are you?"

"I'm fine, but I'd feel a lot better if you did a congratulatory dance with me."

She hesitated. She'd been very careful not to encourage Cotter Eastwood, and his choice of words made her uneasy.

"I promise not to chase you around the dance floor," he laughed. "I can't stay long because I've got a surgery scheduled for this afternoon."

"All right." Mariah put her napkin on the table and stood up. She let Cotter take her hand and lead her to the dance floor.

"I think red is your color." Cotter spoke in low tones as he pulled her into his arms. He turned his head to kiss her cheek. "Congratulations on achieving your goal, Mariah. You are one of the most successful women I know."

She thanked him and got into the spirit of the slow dance. Cotter had always been a skilled and graceful dancer, second only to Ramón.

"So where's your bodyguard?"

"Who?"

"The good buddy, old pal, Ramón."

"Unavoidably detained."

"I was right to be jealous of him, wasn't I?" Cotter asked in a sharp tone.

Astounded, Mariah pushed back to look into his face. "I can't believe you said that."

"Just tell me the truth. He had a lot more than friendship on his mind, didn't he?"

She didn't want to deal with Cotter Eastwood's jealousy. He had no rights as far as she was concerned. She put her hands on Cotter's expensive pin-striped suit and pushed. "I don't like the way this conversation is going. I want to go back to the table."

"No, Mariah, please." He put gentle hands on her shoulders, his troubled gaze meeting hers. "I'm sorry. I won't say anything more. Just let me have this dance."

"All right." She gave in gracefully then, ready to leave him stranded on the dance floor if he continued his negative conversation.

True to his word, Cotter was silent for the rest of the dance. Mariah realized that she wasn't the only person experiencing a bit of negativity when they danced near a table where Imani and Perry's argument could be heard above the music.

"You don't mean it," Perry said, "We've got something special. Don't throw it away."

Imani's voice was cold and vehement. "I do mean it. I don't want to see you. I want you to leave me alone. Why can't you to understand that it's over?"

Cotter swung Mariah in a circle and she saw the tension in their faces. Perry had her sympathy. Imani was ripping him to shreds. She wondered how much the man would take. As if he'd heard her thought, Perry got up from the table, his face a frozen mask. He gazed silently at Imani for a moment, and then strode out of the room.

Later, when Mariah went to the ladies room to freshen up, she heard someone crying softly in one of the stalls. Glancing down at the area near the floor of the stall, she recognized Imani's ice blue heels. The urge to try to comfort her was strong, but Mariah held fast. She'd been highly upset when Imani tried to put in a good word for Ramón. Besides, she'd given out enough advice for the day. There'd been a lot of times lately when she'd felt like crying too. Sometimes a good cry made you feel better.

Mariah flicked the comb through her hair. What was she going to do about Ramón? His absence affected her much more than any friendship should. She'd tried to hold the line on their relationship after letting it slip past the boundaries, and what had it gotten her? In the mirror, she stared into her clear brown eyes and asked, "You are in love with Ramón Richards, aren't you?"

ELEVEN

The ringing just wouldn't stop. The alarm rang, the phone rang, and now the doorbell was ringing. She'd had enough! Abruptly, Mariah sat up on the couch. Someone rang the doorbell so persistently that the sound resembled a broken cuckoo clock. Apparently, the bell had been ringing for some time, the sound moving in and out of her dreams. With sleep-drugged eyes, she looked around her moonlit den. She must have fallen asleep when she got home from the party. Pushing her legs over the side of the couch, she stood up. Her skirt fell to mid-thigh. "Okay, okay!" she called out irritably in the dark. "I'm coming."

She switched on the lamp as she went by the end table, her gaze falling on the clock. It was nine o'clock. She'd been asleep for three hours. Mariah stifled a yawn as she came to the carved oak front door. Leaning forward, she put an eye to the brass-covered peephole and drew back in amazement. Ramón paced back and forth under the bright porch lights, his handsome face twisted with frustration. He was still dressed for work in his charcoal gray business suit. Was she still dreaming? Thank you God! Gasping softly, Mariah turned the locks with shaking fingers. She'd been given another chance. Relief and joy bubbled up from the depths of her soul as she wrenched the door open in excitement. "Ramón!"

Ramón tugged the screen door open and they fell into each other's arms. For a very long time, they just held each other. He came back! He came back! The words played over and over like a song in her mind.

Hidden crickets sang a song of their own in the warm summer night. Mariah closed her eyes, breathed in the scent of him, and enjoyed the sensation of being close to Ramón. Her arms locked around his waist and her cheek rested against his linen-covered chest. How she loved this man. This was where she wanted to be. She tightened her arms, pressing her body as close as she could.

His rough sigh of satisfaction was like the purr of a contented cat. "I didn't think you were going to open the door! I guessed you were still angry about that day near the courthouse." She felt his warm breath close to her ear, his voice husky with fatigue.

"No," she said quickly. "I was asleep. Ramón, you're always welcome, no matter what."

"I missed your celebration because we had a crisis with the case. I just left the office." Gently, he kissed her temple. "Congratulations, Mariah, on the site closing. I knew you could do it. You are the best."

"Thanks!" Mariah's words came out on a sob. A heavy load had been lifted from her shoulders with his return.

"Hey, no tears," Ramón admonished, tilting her chin up with one hand, and pushing the hair from her face with the other. "This isn't like you, Mariah." Fatigue lined his handsome face, and tiny red lines edged the gray eyes that studied her face.

"So I fell off my pedestal, sue me!" she replied feistily, her gaze clouded with tears. "Don't pay me any attention. I'm just h-happy." Touched that he'd come to see her, she reveled in his presence. She'd begun to think their friendship was over.

He pulled a beautiful striped silk handkerchief from his jacket. "Here, take this."

Not wanting to spoil the beautiful silk, she hesitated, but when he started to pat the tears from her face with it, she relented. Quickly, she dabbed at her eyes and blew her nose. He watched her with a tender but wry expression that she normally resented. Sniffling, she managed a smile, recovering enough to take his hand. "Come into the house," she muttered, pulling him in through the entrance and shutting the door.

The lock clicked as she switched on the lights in her front hall. A fat tear rolled down her face, and she quickly brushed it away. Then she stuffed his handkerchief into her pocket. It had all been her fault. She'd been the one to take that first step that landed them in bed together, and then she'd been the one who couldn't handle it. She knew now that she loved him.

Mariah remembered her dream. Would she really have been just another woman in his long line of ex-girlfriends? She couldn't make herself believe that. She clenched her fists, trying to sort through the hot jumble of her emotions. Determined to make things right between them, she turned to Ramón. "I am sorry about everything. I went after you that night, and then I didn't handle things the way I should. I..."

Ramón's pewter gaze met hers, and then he pulled her into his arms, his hands massaging her back in a comforting motion. She leaned into him, rubbing her face against the rough texture of his suit. "I don't want you to apologize, Mariah. I was the one who was wrong. I can't force you to feel something that you don't. I shouldn't have been angry with you." He tilted her chin up, his gaze locking with hers. "I'm sorry, Mariah."

For just a moment, in the depths of his slate gray eyes she saw longing and desire mingled with sadness that was quickly suppressed. In response, Mariah experienced a tingle of excitement. Even now, with Ramón ready to be friends again, she felt the same intense awareness of him. He shifted from one foot to the other and she felt the sinuous movement of his heated body.

Her mind slipped back to that one unforgettable night when she couldn't get enough of him. She still wanted him, and it was foolish to try to think otherwise. She should say something, she thought, tell him how she felt, but how could she? Their time apart had been based on her inability to see Ramón as anything but a brother, and now he seemed determined to play that role. How could she be so fickle? Mariah struggled with guilt. "I virtually ruined our friendship..."

"We're still friends," his voice softened, "aren't we?" His hands clasped Mariah's hands, palms up and flat, but fingers clasped in their version of a high five.

"Yes. Always." Mariah returned the pressure of his fingers. It was a mistake. The warmth of his hands traveled down her arms and spread throughout her body to settle in the nether regions. She shivered involuntarily and forced herself to move away from the potency of his sensual charm. "Have you eaten?"

"No, I planned to grab a carryout on the way home."

"Let me fix you a sandwich."

"You look tired. I know you've had a long day. I don't want to put you to any trouble."

His words surprised her. Her eyes widened. She didn't feel tired, and she didn't view doing something for her friend as trouble. He hadn't been in her house more than a few minutes. She didn't want him to go, not yet. "You're not putting me to any trouble. I haven't seen you in weeks, and I missed you. Come on, let me enjoy your company for a while." She motioned him towards the kitchen. "The McCleary Kitchen is open for business. Want a beer?"

"No, that would really knock me out." Ramón followed her into the kitchen. "I'd better stick to the non-alcoholic stuff. Have you got any lemonade?"

Together, they washed their hands in the kitchen sink, then Mariah gave Ramón a couple of fresh lemons, a pitcher, a knife, and the sugar. While he made fresh-squeezed lemonade, she made her special Dagwood sandwich on a club roll, complete with ham, turkey, bacon, corned beef, eggs, lettuce, tomato, onion, cheese, and mayonnaise. Mariah sat across from him in the small breakfast nook and drank lemonade while he ate his meal.

"Gloria told me that the police found the murder weapon in a locker at Gerald Hatten's country club. Do you think it's all but over for him?" she asked, swiveling her chair to face him.

"A lot of assumptions have been made. Although the police know the gun is the murder weapon, and they've verified that the gun is registered to Hatten, they haven't finished checking all the fingerprints. They need to determine who besides Hatten had access to it. This was a real setback for the defense, but we may still pull this one out of the fire. I still believe Hatten is innocent."

She saw a rocky road ahead for the defense. Mariah lifted her feet and put them in a chair. "What's on the agenda for tomorrow?"

"We'll be cross examining Julie Marsh, his partner's wife. She had as good a reason as any to kill him. He was cheating on her and planning a divorce. Hatten had a party only days before he discovered the gun was missing, and she was there."

"Hmmph." Mariah propped an elbow on the table and set her chin in the palm of her hand. She'd seen Julie Marsh, and knew her as a local businesswoman in her own right, who contributed time and money to the charities. She didn't want Julie to be the guilty one.

"So what have you been doing this past month and a half?" Ramón asked as he finished the last bite of his sandwich.

Mariah shifted her stockinged feet in the chair across from him. "Going crazy trying to get the money for the site. I gave my clients due bills, I had the broker liquidate Mama's stocks, and you know I'd refinanced the house and cleaned out my savings account. It looked as if I wouldn't have enough money last Friday, so I sold my grandmother's ring to Dumouchelle Auction Galleries."

Ramón wiped his mouth and hands with the napkin, then put it down. "I wish you hadn't. I know how much you treasured that ring. Sometimes you're too knuckle-headed for your own good. Mariah, we offered to help you, and you turned us down. Was doing it on your own worth losing the ring?"

She tightened her lips and shot him a defiant look. "Hey, I made a decision and stuck with it."

"But you wish you hadn't," he said matter-of-factly.

"Only because the broker got quite a bit for some of Mother's stock in a company bought out by Starshine Enterprises. As a result, I didn't need to sell the ring after all." The revelation still stung. If she'd waited just a little longer, she'd have had everything.

"Did you try to get the ring back?"

"Of course I did," she answered, thumping her nails on the table. "Someone bought it just like that, and at a significant mark-up. I asked Dumouchelle's to get the ring back. Tally West is looking into it. I never expected the ring to disappear so soon. I kept thinking I'd be able to buy it back." Irritated, she pushed the hair up off her neck and stared down at her toes.

"You won't be able to get married without it, will you?" The odd silkiness in his tone caused her to look up and meet his enigmatic gaze. Puzzled, she stared at him, trying to discern what he really meant. His enigmatic gray gaze never left hers for a second.

"I guess not," she answered in a tone that was much lighter than she felt. Did he believe she was thinking of getting married? Mariah swiveled her chair. "I always dreamed that when I got married, it would be with my grandmother's ring. It would be a blessing of sorts from her, and you know how much I love that ring."

"Yes, I do."

"I guess it's a good thing I'm not planning to get married anytime soon."

"And whom would you marry, since it can't be me?" Ramón asked in a deceptively casual tone of voice.

"Don't tell me you didn't know your mother has a list of eligible bachelors put together especially for me," she said, feeling oddly disloyal. She'd gone out on those dates because she'd grown tired of being alone. The sad thing was that they'd only shown her how special Ramón was, and how much she really cared for him. "It's time I stopped moping around. I was at the racquet club with Larry, Number One on the list, last Friday while you played Phil."

Ramón's facial expression hardened. "And was he worthy of being Number One? Could you see yourself marrying the guy?" his eyes burned with jealousy.

The answer was no. Instinctively she knew that nothing she could ever develop for Larry would even touch the depth of feeling she had for Ramón, but she couldn't bring herself to tell Ramón. She loved Ramón, and wanted him in her life for always, but did she want to marry him? Could Ramón be a faithful husband? Mariah said nothing, as she stirred uneasily in her chair. She rose, took his plate and glass and put them in the sink. Doubts and fears filled her thoughts.

Ramón stood abruptly and stretched. "It's time I got home. I'm facing a difficult day in court tomorrow."

Her heart skipped as she turned to face him, needing to reassure herself that he would be back. "You're not running off in a huff, are you?"

"No," he said firmly, "no, I'm not. I'm just tired, that's all, and I'm still getting used to the way things are."

She knew what he meant. He was back, and she was glad, but it wasn't quite the same. She went to him then, and put her hands on his shoulders, determined to try to explain her feelings as best she could. "Ramón, I—"

"Don't say it. I don't want you to be charitable."

"I wasn't going to be charitable. I just—"

He cut her off again. "Just drop it. We're just going to have to work through this." He tilted her chin with a finger and kissed her forehead. "Good night, Mariah."

"Good night, Ramón." She wrapped her arms around his waist and hugged him hard. "Don't be a stranger."

"I won't." Briefly, he returned the embrace and then smoothly moved away from her. "Maybe we could do lunch, or something this week?" He moved steadily towards the front door.

Mariah followed, reluctant to see him go. "I'd like that."

When he had gone, she sat in the kitchen for a while, reliving his visit. She still felt the adrenaline rush he'd caused. She loved Ramón. She loved Ramón and it frightened her. She hadn't even told him. What did she really want from Ramón Richards? Whatever it was, it was certainly more than friendship.

Too tired for fast maneuvering, Ramón resisted the urge to speed as he drove home. He'd almost lost it and been blinded by jealousy at Mariah's when he'd asked about her new friend Larry. The wary look she'd given him had kept him from going further. He'd left abruptly because he was still too emotionally tied to her.

Mariah's genuine welcome and frank happiness at seeing him was undeniable, and then she'd held onto him as if she'd never let him go again. He'd held on to her, feeling as if he'd come home from a long, difficult journey. She'd certainly lifted his spirits. He felt hopeful again. Maybe they could get the relationship back on track. Her tears touched a chord deep within him; she'd cried for him, no matter how she tried to explain it away.

He grinned as he neared his exit on the freeway. She'd looked sexy as hell in the short red skirt, her long shapely legs begging for his touch. The white silk camisole had hugged her full breasts, the soft material slipping sensuously against his fingers when he'd held her and massaged her back. The grin froze, then disappeared. He was going to have to keep his hands off Mariah, at least until she came around to his way of thinking.

Time to start implementing Plan B. He'd had a serious talk with his meddling mom earlier in the day and formulated Plan B, the path to the surrender of Mariah McCleary. If he listened to Mom, all he had to do was to take Mariah at her word and start acting like the good friend she said she missed. Already he'd trashed the idea of having the usual lunch with Mariah. No, a better, more effective move would be a double date to that new jazz club, and he knew just the date he'd bring.

"Uhhhhh!" Mariah brushed her chocolate brown hair and then rearranged it for the third time. This was definitely a bad hair day! Her short, unruly curls fell all over the place, and she didn't dare use more hairspray. Cardboard hair was worse than hair with a mind of its own. Moaning in frustration, she splayed her fingers and glanced at herself in the full-length mirror.

At least her outfit was stunning. The elegant lime green pants and shirt with the black tank top underneath achieved the casually dressy effect she wanted. She turned on the three-inch heel of one of the strappy black sandals that Anthony had insisted she wear. They did look sexy, but Mariah wondered if she would be able to bear walking in them all night long.

"This is a bad idea!" She flopped back onto her bed and sighed. She hadn't seen Ramón since he stopped to congratulate her on the closing. How in the world had she let him talk her into a double date with him and his ex-girlfriend Rita? She'd already admitted to herself that she loved him. When he dropped by, he hadn't let her discuss her feelings, but she could have told him how she felt when he set up the double date. Why hadn't she? Mariah nibbled on her bottom lip. Could she have made him believe it, after all she'd said to the contrary?

Restlessly, she shifted her hips on the bed. They were all in for a very tense evening. His choice of date bothered her. Of all the women in his past, he'd seemed the most physically and emotionally involved with Rita, the beautiful and passionate daughter of one of Gloria's Puerto Rican friends. Yes, Ramón had been much younger, with his hormones in overdrive, but Rita had broken his heart. Could he be in love with her as he claimed if he were back with Rita? Rita was definitely one hot date.

From the nightstand beside the bed, she retrieved the green and black flowered earrings and snapped them onto her ears. No use harping on the situation, she decided. She took a couple of deep breaths and tried to relax. Then doorbell rang.

It had to be Larry. Mariah got up, grabbed her purse, and answered the door.

"Hello beautiful!" Larry said in his deep sexy voice. He stood on her porch, fashionably dressed in an exclusive designer print shirt and matching pants. A wide smile graced his handsome face.

"Hello yourself." Mariah returned his smile.

Gently he took her hand, leaned forward, and kissed her lips. "Are you ready to go?" He shot a quick glance at his watch. "It's getting late." His appreciative gaze returned to Mariah, wandering over her slowly and waxing eloquent. "You couldn't look more exquisite if you tried," he said with a slow sensual smile.

She enjoyed his smile. Maybe the evening wouldn't be a total loss. Larry was always nice to have around. "Thank you, Larry. I like the way you look too. Just give me a minute to lock the door." She pulled her keys from the evening purse and fitted her key into the deadbolt.

After she'd locked the door, Larry took her hand and led her down the steps. "Tell me about the friends we're meeting at the club."

"Ramón Richards and I have been friends since we were sophomores at U of M, and we're pretty close. He's like the brother I never had." Now that's a lie, she realized after the words tripped off her tongue. Larry opened the door of his silver blue Mercedes and Mariah got in. "He's also the lead lawyer on the Gerald Hatten case."

Closing her door, Larry came around and got into the car. "I think your friend and the other lawyers on the defense team are doing a great job of defending Hatten. With all the articles in the paper before the trial started, I just knew he was guilty, but now, I think someone else could have done it. His wife seems pretty scary. I wouldn't be surprised to hear she did it."

"Me either," Mariah said as she adjusted her seat.

He started the car and headed for the club. "What about your friend's date?"

Mariah thought of the sensual Rita Morales and tried to think of something neutral to say. Though she'd tried, she'd never liked Rita. Drawing upon some things she'd heard Gloria say, she said, "Rita Morales is a nurse. I think she works at Beaumont Hospital."

"I know Rita." A slight smile curved Larry's lips. "Tall and dark-haired, and Hispanic, something on the order of Salma Hayek, the girl with Antonio Banderas in *Desperado*?"

"That's Rita."

"I've been out with her a time or two," he said pleasantly. "She was my nurse when I got into a minor accident last year."

Mariah raised an eyebrow in surprise. Uh-oh, things are worse than I thought. She wouldn't have thought Larry or Ramón would be Rita's type. The woman sure got around. Her thoughts returned to the evening ahead. Would Rita be all over Ramón the way she used to be? Would she try to dangle Larry too? She had never been friends with Mariah, but Ramón had always assured Mariah that Rita's attitude towards her was merely part of her competitive nature.

By the time they got to the jazz club, it was almost eleven o'clock. They passed beneath the flashing sign of colored lights and entered the gray brick building through the black double doors with gold handles.

The smooth sounds of Al Jarreau on the club stereo system and the low buzz of conversation welcomed them into the softly lit interior. Various murals of jazz greats covered the walls, and fancy candles shaped like musical instruments graced the tables. Larry gave their names and the hostess took them past elegant tables filled with couples to a ringside table close to the stage.

Ramón stood up as they neared the table, and she felt a new ripple of excitement. His dark hair was brushed back to display the beautiful planes and angles of his face and he wore a nutmeg and black print dress shirt and black pants. "Mariah." He extended a hand and grasped Mariah's. The very air around her seemed electrified. Her skin tingled as he leaned close and brushed her cheek with his lips. She smiled, caught in the glow of his presence. "Hello gorgeous!" he murmured in a low voice that only she could hear. Holding her hand for a few beats more than necessary, he gave her his very special smile. Releasing her hand, he turned to Larry, his smile fading as he sized him up. In a very subtle way, he seemed to find Larry lacking.

Larry gave Ramón an astute glance, then extended his hand and said, "I'm Larry, how ya doing, man?"

Ramón politely extended his hand and said pleasantly, "Ramón Richards, and I'm just fine." The two men shook hands politely. "I've heard a lot about you from Mariah and my mother."

Larry took Mariah's hand and clasped it to his chest. "Yes, your mother has taken me under her wing and is determined to marry me off. When she introduced me to Mariah, I knew there was no way it could get any better."

"They don't come any better than Mariah." Ramón grinned. "She's been like a sister to me," he said smoothly.

Mariah stiffened. Her own words stung like salt in a raw wound.

Rita stood up then and immediately became the center of attention in a short red tank dress that hugged her petite curvy figure, emphasizing the fullness of her breasts, her tiny waist, and rounded hips. Masses of glossy black waves fell past her shoulders to frame her alluring features. "Mariah, it's been a long time. How are you?"

"I'm fine. You know Larry?"

"Yes, I do." With her eyes full of sensual mischief, Rita turned to Larry and extended her hand. When he clasped it, she used his hand to pull him close and smacked him on the cheek. "It's been much too long."

Larry seemed a little surprised, but he was enjoying his time in the sun. "Yes, but I have memories that I'll always treasure. How have you been?" He positively glowed under Rita's attention. Somehow, this fact didn't bother Mariah in the least. She was so busy trying not to stare at Ramón that she quit listening to their conversation.

Finally risking a glance at Ramón to see how he was taking the exchange between Larry and Rita, she found herself gazing into the murky depths of his slate gray eyes. It was as if they were alone. A spark of some indefinable emotion in his eyes was compellingly magnetic. She forgot all about Larry and Rita.

"Here comes the waitress," Ramón said, breaking the odd silence. "Shall we sit down?" They arranged the chairs around the table and sat down. Then they ordered drinks.

"What do you know about the band?" Mariah asked, watching Rita scoot her chair so close to Ramón's that you couldn't have slid a sheet of paper between them.

"They're called the Detroit Expressions, and they feature the saxophone, electric piano, piano, electric guitar, and flute," Ramón answered, seemingly unaffected by Rita fluffing the curling hair covering his neck and just touching his shirt collar. "I like them."

The waitress approached their table with a tray of drinks. "They've got a new album out," Larry joined in, retrieving his wallet and pulling out a few bills. "I think it's called Saxpressions, and it's a goody." He accepted drinks for himself and Mariah and gave the money to the waitress. Ramón did the same.

"It's going to be quite a show," Rita said in a tone so sultry that Larry and Ramón turned to look at her. She leaned forward till her breasts virtually rested on Ramón's arm and whispered something in his ear. He shook his head and smiled. Briefly, his gaze met Mariah's. She looked away.

They looked like a beautiful pair of Latin lovers with their dark hair and exotic features, Mariah thought, like something out of a magazine. The air between them sizzled. Judging from the atmosphere, they'd probably leave right after the show to go back to Ramón's to make love.

Envy squeezed her heart. She found herself wanting to be in Rita's place. She'd never liked Rita, was that the reason why? Had Ramón ever looked at her that way? She sipped her white wine and tried to think of something else.

Larry's hand covered hers for a moment. "Show time in two minutes," he said in a warm voice.

She caught his gaze and smiled.

"I think you're going to love it."

The house lights dimmed and the stage lights came on. Mariah loved the jazz band. Her favorite instrument, the saxophone, dominated the first three songs. Its smooth, provocative sound was a musical caress that soothed her mind and spirit. Larry scooted closer, put an arm around her shoulders, and shared sporadic comments about the band with her. The only sour note was the occasional husky laugh from Rita, who cuddled with Ramón to her left. Rita draped herself around him like a hot, brightly colored sweater. Mariah kept wishing Ramón would fling her off.

Okay, okay, so she was jealous. Mariah lifted her glass and took a sip of wine. Her nerves were strung so tight that she was beginning to get a headache. Taking a deep breath, she turned her attention to the four men on stage and the refreshing sounds they made.

The applause was thunderous when the lights came back up. "Want to stay for the next show?" Larry's voice rippled with enthusiasm.

The band was good, but she wasn't looking forward to another hour of watching Rita throw herself at Ramón. No, she wasn't going to let Rita cause her to miss an otherwise pleasant evening. She answered, "Sure, how long do we have to wait?"

"About another hour. I think it's worth it."

"Me too." Mariah turned to Rita and Ramón. "Are you guys staying for the next show?"

"What do you want to do?" Ramón asked Rita, who nestled in the crook of his arm.

"I'm a little tired, aren't you?" Rita's voice held a soft, caressing note. Mariah wondered, did she imagine the intimate question in Rita's eyes?

"Not really," Ramón answered, not getting the hint, and obviously missing the disappointment in her expression. "Let's compromise. Why don't we stay and have another drink with Larry and Mariah, and then I take you home?"

"I'm happy if you are."

"Good." Ramón signaled the waitress for another round of drinks. "This round's on me."

"Ramón tells me that you've recently acquired a new site for your agency," Rita said to Mariah. "Where is it located?"

"Off Jefferson Avenue, on the waterfront."

"Do you mean that dilapidated area with all those abandoned buildings and warehouses?"

Mariah's temperature started rising fast. If Rita Morales was trying to belittle her accomplishment, she was going to show her when to shut up. "I mean the Federal Empowerment Zone. Surely you've heard of those areas in the city that they're trying to revitalize with new businesses and housing?" Mariah worked to keep the sarcasm out of her tone.

"Actually, I haven't been paying much attention to the news," Rita put in with an insincere little smile.

Ramón set his glass of Martell on the table. "Mariah got a choice piece of property for a fantastic price."

"Well congratulations! I always thought you had a great head for business," Rita stressed the end of her sentence just long enough for Mariah to notice. The implication was that her head wasn't good for much else. "I really admire your business skills."

Mariah smiled sweetly, her eyes shooting flames at Rita. So it was war, was it? She gritted her teeth and said graciously, "Thank you."

"There's a lot more to Mariah than business." Larry set his glass down. "I'm a bona fide member of the Mariah McCleary Admiration Society. I could go on, and on—"

"I'll take your word for it," Rita smirked with a wink and a smile.

Really annoyed, Mariah said, "You were thinking of going to medical school when I saw you last. Are you still pursuing that dream?"

Rita looked down at her perfect nails. "No, I—I haven't had the time."

"Gee, you must be awfully busy."

Rita nodded, her voice much lower, "Yeah."

Mariah wet her lips and then tossed down the rest of her white wine. Her gaze caught Ramón's when she set the glass down and she noticed the faint glint of humor in the depths of his eyes. He'd obviously enjoyed the exchange. Larry sat drinking his whiskey, apparently unaware of the currents in the conversation swirling around him.

The waitress brought the new round of drinks then, and conversation settled more along its normal lines. Ramón and Larry had the obligatory sports discussion until the bored looks of Rita and Mariah were too pointed to ignore.

Rita and Ramón left ten minutes before show time with everyone politely agreeing that they had to all double date again soon. Mariah had no intention of repeating the torture. In fact, when she figured out exactly what she wanted to say, and the way to say it, she planned to have a long talk with Ramón Richards.

A couple of days later, Mariah sat in her office going through portfolios.

Lynn stuck her head in the doorway. "Mama's here." A nervous smile creased her face. "We've got to leave for lunch soon, so why don't you come out and meet her?"

She gave Lynn a reassuring smile. "Sure. Give me a minute." Then she retrieved her purse, locked the desk, and moved to the outer office.

A petite, ginger-brown woman in a smart black and white suit sat in Lynn's guest chair talking animatedly. The boyish cut of her golden brown hair complemented her fine features. She turned as Mariah entered the room, a warm smile lighting her features. "You must be Mariah. I've heard so much about you. Hello, I'm Linda Ware." Her soft Southern twang fell gently on the ears.

"It's nice to meet you, Mrs. Ware." Mariah extended her hand and clasped the woman's hand. "Lynn is not only my secretary and assistant, she's also my friend."

"Well, it's nice to meet you too. I certainly think you've been a good influence on Lynn. With that new hairdo, and the clothes she's been wearing, she's like the girl I always knew she could be."

"Mama!" The disapproval in Lynn's voice was hard to miss.

"Mrs. Ware, Anthony cut Lynn's hair, and she's been wearing some of his designs," Mariah said carefully.

"I've told you again and again," Lynn said, her voice inches shy of annoyance.

"Yes, I guess you did." Mrs. Ware turned to face Mariah again. "I'm sure you can understand that as a mother I want the best for my oldest child. Lynn sacrificed a lot of her dreams to help me take care of her brother and sister, and put them through college. I—"

"Ready to go?" Anthony lounged casually against the doorframe looking handsome in a severely cut blue suit. His ebony hair was freshly cut.

"Anthony." Lynn got out of her chair and went to him. They stood close, but not touching. The pull between the two was so strong that everyone else was excluded. Mariah wondered, is it like that between Ramón and me?

Anthony's eyes caressed Lynn as he took her hand. Slowly, he leaned forward and gently touched his lips to hers. Lynn visibly trembled. Linda Ware's lips tightened as she watched the couple.

"Hello Mrs. Ware, how are you?" Anthony said quietly. Mariah knew he expected an unpleasant lunch, but was going through with it for Lynn's sake.

"I'm fine, Anthony, and looking forward to lunch. How are you?" Something in her tone belied her pleasant words.

"Better since I've seen Lynn. Mrs. Ware, your daughter is like the sun."

Linda Ware merely smiled.

"Ramón's going to try and meet us at the restaurant, so I thought I'd ride with you and Lynn." Mariah pulled her purse onto her arm and approached Lynn and Anthony.

"Of course you're welcome to come with us." Anthony jingled his keys. "I borrowed my brother's car so we'd have more room."

"Thank you." Anthony was a sweetheart, Mariah thought.

"Are you coming, Mama?" Lynn gazed expectantly at her mother.

"I wouldn't miss it for the world." Linda Ware rose gracefully and strolled to the door. They left the building in companionable silence.

"I love the car," Mariah said, scooting into the back of the dark green Cadillac.

"I do too." Anthony closed Lynn's door. "But I haven't quite gotten over the thrill of a sports car." He closed Mariah's door and then walked around the car to get into the driver's seat. "I really don't need the extra room until I get married."

"That won't be anytime soon, will it?" Mrs. Ware piped up from the back seat.

Anthony gazed at Lynn, who was suddenly very interested in her nails. "I don't know. I've never felt this way before. I love Lynn."

Mariah held her breath. She knew how much Lynn and Anthony loved each other, but was it strong enough to face all the problems they'd encounter by being married?

Lynn lifted her head, her heart in her eyes.

Linda Ware gasped audibly. "So you are serious about my daughter."

"Yes, I am." Anthony gripped the steering wheel. "There's just so much that needs to be resolved." He turned to Lynn and said, "I'm sorry it came up this way. I've been meaning to say something to you."

Lynn put her hand on Anthony's arm. "It's all right. I've got a lot to say to you too. Let's discuss it when we're alone."

He gazed at her for several moments, then said, "Whatever you want." Anthony started the car and headed for the restaurant.

They were all seated and looking at the menus when Ramón arrived, brimming with excitement. "Hello, gorgeous!" Ramón took the empty seat next to Mariah and leaned close to smack her on the lips. He spoke to Lynn and Anthony, then turned his attention to Lynn's mother. "I can see where Lynn gets her looks. You must be Lynn's mother, I'm Ramón Richards." He shook her hand.

Linda Ware bloomed under his attention. "It's nice to meet you."

"It's nice to meet you too. Are you enjoying your visit to Detroit?"

"So far, so good. I've just begun to get around."

"Make sure Lynn takes you to some of the jazz clubs in the city and festivals downtown at Hart Plaza. Those are some of the fun things I like to do here," Ramón said.

"Don't forget Belle Isle, the shows at the Fox, and the gambling across the river," Mariah added.

"Or the Detroit Symphony Orchestra, the African-American Museum, and shows at the Fisher Theatre," Anthony said, closing his menu.

"All your suggestions sound interesting." Mrs. Ware turned to Lynn. "Do you think you'll remember everything?"

Lynn sipped her water, then put the glass down. "Sure. I've got a two-page list at home. All you have to do is let me know which things you want to see."

"I can hardly wait to get started," Mrs. Ware murmured before turning her attention back to the menu.

"All right, what's got you so excited?" Mariah asked Ramón as the others gave their orders to the waitress.

"Other than looking at you?" Ramón leaned closer, his hand covering hers.

"Ramón, I'm serious."

"So am I."

"Then let me guess. Someone's confessed to the murder, and it isn't Gerald Hatten."

"Not exactly." He tilted his head to meet her curious gaze. "Traces of blood were found on the gun used to kill Hatten's partner." At Mariah's nod, he continued, "Those traces have been analyzed to show an RH negative factor, and the blood belongs to neither Hatten nor the murder victim. That's a rare blood factor. It certainly helps to tip the defense end of the scale. The big question now is, whose blood is on the gun? How did it get there?"

The waitress completed Linda Ware's order and moved on to Mariah. "Miss, are you ready to order?"

While Mariah gave her order, Ramón hurriedly scanned the menu. After he'd selected an entrée and ordered, they all chatted amiably until the food arrived. Mariah noticed that the small talk from Anthony was a little stilted due to Mrs. Ware's presence. The woman was noticeably cool to him. Mariah's heart went out to Lynn and Anthony. It wasn't as if he and Lynn were having an easy time making their relationship work. They sat close together, apparently drawing strength from one another.

After the delicious meal, they sat drinking coffee while Lynn, Anthony, and Ramón had chocolate mousse and cheesecake for dessert.

Linda Ware casually stirred her coffee. "Anthony, you've achieved so much with your designs. I know your mother must be proud of you."

Anthony chucked in the last fork of cheesecake, then answered, "She is, Mrs. Ware—believe me."

She turned to face Lynn. "Have you met Mrs. LeFarge? She must be an interesting woman."

"No. Not yet," Lynn answered in even tones.

Anthony looked uncomfortable. He glanced quickly at Lynn, then answered, "Lynn will meet my mother when the time is right."

"I've met his grandmother," Lynn said evenly. "She's a wonderful person."

"Yes, you told me." Mrs. Ware gave Anthony a penetrating stare. "I bet your mother meets all the girls you really like after the first few dates."

"And you'd win the bet, except that Lynn is a special case." Anthony flexed his fingers, his expression tense.

Lynn pushed away her dessert. "Mama, it's no secret that his family, like my own, is having a hard time accepting our relationship. Can't we talk about something else?"

"Lynn, I only want the best for you, not a lifetime of being snubbed or ignored. I've met Anthony, and I talk to him. I'd say I'm miles ahead of anything his mother has done."

Lynn's face was flushed with embarrassment. "Please, Mama."

"I'm sorry Lynn, but that's how I feel. I'm not about to apologize for it."

Anthony signaled for the check. "I think it's time I got back to the office. Lynn, Mariah, Mrs. Ware, are you ready to go?"

Lynn retrieved her purse and stood up. "Yes, just let me make a pit stop." Walking briskly, she took off for the ladies' room.

Mariah quickly followed Lynn. She found her combing her hair in the bathroom mirror.

"No, I'm not in here crying my eyes out," Lynn said in a controlled voice when she spotted Mariah.

"I'm glad." Mariah ran a comb through her own hair.

"Some of the things she said really put Anthony on the spot, but now I know that he's planning to ask me to marry him. In spite of all the problems, it makes me feel good."

"Then that's all that matters." Mariah reapplied Chocolate Cherry lipstick.

Tentatively, Linda Ware entered the ladies room. "Lynn, are you still speaking to me?"

"Of course I am, Mama," Lynn said in warm tones as she went and hugged her mother. "I know that everything you've said was out of concern for me. I just can't agree with your methods."

After the ladies returned to the table, Ramón hurried back to court. Then Anthony took Mrs. Ware to her car, and Mariah and Lynn back to the office.

TWELVE

"Ramón's birthday is next week and you promised to help me!"

The exasperation in Gloria's tone hit Mariah like a volley of arrows. She struggled to answer her friend and substitute mother. "Yes, I know, but I thought you meant with the invitations, food and decorations. I don't know how to get Ramón over to the birthday party without him suspecting anything." She'd hardly heard from him in the last few days. She knew he was busy with the case, but couldn't he call and say hello as he used to? She'd called twice and left messages with no response. Was he avoiding her again?

"Mariah, you're his best friend, and you've got a good head on your shoulders. Think of something!" Gloria spoke so fast with her thick accent that it was a wonder Mariah understood her. She'd seen Gloria excited or upset in the past and knew she was close to meltdown.

Not wanting to see Gloria cry, she said, "I'll see what I can do. Let me sleep on it."

Gloria grabbed her and hugged her tight. "I knew I could count on you."

Mariah mulled it over for a couple of days. How could she lure Ramón to his own surprise party? Was she even the right woman for the job? She used to hear from him at least every other day.

Two days later, a workable idea came to mind. She'd call him at the appropriate time with car trouble and ask for a ride.

On the evening of Ramón' s birthday, she nervously dialed his office, rehearsing in her mind just what she would say.

When she heard him answer, she began. "Hey Ramóndo Beyondo, are you having a happy birthday?"

"Not bad, Mariah, but we should have gone to lunch today." The animation in his voice picked up. He was obviously glad to hear from her.

Mariah breathed a sigh of relief. Smiling to herself, she said. "I agree, why didn't we?"

"Oh, we were in the middle of some important testimony. It turns out that the alibi for Hatten's wife's isn't as ironclad as it seemed. She had ample reason to want his partner dead, and setting it up so that he took the blame would have been the icing on the cake. We spent a working lunch following up on a few of the leads that came up in this morning's testimony." He paused a moment and she imagined him pushing back in his big chair and rocking it back and forth. "You sound excited. What's up?"

"I'm stranded and I need a favor. Could you pick me up? My car got temperamental on me, so I'm stranded on Jefferson Avenue. I wouldn't bother you except that I've got to get an important package to one of the models. He's going out of town and should be leaving for the airport in about half an hour."

"No problem. What are you close to?"

"I'm down from the radio station."

"Sit tight. I'll be right there."

Pleased, Mariah quickly ended the conversation and turned off her cell phone. She stared out at the rush hour traffic. Now all she had to do was discourage passing motorists from stopping to help her.

Ramón pulled up behind her car in less than ten minutes. She got out with a fat package and went around to his opened passenger window to talk. Her heart actually fluttered at the sight of him. Looking especially handsome in a tailor-made black suit with gold undertones, he said, "If you weren't in a hurry, I'd try to start it for you."

"Dressed like that?" she said eyeing his expensive suit. No need to ask where all his extra money went.

"I keep a pair of coveralls in the trunk of my car."

"We'd better get going," Mariah said, getting into the passenger seat of his car. "Tyree can't leave without the package." It amazed her that her bogus car breakdown had worked so well. Ramón should have seen straight through her ruse. She pulled a piece of paper from her purse. "Here's the address."

"You're looking awfully nice this evening." Ramón gave her an appreciative glance as he drove off. "You didn't get all dressed up just to take this guy a package, did you?" He lifted an eyebrow.

Glad he liked her new evening dress, Mariah smiled. Anthony and Lynn had talked her into wearing the short, low-cut, burgundy number. "I was going to dinner and a show with Lynn. What are your plans for the evening?"

"I'm just hanging loose. I haven't heard a thing from Mom, except that she might drop by tomorrow with my gift. I'd have thought she'd plan a party. You know how she loves a celebration."

"Yes, she does." Is he catching on? she wondered, watching him from beneath her lashes.

He caught her looking and gave her an admonishing look. "I remember the time when we used to do something special on each of our birthdays. And you didn't call me to arrange anything." He looked a little hurt.

It made her want to tell him everything. "I did call you, Ramón. I called you twice this week and you never returned my calls."

"Mariah, I never got the message. My secretary has been out sick all week and we've been making do with someone from the temporary agency. I'm going to give that woman a piece of my mind."

"No, don't do that. You're here now."

"I'm happy to help you out, but chauffeur duty isn't what I had in mind."

"What did you have in mind?" She gazed at him expectantly, not quite sure what she wanted to hear.

Ramón turned his head to look at her. A speculative expression crossed his face and then he executed a sexy grin that made her toes curl. She hung on, hoping he'd elaborate and wanting to do whatever it was that put that look on his face.

"All sorts of nasty things that you don't do with your good friends." His low provocative tone sent chills down her spine. The blood rushed to Mariah's face. She imagined herself in bed with Ramón, and it was so good. Mariah moistened her lips. He seemed to catch himself and his smoldering expression cooled. Shaking his head he said, "Forget I said that." He turned his attention back to the road. "Three more lights and turn left?"

Pulse racing, she tried to keep the breathlessness from her voice. "Yes. Have you been to this complex before?"

"Yeah. One of Mom's friends has an apartment there. They're real ritzy, and have a view of the river."

In short order, Ramón made his left turn and went down the street a ways before pulling into the complex parking lot. "Shall I wait for you in the car?"

"Nah, come with me. You need the exercise," she shot back at him.

"Yeah, I do need to exercise," he said suggestively. "Are you volunteering to help with the job?

"Come on, Ramón!" She got out of the car and closed her door. Taking a quick look around, she noticed that there weren't many parking spots left in the lot. She was glad that none of their friends' cars were visible.

Obediently, he got out of the car and trailed her into the second building along the waterfront. "After we drop this off, I'll go back and try to start your car, okay?"

"Okay," she said, feeling only slightly guilty that there was nothing wrong with her car. She led him up the steps to apartment 2C. There was a note on the door. Mariah pulled it off and made a show of reading its contents. "Too bad this is too big to slip under the door. He had to run down to the laundry room. Let's just get this over with by taking it to him."

He followed her down the stairs and to a set of double doors with a laundry room sign on them. "It must be a pretty big laundry room to have double doors," he remarked, giving it a suspicious look.

"You know how these ritzy apartment complexes are." Mariah put her hand on one door and turned the knob, pushing inward. She stopped short. "Ramón?"

"I'm here. What's the matter?" He moved to stand in front of her. Staring into the pitch black of the room, he said, "He's obviously not down here."

Suddenly the room exploded with light and choruses of "Surprise! Happy birthday to you." Ramón's mouth fell open in surprise and his face broke out into a jubilant smile. He loved surprises.

"Happy birthday, Ramón!" she called out as she hugged him quickly and kissed his bronze cheek.

"You..." was all he had a chance to say before a crowd of family and friends surrounded him. He would be busy for a while, she thought. Gloria Richards was the first to pull her son into a big bear hug. She kissed him effusively. Judge Richards patiently waited his turn. In the background, salsa music began to play and was quickly followed by the raucous sounds of laughter and conversation. People began to dance on the hardwood floor in the large area in the center of the room.

Gloria had gone all out on the decorations. Mariah's gaze took in the custom-made gold foil birthday banners with Ramón's name on them, the ceiling covered with streamers and balloons and Ramón's initials in gold. Each table was graced with a white tablecloth and skirt, and an elegant flower arrangement.

The mixed yet discernible mouth-watering aromas of shrimp, wingdings, nachos, jalapeno peppers, and sizzling fajitas turned Mariah's head to the back of the room where a catering staff dished up the delectables. There was even a table filled with fruit and vegetable trays. Following the demands of her grumbling stomach, she dashed to the back of the room to get a plate.

Mariah sat down with her plate full of goodies. She shouldn't eat this much, she knew, but Gloria had managed to provide all her favorite party foods. Turning her chair to get a full view of the dance floor, she started with the shrimp. She saw Rita drag Ramón onto the dance floor.

A passing waiter dropped off a glass of white zinfandel. "Mrs. Richards said you'd be needing this," he murmured.

Scanning the room, she found Gloria chatting with a group of friends near the dance floor. She gave Mariah a grateful smile and then saluted her with a glass of wine. Mariah mirrored her gesture and then turned her attention back to the dance floor.

Tightness gripped her chest at the sight of Ramón and Rita burning up the dance floor with a hot salsa number. Mariah couldn't take her eyes off Ramón and the sensual way his body dipped, rotated, and stepped in a dance that too closely resembled foreplay with the red hot Rita. They laughed and flirted with each other as they danced, obviously enjoying themselves. Dressed in a short, hot pink slip dress and matching spike heels, Rita looked like one of the women in those 1-900 commercials. They danced so close together in their choreographed dance, that they could have been glued together. Nearly visible waves of the chemistry and body heat they generated swirled around them. She watched them through a haze of her own hot emotions and desire. Why hadn't she told Ramón she loved him?

"Mind if we join you?" In a cream silk halter gown, Lynn stood by the table holding three glasses of wine. Dressed in one of his own label's black raw silk suits, Anthony stood behind her with a plate in each hand.

"No, please do," Mariah said clearing her throat. She was happy to see Lynn and Anthony, and glad to have an alternative to the show on the dance floor.

"How are you?" Lynn asked, settling in the chair across from her. Lynn's eyes flicked from Mariah's face to Ramón and Rita.

"Fine." Mariah said brightly without following Lynn's gaze. She gripped the edge of her chair tightly, trying to ride out her intense emotions.

Also seated across from her, Anthony gave her an astute look. "I hope you can tell the difference between a real threat and window dressing."

Drawing in a deep breath, Mariah let it out very slowly. She considered his words, an obvious reference to Ramón and Rita, and said, "I can, but sometimes window dressing is so authentic looking that people settle for it."

"I don't think you have to worry."

There was no doubt where her friends stood on the issue of Rita and Ramón. She was a little embarrassed for being so transparent. The realization of her love for Ramón was still so new that she'd barely admitted it to herself. One corner of her lips quirked up. "I appreciate your support."

"Yes, we support you," Lynn piped up, "But Anthony's just telling it like it is. Mariah, you have nothing to worry about."

Maybe they were right. Opening her aching fingers, she removed them from the edge of the chair and flexed them. Mariah stole one last glance at the couple on the dance floor and changed the subject.

Lynn leaned over and spoke in a low tone. "Have you seen the latest *Tattletale*?"

"No." Mariah shook her head. "Why?"

"Perry's plastered across the front page with his arm around one of those starlets from the movie *Fade*. According to the article, she's pregnant with his kid, so they're getting married."

In her mind's eye Mariah saw Imani crying alone in the bathroom stall after publicly sending Perry away. She was certain that Imani still loved Perry. "How's poor Imani taking it?"

"The way she takes everything." Lynn emphasized her words by tilting her head and shifting her shoulders from side to side. "She said that she didn't give a rat's behind, and I'm using the polite word for it. Then she claimed that their last break-up was permanent because he was never the man she thought he was."

"I know that the article in *Tattletale* must have hurt her badly, because she loved Perry," Mariah said sympathetically. "What can she do but hold her head up high and keep on stepping?"

Lynn shrugged. "I guess that's it—but don't think that she doesn't have a lot of handsome volunteers simply begging to help her forget the pain of it all."

Mariah blew out a puff of air and shrugged, as if to say, "Maybe that'll help."

After a while, Lynn and Anthony got up and danced. When Anthony asked Mariah to dance, she declined, so they sat and talked.

"So tell me Mariah, is there really anything wrong with your car?" a familiar voice asked in an amused tone.

Mariah whirled around. At the sight of Ramón, a warm glow suffused her. Ramón stood behind her with a plate of appetizers and a glass of wine. "What do you think?" she asked coyly as he placed his plate and drink on the table and seated himself in the empty chair next to her.

"I think you were in cahoots with my mother." He shot her a look brimming with humor. "I even offered to put on a pair of coveralls to fix the car for you. You're a good liar, Ms. McCleary."

"Are you complaining about the result?" she quipped smartly.

"No, I was just wondering if you were lying about anything else," he teased.

Mariah crossed her legs. "I guess you'll just have to catch me at it."

Taking in the movement, Ramón lifted an eyebrow. "Don't worry, I'm planning on it."

Slowly, the crowd thinned as the evening wore on. By one o'clock, with most of the people gone, Mariah, Phil, and another friend were helping Ramón pack gifts. He'd also promised to take her back to her car. Gloria and the judge had already said good night and were saying good-bye to the friend who lived in the building.

Ramón had gotten a ridiculous number of gifts. Fortunately, most were things he liked. "Nice tie," Mariah said looking down at the blue and gray silk designer tie topping the mound of boxed gifts she carried out of the banquet room.

"Thanks, Phil knows what I like." Ramón and Phil followed her out with the rest of the gifts. "Thanks for lending a hand."

"No problem," Phil murmured.

"It was the least I could do after you rescued me tonight," Mariah said mockingly as she started up the stairway to the first floor.

Following her up the steps, Ramón chuckled. "I definitely owe you a return favor, and I am going to enjoy it."

"It'll be hard to surprise me because anything you do will be suspect." Mariah made it to the top and pushed the door open with her hip. Warm summer air caressed her face.

Thunder rumbled in the distance. Uh-oh, she thought, looking down at her dress, and remembering Anthony saying it was dry-clean only and likely to shrink if she got it wet. They were halfway to the car when the first few drops of rain fell. Mariah increased her speed, hoping she'd make it to his car before the downpour. Lightning flashed, slashing the darkness, and Ramón moved past her, his car keys jingling beneath his gifts. Phil sped past her as the rain drops increased in number and speed. Just as Ramón opened his trunk, torrents of rain fell from the sky, flooding the parking lot. Phil dumped his load and got into his car.

Mariah squealed as the cold rain beat against her skin with a driving force. With her wet hair plastered to her head, and her sodden dress dripping down her legs, she made it to the car and dumped her load in the trunk. Slamming the trunk shut, Ramón hit the automatic locks on the door. Then both dived into the dry welcome of the car's interior. It was raining so hard they could barely see five feet in front of them.

Ramón pushed wet hair back from his face and turned to face Mariah. "We need to get home and get out of these wet clothes. I think you should wait until the rain lets up a bit before you start home. Why don't we wait out this storm at my place?"

"Sure." What else could she say? She felt like a drowned rat, a drowned rat whose expensive dry clean only dress was already shrinking. Maybe he wouldn't notice. Like hell, he wouldn't. Ramón noticed everything.

Ramón drove slowly through the flooding streets with noisy rain pounding the roof of the car. Mariah shivered in the cool air conditioning, knowing it was required to keep the windshield clear. Goosebumps rose on her arms and legs.

She risked a glance at Ramón, relieved to see that driving took all his attention. As unobtrusively as possible, she tried to pull down her rapidly shrinking hemline. It had already gone up past the tops of her lace-edged thigh highs. At the rate her dress was going, she'd be lucky if her bare essentials were covered when she stepped out of the car. Why had she worn such sexy underwear? The skimpy black lace bikinis revealed more than they concealed.

At a red light she glanced at him and saw his gaze linger on her thighs and travel up to her breasts. Her nipples hardened as liquid warmth pooled between her legs. She wanted him, wanted him to touch her. This time she shivered in excitement. The words of one of her favorite cartoon characters rang in her mind, Uh-oh, we're in deep do-do.

"Cold?" His hand massaged up and down her arm, heating her skin and making her tingle all over.

Shivering, she nodded in answer to his question. Was she imagining the desire in his eyes?

His fingers fell to her palm and smoothed across the surface. "We're almost there."

Within minutes, Ramón pulled into the parking spot and shut off the engine. The rain outside the car displayed no signs of letting up. Relaxing back on the seat with a heartfelt sigh, he turned to Mariah. "I'm glad that's over. I hate driving in rain like that." His gaze caught Mariah's and something hot and intense flared between them. She felt a tingling in the pit of her stomach.

Just then, the steady drum of rain on the roof of the car increased to a frenzied pounding. He turned to check the cascading sheets of rain outside the car, then back to Mariah. "I guess we'll just have to make a run for it, unless you want to spend the time waiting in the car."

"And end up dying of pneumonia?" She released his hand and gathered her purse, mentally preparing herself as he hit the automatic door locks. "Let's go for it."

"Wait a minute." Ramón shrugged out of his jacket and passed the damp garment to her. The inside still held the warmth from his body. "You need this more than I do."

Heat rushed to her face. "I was wondering if you'd noticed."

"Oh, I noticed." A sensual note crept into his tone as he helped her put an arm in the jacket. His gaze touched hers, a sexy light in it. "I could hardly keep my eyes on the road. You could make me forget to breathe, Mariah."

The temperature in car rose several degrees as their gazes held. He leaned towards her, a hungry look in his hot gray eyes. Her lips parted unconsciously, anticipating his kiss. His lips touched hers, and then his tongue was stroking hers in a shockingly sensual dance. The delightfully unique and intoxicating taste of him drove her wild. She moaned, one hand twisting in his thick hair, and the other pulling him closer. She couldn't seem to get close enough. The strap on her dress slid down, exposing the top of her breasts as she wiggled in the seat. His warm hand caressed her thighs, moving higher and higher until he reached their apex. He held her lace-covered sex in his hands, kneading it with his fingers, moving his palm against her mound.

She gasped, panting out his name, "Ramón." Arching against him, she ached to give herself to him, to give him anything and everything he wanted. The car windows steamed up.

He broke their kiss, his lips moving down her neck to the exposed tops of her breasts. Then he stopped so suddenly that she cried out to him, "No, no." She didn't want him to stop.

Ramón spoke urgently, his voice raw with passion. "You're driving me crazy, Mariah. Yes or no?" One finger slipped beneath the elastic of her black lace panties and moved in and out of the moisture in her center.

"Yes," she whispered, melting against him. She saw everything through a sensual haze.

His free hand tilted her chin up, an almost savage look in his burning gray eyes. "No regrets?"

"No regrets." She pulled him closer, her fingers stroking the hardened length of his erection. She'd learned that what she felt for Ramón could not be controlled or denied.

He kissed her hard, his mouth and hands coaxing, caressing, and thrilling her, all the while letting her know just how much he wanted her. This time when he pulled away, he said huskily. "Not here. In the house. We've got all night." His fingers shook as he helped her put the other arm into his jacket and button it.

In a torrent of cold rain, she followed him up the steps and into the house. She stepped into the warm, dry, lighted interior and closed the door. She saw him in the living room as she kicked off her shoes. He was already stripping off the wet shirt and tossing it into the hallway with his shoes. She walked towards him, the sight of him drawing her like a warm fire. The golden skin of his lean muscled chest gleamed in the light, begging for her touch. Giving in to temptation, Mariah extended a hand to stroke his chest, trailing her fingers down to his belt buckle.

Ramón leaned down and kissed her hungrily, the warm velvet of his mouth and wild, exciting taste of him sending warm shivers of desire coursing through her. She met his gaze. With trembling fingers, she unbuckled the belt and pulled down his zipper. Her fingers stroked the hardened length of him. He was more than ready for her.

"Anything you want," he whispered. With enough heat to fuse metal, their lips met in another thrilling kiss. Quickly peeling off the wet pants, he stood before her in a well-filled pair of dark blue briefs. He was beautiful, like an expensive ad for men's underwear.

Wonderingly, she touched him, her mouth skimming across his chest and moving lower until he pulled her into his arms, his hot mouth melting to hers in several lush, wet kisses. "I want you," she whispered against his lips. *I love you.*

His fingers danced along the surface of her skin, smoothing the waterlogged dress down the length of her body. His mouth followed the same path as the dress, warming her as he tasted her skin. Shivering, she stepped out of the dress, reaching for him as he tossed the garment onto the wet pile in the hall.

Ramón dropped to his knees. "I like the underwear," he whispered hoarsely, his lips on her thigh. "Did you wear them just for me?"

Mariah nodded, her legs giving way when he traced the edges of the lace with his tongue. He caught her in his arms and laid her down on the carpet. Nuzzling her sex through the black lace he asked, "Do you taste as good as you smell? Because if you do, I want it all." Hooking his fingers in each side of her lace panties, he pulled them over her hips, down her legs, and off.

Mariah tried to sit up, but Ramón held her ankles firmly. "Let me do this, Mariah. I want a taste of honey. It's all I thought about on the drive home. I want to love you like you've never been loved before."

She moaned, passion and desire rising in her like the hottest fire, clouding her brain. Ramón's lips traced a burning path up her long legs from her ankle to the smooth caramel colored insides of her soft thighs. He buried his face between her thighs and like someone lingering over a bowl of gourmet ice cream, lovingly pleasured her. Her body vibrated with liquid fire, the tight knot within her demanding release as she gripped his head and undulated against him, crying out his name. Her breath came in long, low, surrendering moans of satisfaction.

As she lay limp and spent, Ramón stood and gathered her into his arms. "That was just the appetizer. This is going to be so good," he promised, as he carried her down the hall into his bedroom.

"Put me down," she said, giggling when he dropped her on the high, bouncy bed.

He peeled off his briefs and followed her down on the bed. She gasped at the first full tantalizing contact of their bodies. Thrilled, her hands stroked the warm sculpted length of his body, the satin smoothness of his rock hard erection. They rolled on the bed, kissing and touching each other in divine ecstasy. Ramón's hands explored her breasts intimately. Delicately, his tongue laved the chocolate-colored nipples, his mouth opening to cover one breast while his hand moved between her thighs.

Unable to take much more, she rolled with him until she ended up on top, tracing the hard buds of his nipples with the tips of her fingers. Feeling his body tighten in response, she licked them lovingly. "I want you. I want you inside me now," she whispered, trailing her lips lower and lower.

Ramón slipped out of her arms, moving to the edge of the bed to get a foil package from the nightstand. With quick efficiency, he opened the package, removed the condom, and smoothed it on. "Come and get me," he said with a smile.

Mariah crawled across the bed on her hands and knees. When she reached him, the warm length of his body curved around her.

She cried out his name in sweet agony as he pushed into her, filling her so she thought she'd burst. If only they could stay joined like this forever. Her cries were nearly screams when he began to rock with piston-like precision. Writhing and shaking beneath his sensual assault, Mariah gripped his hard thighs. The wild rocky tempo accelerated until they reached the pinnacle and floated down to earth. Her body hummed like a piece of well-oiled machinery.

In the aftermath, Ramón pulled her into the center of the bed with him. They lay entwined beneath the sheets, their bodies still damp from lovemaking. Curving his arms around her, Ramón kissed her temple and whispered very softly as he drifted off to sleep. "I still love you, Mariah McCleary."

Mariah's eyes flew open. Ramón breathed gently with his eyes closed. Was he asleep? This was the time to take a stand and reveal her feelings. She opened her mouth but the words stuck in her throat. When she could speak, she called his name softly. There was no answer. Hoping he was asleep, she snuggled closer and pressed her lips to his moist skin until she drifted off.

Have I died and gone to heaven? Ramón pressed a button on his remote and then lay as still as possible. On his music system in the background, Barry White sang of love, love, and more love. This was his fantasy. Curled against the naked length of his body was the warm softness of the woman he loved. The fresh fragrance of shampoo mixed with her special scent to stir his blood. He stared at the long dark lashes brushing her caramel-colored cheeks and her lush mouth still swollen from his kisses. They'd made love in his bed twice last night, and once in the shower. Was it any wonder that she still slept deeply?

He'd always considered Mariah a sensuous woman. What a joy to have his thought confirmed so enthusiastically. No matter what she said about loving him like a brother, she still wanted him physically. They'd been all over each other. He'd never loved any woman the way he loved Mariah, physically or emotionally.

Mariah snuggled closer in her sleep, the chocolate-colored tips of her breasts sliding along his chest to further stir his blood. He watched her nipples harden. One long shapely leg draped across his thighs. Ramón cursed under his breath as he drew a shaking hand down the curving length of her body to cup her rounded buttocks. He'd tried to let her sleep hadn't he?

Like a magnet drawing metal, her breasts drew his aching fingers. He massaged the soft globes, his fingers rubbing the sensitive tips. She moaned softly as he shifted beneath her, maneuvering until he bent over her to tantalize the buds which had swollen to their fullest. He took one soft breast into his mouth and sucked gently.

"Ramón," she sighed, her fingers delving into his hair.

He inclined his head and she pulled him forward until their mouths met in dreamy intimacy on a deliciously hot, wet kiss. He moved his mouth over hers, reveling in its softness as his hands stroked the curves of her body. She moaned low in her throat, one hand stroking his chest and the other gripping his buttocks. He was on fire, his body aching with need.

They rolled on the bed in a glorious haze of passion, hungrily touching, feeling, and kissing. Landing on top, she straddled him, a teasing look in her brown eyes. "Good morning," she said in a low provocative tone as she slowly sank onto his throbbing member. He heard her soft gasp of pleasure. His world shifted with pure explosive pleasure. Ramón saw stars.

At first, she rode him slowly, holding his gaze till her eyes glazed over and closed with passion. Then she was a wild woman, racing the wind on her trusty steed. He thrust upwards, with her all the way until they leaped high and soared above the clouds. They held each other as they floated down to earth in a shower of sensation.

Kissing him, Mariah nestled close. Ramón pushed damp wisps of hair away from her face and gently kissed the satiny softness of her lips. "I must be dreaming," he said in low, awestruck tones. "You and me, together like this. I've wanted this for so long. You didn't even want to think about it. Then we had that one, unforgettable night. You brought me to my knees, Mariah. I didn't think I would ever get another chance." Ramón massaged the slender curve of her back.

"I was wrong. You don't know how much I missed you." Her troubled gaze met his. "I wanted you and needed you, but I couldn't admit it, not even to myself." She buried her face against his throat, her soft hands stroking his chest. "I just can't fight this anymore."

Pleasure flooded his senses when Mariah admitted that she wanted and needed him, but the barely concealed threads of fear in her eyes bothered him. She was afraid to love him. He didn't want to be viewed as some inevitable disease or affliction. He wanted her to return his love, freely and joyfully. "I missed you too." Ramón trailed a finger down her cheek. "Mariah, I'm really happy, and for the first time in more weeks than I care to count. You are my heart, do you know that?"

Snuggling closer, she tilted her head back up to look at him. He could have sworn he saw love lingering in the depths of hen sherry brown eyes. "You always did have a way with words."

"Would you want me to be any other way?"

"No, I guess not," she sighed, hugging him tightly. "I like you just the way you are."

"Stay with me for the rest of the day?" It took a lot to keep his tone light. Holding Mariah was like trying to hold water; it was always slipping through your fingers. He was determined not to blow it this time.

Her slight hesitation made him feel as though she'd kicked him in an old war wound. "I guess I could move the Saturday chores to Sunday."

"We can go on a picnic. There's a special place I know that's on a little island. I could borrow my buddy's boat to get there."

Her eyes lit up. "I'd like that."

He clasped her warm hands. "I thought you would. We could go get your car and then go by your place so you can change clothes."

"Don't you have to go into the office today?"

"I'm taking a break. I don't know when you'll come back, so I'm going to enjoy every minute with you."

"I'll be back. I can't deny you any more. There's something really strong between us, Ramón. I know so many things I need to say to you, but I can't. I…I need you to be patient with me."

"I'm not trying to rush you. You know how I feel about you, Mariah. I learned something while we were apart. You have to come to your own conclusions."

The rest of the day was a continuation of his dream with a lazy ride out on Lake St. Clair in the warm afternoon sun. They found a place to themselves on a little island and whiled away the rest of the day. For the first time in several months he simply relaxed and enjoyed being with Mariah and showering her with loving care and attention. He found himself memorizing bits of conversation and the way they were together in case she withdrew from him again.

Saying good night was harder than he'd imagined. His hands wandered all over her body in a search that left his own throbbing with pleasure. Lingeringly, he kissed Mariah in her front hallway. "Want me to stay?" he asked, knowing he shouldn't, but hating to leave her. She needed time alone to think.

"I do, but I need a little time to myself." She rubbed her forehead against his cheek. "I could get used to this."

"Me too." His hands traced the curve of her spine and settled on the rounded curve of her hips. He pulled her closer, his mouth in the hollow of her neck. She trembled against him.

She locked her arms around his neck and he felt the hardened tips of her breasts beneath the thin cotton shirt covering his chest. "Will you call me?"

"Yes," he rasped, tracing the curve of her ear with his tongue. "Try and stop me."

"Mmmmh," she moaned softly. "You're not playing fair."

"You're right." Ramón dropped his hands. "Do you really want me to leave?"

She stood with her head on his chest. "No, stay with me." Mariah took his hand and led him to her bedroom. "You can leave early in the morning."

THIRTEEN

Sunday morning sunshine filled Mariah's kitchen. Ramón skimmed the Sunday paper and drank coffee. The pleasant aromas of butter, ham, green pepper, onions, and cheese filled his nostrils and his stomach grumbled. In the background Mariah hummed an old Smokey Robinson tune as she made omelets. Sunlight warmed his face and arms and a sense of well being and belonging filled him. If every Sunday morning could be like this one, he'd be a happy man. He glanced over to where Mariah performed magic at the stove and a smile creased his face. He liked seeing her happy. He liked having contributed to her mood.

Reluctantly, he switched on his cell phone. Immediately, the voice mail symbol came up and the cell phone began ringing. Pressing the send button, he spoke into the receiver. On the other end, Phil's voice vibrated with excitement. Ramón's mind raced ahead with several questions to be discussed. By the time he hung up, he'd already agreed to come into the office for a special meeting. Ramón bent over the table lost in thought, his fingers drumming the surface at a furious rate.

In a black and gold silk kimono, Mariah shifted into his line of vision and set two fragrantly steaming plates of omelets and toast on the table. "Has something happened with the case?"

"Yes and no. Through further analysis of Marsh's blood, we've discovered he was HIV positive."

"Oh!" Mariah touched her fingers to her lips. "I keep remembering what I read in the newspaper. That man was such a womanizer. All I can think about is the cook's granddaughter, and the baby she's expecting. You don't think it's his, do you? When they did a close up of her going into court, she seemed so young and innocent. Hatten's wife admitted having an affair with him. I don't like her much, but no one deserves to be exposed to HIV. Did he know he was HIV positive?"

"He discussed it with his doctor several months before his death."

"When I think of all the women he messed around with, it just makes me want to gag."

"The man had no conscience. He was the scum of the earth," Ramón said in a disgusted tone.

With sunlight shining in her hair, Mariah settled into the cushioned chair across from him and placed her napkin in her lap. "Sounds like you guys need to have a major strategy session today."

"That's a fact. We're meeting at eleven. It's time to tighten up the story for everyone with a motive. Maybe the end's in sight."

"I hope so. You've all worked so hard."

He clasped one of her soft hands across the table and gently squeezed it. "Well, that's the end to my weekend. I've been living my dreams."

Smiling at him, Mariah returned the pressure of his fingers. She seemed to glow with happiness. "I'm still up on cloud twenty-one."

Warmed by the glow, he leaned closer. "Where do we go from here?" It was too late to call the words back. He watched her expression dim with guilt and frustration. This was obviously not the time to press for a declaration of love or some form of commitment. Would he ever experience such a moment with Mariah? Ramón's spirits sank. They'd come so far in the past two days. Were they going backwards already?

She continued to hold his hand for several beats and then carefully released it. "I—I don't know," she stammered. "Can't we just take one day at a time?"

Ramón grabbed his napkin and placed it in his lap. He'd known it wouldn't be easy, but how much could he take? Trying to be reasonable, he said. "As long as it doesn't fade into forever."

Mariah's anxious gaze met his. "It won't, I promise." She idly fingered the tines of her fork. "I can't seem to think straight when it comes to us."

"That's strange, I've got the same problem," he said in an effort to lighten the mood. "Do you think it'll go away?"

A ghost of a smile eased her lips. "Quit teasing me, Ramón."

"Would I do that?"

She rolled her eyes. "All the time."

Ramón retrieved his fork, dug into the omelet, and shoveled a forkful into his mouth. "Mmmmh, this omelet tastes almost as good as you do."

"I'm not sure that's a compliment." She began to eat her own omelet.

"It is, believe me, it is. You rank right up there with fine wines and the sweetest nectar. You're a feast for the senses."

"Thank you." Mariah's lips curved into a genuine smile. "Flattery may get you another kiss."

He played along. "Is that all? I thought...I thought that maybe—"

"Now I know you're kidding." She set down her fork and took a sip of her coffee. "You've got to be almost as sore as I am. Ramón, it was great, and I enjoyed every minute of it, but we were too enthusiastic." Sensing something in his expression, she paused and put the cup down. "That's the real problem, isn't it? You're afraid I'll run away from you."

"Will you?" He bit into the raisin toast.

She swallowed more coffee. "No. You're just going to have to trust me on this."

"I'll give it my best. You're certainly worth waiting for."

Mariah released her breath in a puff of exasperation. "Huh! What's left to wait for?"

"I love you. I want it all."

"You're pushing again."

The expression accompanying her words warned him that the emotional distance between them was lengthening. "I'm sorry." One hand shot out and covered hers. "Fifteen more minutes and you'll be well rid of me."

"I don't want to be rid of you, Ramón. I care about you, and it is not in the least trivial. My feelings for you are so strong and passionate that it's like being drawn into a whirlpool. Sometimes I'm afraid I'll drown, but I'm not ready to go back to the beach. I need to see you."

"And I need to see you." His mouth caught Mariah's in series of kisses across the table. "Hold on to me, I'll never let you drown."

She caught his face in her hands, her sherry brown eyes pleading with him. "Just be patient with me, okay?"

"Okay." When she looked at him like that he couldn't deny her anything. In many ways he was living his dream. He'd come a long way with Mariah. All he had to do was stay with it till the end.

As soon as Ramón's car pulled off, Mariah locked the door and sagged against the frame. She was heading back to bed and this time she was going to sleep. On the way back to her room she thought of Ramón, and all that had happened within the last two days. It had been inevitable. She was not a person who engaged in casual sex, and besides Ramón, there had only been Cotter. So why couldn't she just swallow her fear and tell the man she loved him? What she felt had more depth than she cared to explore. So what was she afraid of? It wasn't as if Ramón would abandon her as Cotter had. Her stomach clenched at the thought. She'd have to make him understand.

In her bedroom, Mariah slipped off the silk kimono and slid between the beige cotton sheets. The lingering fragrance of Ramón's cologne mixed with the pungent odor of sex clung to the sheets, filling her thoughts with memories.

Wrapping her arms around herself, Mariah sighed and drifted off to sleep.

In the air-conditioned conference room of his law office across town, Ramón shifted in his brown leather chair. On his left sat a secretary, studiously making changes to their list and descriptions of the various suspects in the Gerald Hatten murder trial. The casually dressed members of defense team sat around the conference table, their expressions serious. If they kept the pressure on, they could win this case. He could feel it.

On the other side of the long, carved mahogany table, one of the junior associates went over one of the theories they'd been using to defend Gerald Hatten. "We know that Belle Hatten was having an affair with Marsh. Her husband was planning to divorce her, and because of their prenuptial agreement, she would only get a small settlement. Her friend testified that she'd been calling herself the next Mrs. Marsh. Suppose she found out about the other women and the fact that he may have exposed her to AIDS, killed him, then set herself up for life by framing her husband for the murder. Just prior to a party at her home, she spirited the gun from the case and hid it, then convinced a friend to say she was there when Marsh was murdered."

Phil grabbed the coffeepot from the center of the table and poured himself a cup. "Theory number two: Julie Marsh killed her husband. He was always screwing around with other women and didn't try to hide it. He'd become HIV positive as a result of his activities and possibly infected her. She couldn't take any more. The night of the party she took the gun from Hatten's case, caught her husband alone at the office one night, and shot him. Then she managed to slip back into her house without the neighbors seeing her."

Ramón slowly drew his fingers back and forth across his forehead. They needed more theory, and a lot more evidence to back it up, if they were going to win this case. "We've gone over all the obvious suspects and their motives, so let's try something different."

Phil rubbed his hands together. "Such as?"

"How about someone working in his home who may have been virtually invisible, like one of the maids, the cook, or the cleaning crew?"

The private investigator spoke up. "The cook's seventeen-year-old niece had been working there for about a year. She quit suddenly, but her family claims that it was because she was pregnant and had to get married."

Remembering Mariah's comments about the pregnant teen, Ramón flipped a pencil in his hand, his eyes touching on each of the team members until they settled on the thin, tired-looking private investigator. "Marsh was a real dog around women, especially the young ones. Was she pretty?"

"A real looker." The investigator pulled a photo from his file on the table and passed it around.

"Suppose Marsh messed around with the girl and the baby is his? If it were my daughter, I'd have been tempted to put him away permanently."

The investigator pushed his wire-rimmed glasses back up on his nose and made a note on his pad. "I'll see what I can come up with."

Ramón nodded. "Any other ideas?"

Phil spoke up from the other side of the conference table. "What about his personal assistant? Everyone knew she was sleeping with him. Just because she no longer works for the company doesn't mean she didn't make one last trip back to the office for revenge."

"She's got a good alibi, but I'll check on her again." The investigator added to the notes on his pad.

"It's great that the traces of blood on the gun aren't Hatten's, but we can't hang our hats on that." Ramón continued. "Some blood types are pretty common, so I'm betting that a number of the people involved will share the same blood type. We need statistics on blood type and blood factors. How many people actually have this blood factor? You guys know the drill." One of the associates taking copious notes nodded, and Ramón asked, "Can you handle that?"

After she'd agreed to get the statistics he continued, "The police really need an actual sample from each suspect but don't have enough evidence to get a sample from anyone but Gerald Hatten. If we could make a good case and shake something loose, it's possible they could get a court order to force some of the other suspects to submit a sample for blood and DNA testing." At that moment he spotted his secretary at the door waving and a man behind her with a rolling cart. He said, "Let's break for lunch. After lunch, we can go over the line-up for tomorrow's testimony, and then we can all go home."

It was evening when Ramón let himself into his silent condo. His memories of yesterday were so strong that he almost expected to see Mariah appear from one of the rooms in the back. Glad he'd grabbed a sandwich and eaten on the way home, he went straight to his answering machine and pressed the replay button.

Mariah's warm voice flowed over him like a physical caress. "Hi. I just woke up. I've been sleeping all afternoon. Just wanted to make sure you'd made it back and were resting up for tomorrow. Call me back before you go to bed, okay?"

Quickly, he dialed her number and counted the number of times the phone rang. After the third ring, her answering machine picked up. He left a brief message and hung up in disappointment. With his decision to avoid pressuring her, he'd also decided to let her call him first. The theme of the evening seemed to be telephone tag.

Dragging his tired body into the bathroom, he stripped and threw the clothes into the hamper. Then he stood beneath the hot spray and let the water pound him for several minutes. When he finally stepped out of the shower to grab a towel, he felt refreshed. Wrapping the towel around his waist, he headed for the bedroom. When was the last time he'd had a good night's sleep? By the time she called back to say she'd been playing tennis with Sonia, he was so groggy that they only talked briefly.

In court several days later, Ramón stood up, gathering himself to speak. The prosecution had given its closing remarks yesterday with a moving presentation and impassioned pleas that were quite convincing. They'd made Gerald Hatten look guilty as hell. The media had given them an "A" for effort and effect. Could he top that? He had to. Gerald Hatten was an innocent man, and he would remind everyone of that fact.

The hungry silence in the courtroom stretched towards the heavens, drawing all sound. Ramón glanced quickly at his client whose face appeared calm despite his trembling hands beneath the table. He could almost see the question in some of the jurors' eyes. Did he do it?

Showtime! This was his opportunity to capitalize on all their hard work. Removing moist palms from his pocket, Ramón straightened his shoulders and took a deep breath. Releasing it slowly, he made eye contact with each juror, and began to speak. "Ladies and gentlemen, today you sit in this court as the unique focus and instrument of our justice system. The life of my client, Gerald Hatten, is in your hands. Gerald Hatten is an innocent man.

"Let's look at the evidence against him. He had a partner, John Marsh, who betrayed his trust by pilfering company funds and conducting an affair with Hatten's wife. But on the night of August 10, Gerald Hatten was not in Detroit executing his errant partner, he was in his Huntington Woods home asleep."

With all eyes upon him, Ramón paused dramatically to let his words sink in. The silence roared in his ears. Then he began to walk and talk in a synchronized manner as he ticked off the facts in client's favor. "We have his neighbor's sworn testimony that at the crucial time, his car was parked in his driveway. The weapon used to kill John Marsh was stolen from my client's home, months before the murder, and planted in a locker at his health club, but the real killer left one important clue: a smattering of type AB negative blood on the handle. As shown here in court, neither my client nor the victim possesses this particular blood type, but at least two other people with motive and opportunity have blood type AB negative. Last week in court, we learned that John Marsh recently discovered he had AIDS. He was a promiscuous man, likely to have endangered many women. Among those endangered women with motive and opportunity were his wife, Julie, Gerald Hatten's wife, Belle, and Raina Flanks, his cook's pregnant seventeen-year-old daughter..."

Lifting a voluminous court document from the table, Ramón fluttered the pages and tossed it back. "Does the evidence presented by the prosecution show that Gerald Hatten fatally shot John Marsh on August 10, without a shadow of a doubt? I think not. Belle Hatten, a more likely suspect, had been exposed to the HIV virus by John Marsh and had been threatened with divorce by her husband because of her relationship with Marsh. What better way to get revenge and cut her losses than to steal her husband's gun, shoot Marsh, and conveniently drop her husband's watch at the scene? On the evening of August 10, witnesses saw her with a bandaged index finger where she'd broken the nail so close to the cuticle that it bled. She could have broken that nail while pulling the trigger on her husband's gun. Medical reports show that Belle Hatten has the type AB blood found on the gun, including the RH-negative factor. I'd bet money that blood tests will show that Belle Hatten's blood is on the gun."

"That's not true! That's not true!" Belle Hatten jumped to her feet, screaming shrilly. "He's the murderer. He killed John because of me and the money! Don't let him get away with it!"

The judge swung the gavel several times. When he'd finished, two court officials forcibly removed a kicking and screaming Belle Hatten from the courtroom.

Several moments of stunned silence passed before Ramón turned back to face the jurors. "And what about Marsh's cook, Mary Hanks? Five years of faithful service to John Marsh and he repays her by getting her underage granddaughter pregnant! Mary Flanks has no one to collaborate her alibi for the night of August 10 and records show that she too has the blood type found on the gun! She too had motive and opportunity to get rid of John Marsh..."

When Ramón finished speaking, the emotions in the room were so strong he could almost touch them. Had he accomplished his goal? He'd given it his best. Ramón studied the members of the jury. Two middle-aged women gazed at Gerald Hatten sympathetically. A few of the other jurors looked thoughtful. All he could do now was pray.

Mariah pulled into the lot, parked her car next to Ramón's, and then got out into the cooling evening sun. Ramón was cooking dinner. She smoothed down the short black evening dress with the rhinestoned bodice he'd asked her to wear and flexed her feet in the rhinestoned heels. The outfit made her appear taller, and her legs longer.

Mariah stepped up on the porch and rang the bell. Immediately, Ramón opened the door, looking darkly handsome in an elegant black dress shirt and matching pants. She drank in the scent of Ramón, soap, cologne, and a hint of chocolate mint. The frank love and welcome in his expression made her heart leap. He still loved her. Why was she always so surprised?

"Hello gorgeous!" His gaze wandered over her like a physical caress, lingering on her legs and moving up to her lips. Taking her hand, he gently pulled her into the hall and shut the door.

"Hey there, handsome!" she quipped in return.

"I need my daily dose," he whispered, pulling her into his arms and kissing her senseless.

Mariah moaned with pleasure. When the kiss ended, they simply stood holding each other. "Seems like I haven't seen you in a long time," she sighed, nuzzling her face against the warmth of his neck.

"It's been a long twelve hours and twenty minutes, but who's counting?" he teased.

Tilting her face up, she brushed his lips with a gentle kiss. "Every minute seemed like an hour."

"I feel the same way." He framed her face with his hands. "So what are we going to do about it?"

"Have each other before we have dinner?" she suggested with a mischievous grin as she pressed herself against the length of his body. Her nipples hardened.

"No, I had a special evening planned." His warm hands slid down to cup her hips. "But after that, I'm all yours."

Mariah's lips met his in one last, drugging kiss. She could get used to this. She nearly stumbled when the kiss ended.

"That good, huh?" Ramón took her hand and started towards the dining room.

"Mmm-hmm!" she said, balancing herself on the heels as she followed him into the dining room. The linen-covered table was set for two with his best china and crystal. Carefully, Ramón seated her and then sat down across from her. Then he surprised her by lifting a little bell from the center of the table and ringing it.

Mariah's jaw dropped when the kitchen door opened and a waiter dressed in a black suit appeared with a bottle of wine. Dark-haired and pudgy looking, he introduced himself and then began pouring the wine. Then she heard the sounds of someone moving about in the kitchen and realized that there was at least one other catering staff member.

When the waiter returned to the kitchen, she turned to Ramón and said, "I'm glad you made me wait. What's for dinner?" Whatever it was smelled so good her stomach grumbled.

He gave her an enigmatic smile and said, "Wait and see."

The food was delicious. The first course was French onion soup, followed by a light spinach salad. The mouth-watering main course was paella with chicken, shrimp, crab, and sausage in the saffron rice. Mariah and Ramón flirted shamelessly while they stuffed themselves. Then they congratulated the rosy-cheeked chef, who owned the gourmet catering service. Sipping the rest of her wine, Mariah watched Ramón thank them, discreetly pay them, and then let them out.

After they'd gone, he stood gazing at her, an enigmatic expression on his face. "Ramón," she spoke softly. He walked to her and kissed her gently on the lips. Taking her by the hand, he led her into the living room and settled her into a cushioned chair.

Kneeling by her chair, he framed her face with his hands and covered her lips in a series of soft, feather-light kisses. He gazed into her eyes and said, "You are my heart. I love you, Mariah. I have for a long time. It's the kind of love that's forever and always." His tongue traced her lips and danced with hers, sending shivers of desire racing through her body to form a wild swirl in the pit of her stomach. She fell forward, into his arms. He paused, his fingers trailing along the surface of her skin, only a slight hint of fear in his silvery gray gaze. "I can't imagine being without you. I need to have you with me, sharing your dreams, your love, and laughter with me forever. Can you do that? Will you marry me?" He pressed a small, velvet-covered box into her hands.

The breath she'd been holding came out in a large huff. The backs of her eyelids stung with emotion. Ramón had asked her to many him. With shaking fingers, she swung open the top of the heart-shaped box . For a moment, the world stopped spinning. Mariah gasped. Her grandmother's ring winked at her from the bed of velvet. Her heart swelled with love. Love for Ramón, happiness and joy at the sight of her grandmother's ring, and appreciation for Ramón's thoughtfulness overwhelmed her. She couldn't seem to catch her breath.

"I couldn't bear for you to lose it," he whispered. "When Mom told me that you were thinking of using the ring to get the extra money, I called the auction gallery and made arrangements to buy it. Remember, you said you couldn't get married without it?"

"I remember." Quick tears filled her eyes and spilled down her cheeks in twin rivers of emotion.

Ramón licked the tears from her skin. "Does this mean no?"

Unable to speak, she shook her head and threw her arms around him, hugging him tight. He simply held her then, caressing her back and whispering nonsense until she relaxed a little. She loved him. She did! And she wanted to be with him. Why couldn't she get the words out? How could she let him think she didn't love him? He was a man any woman would be proud to claim and she loved him more than she could ever say.

Pushing back, she reached up to frame his face with her hands. The pain in his eyes burned her like acid, but the words stuck in her throat, almost choking her. "I—I—"

"You want time to think about it," he finished for her in a tone that failed to hide his disappointment. "You love me, Mariah. You and I both know that. I can see it in your eyes when you look at me and in the way you touch me. Why can't you say it? Marry me. Commitment is the highest form of love. Don't you want to commit yourself to us, to all we can be? I'll never love anyone the way I love you and no one will ever love you like I do."

He was right. If she lost Ramón, she'd never find another love like his. She wouldn't want to. Panic like she'd never known welled up in her throat. Every one of her beloved family members was lost; there hadn't been a thing she could do to keep them with her, but she could save her relationship with Ramón. All she had to do was admit her love and agree to many him.

Her stomach churned with anxiety. She couldn't answer his questions. Instead, she endured his words and mentally chastised herself. Finally, she begged off one last time, "I can't imagine saying no to you, Ramón, but I'm not ready to say yes. I need a couple of days."

Ramón took several moments to let it sink in, then his kiss was full of sensual persuasion. "Do you need to go home alone to think about it?" His voice resonated against her skin.

Desire and need overwhelmed her. "I need you," she whispered, pulling his head closer so that their lips met in a deep, searing kiss. "That's all I want to think about now."

Ramón stood, taking her hand, and led her to the bedroom.

Because of her late nights with Ramón, Mariah dragged herself into work late that Monday and Tuesday. To make up for it, she arrived early on Wednesday to do paperwork. When Lynn arrived at nine, they sat at the conference table and had cappuccino and coffee together.

"How's your mother?" Mariah asked, noticing that Lynn seemed more happy and relaxed than she had in ages.

"She's fine." Lynn put her cup down. "She actually went home Monday."

Raising an eyebrow, Mariah paused with her cup halfway to her lips. "How'd you manage that?"

"I guess she finally realized that I didn't need her to stay and direct my life." Lynn smiled. "Remember I told you Mama and I were having dinner with Anthony and his mother?"

Mariah nodded. "You never did tell me how it all turned out."

"Well that's because you disappeared for a few days..."

The blood rushed to Mariah's face. She sighed. "Come on, Lynn, don't change the subject."

Lynn merely grinned and the words tumbled from her lips. "Remember how nervous I was? I just knew it was going to be so awful that it would end everything. Well, I got a big surprise. Anthony's mother was really nice. She said that she knew from the moment Anthony met me that I would be an important part of his life."

Lynn paused, one hand tracing back and forth over the edge of the table while she dreamily stared off in space. "He's talked about me so much that she felt as if she knew me. And can you believe that coming by to say hello to you each day has been his excuse to see me?" Lynn giggled. "He wouldn't let her tell me any more."

Mariah laughed too. "It sure took him a long time to make his move."

"Yes it did." Lynn's smile faded a bit. "Because of the race thing, he took it very slow. He'd never seen me with a white guy before, so he wanted to be sure I was open to the idea."

"Anthony wasn't the only one taking it slow." Mariah sipped her cappuccino. "You've been halfway in love with the man for ages."

It was Lynn's turn to blush. "How did you know?"

"For one thing, you're in another world whenever he comes into the room. You watch him like a starving woman looking at a steak. I remember once having to ask you three times about an appointment while he was in the room."

"Now you're exaggerating," Lynn said, throwing Mariah a look of utter disbelief.

"Am I?" Mariah laughed. "What about that little tiny cheesecake you made for us and the large one you made for Anthony?"

Lynn's hand shot up to cover her mouth. "You're not being fair. His cheesecake was a thank you gift for cutting my hair."

"Of course," Mariah answered in ringing tones of skepticism. Lynn looked so embarrassed then, that she decided to ease up on her teasing. "So how did the two moms get along?"

Lynn shrugged. "Okay. They probably won't call each other to chat, but they were cordial and pleasant to each other."

"Great." Mariah finished her drink. "I wonder when you'll get to meet his dad?"

"He was invited." Lynn swallowed, and when her gaze met Mariah's, her eyes were filled with resignation. "When his dad found out about us, he was upset. I guess they had some serious arguments about it." She twisted her fingers in her lap. "Anthony's been trying to bring him around to the idea, but so far he's had no luck. I may never get to meet him."

"That's just too sad," Mariah said tossing their empty foam cups into the trash. "Would Anthony marry without his father's approval?"

Massaging her bare ring finger, Lynn answered, "He swears that he's not going to let anyone come between us." She hesitated a moment, then blurted out, "We've been talking about getting married. Of course, we still have some things to work out."

Mariah leaned over and hugged Lynn. "I'm glad things are working out for you guys."

Lynn returned her hug and asked slyly, "All right, what's the scoop with you and Ramón?"

Mariah found herself smiling all over again. "We're together now. I…I love him, Lynn."

"I knew it all the time!" Lynn laughed aloud. "So when are you guys getting married? He did ask, didn't he?"

"Yes." Mariah's head dipped and she gripped the edge of her chair. "But I haven't given him an answer yet."

"I thought you said you loved him."

"I do." Mariah fiddled with the carryout bag. "But… the thought of marriage frightens me. I'm poised on the brink of having everything I've ever wanted, and I'm afraid to say yes and afraid to say no. She bit her lip, her fingers drumming the tabletop. "What if he discovers that he doesn't really love me after all? What if I really mess things up and he leaves me? What if he suddenly gets hurt and dies?" Mariah's eyes filled with tears. "I'm no good with relationships of any kind, Lynn. Somehow, some way, I always end up alone."

Lynn gave her a tissue and put both arms around her.

"Mariah McCleary, don't you know that what you're describing is the risk we all take, everyday? If you really love someone, Mariah, love is always worth the risk."

A few days later, the sounds of a joyous celebration filled Mariah's office. They'd just gone through a successful dry run for Cora Belson's Fashion Experience.

As their celebration ended, the television news anchor began a late breaking story about the Gerald Hatten murder trial. Gerald Hatten had been acquitted of murder.

"Yes!" With her short, black skirt whirling, Mariah pranced around her office in the throes of a victory dance. Lynn and Anthony sat at her conference table grinning at the little thirteen-inch color VCR/television set she'd placed on her desk. The red recording light was on. The Hatten jury had just found Gerald Hatten not guilty. What a victory! There was some justice in the world.

The news anchor and several reporters discussed the brilliant tactics of the defense and the effects of the gun on the case for at least another ten minutes while she stood transfixed, too thrilled to sit down. With a smile on her lips, Mariah turned up the sound on the little television.

Exhilarated, she went back to the conference table and dropped into the guest chair near her desk. She was waiting for the defense team to come out of the courthouse and talk to the press. Finally, Gerald Hatten's short, stocky figure emerged from the courthouse surrounded by the defense team. A bevy of reporters surged towards them, with camera bulbs flashing. In the bright afternoon sun, they walked to an impromptu podium and Gerald Hatten began to speak. His dark brown eyes misted as he spoke eloquently of his innocence and the dedicated and intelligent efforts of the defense team. Then he gave a moving statement about his belief in the fairness of the justice system.

As Hatten stepped aside, several reporters began firing questions at Ramón. He was calm, self-assured and confident in the face of his success. Looking incredibly handsome and competent in a black silk designer suit, he stepped to the microphone and began answering questions. The rest of the team surrounded him, ready to join in. Something tugged at her heart as she watched him, wishing she could be there with him. However, the view on television was much better than any she would have gotten by standing in the large crowd behind the reporters.

In the background, a car engine revved. Unease prickled along her spine as a peculiar sense of foreboding filled her. People rev their engines all the time, she told herself. She stared at the crowd of reporters and the onlookers behind them. Police barricades had been set up to keep traffic away.

The background sound of the car grew louder. Suddenly, a white sports utility vehicle smashed through the barricades closest to the podium and ploughed into the reporters. Ramón stood paralyzed in the path of the rampaging automobile. Why wasn't he moving? The car advanced through the crowd like a scene from an action thriller. With her heart in her throat, Mariah jumped to her feet, crying out in horror.

Please God, she prayed, icy fear twisting around her heart as the car smashed toward the podium with bruising force. Ramón just stood there, paralyzed. Panic grew within her, filling her with dread. "Move! Move! Come on, Ramón!" she urged in utter disbelief. How could he just stand there?

At the last minute, he scrambled towards safety, but it was too late. No, no! In slow motion the vehicle slammed into Ramón and several members of the defense team. With the violent impact, they flew backwards into the air to rain down in a heap near the battered and blood-stained white SUV as it finally came to rest.

Dry, heaving sobs shook Mariah. For several moments, not one of the three moved in the stunned silence. Her chest burned with a heavy, crippling ache. She'd just seen the end. Ramón was dead. He had to be. Oh God, I've lost Ramón too. For several agonizing moments she stood on shaking legs clutching her burning chest, unable to catch her breath. How could anyone live through that? Please God, let him be alive!

With an agonized cry, Mariah fell into a conference chair. Heaving, hiccupping sobs shook her. Had she just lost Ramón forever? She couldn't go through this again. If Ramón was dead, she wanted to die, too. Her teeth chattered so hard she couldn't stop them as she wrapped her arms about herself.

Lynn knelt by Mariah in shock. "This can't be happening. This can't be happening," she whispered as she brushed the hair back from Mariah's wet face and gently held her.

In the ensuing confusion, those who were not seriously injured moved away from the wreckage. Among them were a couple of reporters and a few members of the defense team. There was no sign of Ramón.

The screen split to continue showing the accident scene while also featuring the local news anchor. "Ladies and gentlemen, ladies and gentlemen, please bear with us," the news anchor announced in a choked voice. "There's been a terrible accident. A white Ford Expedition driven into the crowd by an unidentified woman has injured the Gerald Hatten defense team and several reporters. Their condition is unknown at this time. The emergency medical service has already been called and several are on their way. We now return to the scene where our reporter, John Corbett, will update you on the current situation."

"I'm so sorry, Mariah." Anthony knelt on the other side of her. "He may still be all right. Try to hold on to that thought," he said as he joined Lynn in placing comforting arms around her.

The television drew all eyes with a replay of the crash. Anthony stood up and moved towards it as if to turn it off. No, she had to see it again. Shaking her head from side to side, Mariah rocked back and forth. She gulped hard, hot tears racing down her cheeks as she endured a repeat showing of the accident. There was nothing to support a hope that any of the people who had been standing on the podium still lived.

Behind the reporter, the cries and moans of the surviving victims filled the background. Her trembling hands went to her face. A number of EMS trucks had arrived on the scene. Several police officers were helping the white uniformed medical personnel remove the injured from the wreckage. In a rare show of decency, the cameraman avoided filming the faces of the victims. A desperate prayer filled her thoughts as she strained her eyes, searching in vain for Ramón's black silk suit. Please let him be all right. Please don't let him leave me.

When the reporter on the scene announced that most of the victims were being taken to Detroit's Receiving Hospital, Mariah jumped to her feet. "I'm going down there. I've got to see him."

"I'll drive." Lynn's voice rang with command as she moved to her desk in the outer office to get her purse.

"I'm coming too," Anthony declared as Mariah went to her desk on spongy legs and retrieved her purse. He put his arms around her and led her to Lynn's blue Toyota.

In the car, Lynn kept the radio on the news station for updates. Mariah curled into a corner of the backseat, her mind churning with thoughts of Ramón. She kept seeing the way his face looked when he'd proposed only two days ago. Why hadn't she just said yes? She'd been afraid to throw her whole heart into her relationship with Ramón, and where had it gotten her? Now he'd never know how much she loved him, how much she wished they'd gotten married. Mariah bit down hard on her lip and tasted blood. She couldn't lose Ramón too! Please God, let Ramón be alive.

Helplessly, Mariah listened with anticipation and dread as the news station broadcast another update.

"Several survivors have been taken to Detroit Receiving Hospital. Two have been declared dead on the scene. Their names are being withheld until their families have been notified. The driver of the white Ford Expedition has been identified as Mrs. Belle Hatten, wife of the defendant. She is in police custody at Detroit Receiving and listed in serious condition, along with Gerald Hatten and two others. In other news today…"

Mariah's hand tightened on the seatbelt. So Belle Hatten had made one last desperate and deranged attempt to get her husband, and hurt several other people in the process. Against her will, her mind replayed the film footage of Ramón being tossed in the air by the impact of the car and disappearing beneath its wheels. A sob choked her. Anthony pulled her into his arms and comforted her.

At the hospital, Mariah was a crazy person, fighting her way through the crowd. Instinctively she said and did whatever was necessary to get her past the hospital staff. When a volunteer led her back into the emergency area, hope sprang within her. He was still alive.

There was no privacy here. The sounds of people crying, moaning, and doctors caring for patients filled the air. Just outside of a curtained area, she saw Judge Richards comforting a tearful Gloria. Mariah stared, trying to read the expression on his face and failing.

Gloria lifted her tear-streaked face and shook her head. "He's…he's just…"

Mariah stared, her mouth opening and closing and no sound coming out. No. She refused to believe he was gone.

Unable to speak, Gloria dissolved into tears.

Briefly, Mariah hugged Gloria. "I've got to see him."

Gloria nodded wordlessly and Mariah pulled open the curtain. A petite, dark- haired nurse stepped out. "We're going to move him in a few minutes. You can go in."

Hesitantly, she stepped into the makeshift area. Frightened of just what she would see, she lifted her eyes to the level of the bed. Slowly and painfully she shifted her gaze from his blanket-covered feet to his knees, to his chest, to his smiling mouth… His smiling mouth?!

"Ramón!" Thank you, God! In mere seconds, she was on the bed and in his arms, kissing him, and burying her face in his neck. His body tensed as he yelled out in pain. "Are you all right?" she cried.

With his good hand, he brushed the moisture from her cheeks. "Just beat up a bit. I've got a mild concussion and several cuts and bruises. They're keeping me overnight for observation."

"I was watching on television when it happened, and I thought, I thought…" Tears blinded her eyes, choking her voice. She pressed her wet face to his chest.

"You thought I was dead?" He lifted a bandaged hand and smoothed it along her back.

Mariah nodded, hugging him tighter, glorying in his warmth and vitality.

"Awowl," Ramón winced. "Careful, I've been abused. I thought I was going to die, too."

She leaned back, gazing into his battered face with love. A large red scrape went down the right half of his face. He had a black eye and several scratches on the left side of his face. With gentle fingers she traced the boundaries of the damage. Despite his injuries, he'd never been more handsome. Wonderingly, she gazed at him. She'd almost lost her chance at a future with him. "I'm glad you didn't. I love you so much. I was afraid I wouldn't get a chance to tell you."

Ramón pulled her to him, his kiss rough and gritty. "I know you love me."

"Really?" Her hands smoothed down the golden flesh of his shoulders.

"Really." His lips softened against hers, his kiss becoming deep and caressing.

A smile trembled over her lips. "I was so afraid you'd left me forever. Two people died. I couldn't be sure you weren't one of them until they led me back here." She held up her hand, showing him the finger with her grandmother's ring. "Suddenly nothing seemed to matter except the fact that I love you, want to be with you forever, and have your children..." A deep shuddering sigh shook her.

He took her hand and kissed her fingers. His eyes were questioning. "Are you sure you want to marry me?"

"Yes, and I'm so glad to have another chance to say it," she said, her tears evaporating. Emotion welled within her as she looked at him. Leaning forward, she brushed her lips against his. "I've been alone too long. You're the only man I've ever loved, Ramón, and as long as you'll have me, I want to be your wife."

His arms tenderly enfolded her. "When?"

"Anytime, any place you want." She nuzzled her face against his cheek.

"Did I hear you guys say you were getting married?" Gloria stepped into the room with the judge close behind her.

"Yes." Mariah moved off the bed to hug her. "I love Ramón, I have for a long time."

"I'm glad. You belong together." Gloria kissed her cheek.

"It's time both of you came to your senses," Judge Richards said from behind them.

"I've been outside this room thanking God for saving my son. When I saw the crash, I thought I'd lost him." Gloria sniffled.

"Me too." Mariah hugged Judge Richards.

"And now I thank him for sending you to us." Gloria began to cry again. "My son is getting married, and we couldn't ask for a better bride."

Mariah went back to the bed to sit beside Ramón. His arm snaked about her waist, pulling her close. "I love you," he whispered close to her ear. Mariah smiled.

"When is the wedding?" the judge asked.

Mariah turned to Ramón and met his loving gaze. She reveled in it, her well of happiness overflowing. Finally Ramón answered, "Just as soon as Mariah can put it together."

"A week? Certainly no more than a month." The words tumbled from her mouth. Her hand gripped Ramón's, drawing from his strength and vitality. "Anthony's designed a wedding dress just for me." Fleetingly she thought of Anthony, and hoped he'd soon be designing a gown for his own bride, Lynn.

"We've got to get started as soon as possible," Gloria said in growing excitement. "I know just the place for a wedding, and a friend of mine has a catering business..."

2007 Publication Schedule

January

Rooms of the Heart
Donna Hill
ISBN-13: 978-1-58571-219-9
ISBN-10: 1-58571-219-1
$6.99

A Dangerous Love
J. M. Jeffries
ISBN-13: 978-1-58571-217-5
ISBN-10: 1-58571-217-5
$6.99

February

Bound By Love
Beverly Clark
ISBN-13: 978-1-58571-232-8
ISBN-10: 1-58571-232-9
$6.99

A Love to Cherish
Beverly Clark
ISBN-13: 978-1-58571-233-5
ISBN-10: 1-58571-233-7
$6.99

March

Best of Friends
Natalie Dunbar
ISBN-13: 978-1-58571-220-5
ISBN-10: 1-58571-220-5
$6.99

Midnight Magic
Gwynne Forster
ISBN-13: 978-1-58571-225-0
ISBN-10: 1-58571-225-6
$6.99

April

Cherish the Flame
Beverly Clark
ISBN-13: 978-1-58571-221-2
ISBN-10: 1-58571-221-3
$6.99

Quiet Storm
Donna Hill
ISBN-13: 978-1-58571-226-7
ISBN-10: 1-58571-226-4
$6.99

May

Sweet Tomorrows
Kimberley White
ISBN-13: 978-1-58571-234-2
ISBN-10: 1-58571-234-5
$6.99

No Commitment Required
Seressia Glass
ISBN-13: 978-1-58571-222-9
ISBN-10: 1-58571-222-1
$6.99

June

A Dangerous Deception
J. M. Jeffries
ISBN-13: 978-1-58571-228-1
ISBN-10: 1-58571-228-0
$6.99

Illusions
Pamela Leigh Starr
ISBN-13: 978-1-58571-229-8
ISBN-10: 1-58571-229-9
$6.99

2007 Publication Schedule (continued)

July

Indiscretions
Donna Hill
ISBN-13: 978-1-58571-230-4
ISBN-10: 1-58571-230-2
$6.99

Whispers in the Night
Dorothy Elizabeth Love
ISBN-13: 978-1-58571-231-1
ISBN-10: 1-58571-231-1
$6.99

August

Bodyguard
Andrea Jackson
ISBN-13: 978-1-58571-235-9
ISBN-10: 1-58571-235-3
$6.99

Crossing Paths, Tempting Memories
Dorothy Elizabeth Love
ISBN-13: 978-1-58571-236-6
ISBN-10: 1-58571-236-1
$6.99

September

Fate
Pamela Leigh Starr
ISBN-13: 978-1-58571-258-8
ISBN-10: 1-58571-258-2
$6.99

Mae's Promise
Melody Walcott
ISBN-13: 978-1-58571-259-5
ISBN-10: 1-58571-259-0
$6.99

October

Magnolia Sunset
Giselle Carmichael
ISBN-13: 978-1-58571-260-1
ISBN-10: 1-58571-260-4
$6.99

Broken
Dar Tomlinson
ISBN-13: 978-1-58571-261-8
ISBN-10: 1-58571-261-2
$6.99

November

Truly Inseparable
Wanda Y. Thomas
ISBN-13: 978-1-58571-262-5
ISBN-10: 1-58571-262-0
$6.99

The Color Line
Lizzette G. Carter
ISBN-13: 978-1-58571-263-2
ISBN-10: 1-58571-263-9
$6.99

December

Love Always
Mildred Riley
ISBN-13: 978-1-58571-264-9
ISBN-10: 1-58571-264-7
$6.99

Pride and Joi
Gay Gunn
ISBN-13: 978-1-58571-265-6
ISBN-10: 1-58571-265-5
$6.99

Other Genesis Press, Inc. Titles

A Dangerous Deception	J.M. Jeffries	$8.95
A Dangerous Love	J.M. Jeffries	$8.95
A Dangerous Obsession	J.M. Jeffries	$8.95
A Drummer's Beat to Mend	Kei Swanson	$9.95
A Happy Life	Charlotte Harris	$9.95
A Heart's Awakening	Veronica Parker	$9.95
A Lark on the Wing	Phyliss Hamilton	$9.95
A Love of Her Own	Cheris F. Hodges	$9.95
A Love to Cherish	Beverly Clark	$8.95
A Risk of Rain	Dar Tomlinson	$8.95
A Twist of Fate	Beverly Clark	$8.95
A Will to Love	Angie Daniels	$9.95
Acquisitions	Kimberley White	$8.95
Across	Carol Payne	$12.95
After the Vows	Leslie Esdaile	$10.95
(Summer Anthology)	T.T. Henderson	
	Jacqueline Thomas	
Again My Love	Kayla Perrin	$10.95
Against the Wind	Gwynne Forster	$8.95
All I Ask	Barbara Keaton	$8.95
Ambrosia	T.T. Henderson	$8.95
An Unfinished Love Affair	Barbara Keaton	$8.95
And Then Came You	Dorothy Elizabeth Love	$8.95
Angel's Paradise	Janice Angelique	$9.95
At Last	Lisa G. Riley	$8.95
Best of Friends	Natalie Dunbar	$8.95
Beyond the Rapture	Beverly Clark	$9.95
Blaze	Barbara Keaton	$9.95
Blood Lust	J. M. Jeffries	$9.95
Bodyguard	Andrea Jackson	$9.95
Boss of Me	Diana Nyad	$8.95
Bound by Love	Beverly Clark	$8.95

Other Genesis Press, Inc. Titles (continued)

Breeze	Robin Hampton Allen	$10.95
Broken	Dar Tomlinson	$24.95
By Design	Barbara Keaton	$8.95
Cajun Heat	Charlene Berry	$8.95
Careless Whispers	Rochelle Alers	$8.95
Cats & Other Tales	Marilyn Wagner	$8.95
Caught in a Trap	Andre Michelle	$8.95
Caught Up In the Rapture	Lisa G. Riley	$9.95
Cautious Heart	Cheris F Hodges	$8.95
Chances	Pamela Leigh Starr	$8.95
Cherish the Flame	Beverly Clark	$8.95
Class Reunion	Irma Jenkins/ John Brown	$12.95
Code Name: Diva	J.M. Jeffries	$9.95
Conquering Dr. Wexler's Heart	Kimberley White	$9.95
Crossing Paths, Tempting Memories	Dorothy Elizabeth Love	$9.95
Cypress Whisperings	Phyllis Hamilton	$8.95
Dark Embrace	Crystal Wilson Harris	$8.95
Dark Storm Rising	Chinelu Moore	$10.95
Daughter of the Wind	Joan Xian	$8.95
Deadly Sacrifice	Jack Kean	$22.95
Designer Passion	Dar Tomlinson	$8.95
Dreamtective	Liz Swados	$5.95
Ebony Butterfly II	Delilah Dawson	$14.95
Echoes of Yesterday	Beverly Clark	$9.95
Eden's Garden	Elizabeth Rose	$8.95
Everlastin' Love	Gay G. Gunn	$8.95
Everlasting Moments	Dorothy Elizabeth Love	$8.95
Everything and More	Sinclair Lebeau	$8.95
Everything but Love	Natalie Dunbar	$8.95
Eve's Prescription	Edwina Martin Arnold	$8.95

Other Genesis Press, Inc. Titles (continued)

Falling	Natalie Dunbar	$9.95
Fate	Pamela Leigh Starr	$8.95
Finding Isabella	A.J. Garrotto	$8.95
Forbidden Quest	Dar Tomlinson	$10.95
Forever Love	Wanda Y. Thomas	$8.95
From the Ashes	Kathleen Suzanne Jeanne Sumerix	$8.95
Gentle Yearning	Rochelle Alers	$10.95
Glory of Love	Sinclair LeBeau	$10.95
Go Gentle into that Good Night	Malcom Boyd	$12.95
Goldengroove	Mary Beth Craft	$16.95
Groove, Bang, and Jive	Steve Cannon	$8.99
Hand in Glove	Andrea Jackson	$9.95
Hard to Love	Kimberley White	$9.95
Hart & Soul	Angie Daniels	$8.95
Heartbeat	Stephanie Bedwell-Grime	$8.95
Hearts Remember	M. Loui Quezada	$8.95
Hidden Memories	Robin Allen	$10.95
Higher Ground	Leah Latimer	$19.95
Hitler, the War, and the Pope	Ronald Rychiak	$26.95
How to Write a Romance	Kathryn Falk	$18.95
I Married a Reclining Chair	Lisa M. Fuhs	$8.95
Indigo After Dark Vol. I	Nia Dixon/Angelique	$10.95
Indigo After Dark Vol. II	Dolores Bundy/ Cole Riley	$10.95
Indigo After Dark Vol. III	Montana Blue/ Coco Morena	$10.95
Indigo After Dark Vol. IV	Cassandra Colt/ Diana Richeaux	$14.95
Indigo After Dark Vol. V	Delilah Dawson	$14.95
Icie	Pamela Leigh Starr	$8.95
I'll Be Your Shelter	Giselle Carmichael	$8.95

Other Genesis Press, Inc. Titles (continued)

I'll Paint a Sun	A.J. Garrotto	$9.95
Illusions	Pamela Leigh Starr	$8.95
Indiscretions	Donna Hill	$8.95
Intentional Mistakes	Michele Sudler	$9.95
Interlude	Donna Hill	$8.95
Intimate Intentions	Angie Daniels	$8.95
Jolie's Surrender	Edwina Martin-Arnold	$8.95
Kiss or Keep	Debra Phillips	$8.95
Lace	Giselle Carmichael	$9.95
Last Train to Memphis	Elsa Cook	$12.95
Lasting Valor	Ken Olsen	$24.95
Let Us Prey	Hunter Lundy	$25.95
Life Is Never As It Seems	J.J. Michael	$12.95
Lighter Shade of Brown	Vicki Andrews	$8.95
Love Always	Mildred E. Riley	$10.95
Love Doesn't Come Easy	Charlyne Dickerson	$8.95
Love Unveiled	Gloria Greene	$10.95
Love's Deception	Charlene Berry	$10.95
Love's Destiny	M. Loui Quezada	$8.95
Mae's Promise	Melody Walcott	$8.95
Magnolia Sunset	Giselle Carmichael	$8.95
Matters of Life and Death	Lesego Malepe, Ph.D.	$15.95
Meant to Be	Jeanne Sumerix	$8.95
Midnight Clear (Anthology)	Leslie Esdaile Gwynne Forster Carmen Green Monica Jackson	$10.95
Midnight Magic	Gwynne Forster	$8.95
Midnight Peril	Vicki Andrews	$10.95
Misconceptions	Pamela Leigh Starr	$9.95
Montgomery's Children	Richard Perry	$14.95
My Buffalo Soldier	Barbara B. K. Reeves	$8.95

Other Genesis Press, Inc. Titles (continued)

Naked Soul	Gwynne Forster	$8.95
Next to Last Chance	Louisa Dixon	$24.95
No Apologies	Seressia Glass	$8.95
No Commitment Required	Seressia Glass	$8.95
No Regrets	Mildred E. Riley	$8.95
Nowhere to Run	Gay G. Gunn	$10.95
O Bed! O Breakfast!	Rob Kuehnle	$14.95
Object of His Desire	A. C. Arthur	$8.95
Office Policy	A. C. Arthur	$9.95
Once in a Blue Moon	Dorianne Cole	$9.95
One Day at a Time	Bella McFarland	$8.95
Outside Chance	Louisa Dixon	$24.95
Passion	T.T. Henderson	$10.95
Passion's Blood	Cherif Fortin	$22.95
Passion's Journey	Wanda Y. Thomas	$8.95
Past Promises	Jahmel West	$8.95
Path of Fire	T.T. Henderson	$8.95
Path of Thorns	Annetta P. Lee	$9.95
Peace Be Still	Colette Haywood	$12.95
Picture Perfect	Reon Carter	$8.95
Playing for Keeps	Stephanie Salinas	$8.95
Pride & Joi	Gay G. Gunn	$15.95
Pride & Joi	Gay G. Gunn	$8.95
Promises to Keep	Alicia Wiggins	$8.95
Quiet Storm	Donna Hill	$10.95
Reckless Surrender	Rochelle Alers	$6.95
Red Polka Dot in a World of Plaid	Varian Johnson	$12.95
Reluctant Captive	Joyce Jackson	$8.95
Rendezvous with Fate	Jeanne Sumerix	$8.95
Revelations	Cheris F. Hodges	$8.95
Rivers of the Soul	Leslie Esdaile	$8.95

Other Genesis Press, Inc. Titles (continued)

Rocky Mountain Romance	Kathleen Suzanne	$8.95
Rooms of the Heart	Donna Hill	$8.95
Rough on Rats and Tough on Cats	Chris Parker	$12.95
Secret Library Vol. 1	Nina Sheridan	$18.95
Secret Library Vol. 2	Cassandra Colt	$8.95
Shades of Brown	Denise Becker	$8.95
Shades of Desire	Monica White	$8.95
Shadows in the Moonlight	Jeanne Sumerix	$8.95
Sin	Crystal Rhodes	$8.95
So Amazing	Sinclair LeBeau	$8.95
Somebody's Someone	Sinclair LeBeau	$8.95
Someone to Love	Alicia Wiggins	$8.95
Song in the Park	Martin Brant	$15.95
Soul Eyes	Wayne L. Wilson	$12.95
Soul to Soul	Donna Hill	$8.95
Southern Comfort	J.M. Jeffries	$8.95
Still the Storm	Sharon Robinson	$8.95
Still Waters Run Deep	Leslie Esdaile	$8.95
Stories to Excite You	Anna Forrest/Divine	$14.95
Subtle Secrets	Wanda Y. Thomas	$8.95
Suddenly You	Crystal Hubbard	$9.95
Sweet Repercussions	Kimberley White	$9.95
Sweet Tomorrows	Kimberly White	$8.95
Taken by You	Dorothy Elizabeth Love	$9.95
Tattooed Tears	T. T. Henderson	$8.95
The Color Line	Lizzette Grayson Carter	$9.95
The Color of Trouble	Dyanne Davis	$8.95
The Disappearance of Allison Jones	Kayla Perrin	$5.95
The Honey Dipper's Legacy	Pannell-Allen	$14.95
The Joker's Love Tune	Sidney Rickman	$15.95

Other Genesis Press, Inc. Titles (continued)

The Little Pretender	Barbara Cartland	$10.95
The Love We Had	Natalie Dunbar	$8.95
The Man Who Could Fly	Bob & Milana Beamon	$18.95
The Missing Link	Charlyne Dickerson	$8.95
The Price of Love	Sinclair LeBeau	$8.95
The Smoking Life	Ilene Barth	$29.95
The Words of the Pitcher	Kei Swanson	$8.95
Three Wishes	Seressia Glass	$8.95
Ties That Bind	Kathleen Suzanne	$8.95
Tiger Woods	Libby Hughes	$5.95
Time is of the Essence	Angie Daniels	$9.95
Timeless Devotion	Bella McFarland	$9.95
Tomorrow's Promise	Leslie Esdaile	$8.95
Truly Inseparable	Wanda Y. Thomas	$8.95
Unbreak My Heart	Dar Tomlinson	$8.95
Uncommon Prayer	Kenneth Swanson	$9.95
Unconditional	A.C. Arthur	$9.95
Unconditional Love	Alicia Wiggins	$8.95
Until Death Do Us Part	Susan Paul	$8.95
Vows of Passion	Bella McFarland	$9.95
Wedding Gown	Dyanne Davis	$8.95
What's Under Benjamin's Bed	Sandra Schaffer	$8.95
When Dreams Float	Dorothy Elizabeth Love	$8.95
Whispers in the Night	Dorothy Elizabeth Love	$8.95
Whispers in the Sand	LaFlorya Gauthier	$10.95
Wild Ravens	Altonya Washington	$9.95
Yesterday Is Gone	Beverly Clark	$10.95
Yesterday's Dreams, Tomorrow's Promises	Reon Laudat	$8.95
Your Precious Love	Sinclair LeBeau	$8.95

Order Form

Mail to: Genesis Press, Inc.
P.O. Box 101
Columbus, MS 39703

Name ____
Address ______________________________________
City/State ______________________ Zip ______________
Telephone ______________________

Ship to (if different from above)
Name ____
Address ______________________________________
City/State ______________________ Zip ______________
Telephone ______________________

Credit Card Information
Credit Card # ____________________ ☐ Visa ☐ Mastercard
Expiration Date (mm/yy) ______________ ☐ AmEx ☐ Discover

Qty.	Author	Title	Price	Total

Use this order form, or call 1-888-INDIGO-1

Total for books ______________
Shipping and handling:
$5 first two books,
$1 each additional book ______________
Total S & H ______________
Total amount enclosed ______________

Mississippi residents add 7% sales tax